Mother Aegypt

and Other Stories

Other books by Kage Baker

Novels:
The Anvil of The World
Empress of Mars (novella)
The Graveyard Game
Mendoza In Hollywood (AKA *At The Edge of the West*)
Sky Coyote
In The Garden of Iden

Collections:
The Company Dossiers: Black Projects, White Knights

Mother Aegypt

and Other Stories

by

Kage Baker

NIGHT SHADE BOOKS
San Francisco & Portland

First Edition

ISBN
1-892389-75-4 (Trade Hardcover)
1-892389-76-2 (Limited Edition)

Night Shade Books
http://www.nightshadebooks.com

Contents

In Memory of
LINDA UNDERHILL
1955-2004

"It was the nightingale… Nightly she sings on yond pomegranate tree."

Leaving His Cares Behind

The young man opened his eyes. Bright day affronted them. He groaned and rolled over, pulling his pillow about his ears.

After thirty seconds of listening to his brain pound more loudly than his heart, he rolled over again and stared at his comfortless world.

It shouldn't have been comfortless. It had originally been a bijou furnished residence, suitable for a wealthy young person-about-town. That had been when one could see the floor, however. Or the sink. Or the tabletops. Or, indeed, anything but the chilly wasteland of scattered clothing, empty bottles and unwashed dishes.

He regarded all this squalor with mild outrage, as though it belonged to someone else, and crawled from the strangling funk of his sheets. Standing up was a mistake; the top of his head blew off and hit the ceiling. A suitable place to vomit was abruptly a primary concern.

The kitchen? No; no room in the sink. Bathroom? Too far away. He lurched to the balcony doors, flung them wide and leaned out. A delicate peach soufflé, a bowl of oyster broth, assorted brightly colored trifles that did not yield their identities to memory and two bottles of sparkling wine spattered into the garden below.

Limp as a rag he clung to the rail, retching and spitting, shivering in his nakedness. Amused comment from somewhere roused him; he lifted his eyes and saw that half of Deliantiba (or at least the early-morning tradesmen making their way along Silver Boulevard) had watched his performance. He glared at them. Spitting out the last of the night before, he stood straight, turned his affronted back and went inside, slamming the balcony doors behind him.

With some effort, he located his dressing gown (finest velvet brocade, embroidered with gold thread) and matching slippers. The runner answered his summoning bell sooner than he had expected and her thunder at his door

1

brought on more throbbing in his temples. He opened to see the older one, not the young one who was so smitten with him, and cursed his luck.

"Kretia, isn't it?" he said, smiling nonetheless. "You look lovely this morning! Now, I'd like a carafe of mint tea, a plate of crisp wafers and one green apple, sliced thin. Off you go, and if you're back within ten minutes you'll have a gratuity of your very own!"

She just looked at him, hard-eyed. "Certainly, sir," she replied. "Will that be paid for in advance, sir?"

"There goes *your* treat," he muttered, but swept a handful of assorted small coins from the nearest flat surface and handed them through the doorway. "That should be enough. Kindly hurry; I'm not a well man."

He had no clean clothing, but while poking through the drifts of slightly less foul linen he found a pair of red silk underpants he was fairly certain did not belong to him, and pulling them on cheered him up a great deal. By the time he had breakfasted and strolled out to meet the new day, Lord Ermenwyr was nearly himself again, and certainly capable of grappling with the question of how he was going to pay his rent for another month.

And grappling was required.

The gentleman at Firebeater's Savings and Loan was courteous, but implacable: no further advances on my lord's quarterly allotment were to be paid, on direct order of my lord's father. Charm would not persuade him; neither would veiled threats. Finally the stop payment order itself was produced, with its impressive and somewhat frightening seal of black wax. Defeated, Lord Ermenwyr slunk out into the sunshine and stamped his foot at a pigeon that was unwise enough to cross his path. It just stared at him.

He strode away, hands clasped under his coattails, thinking very hard. By long-accustomed habit his legs bore him to a certain pleasant villa on Goldwire Avenue, and when he realized where he was, he smiled and rang at the gate. A laconic porter admitted him to Lady Seelice's garden. An anxious-looking maidservant admitted him to Lady Seelice's house. He found his own way to Lady Seelice's boudoir.

Lady Seelice was sitting up in bed, going over the books of her shipping company, and she had a grim set to her mouth. Vain for him to offer to distract her with light conversation; vain for him to offer to massage her neck, or brush her hair. He perched on the foot of her bed, looking as winsome as he could, and made certain suggestions. She declined them in an absent-minded sort of way.

He helped himself to sugared comfits from the exquisite little porcelain jar on her bedside table, and ate them quite amusingly, but she did not laugh. He pretended to play her corset like an accordion, but she did not laugh at that either. He fastened her brassiere on his head and crawled around the room on his hands and knees meowing like a kitten, and when she took absolutely no notice of that, he stood up and asked her outright if she'd loan him a hundred crowns.

She told him to get out, so he did.

As he was stamping downstairs, fuming, the anxious maidservant drifted into his path.

"Oh, dear, was she cross with you?" she inquired.

"Your mistress is in a vile mood," said Lord Ermenwyr resentfully, and he pulled her close and kissed her very hard. She leaned into his embrace, making soft noises, stroking his hair. When they came up for air at last, she looked into his eyes.

"She's been in a vile mood these three days. Something's wrong with her stupid old investments."

"Well, if she's not nicer soon, she'll find that her nimble little goat has capered off to greener pastures," said Lord Ermenwyr, pressing his face into the maidservant's bosom. He began to untie the cord of her bodice with his teeth.

"I've been thinking, darling," said the maidservant slowly, "that perhaps it's time we told her the truth about... you know... *us.*"

Unseen under her chin, the lordling grimaced in dismay. He spat out a knot and straightened up at once.

"Well! Yes. Perhaps." He coughed, and looked suddenly pale. "On the other hand, there is the danger—" He coughed again, groped hurriedly for a silk handkerchief and held it to his lips. "My condition is so, ah, *tentative.* If we were to tell of our forbidden love—and then I were to collapse unexpectedly and die, which I might at any moment, how could I rest in my grave knowing that your mistress had turned you out in the street?"

"I suppose you're right," sighed the maidservant, watching as he doubled over in a fit of coughing. "Do you want a glass of wine or anything?"

"No, my darling—" Wheezing, Lord Ermenwyr turned and made his unsteady way to the door. "I think—I think I'd best pay a call on my personal physician. Adieu."

Staggering, choking, he exited, and continued in that wise until he was well out of sight at the end of the avenue, at which time he stood straight and walked on. A few paces later the sugared comfits made a most unwelcome return, and though he was able to lean quickly over a low wall, he looked up directly into the eyes of someone's outraged gardener.

Running three more blocks did not improve matters much. He collapsed on a bench in a small public park and fumed, considering his situation.

"I'm fed up with this life," he told a statue of some Deliantiban civic leader. "Independence is all very well, but perhaps...."

He mulled over the squalor, the inadequacy, the creditors, the wretched *complications* with which he had hourly to deal. He compared it with his former accustomed comforts, in a warm and loving home where he was accorded all the consideration his birth and rank merited. Within five minutes, having given due thought to all arguments pro and con, he rose briskly to his feet and set off in the direction of Silver Boulevard.

Ready cash was obtained by pawning one of the presents Lady Seelice had given him (amethysts were not really his color, after all). He dined pleasantly at his favorite restaurant that evening. When three large gentlemen asked at the door whether or not Lord Ermenwyr had a moment to speak with them, however, he was obliged to exit through a side door and across a roof.

Arriving home shortly after midnight, he loaded all his unwashed finery into his trunks, lowered the trunks from his window with a knotted sheet, himself exited in like manner, and dragged the trunks a quarter-mile to the caravan depot. He spent the rest of the night there, dozing fitfully in a corner, and by dawn was convinced he'd caught his death of cold.

But when his trunks were loaded into the baggage cart, when he had taken his paid seat amongst the other passengers, when the caravan master had mounted into the lead cart and the runner signaled their departure with a blast on her brazen trumpet—then Lord Ermenwyr was comforted, and allowed himself to sneer at Deliantiba and all his difficulties there as it, and they, fell rapidly behind him.

*   *   *

The caravan master drew a deep breath, deciding to be patient.

"Young man, your friends must have been having a joke at your expense," he said. "There aren't any country estates around here. We're in the bloody *Greenlands*. Nobody's up here but bandits, and demons and wild beasts."

"No need to be alarmed on my behalf, good fellow," the young man assured him. "There'll be bearers along to meet me in half an hour. That's their cart-track right there, see?"

The caravan master peered at what might have been a rabbit's trail winding down to the honest paved road. He followed it up with his eyes until it became lost in the immensity of the forests. He looked higher still, at the black mountain towering beyond, and. shuddered. He knew what lay up there. It wasn't something he told his paying passengers about, because if he were ever to do so, no amount of bargain fares could tempt them to take this particular shortcut through the wilderness.

"Look," he said, "I'll be honest with you. If I let you off here, the next thing anyone will hear of you is a note demanding your ransom. *If* the gods are inclined to be merciful! There's a Red House station three days on. Ride with us that far, at least. You can send a message to your friends from there."

"I tell you this is my stop, Caravan Master," said the young man, in such a snide tone the caravan master thought: *To hell with him.*

"Offload his trunks, then!" he ordered the keymen, and marched off to the lead cart and resumed his seat. As the caravan pulled away, the other passengers looked back, wondering at the young man who sat down on his luggage with an air of unconcern and pulled out a jade smoking-tube, packing it with fragrant weed.

"I hope his parents have other sons," murmured a traveling salesman. Something howled in the depths of the forest, and he looked fearfully over his shoulder. In doing so, he missed seeing the young man lighting up his smoke with a green fireball. When he looked back, a bend in the road had already hidden the incautious youth.

Lord Ermenwyr, in the meanwhile, sucked in a double lungful of medicinal smoke and sighed in contentment. He leaned back, and blew a smoke ring.

"That's my unpaid rent and cleaning fee," he said to himself, watching it dissipate and wobble away. He sucked smoke and blew another.

"That's my little misunderstanding with Brasshandle the moneylender," he said, as it too faded into the pure air. Giggling to himself, he drew in a deep, deep store of smoke and blew three rings in close formation.

"Your hearts, ladies! All of you. Byebye now! You'll find another toy to amuse yourselves, I don't doubt. All my troubles are magically wafting away— oh, wait, I should blow one for that stupid business with the public fountain—"

When he heard the twig snap, however, he sat up and gazed into the darkness of the forest.

They were coming for him through the trees, and they were very large. Some were furred and some were scaled, some had great fanged pitilessly grinning mouths, some had eyes red as a dying campfire just before the night closes in. Some bore spiked weapons. Some bore treebough clubs. They shared no single characteristic of feature or flesh, save that they wore, all, livery black as ink.

"It's about time you got here," said Lord Ermenwyr. Rising to his feet, he let fall the glamour that disguised his true form.

"Master!" cried some of that dread host, and "Little Master!" cried others, and they abased themselves before him.

"Yes, yes, I'm glad to see you too," said Lord Ermenwyr. "Take special care with my trunks, now. I'll have no end of trouble getting them to close again, if they're dropped and burst open."

"My little lord, you look pale," said the foremost creature, doffing his spiked helmet respectfully. "Have you been ill again? Shall we carry you?"

"I haven't been well, no," the lordling admitted. "Perhaps you ought."

The leader knelt immediately, and Lord Ermenwyr hopped up on his shoulder and clung as he stood, looking about with satisfaction from the considerable height.

"Home!" he ordered, and that uncouth legion bore him, and his trunks, and his unwashed linen, swiftly and with chants of praise to the great black gate of his father's house.

*   *   *

The Lord Ermenwyr was awakened next morning by an apologetic murmur, as one of the maidservants slipped from his bed. He acknowledged her departure with a sleepy grunt and a wave of his hand, and rolled over to luxuriate in dreams once more. Nothing disturbed his repose further until the black and purple curtains of his bed were drawn open, reverently, and he heard a sweet chime that meant his breakfast had just arrived on a tray.

"Tea and toast, little Master," someone growled gently. "The toast crisp, just as you like it, and a pot of hyacinth jam, and Hrekseka the Appalling remembered you like that shrimp-egg relish, so here's a puff pastry filled with it for a savory. Have we forgotten anything? Would you like the juice of blood oranges, perhaps?"

The lordling opened his eyes and smiled wide, stretched lazily.

"Yes, thank you, Krasp," he said, and the steward—who resembled nothing so much as an elderly werewolf stuck in mid-transformation—bowed and looked sidelong at an attendant, who ran at once to fetch a pitcher of juice. He meanwhile set about arranging Lord Ermenwyr's tray on his lap, opening out the black linen napery and tucking it into the lace collar of the lordling's nightshirt, and pouring the tea.

"And may I say, Master, on behalf of the staff, how pleased we are to see you safely returned?" said Krasp, stepping back and turning his attention to laying out a suit of black velvet.

"You may," said Lord Ermenwyr. He spread jam on his toast, dipped it into his tea and sucked at it noisily. "Oh, bliss. It's good to be back, too. I trust the parents are both well?'

Krasp genuflected. "Your lord father and your lady mother thrive, I rejoice to say."

"Mm. Of course. Siblings all in reasonably good health, I suppose?"

"The precious offspring of the Master and his lady continue to grace this plane, my lord, for which we in the servant's hall give thanks hourly."

"How nice," said Lord Ermenwyr. He sipped his tea and inquired further: "I suppose nobody's run a spear through my brother Eyrdway yet?"

The steward turned with a reproachful look in his sunken yellow eye. "The Variable Magnificent continues alive and well, my lord," he said, and held up two pairs of boots of butter-soft leather. "The plain ones, my lord, or the ones with the spring-loaded daggers in the heels?"

"The plain ones," Lord Ermenwyr replied, yawning. "I'm in the bosom of my family, after all."

When he had dined, when he had been washed and lovingly groomed and dressed by a succession of faithful retainers, when he had admired his reflection in a long mirror and pomaded his beard and moustaches—then Lord Ermenwyr strolled forth into the corridors of the family manse, to see what amusement he might find.

He sought in vain.

All that presented itself to his quick eye was the endless maze of halls, hewn through living black basalt, lit at intervals by flickering witchlight or smoking flame, or here and there by a shaft of tinted sunbeam, from some deep-hewn arrowslit window sealed with panes of painted glass. At regular intervals armed men—well, armed *males*—stood guard, and each bowed respectfully as he passed, and bid him good-morning.

He looked idly into the great vaulted chamber of the baths, with its tiled pools and scented atmosphere from the orchids that twined, luxuriant, on trellises in the steamy air; but none of his sisters were in there.

He leaned on a balustrade and gazed down the stairwell, at the floors descending into the heart of the mountain. There, on level below level to the vanishing point of perspective, servants hurried with laundry, or dishes, or firewood. It was reassuring to see them, but he had learned long since that they would not stop to play.

He paused by a window and contemplated the terraced gardens beyond, secure and sunlit, paradise cleverly hidden from wayfarers on the dreadful slopes below the summit. Bees droned in white roses, or blundered sleepily in orchards, or hovered above reflecting pools. Though the bowers of his mother were beautiful beyond the praise of poets, they made Lord Ermenwyr want to scream with ennui.

He turned, hopeful, at the sound of approaching feet.

"My lord." A tall servant bowed low. "Your lord father requests your presence in his accounting chamber."

Lord Ermenwyr bared his teeth like a weasel at bay. All his protests, all his excuses, died unspoken at the look on the servant's face. He reflected that at least the next hour was unlikely to be boring.

"Very well, then," he said, and followed where the servant led him.

By the time he had crossed the threshold, he had adopted a suitably insouciant attitude and compiled a list of clever things to say. All his presence of mind was required to remember them, once he had stepped into the darkness beyond.

His father sat in a shaft of light at the end of the dark hall, behind his great black desk, in his great black chair. For all that was said of him in courts of law, for all that was screamed against him in temples, the Master of the Mountain was not in his person fearful to look upon. For all that his name was spoken in whispers by the caravan-masters, or used to frighten their children, he wore no crown of sins nor cloak of shades. He was big, black-bearded, handsome in a solemn kind of way. His black eyes were calm, patient as a stalking tiger's.

Lord Ermenwyr, meeting those eyes, felt like a very small rabbit indeed.

"Good morning, Daddy," he said, in the most nonchalant voice he could summon.

"Good afternoon, my son," said the Master of the Mountain.

He pointed to a chair, indicating that Lord Ermenwyr should come forward and sit. Lord Ermenwyr did so, though it was a long walk down that dark hall. When he had seated himself, a saturnine figure in nondescript clothing stepped out of the shadows before him.

"Your report, please," said the Master of the Mountain. The spy cleared his throat once, then read from a sheaf of notes concerning Lord Ermenwyr's private pastimes for the last eight months. His expenses were listed in detail, to the last copper piece; his associates were named, their addresses and personal histories summarized; his favorite haunts named too, and the amount of time he spent at each.

The Master of the Mountain listened in silence, staring at his son the whole time, and though he raised an eyebrow now and then he made no comment. Lord Ermenwyr, for his part, with elaborate unconcern, drew out his smoking-tube, packed it, lit it, and sat smoking, with a bored expression on his face.

Having finished at last, the spy coughed and bowed slightly. He stepped back into the darkness.

"Well," said Lord Ermenwyr, puffing smoke, "I don't know why you bothered giving me that household accounts book on my last birthday. He kept *much* better records than I did."

"Fifteen pairs of high-heeled boots?" said the Master of the Mountain, with a certain seismic quality in the bass reverberation of his voice.

"I can explain that! There's only one cobbler in Deliantiba who can make really comfortable boots that give me the, er, dramatic presence I need," said Lord Ermenwyr. "And he's poor. I felt it was my duty to support an authentic craftsman."

"I can't imagine why he's poor, at these prices," retorted his father. "When I was your age, I'd never owned a pair of boots. Let alone boots 'of premium-grade elkhide, dyed purple in the new fashion, with five-inch heels incorporating the unique patented Comfort-Spring lift.' "

"You missed out on a lot, eh? If you wore my size, I'd give you a pair," said Lord Ermenwyr, cool as snowmelt, but he tensed to run all the same.

His father merely stared at him, and the lordling exhaled another plume of smoke and studied it intently. When he had begun to sweat in spite of himself, his father went on:

"Is your apothecary an authentic craftsman too?"

"You can't expect me to survive without my medication!" Lord Ermenwyr cried. "And it's damned expensive in a city, you know."

"For what you spent, you might have kept three of yourselves alive," said his father.

"Well—well, but I've been ill. More so than usually, I mean. I had fevers—and I've had this persistent racking cough—blinding headaches when I wake up every morning—and see how pale I am?" Lord Ermenwyr stammered. His father leaned forward and grinned, with his teeth very white in his black beard.

"There's nothing wrong with you, boy, that a good sweat won't cure. The exercise yard, quick march! Let's see if you've remembered your training."

*   *   *

"Just what I expected," said the Master of the Mountain, as his son was carried from the exercise yard on a stretcher. Lord Ermenwyr, too winded to respond, glared at his father.

"And get that look off your face, boy. This is what comes of all those bottles of violet liqueur and vanilla éclairs," continued his father, pulling off his great gauntlets. "And the late nights. And the later mornings." He rubbed his chin thoughtfully, where a bruise was swelling. "Your reflexes aren't bad, though. You haven't lost any of your speed, I'll say that much for you."

"Thank you," Lord Ermenwyr wheezed, with as much sarcasm as he could muster.

"I want to see you out there again tomorrow, one hour after sunrise. We'll start with saber drill, and then you'll run laps," said the Master of the Mountain.

"On my sprained ankle?" Lord Ermenwyr yelled in horror.

"I see you've got your breath back," replied his father. He turned to the foremost guard bearing the stretcher. "Take my son to his mother's infirmary. If there's anything really the matter with him, she'll mend it."

"But—!" Lord Ermenwyr cried, starting up. His father merely smiled at him, and strode off to the guardroom.

*   *   *

By the time they came to his mother's bower, Lord Ermenwyr had persuaded his bearers to let him limp along between them, rather than enter her presence prostrate and ignominious.

But as they drew near to that place of sweet airs, of drowsy light and soft perfumes, those bearers must blink and turn their faces away; and though they propped him faithfully, and were great and horrible in their black livery and mail, the two warriors shivered to approach the Saint of the World. Lord Ermenwyr, knowing well that none of his father's army could meet his mother's gaze, sighed and bid them leave him.

"But, little Master, we must obey your lord father," groaned one, indistinctly through his tusks.

"It's all right; most of the time I can't look her in the eye, myself," said Lord Ermenwyr. "Besides, you were only told to bring me to the *infirmary*, right? So there's a semantic loophole for you."

Precise wording is extremely important to demons. Their eyes (bulging green and smoldering red respectively) met, and after a moment's silent debate the two bowed deeply and withdrew, murmuring their thanks. Lord Ermenwyr sighed, and tottered on through the long grass alone.

He saw the white-robed disciples walking in the far groves, or bending between the beds of herbs, gathering, pruning, planting. Their plain-chant hummed through the pleasant air like bee song, setting his teeth on edge somehow. He found his mother at last, silhouetted against a painfully sunlit bower of blossoming apple, where she bent over a sickbed.

"…the ointment every day, do you understand? You must have patience," she was saying, in her gentle ruthless voice. She looked over her shoulder and saw her son. He felt her clear gaze go through him, and he stood still and fidgeted as she turned back to her patient. She laid her hand upon the sufferer's brow, murmured a blessing; only then did she turn her full attention to Lord Ermenwyr.

He knelt awkwardly. "Mother."

"My child." She came forward and raised him to his feet. Having embraced him, she said:

"You haven't sprained your ankle, you know."

"It hurts," he said, and his lower lip trembled. "You think I'm lying again, I suppose."

"No," she said, patiently. "You truly believe you're in pain. Come and sit down, child."

She led him into the deeper shade, and drew off his boot (looking without comment on its five-inch heel). One of her disciples brought him a stoneware cup of cold spring water, and watched with wide eyes as she examined Lord Ermenwyr's ankle. Where her fingers passed, the lordling felt warmth entering in. His pain melted away like frost under sunlight, but he braced himself for what else her healing hands would learn in their touch.

"I know what you'll tell me next," he said, testily. "You'll say I haven't been exercising enough. You'll tell me I've been eating and drinking too much. You'll tell me I shouldn't wear shoes with heels this high, because it doesn't matter how tall I am. You'll tell me I'm wasting myself on pointless self-indulgences that leave me sick and depressed and penniless."

"Why should I tell you what you already know?" his mother replied. He stared sullenly into his cup of water.

"And you'll *reproach* me about Lady Seelice and Lady Thyria. And the little runner, what's-her-name, you'll be especially sorrowful that I can't even remember the name of a girl I've seduced. Let alone chambermaids without number. And... and you'll tell me about all those poor tradesmen whose livelihoods depend on people like me paying bills on time, instead of skipping town irresponsibly."

"That's true," said his mother.

"And, of course, you'll tell me that I don't really need all those drugs!" Lord Ermenwyr announced. "You'll tell me that I imagine half of my fevers and coughs and wasting diseases, and that neither relief nor creative fulfillment will come from running around artist's salons with my pupils like pinpoints. And that it all comes from my being bored and frustrated. And that I'd feel better at once if I found some honest work putting my *tremendous* talents to good use."

"How perceptive, my darling," said his mother.

"Have I left anything out?"

"I don't think so."

"You see?" Lord Ermenwyr demanded tearfully, turning to the disciple. "She's just turned me inside out, like a sock. I can't keep one damned secret from her."

"All things are known to Her," said the disciple, profoundly shocked at the lordling's blasphemy. He hadn't worked there very long.

"And now, do you know what else she's going to do?" said Lord Ermenwyr, scowling at him. "She's going to nag at me to go to the nursery and visit my bastard children."

"Really?" said the disciple, even more shocked.

"Yes," said his mother, watching as he pulled his boot back on. He started to stamp off, muttering, but turned back hastily and knelt again. She blessed him in silence, and he rose and hurried away.

"My son is becoming wise," said the Saint of the World, smiling as she watched him go.

*   *   *

The way to the nursery was mazed and obscured, for the Master of the Mountain had many enemies, and hid well where his seed sheltered. Lord Ermenwyr threaded the labyrinth without effort, knowing it from within. As he vaulted the last pit, as he gave the last password, his heart grew more cheerful. He would shortly behold his dear old nurse again!

Twin demonesses guarded the portal, splendid in black livery and silver mail. The heels of their boots were even higher than his, and much sharper. They grinned to see him, baring gold-banded fangs in welcome.

"Ladies, you look stunning today," he told them, twirling his moustaches. "Is Balnshik on duty?"

"She is within, little lord," hissed the senior of the two, and lifted her blade to let him pass.

He entered quite an ordinary room, long and low, with a fire burning merrily in the hearth behind a secure screen. Halfway up the walls was a mural painted in tones of pink and pale blue, featuring baby rabbits involved in unlikely pastimes.

Lord Ermenwyr curled his lip. Three lace-gowned infants snuffled in cots here; four small children sat over a shared game there, in teeny-tiny chairs around a teeny-tiny table; another child rocked to and fro on a ponderous wooden beast bright-painted; three more sat before a comfortable-looking chair at the fireside, where a woman in a starched white uniform sat reading to them.

"…but the people in *that* village were very naughty and tried to ambush his ambassadors, so he put them all to the sword," she said, and held up the picture so they could all see.

"Ooo," chorused the tots.

She, having meanwhile noticed Lord Ermenwyr, closed the book and rose to her feet with sinuous grace.

"Little Master," she said, looking him up and down. "You've put on weight."

He winced.

"Oh, Nursie, how unkind," he said.

"Nonsense," Balnshik replied. She was arrogantly beautiful. Her own body was perfect, ageless, statuesque and bosomy as any little boy's dream, or at least Lord Ermenwyr's little boy dreams, and there was a dangerous glint in her dark eye and a throaty quality to her voice that made him shiver even now.

"I've come about the, er, the… those children I—had," he said. "For a sort of visit."

"What a delightful surprise!" Balnshik said, in well-bred tones of irony. She turned and plucked from the rocking beast a wretched-looking little thing in a green velvet dress. "Look who's come to see us, dear! It's our daddy. We scarcely knew we had one, did we?"

Baby and parent stared at one another in mutual dismay. The little boy turned his face into Balnshik's breast and screamed dismally.

"Poor darling," she crooned, stroking his limp curls. "We've been teething again and we're getting over a cold, and that makes us fretful. We're just like our daddy, aren't we? Would he like to hold us?"

"Perhaps not," said Lord Ermenwyr, doing his best not to run from the room. "I might drop it. Him. What do you mean, he's just like me?"

"The very image of you at that age, Master," Balnshik assured him, serenely unbuttoning her blouse. "Same pasty little face, same nasty look in his dear little eyes, same tendency to shriek and drum his little heels on the floor when he's cross. And he gets that same rash you did, all around his little—"

"Wasn't there another one?" inquired Lord Ermenwyr desperately.

"You know perfectly well there is," said Balnshik, watching tenderly as the baby burrowed toward comfort. "Your lord father's still paying off the girl's family, and your lady sister will never be able to hold another slumber party for her sorority. Where is he?" She glanced over at the table. "There we are! The one in the white tunic. Come and meet your father, dear."

The child in question, one of those around the table, got up reluctantly.

He came and clung to Balnshik's leg, peering up at his father.

"Well, you look like a fine manly little fellow, anyway," said Lord Ermenwyr.

"You look like a very bad man," stated the child.

"And he's clever!" said Lord Ermenwyr, preening a bit. "Yes, my boy, I am rather a bad man. In fact, I'm a famous villain. What else have you heard about your father?"

The boy thought.

"Grandpapa says when I'm a man, I can challenge you to a fight and beat you up," he said gravely. "But I don't think I want to."

"You don't eh?" A spark of parental feeling warmed in Lord Ermenwyr's heart. "Why not, my boy?"

"Because then I will be bigger than you, and you will be old and weak and have no teeth," the child explained. "It wouldn't be fair."

Lord Ermenwyr eyed him sourly. "That hasn't happened to your Grandpapa, has it?"

"No," the child agreed, "But he's twice as big as you." He brightened, remembering the other thing he had heard about his father. "And Grandmama says you're so smart, it's such a shame you don't do something with your life!"

Lord Ermenwyr sighed, and pulled out his jade tube. "Do you mind if I smoke in here?" he asked Balnshik.

"I certainly do," she replied, mildly but with a hint of bared fangs.

"Pity. Well, here, son of mine; here's my favorite ring for your very own." He removed a great red cabochon set in silver, and presented it to the child. "The top is hinged like a tiny box, see the clever spring? You can hide sleeping powders in it to play tricks on other little boys. I emptied out the poison, for heaven's sake," he added indignantly, seeing that the hint of bared fangs was now an open suggestion.

"Thank you, Father," piped the child.

*   *   *

Disconsolate, Lord Ermenwyr wandered the black halls.

He paused at a window that looked westward, and regarded the splendid isolation of the Greenlands. Nothing to be seen for miles but wave upon wave of lesser mountains, forested green as the sea, descending to the plain. Far away, far down, the toy cities behind their walls were invisible for distance, and when night fell their sparkling lights would glimmer in vain, like lost constellations, shrouded from his hopeful eye.

Even now, he told himself, even now down there the taverns would be opening. The smoky dark places would be lighting their lanterns, and motherly barmaids would serve forth wine so raw it took the paint off tables. The elegant expensive places would be firing up the various patent devices that glared in artificial brilliance, and the barmaids there were all thin, and young, and interestingly depraved-looking. What *they* served forth could induce visions, or convulsions and death if carelessly indulged in.

How he longed, this minute, for a glass of dubious green liqueur from the Gilded Clock! Or to loll with his head in the lap of an anonymous beauty who couldn't care less whether he did something worthwhile with his life. What had he been thinking, to desert the cities of the plain? They had everything his heart could desire. Theaters. Clubs. Ballrooms. Possibilities. Danger. Fun....

Having made his decision to depart before the first light of dawn, Lord Ermenwyr hurried off to see that his trunks were packed with new-laundered clothes. He whistled a cheery little tune as he went.

*   *   *

The Master and the Saint sat at their game.

They were not Good and Evil personified, nor Life and Death; certainly not Order and Chaos, nor even Yin and Yang. Yet most of the world's population believed that they were. Their marriage, therefore, had done rather more than raise eyebrows everywhere.

The Master of the Mountain scowled down at the game board. It bore the simplest of designs, concentric circles roughly graven in slate, and the playing pieces were mere pebbles of black marble or white quartz. The strategy was fantastically involved, however. So subtle were the machinations necessary to win that this particular game had been going on for thirty years, and a decisive conquest might never materialize.

"What are we going to do about the boy?" he said.

The Saint of the World sighed in commiseration, but was undistracted. She slid a white stone to a certain position on the board.

High above them, three white egrets peered down from the ledge that ran below the great vaulted dome of the chamber. Noting the lady's move, they looked sidelong at the three ravens that perched opposite, and stalked purposefully along the ledge until the ravens were obliged to sidle back a pace or two.

"To which of your sons do you refer, my lord?" the Saint inquired.

"The one with the five-inch heels to his damned boots," said the Master of the Mountain, and set a black stone down, *click,* between a particular pair of circles. "Have you seen them?"

One of the ravens bobbed its head derisively, spread its coal-black wings and soared across the dome to the opposite ledge.

"Yes, I have," admitted the Saint.

"They cost me a fortune, and they're purple," said the Master of the Mountain, leaning back to study the board.

"And when you were his age, you'd never owned a pair of boots," said the Saint serenely, sliding two white stones adjacent to the black one.

Above, one egret turned, retraced its way along the ledge, and the one raven cocked an eye to watch it. Three white stars shone out with sudden and unearthly light, in the night heavens figured on the surface of the arching dome.

"When I was his age, I wore chains. I never had to worry about paying my tailor; only about living long enough to avenge myself," said the Master of the Mountain. "I wouldn't want a son of mine educated so. But we've spoiled the boy!"

He moved three black stones, lining them up on successive rings. The two ravens flew to join their brother. Black clouds swirled under the dome, advanced on the floating globe of the white moon.

"He needs direction," said the Saint.

"He needs a challenge," said the Master. "Pitch him out naked on the mountainside, and let him survive by his wits for a few years!"

"He would," pointed out the Saint. "Do we want to take responsibility for what would happen to the innocent world?"

"I suppose not," said the Master with a sigh, watching as his lady moved four white stones in a neat line. The white egrets advanced on the ravens again. The white moon outshone the clouds.

"But he does need a challenge," said the Saint. "He needs to put that mind of his to good use. He needs *work*."

"Damned right he does," said the Master of the Mountain. He considered the board again. "Rolling up his sleeves. Laboring with his hands. Building up a callus or two."

"Something that will make him employ his considerable talent," said the Saint.

There was a thoughtful silence. Their eyes met over the board. They smiled. Under the vaulted dome, all the birds took flight and circled in patterns, white wings and black.

"I'd better catch him early, or he'll be down the mountain again before cockcrow," said the Master of the Mountain. "To bed, madam?"

*   *   *

L ord Ermenwyr rose sprightly by candlelight, congratulating himself on
the self-reliance learned in Deliantiba: for now he could dress himself
without a valet. Having donned apparel suitable for travel, he went to his
door to rouse the bearers, that they might shoulder his new-laden trunks
down the gorge to the red road far below.

Upon opening the door, he said:

"Sergeant, kindly fetch—Ack!"

"Good morning, my son," said the Master of the Mountain. "So eager
for saber drill? Commendable."

"Thank you," said Lord Ermenwyr. "Actually, I thought I'd just get in
some practice lifting weights, first."

"Not this morning," said his father. "I have a job for you, boy. Walk with
me."

Gritting his teeth, Lord Ermenwyr walked beside his father, obliged to
take two steps for every one the Master of the Mountain took. He was
panting by the time they emerged on a high rampart, under faint stars, where
the wall's guard were putting out the watch-fires of the night.

"Look down there, son," said the Master of the Mountain, pointing to
three acres' space of waste and shattered rock, hard against the house wall.

"Goodness, is that a bit of snow still lying in the crevices?" said Lord
Ermenwyr, watching his breath settle in powdered frost. "So late in the year,
too. What unseasonably chilly weather we've had, don't you think?"

"Do you recognize the windows?" asked his father, and Lord Ermenwyr
squinted down at the arrowslits far below. "You ought to."

"Oh! Is that the nursery, behind that wall?" Lord Ermenwyr said. "Well,
what do you know? I was there only yesterday. Visiting my bastards, as a
matter of fact. My, my, doesn't it look small from up here?"

"Yes," said the Master of the Mountain. "It does. You must have noticed
how crowded it is, these days. Balnshik is of the opinion, and your mother
and I concur with her, that the children need more room. A place to play
when the weather is fine, perhaps. This would prevent them from growing
up into stunted, pasty-faced little creatures with no stamina."

"What a splendid idea," said Lord Ermenwyr, smiling with all his sharp
teeth. "Go to it, old man! Knock out a few walls and expand the place.
Perhaps Eyrdway would be willing to give up a few rooms of his suite, eh?"

"No," said the Master of the Mountain placidly. "Balnshik wants an
outdoor play area. A garden, just there under the windows. With lawns and a
water feature, perhaps."

He leaned on the battlement and watched emotions conflict in his son's face. Lord Ermenwyr's eyes protruded slightly as the point of the conversation became evident to him, and he tugged at his beard, stammering:

"No, no, she can't be serious! What about household security? What about your enemies? Can't put the little ones' lives in danger, after all. Mustn't have them out where they might be carried off by, er, eagles or efrits, can we? Nursie means well, of course, but—"

"It's an interesting problem," said the Master of the Mountain. "I'm sure you'll think of a solution. You're such a clever fellow, after all."

"But—!"

"Krasp has been instructed to let you have all the tools and materials you need," said the Master of the Mountain. "I do hope you'll have it finished before high summer. Little Druvendyl's rash might clear up if he were able to sunbathe."

"Who the hell is Druvendyl?" cried Lord Ermenwyr.

"Your infant son," the Master of the Mountain informed him. "I expect full-color renderings in my study within three days, boy. Don't dawdle."

*   *   *

Bright day without, but within Lord Ermenwyr's parlor it might have been midnight, so close had he drawn his drapes. He paced awhile in deep thought, glancing now and then at three flat stones he had set out on his hearth-rug. On one, a fistful of earth was mounded; on another, a small heap of coals glowed and faded. The third stone held a little water in a shallow depression.

To one side he had placed a table and chair.

Having worked up his nerve as far as was possible, he went at last to a chest at the foot of his bed and rummaged there. He drew out a long silver shape that winked in the light from the few coals. It was a flute. He seated himself in the chair and, raising the flute to his lips, began to play softly.

Summoning music floated forth, cajoling, enticing, music to catch the attention. The melody rose a little and was imperious, beckoned impatiently, wheedled and just hinted at threatening; then was coy, beseeched from a distance.

Lord Ermenwyr played with his eyes closed at first, putting his very soul into the music. When he heard a faint commotion from his hearth, though, he opened one eye and peered along the silver barrel as he played.

A flame had risen from the coals. Brightly it lit the other two stones, so he had a clear view of the water, which was bubbling upward as from a concealed fountain, and of the earth, which was mounding up too, for all the world like a molehill.

Lord Ermenwyr smiled in his heart and played on, and if the melody had promised before, it gave open-handed now; it was all delight, all ravishment. The water leaped higher, clouding, and the flame rose and spread out, dimming, and the earth bulged in its mound and began to lump into shape, as though under the hand of a sculptor.

A little more music, calling like birds in the forest, brightening like the sun rising over a plain, galloping like the herds there in the morning! And now the flame had assumed substance, and the water had firmed beside it. Now it appeared that three naked children sat on Lord Ermenwyr's hearth, their arms clasped about their drawn-up knees, their mouths slightly open as they watched him play. They were, all three, the phantom color of clouds, a shifting glassy hue suggesting rainbows. But about the shoulders of the little girl ran rills of bright flame, and one boy's hair swirled silver, and the other boy had perhaps less of the soap bubble about him, and more of wet clay.

Lord Ermenwyr raised his mouth from the pipe, grinned craftily at his guests, and set the pipe aside.

"No!" said the girl. "You must keep playing."

"Oh, but I'm tired, my dears," said Lord Ermenwyr. "I'm all out of breath."

"You have to play," the silvery boy insisted. "Play right now!"

But Lord Ermenwyr folded his arms. The children got to their feet, anger in their little faces, and they grew up before his eyes. The boys' chests deepened, their limbs lengthened, they overtopped the girl; but she became a woman shapely as any he'd ever beheld, with flames writhing from her brow.

"Play, or we'll kill you," said the three. "Burn you. Drown you. Bury you."

"Oh, no, that won't do," said Lord Ermenwyr. "Look here, shall we play a game? If I lose, I'll play for you again. If I win, you'll do as I bid you. What do you say to that?"

The three exchanged uncertain glances.

"We will play," they said. "But one at a time."

"Ah, now, is that fair?" cried Lord Ermenwyr. "When that gives you three chances to win against my one? I see you're too clever for me. So be it." He picked up the little table and set it before him. Opening a drawer, he brought out three cards.

"See here? Three portraits. Look closely: this handsome fellow is clearly me. This blackavised brigand is my father. And *this* lovely lady—" he held the card up before their eyes, "is my own saintly mother. Think you'd recognize her again? Of course you would. Now, we'll turn the cards face down. Can I find the lady? Of course I can; turn her up and here she is. That's no game at all! But if you find the lady, you'll win. So, who'll go first? Who'll find the lady?"

He took up the cards and looked at his guests expectantly. They nudged one another, and finally the earthborn said: "I will."

"Good for you!" Lord Ermenwyr said. "Watch, now, as I shuffle." He looked into the earthborn's face. "You're searching for the lady, understand?"

"Yes," said the earthborn, meeting his look of inquiry. "I understand."

"Good! So, here she is, and now here, and now here, and now—where?" Lord Ermenwyr fanned out his empty hands above the cards, in a gesture inviting choice.

Certain he knew where the lady was, the earthborn turned a card over.

"Whoops! Not the lady, is it? So sorry, friend. Who's for another try? Just three cards! It ought to be easy," sang Lord Ermenwyr, shuffling them again. The earthborn scowled in astonishment, as the others laughed gaily, and the waterborn stepped up to the table.

*   *   *

"Stop complaining," said Lord Ermenwyr, dipping his pen in ink. "You lost fairly, didn't you?"

"We never had a chance," said the earthborn bitterly. "That big man on the card, the one that's bigger than you. He's the Soul of the Black Rock, isn't he?"

"I believe he's known by that title in certain circles, yes," said Lord Ermenwyr, sketching in a pergola leading to a reflecting pool. "Mostly circles chalked on black marble floors."

"He's supposed to be a *good* master," said the waterborn. "How did he have a son like you?"

"You'll find me a good master, poppets," said Lord Ermenwyr. "I'll free you when you've done my will, and you've my word as my father's son on that. You're far too expensive to keep for long," he added, with a severe look at the fireborn, who was boredly nibbling on a footstool.

"I hunger," she complained.

"Not long to wait now," Lord Ermenwyr promised. "No more than an hour to go before the setting of the moon. And look at the pretty picture I've made!" He held up his drawing. The three regarded it, and their glum faces brightened.

When the moon was well down, he led them out, and they followed gladly when they saw that he carried his silver flute.

The guards challenged him on the high rampart, but once they recognized him they bent in low obeisance. "Little master," they growled, and he tapped each lightly on the helmet with his flute, and each grim giant nodded its head between its boots and slept.

"Down there," he said, pointing through the starlight, and the three that served him looked down on that stony desolation and wondered. All doubt fled, though, when he set the flute to his lips once more.

Now they knew what to do! And gleeful they sprang to their work, dancing under the wide starry heaven, and the cold void warmed and quickened under their feet, and the leaping silver music carried them along. Earth and Fire and Water played, and united in interesting ways.

*   *   *

Lord Ermenwyr was secure in bed, burrowed down under blankets and snoring, by the time bright morning lit the black mountain. But he did not need to see the first rays of the sun glitter on the great arched vault below the wall, where each glass pane was still hot from the fire that had passionately shaped it, and the iron frame too cooled slowly.

Nor did he need to see the warm sleepy earth under the vault, lying smooth in paths and emerald lawns, or the great trees that had rooted in it with magical speed. Neither did he need to hear the fountain bubbling languidly. He knew, already, what the children would find when they straggled from the dormitory, like a file of little ghosts in their white nightgowns.

He knew they would rub their eyes and run out through the new doorway, heedless of Balnshik's orders to remain, and knew they'd rush to pull down fruit from the pergola, and spit seeds at the red fish in the green lily-pool, or climb boldly to the backs of the stone wyverns, or run on the soft grass, or vie to see how hard they could bounce balls against the glass without breaking it. Had he not planned all this, to the last detail?

*   *   *

The Master of the Mountain and the Saint of the World came to see, when the uneasy servants roused them before breakfast.

"Too clever by half," said the Master of the Mountain, raising his eyes to the high vault, where the squares of bubbled and sea-clear glass let in an underwater sort of light. "Impenetrable. Designed to break up perception and confuse. And... what's he done to the time? Do you feel that?"

"It's slowed," said the Saint of the World. "Within this garden, it will always be a moment or so in the past. As inviolate as memory, my lord."

"Nice to know he paid attention to his lessons," said the Master of the Mountain, narrowing his eyes. Two little boys ran past him at knee level, screaming like whistles for no good reason, and one child tripped over a little girl who was sprawled on the grass pretending to be a mermaid.

"You see what he can do when he applies himself?" said the Saint, lifting the howling boy and soothing him.

"He still cheated," said the Master of the Mountain.

*   *   *

It was well after noon when Lord Ermenwyr consented to rise and grace the house with his conscious presence, and by then all the servants knew. He nodded to them as he strolled the black halls, happily aware that his personal legend had just enlarged. Now, when they gathered in the servant's halls around the balefires, and served out well-earned kraters of black wine at the end of a long day, *now* they would have something more edifying over which to exclaim than the number of childhood diseases he had narrowly survived or his current paternity suit.

"By the Blue Pit of Hasrahkhin, it was a miracle! A whole garden, trees and all, in the worst place imaginable to put one, and it had to be secret and secure—and the boy did it in just one night!" That was what they'd say, surely.

So it was with a spring in his step that nearly overbalanced him on his five-inch heels that the lordling came to his father's accounting chamber, and rapped briskly for admission.

The doorman ushered him in to his father's presence with deeper than usual obeisances, or so he fancied. The Master of the Mountain glanced up from the scroll he studied, and nodded at Lord Ermenwyr.

"Yes, my son?"

"I suppose you've visited the nursery this morning?" Lord Ermenwyr threw himself into a chair, excruciatingly casual in manner.

"I have, as a matter of fact," replied his lord father. "I'm impressed, boy. Your mother and I are proud of you."

"Thank you." Lord Ermenwyr drew out his long smoking-tube and lit it with a positive jet of flame. He inhaled deeply, exhaled a cloud that writhed about his head, and fixed bright eyes upon the Master of the Mountain. "Would this be an auspicious time to discuss increasing an allowance, o my most justly feared sire?"

"It would not," said the Master of the Mountain. "Bloody hell, boy! A genius like you ought to be able to come up with his own pocket money."

*   *   *

Lord Ermenwyr stalked the black halls, brooding on the unfairness of life in general and fathers in especial.

"Clever enough to come up with my own pocket money, am I?" he fumed. "I'll show *him.*"

He paused on a terrace and looked out again in the direction of the cities on the plain, and sighed with longing.

The back of his neck prickled, just as he heard the soft footfall behind him.

He whirled around and kicked, hard, but his boot sank into something that squelched. Looking up into the yawning, dripping maw of a horror out of legend, he snarled and said:

"Stop it, you moron! Slug-Hoggoth hasn't scared me since I was six."

"It has too," said a voice, plaintive in its disappointment. "Remember when you were twelve, and I hid behind the door of your bedroom? You screamed and screamed."

"No, I didn't," said Lord Ermenwyr, extricating his boot.

"Yes, you did, you screamed just like a girl," gloated the creature. "Eeeek!"

"Shut up."

"Make me, midget." The creature's outline blurred and shimmered; dwindled and firmed, resolving into a young man.

He was head and shoulders taller than Lord Ermenwyr, slender and beautiful as a beardless god, and stark naked except for a great deal of gold and silver jewelry. That having been said, there was an undeniable resemblance between the two men.

"Idiot," muttered Lord Ermenwyr.

"But prettier than you," said the other, throwing out his arms. "Gorgeous, aren't I? What do you think of my new pectoral? Thirty black pearls! And the bracelets match, look!"

Lord Ermenwyr considered his brother's jewelry with a thoughtful expression.

"Superb," he admitted. "You robbed a caravan, I suppose. How are you, Eyrdway?"

"I'm always in splendid health," said Lord Eyrdway. "Not like you, eh?"

"No indeed," said Lord Ermenwyr with a sigh. "I'm a wreck. Too much fast life down there amongst the Children of the Sun. Wining, wenching, burning my candle at both ends! I'm certain I'll be dead before I'm twenty-two, but what memories I'll have."

"Wenching?" Lord Eyrdway's eyes widened.

"It's like looting and raping, but nobody rushes you," explained his brother. "And sometimes the ladies even make breakfast for you afterward."

"I know perfectly well what wenching is," said Lord Eyrdway indignantly. "What's *burning your candle at both ends?*"

"Ahhh." Lord Ermenwyr lit up his smoking tube. "Let's go order a couple of bottles of wine, and I'll explain."

*   *   *

Several bottles and several hours later, they sat in the little garden just outside Lord Ermenwyr's private chamber. Lord Ermenwyr was refilling his brother's glass.

"...so then I said to her, 'Well, madam, if you insist, but I really ought to have another apple first,' and that was the exact moment they broke in the terrace doors!" he said.

"Bunch of nonsense. You can't do that with an apple," Lord Eyrdway slurred.

"Maybe it was an apricot," said Lord Ermenwyr. "Anyway, the best part of it was, I got out the window with both the bag *and* the jewel case. Wasn't that lucky?"

"It sounds like a lot of fun," said Lord Eyrdway wistfully, and drank deep.

"Oh, it was. So then I went round to the Black Veil Club—but of course you know what goes on in *those* places!" Lord Ermenwyr pretended to sip his wine.

" 'Course I do," said his brother. "Only maybe I've forgot. You tell me again, all right?"

Lord Ermenwyr smiled. Leaning forward, lowering his voice, he explained about all the outré delights to be had at a Black Veil Club. Lord Eyrdway began to drool. Wiping it away absentmindedly, he said at last:

"You see—you see—that's what's so awful unflair. Unfair. All this fun you get to have. 'Cause you're totally worthless and nobody cares if you go down the mountain. You aren't the damn Heir to the Black Halls. Like me. I'm so really important Daddy won't let me go."

"Poor old Way-Way, it isn't fair at all, is it?" said Lord Ermenwyr. "Have another glass of wine."

"I mean, I'd just love to go t'Deliatitatita, have some fun," said Lord Eyrdway, holding out his glass to be refilled, "But, you know, Daddy just puts his hand on my shoulder n' says, 'When you're older, son,' but I'm older'n you by four years, right? Though of course who cares if *you* go, right? No big loss to the Family if *you* get an arrow through your liver."

"No indeed," said Lord Ermenwyr, leaning back. "Tell me something, my brother. Would you say I could do great things with my life if I only applied myself?"

"What?" Lord Eyrdway tried to focus on him. "You? No! I can see three of you right now, an' not one of 'em's worth a damn." He began to snicker. "Good one, eh? Three of you, get it? Oh, I'm sleepy. Just going to put my head down for a minute, right?"

He lay his head down and was promptly unconscious. When Lord Ermenwyr saw his brother blur and soften at the edges, as though he were a waxwork figure that had been left too near the fire, he rose and began to divest him of his jewelry.

"Eyrdway, I truly love you," he said.

*   *   *

The express caravan came through next dawn, rattling along at its best speed in hopes of being well down off the mountain by evening. The caravan master spotted the slight figure by the side of the road well in advance, and gave the signal to stop. The lead keyman threw the brake; sparks flew as the wheels slowed, and stopped.

Lord Ermenwyr, bright-eyed, hopped down from his trunks and approached the caravan master.

"Hello! Will this buy me passage on your splendid conveyance?" He held forth his hand. The caravan master squinted at it suspiciously. Then his eyes widened.

"Keymen! Load his trunks!" he bawled. "Lord, sir, with a pearl like that you could ride the whole route three times around. Where shall we take you? Deliantiba?"

Lord Ermenwyr considered, putting his head on one side.

"No... not Deliantiba, I think. I want to go somewhere there's a lot of trouble, of the proper sort for a gentleman. If you understand me?"

The caravan master sized him up. "There's a lot for a gentleman to do in Karkateen, sir, if his tastes run a certain way. You've heard the old song, right, about what *their* streets are paved with?"

Lord Ermenwyr began to smile. "I have indeed. Karkateen it is, then."

"Right you are, sir! Please take a seat."

So with a high heart the lordling vaulted the side of the first free cart, and sprawled back at his ease. The long line of carts started forward, picked up speed, and clattered on down the ruts in the red road. The young sun rose and shone on the young man, and the young man sang as he sped through the glad morning of the world.

The Briscian Saint

"We shouldn't have killed the priest," said the first soldier. He was one of three who fled from the long high smoke-pall of the burning city, and he glanced back now to see what white rider might be flying over the fissured plain, following them.

"Don't be stupid, what else could we have done?" said the second soldier. "He swung an axe at us. That made him a Combatant, see? So it was all right."

"But he cursed us, before he died," said the first soldier uneasily.

"So what?"

"So then the earthquake hit!"

"It didn't get us, did it?" said the third soldier, as he jogged steadily on.

"It got our side," said the first soldier, whose name was Spoke. "One minute we're a conquering army, the next minute the Duke's buried under a wall and we're on the run!"

"It got plenty of the Briscians too," said Mallet, the second soldier, panting from the weight of the burden he carried. "And the Duke never paid us much anyway, did he? So to hell with him, and the priest, and the whole business. We're clear away with a fortune, that's all I know. That's called *good* luck."

"We're not clear yet," said Spoke, and an aftershock followed as if on cue, making them all stagger.

"Shut up!" said the other two soldiers, and they ran on, and Spoke turned his face too and ran on, peering desperate up at the hills. Only he who rode behind Mallet regarded the flaming devastation, now, staring from the leather pack with wide sapphire-colored eyes. If the prayers of the dying reached his golden ears, he gave no sign, for his faint smile altered not in the least.

* * *

27

By nightfall they had made the cover of the trees and followed a stream up its course, crossing back and forth to throw off anything that might be tracking them by scent. They crawled the face of the wide-exposed stone gorge, expecting any moment to be nailed in place by pistol-bolts; but no one attacked, and when they lay gasping at the top Spoke said:

"I don't like this. It's too easy."

"Easy!" said Mallet, who had carried on his back a statue weighing more than a child. He slipped off his pack with a groan and set it upright, but it toppled over and the golden figure struck the rock, ringing hollowly. Spoke cringed.

"And that's a bad omen!" he said.

The third soldier, whose name was Smith, sat up. "If it was," he said, "I'd think it'd be a bad omen for the Briscians, wouldn't you? Their saint falling over?"

"You're both idiots," said Mallet. "Omens! Portents! My ass."

"If you'd seen what I've seen over the years, you'd be a little more respectful," Spoke persisted.

"My ass," Mallet repeated.

Spoke crawled to the statue and slipped it from the pack, handling it gingerly. He set it upright before them, knelt, and cleared his throat.

"Blessed saint, have mercy on us. We are poor men in need, and we fought only for pay. Our Duke is dead, maybe by your just anger; so be appeased, and take no further revenge on us. We promise to atone."

Mallet snorted. "*I* promise to take that thing straight to the first goldsmith I find. The eyes alone are probably worth a farm."

Wincing, Spoke cried: "Judge us separately, blessed saint! Rebuke his blasphemy as you see fit, but accept my contrition and spare me."

"Oh, that's lovely," said Smith. "So much for being comrades-in-arms, eh?"

"Haven't you ever heard any stories about this kind of thing?" said Spoke. "Remember what happened to Lord Salt when he mocked the Image at Rethkast?"

Mallet just shook his head in disgust and got up, looking about them. He moved off into the trees, picking up broken branches as he went.

Smith slipped off his own pack and rummaged in it for flint and steel. "Have you ever noticed," he said, "how those stories are never about ordinary people like us? It's always Lord This and Prince That who piss off the gods and get blasted with balefire."

"Well, there could be a good reason for that," said Spoke. "Highborn people get noticed, don't they? If they're punished for sin, everyone sees. Makes a better example than if the punishment fell on nobodies."

"So the gods think like men?" said Smith, standing up to peer through the shadows. He pulled down a low bough and yanked free a handful of trailing moss, rubbing it between his fingers to see whether it was dry enough to take a spark.

"They must think like men," argued Spoke seriously. "At least, when they're dealing with us. They have to use logic we'll understand, don't they?"

Smith ignored him, breaking off dry twigs and settling down to the business of starting a fire. He had a little creeping flame established by the time Mallet came back with an armload of dead wood. The wood caught, the flames leaped up; the clearing above the gorge lit in a small circle, and the black shadows of the trees leaned back from it all around.

"Good," grunted Smith, stretching out his hands. He slipped off his helmet and went down to the water's edge, where it ran shallow and transparent over the smooth rock before plummeting down in mist. Here he rinsed his helmet out, and brought it back full of water. Arranging three stones close against the flames, he propped it there where it would take heat. After a moment, the other two men followed his example.

They sat in silence, watching for the water to steam. Spoke, however, turned his troubled gaze now and again to the image of the saint.

"Was his face pointed toward us, before?" he said at last.

"Of course it was."

"I thought—it was looking straight ahead."

The other two glanced over their shoulders at the statue.

"You're right!" said Mallet. "Oh dear, what'll we do now? There Holy Saint Foofoo sits, taking advantage of the fact that all these jumping shadows make him look eerie as hell. As soon as he's got us good and scared, you know what he's going to do? He'll start creeping toward us, a little at a time. Only when we're not looking, naturally."

"Shut your face!"

"He'll come closer, and closer, and then—"

"Stop it!"

"Then he'll realize he's two feet tall and armed with a teeny little golden tambourine in one hand and a—what is that thing in his other hand?" Mallet squinted at it. "A silver toothpick?"

"It's supposed to be a dagger," said Smith.

"Oh, I don't know how I'm ever going to fall asleep tonight, with a supernatural menace like that around," said Mallet.

Spoke stared into the fire.

"It *was* looking straight ahead," he murmured.

"You couldn't have seen that, as dark as it was here," said Mallet.

Smith shrugged and took up his pack again. He pulled out a ration-block wrapped in oiled paper, a little the worse for wear after being knocked around in the company of his other gear. He opened it, picked off dirt and lint, and broke a few chunks into the water in his helmet, which was beginning to steam slightly.

"Let me tell you about something that happened in our village," said Spoke. "All right? We had a saint of our own. She watched over the harvest and she kept away the marsh fevers. And if you had a toothache, you could pray to her, and she'd heal you *every time*. All you had to do was leave offerings in her shrine. And make sure her image was kept polished.

"Well, one time, somebody's little boy went in there and left a lump of butter in the statue's open hand. He thought she'd like it. But it was summer, and the butter melted, and then dust blew in from the road and stuck to the mess. When the old priest saw it, he thought somebody'd been disrespectful, and he cursed whoever'd done it. And, do you know, the child was taken ill that very night? And he burned with fever until his mother figured out what he'd done, and she went and made an offering in apology? And right away the child got better."

"Some saint!" said Mallet, stirring bits of ration block into his helmet.

"Well, it would have been the priest's mistake, not the saint's," conceded Smith.

"Damn right; a statue can't make mistakes," said Mallet.

"And I'll tell you something else that happened!" said Spoke. "The old priest died, and we got a new one. But he wasn't a holy man. He was greedy, and people began to notice that the offerings were disappearing from the shrine, almost as soon as they were put out. When pig-slaughtering time came around, somebody left a beautiful plate of blood sausages in front of the saint's image; but they disappeared the same night."

"Was this shrine outdoors, by any chance?" asked Mallet.

"Listen to what happened, before you laugh!" said Spoke. "This priest had a mole on his face—"

Mallet began to chortle.

"And from that night it began to grow, you see? It got huge, hanging down the front of his face, and it turned dark red and looked *exactly* like a blood sausage!"

Mallet fell back, guffawing, and Smith snickered. Spoke stared at them, outraged.

"You think this is funny?" he demanded. "This really happened! I saw it with my own eyes! And finally the priest died of shame, but before he did, he confessed he'd been stealing the offerings left for the saint."

"Sounds like he died of a tumor, to me," said Mallet. "And I have news for you: all priests feed themselves on the stuff left at shrines. In my city, they did it openly. And what's so unusual about a child getting a fever? Children are always getting fevers. Especially in marshy country. Especially where people are too ignorant and superstitious to go to a doctor instead of a priest."

"So you're a skeptic," said Spoke, as though the word had a bad taste.

"I'm a sane man," said Mallet. "And proud of it, brother."

"I did see something I couldn't explain, once, though," said Smith thoughtfully.

"I've seen—" began Mallet.

Spoke made a strangling noise and jumped to his feet. He pointed at the statue.

"It turned its head!" he cried.

"No, it didn't," said Mallet wearily, tasting his soup. Smith turned to look, and went a little pale.

"It is facing the other way, now," he said.

"It's just your imagination," said Mallet.

"No, I'm sure—"

"I saw it move!" said Spoke. "Are you both crazy? Look at it!"

"It looks the same to me," said Mallet. "But if it did move—well, it's sitting on an uneven surface, right? And we're outdoors. The wind could have shifted it."

"It's too heavy for the wind to shift," said Smith.

"Then, it didn't move," said Mallet with finality. "And if you think you saw it move, then your eyes were playing tricks on you, because statues don't move."

"Look at it," said Smith. "I'm not joking, Mallet."

Mallet turned and looked. "I didn't notice which way it was facing before. It might have been facing that way, for all I know. We're dead-tired, we haven't eaten in hours, and we breathed in a lot of smoke. How can we trust what we see?"

Smith looked from Mallet to the statue, shook his head, and leaned forward to stir his soup. Spoke backed away a few paces, watching the statue in silence. After a long moment he sat down again, and without taking his eyes off the statue reached for his helmet. It was hot, and he drew back his hand with a cry of pain.

"Uh-oh! Another bad omen," said Mallet.

"Just shut up," said Spoke.

Smith slipped out of his jacket and used it to lift his helmet from the fire, gingerly, and propped the helmet between his boots as he dug in his pack for a tin cup. He dipped out some of the soup and blew on it to cool it. Mallet followed his example. Spoke did not. The statue watched them all without comment, as the light danced on its golden face.

"Aren't you going to eat?" Smith inquired of Spoke.

"Not yet," said Spoke.

"Can we have your soup, then?" asked Mallet.

"Go ahead," said Spoke.

"Oh, come on!" said Smith. "You can't be so scared of that thing you don't eat. That's stupid."

"Let him suit himself," said Mallet, slurping his portion.

"I'll have it later, then," said Spoke. Mallet looked sidelong at Smith.

"So," he said, "How'll we divide watches?"

"I'll take first watch," said Spoke.

"All right," said Mallet slyly. "That all right with you, Smith?"

"Fine," said Smith. He glanced over at the statue.

They finished their soup, tilting the helmets to get out the bits that hadn't dissolved, and pulled blankets out of their packs.

"I'm dead tired," said Mallet. "Aren't you, Smith?"

"Too bloody right I am," Smith replied. He felt about on the rock with his hands, trying to find a place where its bumps and hollows roughly corresponded with his own. Giving up at last, he wrapped himself in his blanket and settled down. Mallet spread his blanket out, and opened Spoke's pack.

"I'll just borrow your blanket, then, Spoke, since you'll be sitting up," he said. "You won't mind, eh?"

"No, I won't mind," said Spoke.

Mallet fed a couple of sticks into the fire. He stretched out beside it. Smith shifted to make room for him, glancing one more time at the statue. It did not seem to have moved, but he couldn't be sure.

An hour went by. Tired as he was, Smith couldn't drop off. The stone on which he lay seemed to suck all the heat from his body. As he was debating whether to get up and move closer to the fire, he felt Mallet sit up abruptly.

"Drop that right now," said Mallet. Smith rolled over and saw Spoke, backing away from the fire, clutching the statue in his arms.

"I'm saving all our lives," said Spoke. "I'm taking this back."

"Are you crazy?" Smith said. "The Briscians will cut you to pieces!"

"You idiot, that's our retirement pay," said Mallet, who had thrown the blanket aside and scrambled to his feet. He was holding a spike-axe in his hand. "I knew you were going to do something stupid. Give it here!"

"I—" said Spoke, but Mallet lunged forward and grabbed the statue by one raised arm, the one bearing a tiny dagger.

"Give it here!"

"No!"

And it seemed to Smith, as he stared at them, that the golden figure writhed like a living thing between them, turned its shining body, and Spoke must have seen it too because he gasped and let go. Mallet pulled it away from him.

"I'll tell you what," he said, "I'll fix your holy saint right now. I'll pound the damn thing into pieces right here. The goldsmiths won't care—"

He knelt and set the statue on the rock, preparing to hit it with his spike-axe, but Spoke leaped forward.

"You mustn't—"

Mallet turned and swung at him in exasperation, hitting him squarely between the eyes with the spike end of the weapon. Spoke halted where he was, staring, and Smith sat bolt upright.

"Holy gods, what've you done?"

"Shit," said Mallet. He pushed at Spoke, who toppled backward on his heels and fell, smacking his head on the rock, carrying with him Mallet's spike-axe that was firmly stuck in his skull.

"I didn't mean to do that," said Mallet, breathing hard.

"You killed him," said Smith in horror.

"I didn't even hit him that hard," said Mallet. "Stupid bastard! If he hadn't been so superstitious—"

"Spoke!" Smith crawled to his side. He pulled the axe free; slow blood rose from the neat squared hole, ran down into Spoke's left eye.

"It was his own fault," said Mallet. "You saw."

"Well, he's dead, whoever's fault it was," said Smith. He dropped the weapon in disgust. "What do we do now?"

"Pitch him over the edge," said Mallet, nodding at the falls. "I'm not sleeping by a corpse."

"What, without even saying a prayer?" demanded Smith. "You can't be afraid his ghost is going to come make faces at you!"

"Of course I don't believe in ghosts!" said Mallet. "But it's stupid to camp by dead meat in a forest. The smell will attract wolves. Lions. Who knows?"

Smith swore at him. He dragged the body to the edge of the rock and arranged its limbs in a less undignified way. After searching through the pockets, he crossed the hands on its chest and stood with head bowed, murmuring a prayer under his breath.

"As though that'll help him," muttered Mallet. "That's what got him killed, you know. That kind of thinking. And he'd have died anyway, if he'd gone back to the city. The Briscians would have killed him, and not quickly either. As it was, he died in a split-second. Didn't he?"

Smith glared at him but did not miss a word of his prayer. When he had finished, he nudged the body forward with his boot, over the edge, and it rolled from the firelight and dropped, vanished into the shadow. A moment later, from far below, he heard a *smack* and winced, hoping the body had landed in the water at least.

He walked back to the fire and sat down across from Mallet. The statue lay still where Mallet had dropped it, smiling up at the forest canopy and the few stars.

"Well, that's done it for me sleeping here tonight," Smith said. "I'll keep watch and you can sleep, or we can both push on."

"Maybe it'd be wisest to go," Mallet agreed. He looked at the statue again and cleared his throat. "But it would still be a good idea to break the damn thing up, don't you agree? That way we can split the weight. You'll get your share, I'll get mine, and if we decide to go our separate ways, well, the loot's already divided. You can have one of the eyes. I'll take the other."

"Whatever you say," Smith replied curtly.

"I think they must be aquamarines," said Mallet, reaching for his spike-axe. "The Tyrant at Deliantiba buys them for his mistress, did you know? Has a standing offer out for good ones. Maybe I'll go there."

He put his hand down to steady the image before he struck.

There was a flash of gold, a glint in the firelight, and Mallet howled and drew his hand back. Smith jumped to his feet.

"It stabbed you!"

"No, it didn't," said Mallet, clutching his hand. "A coal popped in the fire, that's all. A spark jumped."

"I saw its arm move! It stabbed you with that little dagger!"

"Don't be stupid," said Mallet, lifting his hand to his mouth. He sucked the flesh at the base of his thumb. Smith stared at him a moment, and then grabbed for Mallet's hand. Mallet ducked away, rolling over.

"Let it alone!" he said, putting his hand inside his shirt, but Smith glimpsed the bright blood-bead.

"That's not a burn, that's a wound," he said. "It could be poisoned! What's the matter with you?"

"There's nothing the matter with me," said Mallet, evening his breath. "But I'll tell you what's wrong with *you*. It's the power of suggestion, isn't it?

You and Spoke, the pair of you, you were raised to buy into everything the priests said. So all that, that superstitious horseshit preys on your minds. See? Even though you know better now. Here we are in the dark in the woods, and we've been seeing death all day, and—wouldn't you think Spoke'd have had more sense than to start scaring himself? And you?"

"Look, I know what I saw," said Smith.

"No; you know what you *think* you saw," said Mallet doggedly. "It's all in your mind. You're so worked up, after what happened, that your brain's making ghosts out of everything. The mind does that. It's not reliable."

"Well, your burn is bleeding through your shirt," said Smith.

"No," said Mallet, with elaborate patience, "You only think you see blood."

"Oh, you jackass," said Smith, and went back to his side of the fire, but he gave the statue a wide berth.

There was a long moment of silence. Mallet stared into the fire.

"Or I'll tell you what else it might be," he said at last. "There was an earthquake today, right? And we're still getting aftershocks. Well, that could be affecting our minds too. Making us hallucinate. Something in the rocks maybe, quartz veins clashing together and all. I've heard it makes animals go crazy. Hell, aren't we sitting on a big rock? So there you are."

He was sweating, and his face had gone pale under the soot and dust of the day.

Smith spoke in as reasonable a voice as he could.

"I'm not arguing with you," he said. "I don't believe in omens any more than you do, and I don't think the saint in Spoke's village worked miracles. I'm just saying there might be something going on we don't understand."

"No!" said Mallet. "Don't you see that the minute you believe in craziness like this, you open the door and let in the monsters? Give in this much and you'll believe anything. What you can see with your own eyes is all there is, man."

"But you just got through telling me I couldn't trust my eyes," said Smith. "Or my mind. And if we can't believe our senses, then how can we perceive anything? There might really be fairies in the flowers. How would we know?"

"The point is," said Mallet, with some difficulty, "the point is, everything can be explained. All right? Real things can be measured with calipers. We live in a rational world."

Smith stared at him. "You're a *soldier*," he said. "How the hell can you think we live in a rational world?"

Mallet just gazed at the fire. He sighed, and his hand dropped down on his lap. Smith saw clearly the dried blood, the livid swelling that had spread up his arm.

"That thing's poisoned you," he stated.

"No," said Mallet thickly. "Scorpion hiding in the firewood. Maybe. And we didn't see it."

There was a tiny noise, like the muffled chime of a bell. Smith glanced over to see that the image had indeed turned its head, was looking straight at Mallet now. Mallet raised his eyes too, looked into the statue's bright eyes.

"Scorpion," he repeated. "S'all."

The chime came again. The statue was raising its arm, the one with the tambourine, slow but unmistakable.

"Mallet," said Smith, very quietly, "Let's get out of here."

"What?" said Mallet. "Nothing there. Nothing to be scared of. It's just the play of the light."

"Mallet, the damn thing's moving *right now.*"

Mallet said nothing else. He leaned over and lay down, as though he were tired, and his breath began to rattle in his throat.

Smith got up, edged his way around the far side of the fire, and caught hold of Mallet's leg.

"Come on," he whispered. Mallet didn't reply. He dragged Mallet a few feet and realized he was dragging dead weight; Mallet stared up sightless, and now Smith could see that the livid swelling had spread all the way to his throat.

Smith let go; Mallet's leg dropped like a sandbag. Smith looked over at the statue. It smiled still. Was it moving?

He backed away, crouching as he went, not taking his eyes off the statue, into the running shallows until water rushed over the tops of his boots. He felt around for a rock. Here: his hands told him he had hold of a good one, the size of a melon, water-smoothed and flat on one side. He hefted it experimentally. Then he lifted it over his head and pitched it at the statue.

It landed with a crash, and the distinct sound of breaking pottery. The fire leaped up, bright, shining on Mallet's dead face.

Smith walked up the bank slowly, but nothing happened. He squelched around the perimeter of the fire. Picking up a long branch from the pile of firewood, he levered the rock to one side.

The image of the saint lay in pieces. It wasn't gold after all, only gilded; though the gears and springs inside it, all its subtle mechanisms, shone like something precious.

Smith poked through it with the stick. Here was the little glass reservoir, shattered, leaking green venom now, and here was the clever tube that had sent its charge of poison up into the hollow dagger. Here was the lead weight in the base, where the pulleys had anchored that moved the golden limbs. Was this a switch, here, cleverly concealed? Had it been jostled in the rout, or when it had fallen over? What were these characters, inscribed to either side of it? Did they spell out, in fabulously archaic Briscian, BLESS and CURSE?

Or merely ON and OFF?

The face had been cracked open, and both blue stones knocked loose. Smith prodded them each a safe distance from the rest of the debris, and bent and slipped them into his pocket. He pushed the rest of it into the coals, adding more wood to the fire. Then he went back to his blanket and sat down, and pulled off his wet boots.

For a while there were strange popping and chiming noises from the fire, and every so often the flames leaped up in peculiar colors. The wood lasted until morning.

He walked all the way to Deliantiba to see if he could find a buyer for the stones, but the jeweler he consulted laughed in his face. He was kind enough to show Smith a case of real aquamarines; then he showed him foil-backed paste stones, and invited Smith to judge for himself what he had.

A girl in a public house admired them, so he gave them to her in exchange for a plate of fried fish.

Desolation Rose

Everyone knows that if a woman goes out on Winter's Eve, and makes a fire in some wild place where gods walk, Fate will notice her. She'll huddle beside that fire, waiting: and, some time before dawn, a god will come.

In the morning, the woman will not be the same.

It isn't always good, what happens beside that fire. Sometimes, when morning light comes, there's a dead woman lying in the wilderness. Maybe only a few and closely gnawed bones.

Even, sometimes, a woman comes away alive but raving mad: hair white overnight, tangling the flowers together forever, her hands restless.

But sometimes a woman walks home having given and taken, having got something in a secret bargain. Sometimes a woman comes back smiling in secret; nine months later a child of amazing destiny is born.

It's how the god deals with the woman that makes the difference, and he deals according to what he finds waiting at the fire.

Fearing the unknown, most women stay in their beds on Winter's Eve, or beside their own hearth fires, where no cold hand is likely to come reaching in the night. But, now and then, a girl grows to womanhood restless-hearted. Maybe she yearns after an eternal something she can't put a name to; maybe she is in dreadful need; maybe she's bored, or just too silly to know better. Whatever the cause, one Winter's Eve, out she'll go: and it's another one for the storytellers.

The Yendri, in their forest bowers, knew this custom. The Children of the Sun in their cities knew it. It was known to the Master of the Mountain and to his blessed wife, the Saint of the World, and to their very mixed bag of children. Especially and personally, it was known to Lord Ermenwyr, their third son.

*   *   *

The mage Ermenwyr was wise, cunning and controlled. He was not madly magical, like his brother Eyrdway; not noble and spiritual like his brother Demaledon. He was a man of craft, prudent, deeply cautious. By careful stratagems he worked his will, and sorceries rather than feats of arms. He was not a coward, exactly; but if argument or lies could do the trick (he reasoned), why put on all that heavy armor?

Still, he had a weakness, this subtle man. He was incautious in one thing: Lechery.

He was a ladies' man, was Ermenwyr! His beard was combed, perfumed; his sorcerer's robes were cut with style and elegance. He was small of stature but well-made and handsome, and his manners were oil-smooth and charming when he wanted them to be. When he wasn't brewing careful spells or plotting politics or studying his investments (and sometimes even then) he was attempting to slip into some lady's bed. Successfully, as a rule.

But he never stayed long in a bed once he'd got in, seldom came back to one he'd tried. He was faithless by inclination.

Ermenwyr was often sent down alone from the Master's mountain, into the lands below: he'd spy for his father, conducting that business with cold-hearted skill, or do his own shady deals. Once, on such a journey, he was benighted on a dark road as a storm broke fearfully.

His brother Eyrdway would have laughed, dancing between the lightning bolts; his brother Demaledon would have plodded on bravely through the rain. But fastidious Ermenwyr had a horror of catching cold. So when he saw a light in the darkness he hurried toward it, shouldering through black dripping leaves, pulling his cloak close.

Crack cried the wet sky, and purple lights danced above the wet trees, and the wet sorcerer waded up to the gate of a vast wet house. It was high-walled and frowning, but the gates were rusty: only one lamp flared above the wall. Clearly it was some place fallen on bad times.

Ermenwyr wondered—briefly—whose ancient house was in the middle of nowhere; more, he wondered what he had to do to get someone to open the door. He hammered at the great gates without getting any response. The rain soaked him. Finally, at a barred grate, he saw two pale faces peer out. Someone with a thin sad voice called: "What do you want?"

Ermenwyr called: "Shelter!" thinking that folk were certainly suspicious in these parts. "I beg only a dry place beside your fire! In High God's name, let me in!"

At last the sad voice replied:

"In High God's name, then." The two faces disappeared from the grate.

A long while later he heard slow footsteps, stumbling up behind the gate. It creaked open a little, and he saw three hands straining to push. He got his fingers round it too and pulled it with all his wiry strength, and slipped through nimbly as a weasel going down a hole.

The gate crashed to behind him, and he stood in a rainy courtyard. *Flash*, lightning blued the world: standing before him were a man and a girl. The girl was beautiful. The man was hideous. Half his face was gone, only a ropy mass of scars where it had been.

Ermenwyr wheezed with exertion, and said: "Thank you. Where is your fire, good people? I must get dry."

"You can come in, but I can't guarantee you'll get dry," muttered the man. He turned and shuffled through a dark doorway. The girl followed. Ermenwyr hurried after, watching the girl's lovely back.

Deep they went into the dark house, through narrow stone corridors, through echoing rooms that dripped rain. At last they came to a bare room where a tiny fire struggled on the hearth. It threw dim red light on no carpets, no tapestries, no cushions nor chairs. Rain hissed in the chimney.

"Ahem! What a fine cheerful fire," said Ermenwyr, being a good guest. "But it will never dry my cloak, you were right about that. I'll build it up for you."

He gestured, and the fire blazed up as if fed with seasoned wood. Smiling, for he was proud of the effect, he turned to his hosts. But they weren't staring in open-mouthed admiration; they had drawn together and regarded him with weary resigned faces, the beauty and the horror alike.

"Ah—do not be surprised," he said anyway.

"We're not," said the man.

After a discomfited pause, Ermenwyr added meaningfully, "For, you see, I am a powerful sorcerer."

"Yes," said the girl. "We'd guessed."

"Yes. Well." Ermenwyr was taken aback. He looked about the room. He saw only a leaning table, bearing the remains of a paltry meal. A torn curtain hung across a broken window, flapping in the wind, letting in the rain.

His hosts wore raiment that had once been fine, but was now worn to threadbare cobwebs, through which Ermenwyr saw that the girl was lovely indeed: but as sad music is lovely, or the twilight. The man looked worse. Not only half his face was gone; half his body was maimed, one arm missing, one leg crooked.

Ermenwyr, trying to make the best of an awkward social situation, cleared his throat and said:

"I don't suppose you see sorcerers very often, out here."

The girl trembled but the man laughed, a dreadful long rusted laugh.

"Oh, we've seen our share of sorcerers. We've seen more sorcerers than most people! So, what have you come to inflict on us?"

Ermenwyr was taken aback at this, and stammered:

"I mean you no harm at all, man! Who are you, and what is this place?"

The man drew himself up, as far as he was able.

"Sir, we are the last of what was once a noble house. We were the Aronikai, governors in the city of Brogoun. My brother was the lord, but he made terrible enemies: Assassins. Sorcerers. Politicians. They were powerful, inventive in their revenge, and they have wasted us. One by one we have been slain or exiled, ruined or driven mad. This ruin was the least of our properties: but here we hide, my niece and I, in its dead hulk, and I am more ruined than the house. We alone are left of the Aronikai.

"You would think, sir, that this was enough revenge; but someone ensures that we grow ever poorer. The trees in the orchard died, the game hereabouts has fled, the well's dry. Some vigilant mage tightens the screw daily and kills us by inches. You, maybe."

"Not I, sir, on my honor as a lord's son!" Ermenwyr protested. "And my father is a powerful lord indeed. As your guest, I will protect you."

He cast about him with his bright mage's eye, and perceived a sullen hating Presence that watched. Whatever it was, it recognized the son of the Master of the Mountain, and withdrew its influence under his cold scrutiny.

The girl said, in her voice as sad as violets, "If you're not lying, we'll have one night in peace. Last night a pack of wolves howled beyond the wall until sunrise. The night before that an army of rats fought in the walls for hours. This morning a hailstone fell from a clear sky, right through our last whole window. You see how it is."

She said it simply, straightforward: she had learned that to complain is to send a message written in invisible ink to a blind man.

Ermenwyr turned his expression of greatest benevolence to her.

"My dear child, have no fear; I am respected and honored in my profession. See now! I can summon cheer even in this dank abode."

He flexed the muscles of his glittering mind, and the room was filled with good things. There were cushions and carpets and a cloth spread with a glorious feast, and many bottles of fine wine. It was all illusory, but Ermenwyr was not only boasting for effect when he claimed prowess as a sorcerer: it was the very best illusion. Every sense was fooled and gratified by his display.

His hosts cried out and ran to partake of the repast: hot bread, roasted meats and fowl, fruit melting-ripe. There for an hour they were a little happy, dining in comfort as Ermenwyr poured wine and regaled them with traveler's tales.

It is a curious fact that illusory food satisfies better than real fare, and illusory wine intoxicates faster than real vintages. Ermenwyr was particularly solicitous in refilling the glass of the noble uncle, who shortly lay snoring on illusory cushions before the fire.

This suited Ermenwyr perfectly, of course (he had already decided on his own treat), and he turned his attentions to the girl. He didn't care that she wore rags; he could see her pale skin peeping through like stars through clouds. He didn't care that she sat sad and dignified as a figure on a tomb; his design was to warm that marble.

"Now, my dear," he purred, "you've told me nothing of yourself, not even your name!" He made to pour her more wine; but she set aside her glass.

"No, thank you, my lord," she said. "I am a little drunk. As for my name: I was Golden Rose of the Aronikai once, but now I am Desolation Rose."

"Desolation Rose!" Ermenwyr exclaimed, and drank her health from his own glass. "Truly an original and beautiful name, though not so beautiful as its bearer."

She smiled bitterly.

"My name will be my death, and my beauty will last only until our enemies find a way to wither it. My poor uncle was handsome, once. Do you know what they did to him?"

"Something dreadful, obviously. But please, don't make yourself more sorrowful. Be safe with me, lady! Steal delight, while I stand guard against despair. Shall we not be thieves of felicity together, tonight, though tomorrow brings another bleak day? Why, your enemies may even withdraw if I take you under my protection."

Desolation Rose shook her head. "They won't. You don't know them. Tomorrow something will die under the floor, or a black fungus will begin to grow in the pantry, or another corner of the house will collapse. Every morning, a new and miserable surprise."

"It sounds perfectly dreadful," sympathized Ermenwyr, hitching himself closer. She stared at him thoughtfully.

"I suppose, even now, you might be some agent of theirs," she said, "come to sharpen pain by giving us this brief respite. I don't care if you are. Anything you do to us will only bring us closer to the end of our sufferings. Tell that to your masters, if they are your masters, and tell them we still spit on them."

This sort of talk was not very conducive to a seduction, so Ermenwyr decided to abandon subtlety.

"I am no enemy of yours, Desolation Rose, on my life. Won't you make the night sweet with me, here upon the hearth? For I tell you truly, you are the loveliest girl I've seen in weeks, and I feel sincerest desire for you. Such beauty, and such bravery too, is worth gold. Let me pleasure you here, and give you a rich gift. Your uncle sleeps soundly."

Some fine ladies would have gone white with shame, and some red with anger. Desolation Rose only looked him in the eye and said:

"If I thought I could benefit from lying with you, I'd do it, make no mistake. But I've a reason to keep my maidenhead; and since you've made me such a kind offer, I'll tell you what it is."

She said, "I mean to go out Winter's Eve and present myself to the god. As I am a virgin, I'll beg him in trade to save our poor house. And if the sacrifice is not acceptable to him and he kills me, at least our enemies will lose a victim. My uncle can't last long, alone. So our torment will end."

Ermenwyr sighed and cursed the fate benighting him among the Children of the Sun, a race for whom the vendetta was an art form.

"You're foolish, Desolation Rose, but you have a brave heart. All the same—Winter's Eve is only a few nights away. Will you end your life so soon, never having known bliss? Where is it written that the god demands only virgins? Won't he be just as impressed by your laudable sense of familial piety?"

But Desolation Rose said, "I must make the best offering I can, and my maidenhead is all I have left. Thank you all the same."

"Well, may the god reward you," said Ermenwyr sullenly. They settled down some distance from each other, and soon Desolation Rose was asleep.

Ermenwyr, though, lay awake, still desiring her very much and musing to himself how he might have her.

In the morning he got up, thanked his hosts and pushed on, leaving them a purse of gold. The gold was real enough; he was crafty, but he wasn't cheap.

As Ermenwyr left the pitiful House of the Aronikai behind him, he heard a howling in the woods, as if glad wolves were let off some leash; and a flock of carrion crows rose from the trees where they had waited, and went back to perch on the crumbling battlements.

Ermenwyr came to the city and his father's errands took little time. The temple porter was easily bribed, the worthless stock soon sold to the eager merchant, and the spy had his report neatly written out and ready with a visual presentation. Nobody was sufficiently offended by his presence to challenge him to any duels. Ermenwyr enjoyed a leisurely evening at the theatre and breakfast on a sunlit terrace the next morning, before making his return.

And at sunset on Winter's Eve he waited in the forest, watching the gates of the House of the Aronikai. Presently he saw Desolation Rose creeping out, looking about her as the field mouse watches for the owl; she hurried away into the darkness. Ermenwyr tore down a piece of the sky—a corner, with no stars—for a cloak of invisibility, and went after her.

She walked a long way, up into high cold hills, gathering dry sticks as she went. In a bare open place she stopped. He watched from behind a standing stone as she made her small fire, and settled down by its meager warmth to wait.

Ermenwyr let her sit there until the stars had drifted far overhead and the mists were rising. (He was always scrupulous as to timing and effect.) Then he summoned his powers to him. Out of the night mist he conjured the illusion she expected to see: a towering figure of mysterious gloom. Then he walked out, just beyond the circle of firelight.

Desolation Rose looked up from where she crouched, shivering. Her eyes were wide. Motionless, like a small trapped thing, she watched his slow approach. He stood at last on the other side of the fire. Wordless. Waiting.

She drew all her strength into her heart, but couldn't make a sound. She knelt to him and her heart spoke instead, trusting that the god would know her prayer.

Ermenwyr smiled in his beard and kept his silence, as any god does. He came forward, and indicated to the girl that she should pleasure him.

So he lay with Desolation Rose, passing himself off as a god, and a very creditable job he did of it. Faint with terror and delight, she held him all night long.

When gray morning came she lay asleep; but Ermenwyr got up and made his departure, having had what he'd wanted. Beside the fire he left a bag with more gold, reasoning it would do her more good than revenge on her enemies, which he couldn't give her anyway. Still, for dramatic effect, he wrote the god's name in the ashes of her fire.

All lighthearted Ermenwyr went his way, and journeyed until under smirking stars he returned to his dread father's house. There he went straight to his apartments, flung himself into bed, and slept the sleep of the just.

He woke greatly refreshed, in broad morning. He bathed and dressed himself with more than usual care, for he was to make a report to his father on his affairs among the Children of the Sun. Then Ermenwyr went to his long mirror to comb his beard and preen a little.

He looked once—What? He rubbed his eyes, peered in the glass, and let out a cry of horror. Instead of the small dapper sorcerer he was so fond of looking at, there in the mirror was reflected a looming darkness with eyes. Distant lightnings crackled in its heart.

Now Ermenwyr was terrified. He looked down at himself but could see nothing different. He looked back in the mirror and there It was still. He ran to his dresser and found a hand mirror to peruse: there It was with Its cloudy head. He ran to his washbasin and looked in at his reflection: even yet It looked out at him with Its hollow eyes. He found a crystal ball and glanced at its surface: it roiled and boiled so with the phantom image that he thrust it hastily into a sock drawer.

Ermenwyr's heart hammered. In every reflective surface in the room clouds shifted; stars burned there.

Cautiously he opened his door. He stepped out in the corridor; looked this way, looked that way. His father's guards were posted down at one end, and they saluted him as they were wont to do.

He went up to them and said, with a terrible effort at calm:

"Do I look different today? Is there anything a little, well, unusual about my appearance?"

One of them was a big scaly reptilian fellow with fanged jaws that did not permit light conversation; nonetheless, he rumbled and shook his head No. The other guard blinked his small red eyes thoughtfully, and said:

"You've trimmed your beard, my lord?"

"Thank you," said Ermenwyr, "I just wondered if anyone would notice. Where is my father?"

The guards bowed deeply, and the one said, "Your lord father is in the exercise yard, sir."

Ermenwyr set off at a run.

He found Shadlek his father armed, raining blows on his practice opponent. Ermenwyr waited on the sidelines, fidgeting, until the bout was concluded. As Shadlek stood back and removed his helmet, Ermenwyr hurried up to him.

"Um.... Father?"

The Master of the Mountain looked down at his son, and knit his black brows in a frown.

"What have you done, Ermenwyr?" he said in a voice like thunder.

Ermenwyr cried out in relief and fear.

"You see it too? Oh, Father, what is it?"

Shadlek scowled and made a few passes in the air with his gauntleted hand.

"It will not leave you. Did you steal something?"

"Only what you told me to!"

"Did you trespass in some sacred place?"

"Only where you bid me to!"

"Did you summon powers greater than your own?"

"No!"

"Then what crime did you commit other than the necessary crimes I sent you to commit?" said his father. "Tell me the truth, boy."

Shamefacedly Ermenwyr told his father about Desolation Rose, as they walked up and down the length of the exercise yard. Shadlek nodded thoughtfully.

"I did something like that once," he reminisced. "A wealthy man died and his wife went mad for grief. She had his heart placed in a gold reliquary covered with red sapphires, very fine. She went out lamenting, to wander the world with it.

"Hearing of the sapphires, I went down in search of her. I found her inching along a road, barefoot and ragged, weeping for her love.

"I put a glamour on myself and appeared as her dead husband's ghost; persuaded her I could not rest until my heart, and its handsomely decorated container, was returned to me. She complied, with many touching avowals of eternal passion. I sent her safely home."

Ermenwyr was curious despite himself. "What did you do then?"

"Burned the dead heart and kept the reliquary, of course. It's around here somewhere, I saw it only the other day...."

"Mother must have been angry with you," said Ermenwyr.

"Not at all," replied the sorcerer lord. "Consider, my son: the man's true heart dwelt in the bosom of the lady, beyond theft. It was not that lump of carrion, nor its house of gold. By relieving her of that macabre ornament I spared her the danger of carrying such a thing. She might have met with thieves, after all! So, no, your mother was not angry with me.

"But she'll certainly be angry with you. You did a stupid thing, boy: you impersonated a god, on the one night and in the one place it would be truly imprudent to do so. I thought I had trained you better!"

Ermenwyr said hastily:

"Yes, sir, but surely the thing now is to relieve me of this condition with all possible speed. What's to be done?"

His father grinned down at him and dusted his hands.

"I have no idea. You must go to your mother and ask her advice. Gods have never been my particular field of study."

"But she will reproach me," Ermenwyr said in a stricken voice.

"Even so." Shadlek nodded. "Run along now, my child."

Miserably Ermenwyr went to his mother's bower. It was peaceful there;

white rosemary flowered thick, bees droned in the still air. Inside, the sunlight filtered soft through the white flower petals: a place of utter calm, though Ermenwyr was far from tranquil as he beheld his lady mother.

The Saint knelt at her writing desk, composing a letter to her disciples. Her youngest grandchild slept near her in a willow basket.

Ermenwyr wondered nervously whether the baby was one of his. "H'em! Mother," he said, kneeling for her blessing.

"My child," she responded, placing her hand on his head. She sighed, and when he looked up he saw she was sadly regarding him. She knew exactly what was wrong with him and how he'd got that way, too. There was no fooling her.

"Oh, my son, you have done another wicked thing."

"Yes, Mother, I'm afraid so," Ermenwyr said meekly.

"I did not form a child with no heart in my womb, I know; how are you so cold and faithless? Now your behavior has set a wrathful god on your back."

"What has this god got to be angry about, anyway?" muttered Ermenwyr. "I was good to the poor girl. I gave her a pleasant night and ever so much money!"

"That is not the point," said the Saint. "You mocked her in your heart, which was cruel. But you have paid for it, my darling, and this time it's more than your father or I can mend. The girl opened a door to let in a god. You stood in that doorway and so the god moves through you, and all against your will you must do his Will."

Ermenwyr tugged at his beard in panic. "But what must I do to be free?" he cried. The baby woke up and began to wail. The Saint hushed and comforted it.

"Make reparation to that poor girl. She gave her body to the god in good faith; he intends to give her something in return. You must find out what it is, and bring it to her. Only then will the god leave you."

"But how will I know what the god wants?" Ermenwyr pleaded.

"You could break the habit of a lifetime and pray," said his mother. "Even your father prays, when it suits his purpose. No, don't look at me like that, with your eyes popping out of your head. You don't have a headache."

"Yes, I do!" wept Ermenwyr, but he hid his face in his hands.

"You're a sorcerer," the Saint reminded him. "Do a casting, if you can't bring yourself to meditate. My child, what will become of you? With all the disciplines to which you have applied yourself...."

You can imagine the rest. Covered in gloom, psychic as well as spiritual, Ermenwyr went to his study and prepared. In the magic mirrors, in the seeing spheres, in the curved surfaces of the retorts and alembics, the god's reflection glared thunderous.

Ermenwyr lit candles. He cast spells. The room filled with unearthly blue light.

The light emanated from three objects, in a corner of the casting chamber. Ermenwyr peered through the brilliance to see what they were, and cried out in real pain.

*   *   *

Desolation Rose of the Aronikai sat watching storm clouds cross the sky. She heard a cry from the gate; Ermenwyr standing there with a bundle in his arms.

She scrambled down, over missing bricks, and ran to let him in. The rain hadn't helped the gate. When at last he was inside and had caught his breath, Ermenwyr said:

"I suppose you didn't expect to see me again. But, as it happens, I've got something to deliver.

"On Winter's Eve, as I slept, a god appeared to me. He said: 'Go thou, dig beneath the first black stone that thou findest in thy path. Take what thou shalt find thereunder to Desolation Rose of the Aronikai, for she has pleased me.'

"I rose and went out and dug beneath the first black stone I saw and, would you believe it, there was an ancient chest with some things in it—" Ermenwyr set down and unwrapped his bundle, "which I thought I had better bring you—"

Desolation Rose looked on in wonder as he took out a small sword, a crystal pendant on a chain, and a flask of white glass. Ermenwyr held up the sword.

"This sword," he said, "is magical. It brings the strength of five warriors to its wielder."

He gave her the sword and took up the pendant.

"This pendant," he said, "is also magical. It wards off danger and brings wealth to its wearer."

He gave her the pendant and held up the flask.

"This flask," he said, "as you might have guessed, is magical too. The inexhaustible cordial within has great healing powers."

Desolation Rose took the flask, crying: "But how do you know these things?"

"I'm a sorcerer, after all," said Ermenwyr in some irritation. "I can vouch for their puissance."

Which was certainly true, for he himself had crafted them, with many hours of painstaking labor. He had been particularly proud of them, too.

Desolation Rose swept the sword through the air. It balanced to her hand as if it had been made for her (which it had not been).

"I gave myself to the god, as I said I'd do. Did you know that, sorcerer? And I doubted him, afterward."

"Never doubt the god," said Ermenwyr, solemn as a high priest. "He honors bargains."

Desolation Rose arranged the gifts on the cracked pavement and looked at them.

"With these things, all the fortunes of my house will be restored," she said. "Now our enemies may tremble. Great is the god, blessed is his name!"

"Amen!" said Ermenwyr ruefully.

Desolation Rose took up the gifts and went running in to see what the cordial could do for her uncle.

*   *   *

After that Desolation Rose became Fire Rose, the Fire Rose of the songs, and of course the story is well known how she avenged her family, brought her enemies to ignominious and horrible ends, and served her god bravely through many glorious adventures.

But Ermenwyr went back to his father's house; and the first thing he did there was look in his mirror.

There he stood, himself and no other. So great was his joy and his relief that he hurried off and tumbled one of the housemaids.

Ermenwyr was thenceforth prudent, and never again impersonated a god; save once at a costume ball in Troon, when he seduced the vice-regent's sister. But she knew perfectly well who was under the mask....

Miss Yahoo Has Her Say

Where you come from? Out of *me,* silly. Where I come from? From the field by the lake, on the day the Houyhnhnms came and kill Mama. I tell you about them.

We all swimming, except me. My skin burn red in the sun and hurt, so Mama show me how to put clay on. I all smear up nice and sit in shade. Then screaming start. Look up and see Masters all around the field, tramping stamping on people's heads. Some of the people jump in the water, swim; no good, because Masters on other side too, catch them all. Kill lots, everybody but me and two little boys. Brown Master stamp Mama dead with her head all red and I cry and cry.

So then, Masters tell us in their special talk: *You must obey us or you will die too.* They put nooses around our necks and made us walk away with them. They don't talk to us again. We all crying and screaming but they walk us down to wide land where we see big oat fields with lots of Yahoos working there, cutting down grass, and white Servants watching them. I see lots of Yahoos working hard, different work, and they all going on hands and feet, not standing up!

We come to house and there's little house too, off under some trees, and Masters make us go there and go inside. I never seen house yet then. They tie nooses to wall so we can't get out, and then big brown Master says: *Listen, young Yahoos. We wish to see if you can be improved. You will be fed as rational creatures feed, to see if your savage appetites can be reformed.* What that mean? Means they gave us big bowls milk, and boxes grass and oats. Then they went away.

We drank milk, but grass and oats taste bad. Pretty soon we eat them anyway, because that's all they give us to eat. No roots, no meat, no berries! Days and nights and days and nights, just grass and oats! Make our stomachs sick. Sometimes Masters come look at us and talk in their talk. Big brown Master shakes his head up and down, black and red Masters shake their heads to and fro. We starve. But I learn catch little mousies come in eat the oats, and I climb up to roof bars and catch birds land there. Little boys get weak, pretty soon they die. I don't die. Master comes and says: *My experiment is not a complete failure. It may be that the male Yahoos are incurably savage in their habits, to the point of being unable to thrive on civilized food; but you females are more docile and tractable, as are our own mares, and our diet agrees with you. Very well, Yahoo child. We will now see if you can learn rational behavior.*

What *that* means is, he don't know I catching my own food, so he think he can make me like a Houyhnhnm. I cry and yell. He say: *This is not an auspicious beginning! What do you hope to accomplish by howling like that?*

And I tell him, I mad because he kill my Mama and all the uncles and aunts. He tell me, good thing they died—they were bad Yahoos who wouldn't work for Masters. I tell him I love my Mama.

He say: *If you are to become a rational creature, you must learn that this foolish fondness is one of the things that makes you beasts. I felt not the least distress when my own Dam went to her first mother; since death is inevitable, wild behavior on that account is sheerest unreason. And in any case, I did not kill your mother.*

What he means is, crying and missing people is stupid Yahoo thing. And I say: But you did kill my Mama, I saw you. He shakes his head. *You are saying the thing which is not,* he says. When Houyhnhnms do something they don't want anybody to know about, see, they call it *The Thing Which Is Not,* and then it just never happen. They think. And he say: *If you say the thing which is not again, you will be sent to work in the sun with the other Yahoos. If, however, you refrain from such talk and speak truth like a Houyhnhnm, I will continue my experiment with you, and you will not be treated like a brute beast.*

So I said I be good, because I *cunning and treacherous.* That mean, not dumb. And after that I live in little house all alone, but every day white Servant name Yhlee come take me out for *Improvement.* That means he try make me more like Houyhnhnm, every day. I can't stand up; must bend over and try walk on hands and feet, just like poor Yahoos working in field. It hurt my hands but Yhlee say I get used to it. And he teach me talk Master talk, and he teach me all about how we Yahoos stupid and bad and how Houyhnhnm good and wise, and that's why they Masters, and we Yahoos must work hard for them.

And he take me to wash every day in the lake, but I can't swim because he make me wear noose. I sad, seeing field where everybody die. I sad think of Mama's bones in the dirt with bugs crawling on them.

But—this funny, listen. When we up there all alone by lake, Yhlee tell me scratch him all over, and smack and kill flies. Flies are *the thing which is not,* see. They bite and itch Houyhnhnms bad, all over, but nobody supposed notice and NEVER EVER scratch bites. So when Yhlee make me scratch him, it *the thing which is not*. When he make me take little stones out of his feet, that *the thing which is not* too. And best *thing which is not* of all is when he make me dig him up Crazyroot, and he eat it and get silly and tell me *Poetry*. That's song-talk about how nice Houyhnhnms are to friends, or how fast they run, or how they better than anybody else. When Crazyroot wears off he take me back down again, and of course I say nothing to anybody because it all *the thing which is not*.

All this time they only giving me grass and oats to eat, so I catching birds and mice too, and soon I figure out how get noose untied and I go out at night get more food. I be careful careful, because Servants watch all time. Sometimes I see other Yahoos sneaking around, but all scared of us and run away. But I don't run away. I always go back little house. I like not working hard and not dirty like other Yahoos.

Yahoos not *Improved* like me work so hard! Men must pull plows, and sledges to drag old Masters around. Women must make bowls and pots and fire for Masters, and they must cook oats for old Masters. Everybody must cut poles and branches make houses for Masters, and weave hurdles for walls and dig big holes put posts in. Masters can't do these because they got no hands, but Yhlee says that why Nature made us to do things for them. Sometimes he bring in old Yahoo woman show me how be *useful* with my hands. She mad, she mean, but Yhlee not let her hit me, he make her show me how weave things and braid things, and how take flint and smack it just the way make all little sharp cutters and scrapers.

Sometimes Yhlee fall asleep, though, standing up, and old lady make mean faces at me. She say: Stuck up little bitch! Why YOU so special? Why you get to wash and not work in Houses? I tell her, I being *Improved*. I an *Experiment*. She say, Ha Ha, Master always try that but it never work. Yahoos not Houyhnhnms. You a Yahoo even if they treat you special.

I scared, so I tell her: Not treated special! All I get to eat is oats and grass like Masters! I must sneak out at night get bird and rats and fruit to eat! When I tell her this, she smile, mean smile, and I scared again.

She go back to House and tell Master's Mare about me going out at night for food. Next thing, Yhlee coming out, say I not being *Improved* any more, Master very *sickened and disappointed at my relapse into brute nature*. That means he giving me to new Master to work in House.

So he did, but you know what? Me escaping at night is *the thing which is not*, because old Master embarrassed anybody know I fool him! So new Master not know I can get out of noose! So first night in new House, I untie and sneak out while Master and family asleep. I sneak real good now, I know how get past Servants, and before light comes I get up to lake where Mama and everybody died.

I want look for Mama's bones, but wild Yahoos up there and they see me and come down, grab me to play Bumpbump. First time anybody does that with me and hurts some, but they not so mean as tame Yahoos and not stink like them either. When they all through they ask where I come from, why I there. I tell them. They help me dig and dig for bones. Pretty soon we find some must be my Mama's, so beautiful, and I wash them and wrap up careful in grass and hide in tree so not lost. They find others, because lots Yahoo die there, and they wash and hide them in tree too so dead Yahoos not be sad.

And I was wild Yahoo after that, and so happy! Eat good things whenever I want, run and play with other Yahoos, never ever must go on hands and feet like Houyhnhnm but standing up! Back hurt no more. I show wild Yahoos how weave and we make houses up trees, where woods too thick for Houyhnhnms to go in catch us. They can't climb trees! Safe and not afraid all time. I make nice place for Mama's bones, put flowers all around.

Sometimes we go down lake to swim, catch fish, be so careful! But Yhlee never there. His bites itch him, ha ha.

Sometimes we go down through trees, branch to branch, never climb down, and watch poor Yahoos work for Masters. Oats are green, then oats turn yellow, then Yahoos must cut down with sharp sticks and carry away to Masters' houses. When fields all empty, Yahoos herded back by Masters and BAD thing happen: all Yahoos told lie down and Masters go along, stamp on heads of ones they don't want. Mostly old Yahoos but sometimes young Yahoos too, sometimes even baby Yahoos. Then ones not killed must carry all dead to big pile and set on fire, and after rake ashes into field so rain wash them in. We cry see this, and at night go down dig for bones. Sometimes Servants chase us, almost catch us.

But wild Yahoos show me how put clay on, smeary, stripy, so if we hide in bushes we hard to see, so we not caught ever, find lots of bones. We happy, and dead Yahoos happy.

Long time happy like this, until new thing, worse thing happen. Lake where bad things happen, always.

I go down for wash, catch fish, swim a long time under the cool water. Then I come up and see big Yahoo on shore, and Servant with him. Yahoo sees me but Servant not. I think, he must be old Master's new *Experiment,* up here wash like I was, but no noose on his neck. I hope he not tell Servant, and I swim away so quiet to find bushes climb out by. But big Yahoo jumps in water, swims to me, pulls me out and tries make Bumpbump. But he puts it in wrong place, and it hurts! I yell and yell. Servant comes clopping up and sees, laughs at us HEEhaw Heehaw Heehaw! Big Yahoo pushes me away and yells in Houyhnhnm: *She attacked me! The vile lewd minx assaulted my person!*

That means he tells Servant I Bumpbump HIM, which is silly, and Servant keeps laughing. I very surprised; laughing is *the thing which is not* for Masters, because they know it make them look dumb. But this only Servant anyhow. Strange Yahoo he so funny-looking, thin white face and little thin nose like flint scraper, and no hair on face, just like me! Soft like me, too, but he man all the same—big dumb thing hanging down scared now.

I try run away fast, but Servant stop laughing and chase me down—and he tell big Yahoo help him, and he does! And they catch me and big Yahoo makes noose and puts around my neck. Big Yahoo pulls on bags all over his body, cover up his thing. He ask Servant why catch me, Servant says this bad Yahoo ran away from Master one time. I scared then. They take me down old way like long time ago, and soon we see house and little house where I lived.

They take me in and Servant tells Master all what happen. Everybody there make snorting in their nose, it so funny to them, though nobody Heehaw laugh out loud. Big Yahoo turn all red in face, get mad.

Master say: *This is the second time you have attempted to mate with a Yahoo. Both times, however, you have attempted the act with children—and one of them male!—rather than with a female of procreative age! What reason can you give us for such acts of unreason, gentle Yahoo?* That mean, Master want to know why he play Bumpbump with me and not Yahoo with titties. Big Yahoo get redder still and say: *The Servant is mistaken in what he saw; this young wench made amorous advances to ME, and, when violently rebuffed, turned her posterior to discharge her excrement upon me. It was the same with the boy, as I told you.* This mean, same lie as before, only dirtier.

Servants think this so funny they pull lips up to show teeth, and even Master turns his head. Then he say: *I think you have said the thing which is not again. See here, Gentle Yahoo, it goes against reason to deny Nature. You are a male, with all the urges a male must feel, and by your account you have gone some years without a mate. This cannot be conducive to peace. I command you to take a mate to provide for your need.*

Big Yahoo look at me like he want Bumpbump right there, but then he make all kinds faces and whine and cry to Master that he can't Bumpbump with *hideous* Yahoos because we so *vile and revolting* to him. Master just shake his head and say: *Take this female, then. You will observe she is cleaner and younger than most, and I believe you will find her less savage in disposition than most of her race; for she had some training in that regard some years ago. However, you will need to bind her securely. She is cunning and restive, as we know too well.* That mean, he give me to big Yahoo for Bumpbump, tell him tie me up good so I don't get away.

He take me back little House, tie my hands tight with hard rope, and go Bumpbump right way this time. I scared look at his face—not happy Bumpbump like wild Yahoo but mean, like tame Yahoo. When he done he go sit other side House. I look around: all nice with fresh straw and place to have fire, and bowls of food. I talk to him in Houyhnhnm: *What kind of Yahoo are you?*

He jump! He say: *Good God, you have the power of speech!* He mean, I talk too.

I tell him I learn from Yhlee. Ask him again what he is and he say: *I am no Yahoo! I am a man, a British subject, and my name is Lemuel Gulliver.* That mean he not Yahoo like me but other thing, and he have name, like Houyhnhnm. I think he lie, but I want not make him mad. *Please untie my hands,* I cry, *They hurt.*

He says: *I think not! Simply because you have the ability to converse with me like a rational creature, do not presume to imagine you are less abhorrent to me than the rest of your filthy race. I'll not have you doing me some mischief while I sleep. Nor presume to address me again.* That mean, he not like me and won't let me loose. Then he lie down and sleep. I cry until he wake up and throw stone at me.

Well, so bad time then. All night I tied up, and in morning my hands cold and blue. Servant come in and see, tell Lemuel Gulliver to untie me. My hands hurt so bad I cry. Servant mad, tell Lemuel Gulliver my hands no use like that. Tell him to tie my leg tight to bars, then I can work but not run away. Lemuel Gulliver say: *Do you mean to tell me the hussy has been trained to useful domestic industry?* That means, he didn't know I make things with my hands. Servant tell him yes. He look more happy at that. He tie me up by leg and go out with Servant. Gone all day. Gone all day every day, but they put another Servant outside door so I not run away.

I think Lemuel Gulliver must be going for his *Improvement*, because by and by he looks and talks like Houyhnhnm more and more. I think he Yahoo who hate all Yahoos, want to be Houyhnhnm all the way. But he only pretend! And he look silly when he walk, with knees up and hands up, prance stamp, and he talk silly with *whhuhuhuh* voice like Houyhnhnm. I laugh, only he hit me and call me dirty Yahoo. I dirty now, because I can't go out to wash, but he not let me.

He keep making Bumpbump, though, so hard, and soon I bleeding there. I scared, hurt, think I die. Two, three days, bleeding go away. Next month I bleed again, but it go away. After a while I not scared of bleeding.

Lemuel Gulliver bring home stems of grass and tell me weave it into big bag. He bring home dead birds, lots, and tell me pull feathers out; then put all feathers in bag. He takes it and sleeps on it, nice soft bag. I sleep on straw. He bring home little dead animals and cut skins off, make me scrape and soften hides; then make me sew them for bags he wear on himself. I copy them good from his old bags, but he not happy. Always mad.

I wonder when he stop being mad. I think, if I quiet and good, he happy; but he never happy. Maybe because he not Houyhnhnm.

But Lemuel Gulliver try very hard to be Houyhnhnm. Master come to talk with him all time, and he tell Master how he come from England place, and Master tell him how bad it is, and how England Yahoos worse than our kind. Sometimes Master tell him about us Yahoos, and he says lies. He says about killing Yahoos in fields after oats cut, but says other Yahoos do the killing because they *vicious*.

Lemuel Gulliver think about this, then he say: *I wonder, sir, whether I might propose an economical use of the dead brutes? You have perhaps noticed that I have supplied the want of covering for my body with the furs of small beasts. In my country, the skins of larger animals are taken and prepared in such a way as to provide a substance called leather, that hath divers uses both practical and ornamental. The fat of such beasts hath also serviceable qualities when rendered down into tallow. Perhaps the dead Yahoos might be turned to a like utility?*

I didn't know what all that mean, but next day Lemuel Gulliver and Servant bring home dead Yahoo. Lemuel Gulliver untie me and bring me out, tie noose to tree, say: *Take these tools and skin this creature, as you have skinned the others.* That means I have to cut up poor dead Yahoo. I feel bad, but he dead, can't hurt him. Lemuel Gulliver and Servant cut wood in field and make big rack; when I have skin off they take away tools and tie skin to rack and scrape it. I sit by dead Yahoo and cry.

So bad! So bad! Makes me cry now. Too many bad things tell you. But soon Lemuel Gulliver has *factory* in field where he makes dead Yahoos into *candles* and *leather* and *parchment*. He think Houyhnhnms be *impressed by his diligence and industry*. That mean he want them think him Houyhnhnm like them. They don't. He try harder, he tell Master about good way to get rid of too many Yahoos by cutting off boys' danglies. He says they do this beasts in England all the time. Master listen and say nothing. I scared what they do girls in England, be very quiet all time. Only good thing is, bleeding every month stops.

Lemuel Gulliver almost not like Yahoo now: sound just like Houyhnhnms when he talk and walk, nod his head like them, shake his hair out of his face like them, look sideways like them. He try not eating with hands, make a mess, get mad. I not laugh though. He mad I get sick in mornings.

Then one day I scraping Yahoo skin outside and Servant come up to me and smell me all over. He see me with this eye, then turn head and see that eye. Then he go trotting off fast, and Lemuel Gulliver busy pouring hot fat into bowl, not notice.

By and by Master comes out with Servant and looks at me. *Gentle Yahoo,* he says to Lemuel Gulliver, *what have you done? This Yahoo female is going to bear young.* That mean he see I have baby soon.

Lemuel Gulliver stare and stare, then say: *It isn't mine! The dirty wench must have coupled with a Yahoo before her capture, or admitted some beast whilst I was out!* That means, he not Bumpbump me. Master shake his head. He say:

She has been guarded in your absence, Gentle Yahoo, and when I gave her to you she was not yet fertile. There can be no doubt that her condition is your doing. This is most troublesome; it was hoped that her extreme youth, and your penchant for unnatural congress, would prevent conception. That mean, you DID TOO Bumpbump her, and it bad. Lemuel Gulliver fall on the ground at Master's feet, kiss them, cry.

He say: *Pardon! Pardon, oh my Master! Never would I give you the slightest cause to reproach me!* That means, don't hurt me. Master prods him with hoof and says: *Do not indulge yourself in such fits of passion. It was I who advised you to satisfy your natural appetites. Unfortunately, my neighbors will hear of this. Greatly as they have disapproved of my keeping a tame Yahoo for my diversion (albeit one nominally more civilized and rational than the common breed) they will positively censure me for allowing one to reproduce. What should we do if a race of such monsters arose, cleverer than those we govern with such effort? What am I to do?* All that means was, other Masters not want me have baby.

Lemuel Gulliver get up on hands and knees, dropping big tears. He say: *Dear Master, do not imagine that I entertain any foolish fondness for the creature! Say but the word and I'll stifle the wench with my own hands! Then I might be provided with a boy to my purpose, and—*He mean he kill me! Master snort and stamp his feet. He say: *Gentle Yahoo, you are saying the thing which is not again!*

I hear all this, I take scraper and put it in my mouth, sneaky so they don't see. Lemuel Gulliver look at Master and his face get sneaky too. He say, *I understand you, best and wisest of Masters.*

Master says: *Secure the female in your stall and then we will discuss the matter in greater detail, you and I.* That mean, he going to tell Lemuel Gulliver how to kill me. They send Servant away and Lemuel Gulliver take me into House and tie my leg. He not see I hid scraper! He go out. I spit out scraper and cut, cut, cut at rope so hard!

It comes loose and I go out. Run for hills, big trees. I hear yell, Lemuel Gulliver sees I running, he shout and run. Master run too but quiet. He fast. I not fast now, legs hurt, fat tummy. I run all the way over field and Master run up behind me. I think he catch me soon.

BUT!!! Out from trees come wild Yahoos! They run out, grab me! Two pull me into trees, others yell and throw shit at Master and Lemuel Gulliver. Up and up and up we go, all green leaves, free air, blue sky. Away into big trees. When we safe I so happy, we all play Bumpbump.

I tell wild Yahoos what happen. By and by many Houyhnhnm come under trees looking for me. They talk how Lemuel Gulliver sent away, crying all sad, go back over sea to England. They want kill me so I never have smart baby, but they never catch me, because we go away from there, go up in mountain trees, far far. We find this place by big rocks and falling water. Lots to eat. Safe. Happy.

Then you come out, and you so pretty! Little face like flower. You talk so soon and you so smart! Look at pictures you make on stones, look at animals you make in clay. Mama love Baby and never, never let Houyhnhnm get her. But if ever big Yahoo come with nose like scraper blade, talking like Houyhnhnm, Baby must run far and fast and climb highest tree. That Yahoo name Lemuel Gulliver, and he not like us. He never love anything, ever.

Don't be scared! He far away now. Look, uncle Yahoo catch big fish! Let's go see.

What The Tyger Told Her

"**Y**ou must observe carefully," said the tyger.

He was an old tyger. He had survived in captivity more years than he might have been expected to, penned in his narrow iron run in such a cold wet country, in all weathers. He was just the color of toast, and white underneath like bread too. His back was double-striped with black streaks and the rippling shadows of the bars as he paced continually, turn and turn again.

The little girl blinked, mildly surprised at being addressed. She had a round face, pale and freckled like a robin's egg. She had been squatting beside the tyger's pen for some minutes, fascinated by him. If anyone had seen her crouched there, crumpling the silk brocade of her tiny hooped gown, she'd have been scolded, for the summer dust was thick in the garden. But no one had noticed she was there.

"Power," said the tyger, "Comes from knowledge, you see. The best way to learn is to watch what happens. The best way to watch is unseen. Now, in my proper place, which is jungle meadow and forest canes, I am very nearly invisible. That," and he looked with eyes green as beryls at the splendid house rising above the gardens, "is your proper place. Are you invisible there?"

The little girl nodded her head.

"Do you know why you're invisible?"

She thought about it. "Because John and James were born."

"Your little brothers, yes. And so nobody sees you now?"

"And because...." The child waved her hand in a gesture that took in the house, the garden, the menagerie and the immense park in which they were set. "There's so many uncles and people here. Mamma and I used to live in the lodging-house. Papa would come upstairs in his uniform. It was red. He was a poor officer. Then he got sick and lived with us in his nightgown. It was white. He would drink from a bottle and shout, and I would hide behind the chair when he did. And John and James got born. And Papa went to heaven. And Mamma said oh, my dear, whatever shall we do?"

"What did you do?" the tyger prompted.

"I didn't do anything. But Grandpapa forgave Mamma and sent for us."

"What had your Mamma done, to be forgiven?"

"She wasn't supposed to marry Papa because she is," and the child paused a moment to recollect the big words, "an indigent tradesman's daughter. Papa used to tell her so when he drank out of the bottle. But when she had John and James, that made it all right again, because they're the only boys."

"So they're important."

"They will inherit it all," the child explained, as though she were quoting. "Because Papa died and Uncle John is in India, and Uncle Thomas only has Louise."

"But they haven't inherited yet."

"No. Not until Grandpapa goes to heaven."

"Something to think about, isn't it?" said the tyger, lowering his head to lap water from his stone trough.

The little girl thought about it.

"I thought Grandpapa was in heaven when we went to see him," she said. "We climbed so many stairs. And the bed was so high and white and the pillows like clouds. Grandpapa's nightgown was white. He has white hair and a long, long beard. He shouted like Papa did. Mamma turned away crying. Mr. Lawyer said It's only his pain, Mrs. Edgecombe. Uncle Thomas said Dear sister, come and have a glass of cordial. So she did and she was much better."

"But nobody saw you there, did they?"

"No," said the child.

"Who's that coming along the walk?" the tyger inquired.

"That is Uncle Thomas and Aunt Caroline," the child replied.

"Do you notice that she's not as pretty as your Mamma?"

"Yes."

"And quite a bit older."

"Yes. And she can't have any children but Cousin Louise."

"I think perhaps you ought to sit quite still," advised the tyger.

The woman swept ahead in her anger, long skirts trailing in the tall summer grass at the edge of the walk, white fingers knotting on her lace apron, high curls bobbing with her agitation. The man hurried after her, tottering a little because of the height of his heels, and the skirts of his coat flapped out behind him. He wore bottlegreen silk. His waistcoat was embroidered with little birds, his wig was slightly askew. He looked sullen.

"Oh, you have a heart of stone," cried Aunt Caroline. "Your own child to be left a pauper! It's too unjust. Is this the reward of filial duty?"

"Louise is not an especially dutiful girl," muttered Uncle Thomas.

"I meant your filial duty! One is reminded of the Prodigal Son. *You* have obeyed his every wish, while he thundered up there. Wretched old paralytic! And Robert disgraces himself, and dies like a dog in a ditch with that strumpet, but all's forgiven because of the twins. Are all our hopes to be dashed forever?"

"Now, Caroline, patience," said Uncle Thomas. "Consider: life's uncertain."

"That's true." Aunt Caroline pulled up short, looking speculative. "Any childish illness might carry off the brats. Oh, I could drown them like puppies myself!"

Uncle Thomas winced. He glared at Aunt Caroline's back a moment before drawing abreast of her, by which time he was smiling.

"You'll oblige me by doing nothing so rash. Robert was never strong; we can pray they've inherited his constitution. And after all it would be just as convenient, my dear, if the wench were to die instead. I would be guardian of John and James, the estate in my hands; what should we have to worry about then?"

They walked on together. The little girl stared after them.

"Do you think they're going to drown my Mamma?" she asked uneasily.

"Did you see the way your uncle looked at your aunt behind her back?" replied the tyger. "I don't think he cares for her, particularly. What do you think?"

*   *   *

There were fruit trees espaliered all along the menagerie wall, heavy now in apricots and cherries, and when the chimpanzee had been alive it had been driven nearly frantic in summers by the sight and the smell of the fruit. Now stuffed with straw, it stared sadly from a glass-fronted cabinet, through a fine layer of dust.

The little girl, having discovered the fruit was there, wasted no time in filling her apron with all she could reach and retiring to the shade under the plum tree. The largest, ripest apricot she bowled carefully into the tyger's cage. The others she ate in methodical fashion, making a small mound of neatly stacked pits and cherry stones.

The tyger paused in his relentless stride just long enough to sniff the apricot, turning it over with his white-bearded chin.

"Your baby brothers have not died," he said.

"No," the little girl affirmed, biting into a cherry.

"However, your Aunt Caroline has been suffering acute stomach pains, especially after dinner. That's interesting."

"She has a glass of port wine to make it better," said the child. "But it doesn't get better."

"And that's your Mamma coming along the walk now, I see," said the tyger. "With Uncle Thomas."

The child concealed the rest of the fruit with her apron and sat still. She needn't have worried: neither her mother nor her uncle noticed her.

Like her daughter, Mamma had a pale freckled face but was otherwise quite attractive, and the black broadcloth of her mourning made her look slender and gave her a dignity she needed, for she was very young. She was being drawn along by Uncle Thomas, who had her by the arm.

"We ought never to question the will of the Almighty," Uncle Thomas was saying pleasantly. "It never pleased Him that Caroline should bear me sons, and certainly that's been a grief to me; but then, without boys of my own, how ready am I to do a father's duty by dear little John and James! All that I might have done for my sons, I may do for yours. Have no fear on that account, dear Lavinia."

"It's very kind of you, brother Thomas," said Mamma breathlessly. "For, sure we have been so poor, I was at my wit's end—and father Edgecombe is so severe."

"But Robert was his favorite," said Uncle Thomas. "The very reason he disowned him, I think; Father couldn't brook disobedience in one he loved above all. If Henry or I had eloped, he'd have scarcely noticed. And Randall does what he likes, of course. Father was too hard on Robert, alas."

"Oh, sir, I wish someone had said so whiles he lived," said Mamma. "He often wept that he had no friends."

"Alas! I meant to write to him, but duty forbid." Uncle Thomas shook his head. "It is too bad. I must endeavor to redress it, Lavinia."

He slipped his arm around her waist. She looked flustered, but said nothing. They walked on.

"Mamma is frightened," said the child.

"There are disadvantages to being pretty," said the tyger. "As you can see. I imagine she wishes she could be invisible, occasionally. Your uncle's a subtle man; notice how he used words like *duty* and *alas*. No protestations of ardent passion. It's often easier to get something you want if you pretend you don't want it. Remember that."

The little girl nodded.

She ate another cherry. A peahen ventured near the wall, cocking her head to examine the windfall fruit under the little trees. As she lingered there, a peacock came stalking close, stiffened to see the hen; his whole body, bright as blue enamel, shivered, and his trailing train of feathers rose and spread behind him, shimmering in terrifying glory. Eyes stared from it. The little girl caught her breath at all the green and purple and gold.

"You mustn't allow yourself to be distracted," the tyger cautioned. "It's never safe. You see?"

"What, are you lurking there, you little baggage?"

The little girl looked around sharply, craning her head back. Uncle Randall dropped into a crouch beside her, staring at her. He was young, dressed in tawny silk that shone like gold. His voice was teasing and hard. He smelled like wine.

"Ha, she's stealing fruit! You can be punished for that, you know. They'll pull your skirt up and whip your bare bum, if I tell. Shall I tell?"

"No," said the child.

"What'll you give me, not to tell?"

She offered him an apricot. He took it and rolled it in his hand, eyeing it, and hooted in derision.

"Gives me the greenest one she's got! Clever hussy. You're a little woman, to be sure."

She didn't know what to say to that, so she said nothing. He stared at her a moment longer, and then the tyger drew his attention.

"Aren't you afraid of old Master Stripes? Don't you worry he'll break his bounds, and eat you like a rabbit? He might, you know. But I'm not afraid of him."

The tyger growled softly, did not cease pacing.

"Useless thing! I'd a damn sight rather Johnnie'd sent us one of his blacks," said Uncle Randall. He looked down at her again. "Well, poppet. What's your Mamma's favorite color?"

"Sky blue," said the child.

"It is, eh? Yes, with those eyes, she'd wear that to her advantage. D'you think she'd like a velvet scarf in that color, eh? Or a cape?"

"She has to wear black now," the child reminded him.

"She'll wear it as long as it suits her, I've no doubt. What about scent? What's her fancy? Tell me, does she ever drink strong waters in secret?"

The child had no idea what that meant, so she shook her head mutely. Uncle Randall snorted.

"You wouldn't tell if she did, I'll wager. Well. Does she miss your Papa very much?"

"Yes."

"You must say 'Yes, Uncle dear.' "

"Yes, Uncle dear."

"There's a good girl. Do you think you'd like to have another Papa?"

The child thought about it. Remembering the things Papa had said when he raved, that had made her creep behind the chair to hide, she said: "No."

"No? But that's wicked of you, you little minx. A girl must have a Papa to look after her and her Mamma, or dreadful things might happen. They might starve in the street. Freeze to death. Meat for dogs, you see, do you want your Mamma to be meat for dogs?"

"No," said the child, terrified that she would begin to cry.

"Then you'll tell her she must get you another Papa as soon as ever she may," Uncle Randall ordered. "Do you understand me? Do it, and you'll have a treat. Something pretty." He reached down to stroke her cheek, and his hand lingered there.

"What a soft cheek you've got," he said. "I wonder if your Mamma's is as soft."

The peacock was maneuvering up behind the hen, treading on her feathers. Seeing it, Uncle Randall gave a sharp laugh and shied the apricot at her, and she bolted forward, away from the peacock.

Uncle Randall strode off without another word.

"Now, your Uncle Randall," said the tyger, "is not a subtle man. Nor as clever as he thinks he is, all in all. He talks far too much, wouldn't you say?"

The child nodded.

"He uses fear to get what he wants," said the tyger. "And he underestimates his opponents. That's a dangerous thing to do. A bad combination of strategies."

Wasps buzzed and fought for the apricot at his feet.

*   *   *

The summer heat was oppressive. All the early fruit had fallen from the trees, or been gathered and taken in to make jam. There were blackberries in the hedge, gleaming like red and black garnets, but they were dusty and hard for the child to reach without scratching herself on the brambles.

There was a thick square of privet in the center of the menagerie courtyard, man-high. Long ago it had been a formal design, clipped close, but for one reason or another had been abandoned to grow unchecked. Its little paths were all lost now except at ground level, where they formed a secret maze of tunnels in the heart of the bush. There was a sundial buried in the greenery, lightless and mute: it told nobody anything.

The little girl had crawled in under the branches and lay there, pretending she was a jungle beast hiding in long grass. She gazed out at the tyger, who had retreated to the shade of the sacking the grooms had laid across the top of his pen. He blinked big mild eyes. He looked sleepy.

"How fares your Aunt Caroline?" he inquired.

"She's sick," the child said. "The doctor was sent for, but he couldn't find anything wrong with her. He said it might be her courses drying up."

"Do you know what that means?"

"No," said the child. "But that's what Uncle Thomas is telling everybody. And he says, you mustn't mind what a woman says because of it. He's very kind to her."

"How clever of him." The tyger yawned, showing fearful teeth, and stretched his length. "And he's even kinder to your Mamma, isn't he?"

"Yes. Very kind."

"What do you suppose will happen if your Aunt Caroline dies?"

"She will be buried in the graveyard."

"So she will."

They heard footsteps approaching, two pair.

The child peered up from under the leaves and saw Cousin Louise with one of the stableboys. She was a tall girl with a sallow complexion, very tightly laced into her gown in order to have any bosom at all. The stableboy was thickset, with pimples on his face. He was carrying a covered pail. He smelled like manure.

"It be under here," he said, leading Cousin Louise around the side of the privet square. "The heart of it's all hollow, you see? And you can lie inside in the shade. It's a rare nice place to hide, and there ain't nobody knows it's here but me."

"Audacious rogue!" Cousin Louise giggled. "I'll tear my gown."

"Then the Squire'll buy thee a new one, won't he? Get in there."

The child lay very still. She heard the branches parting and the sound of two people awkwardly arranging themselves inside the privet. Turning her head very slightly, she caught a glimpse of them six feet away from her, mostly screened off by green leaves and the base of the sundial. She watched from the corner of her eye as they made themselves comfortable, handing the pail back and forth to drink from it.

"Aah! I like a cool drop of beer, in this heat," the stableboy sighed.

"It's refreshing," said Cousin Louise. "I've never had beer before."

"Like enough you wouldn't," said the stableboy, and belched. "Sweet wines and gin, ain't that what the fine folk have to themselves? The likes of me don't get a taste of your Madeira from one year's end to the next." He chuckled. "That's all one; I'll get a taste of something fine anyway."

There was a thrashing of bushes and Cousin Louise gave a little squeal of laughter.

"Hush! The keeper'll hear, you silly slut."

"No, no, he mustn't."

There was heavy breathing and a certain ruffling, as of petticoats. Cousin Louise spoke in an almost trancelike voice.

"How if you were a bold highwayman? You might shoot the driver, and there might be no other passengers but me, and I might be cowering within the coach, in fear of my very life. You'd fling the door wide—and you might look at me and lick your chops, as a hungry dog might—and you might say—you'd say—"

"Here's a saucy strumpet wants a good futtering, I'd say," growled the stableboy.

"Yes," Cousin Louise gasped, hysteria coming into her voice, "and I'd protest, but you would be merciless. You'd drag me from the coach, and throw me down on the ferns in the savage forest, and tear my gown to expose my bosom, and then—"

"Oh, hush your noise," the stableboy told Cousin Louise, and crawled on top of her. When they'd finished, he rolled off and reached for the beer pail. Cousin Louise was laughing, breathless, helpless, but her laughter began to sound a little like crying, and a certain alarm was in the stableboy's voice when he said:

"Stop your fool mouth! Do you want to get me whipped? If you start screaming I'll cut your throat, you jade! What's the matter with you?"

Cousin Louise put her hands over her face and fell silent, attempting to even her breath. "Nothing," she said faintly. "Nothing. All's well."

There was silence for a moment, and the stableboy drank more beer.

"I feel a little ill with the heat," explained Cousin Louise.

"That's like enough," said the stableboy, sounding somewhat mollified.

Another rustling; Cousin Louise was sitting up, putting her arms around the stableboy.

"I do love you so," she said, "I could never see you harmed, dearest. Say but the word and I'll run away with thee, and be thy constant wife."

"Art thou mad?" The stableboy sounded incredulous. "The likes of you wedded to me? The Squire'd hunt us sure, and he'd have my life. Even so, how should I afford to keep a wife, with my place lost? It ain't likely you'd bring much of a dowry, anyhow, be the Squire never so willing. Not with everything going to them little boys, now."

"I have three hundred pounds a year from my mother, once she's dead and I am married." Cousin Louise sounded desperate. "I have! And she's grievous sick. Who knows how long she will live?"

"And what then? Much good that'd do me, if I was hanged or transported," said the stableboy. "Which I will be, if you don't keep quiet about our fun. Better ladies than you knows how to hold their tongues."

Cousin Louise did not say another word after that. The stableboy drank the rest of the beer, and sighed.

"I've got the mucking out to do," he announced, and buttoned himself and crawled from the bush. His footsteps went away across the paving-stones, slow and heavy.

Cousin Louise sat perfectly still for a long time, before abruptly scrambling out and walking away with quick steps.

The little girl exhaled.

"He didn't speak to her very nicely," said the tyger.

"No."

"And she didn't seem to have much fun. Why do you suppose she'd go into the bushes with a person like that?"

"She said she loved him," said the child.

"Does she?" The tyger licked his paw lazily. "I wonder. Some people seem to feel the need to get manure on their shoes."

The child wrinkled her nose. "Why?"

"Who knows? Perhaps they feel it's what they deserve," said the tyger.

*   *   *

The little girl had found broken china hidden in the green gloom behind the potting shed: two dishes, a custard-cup and a sauceboat. She carried them out carefully and washed them in the horse-trough, and then retired to the bed of bare earth under the fruit trees with them. There she set out the broken plates to be courtyards, and inverted the cup and sauceboat on them to be houses. Collecting cherry pits, she arranged them in lines: they were soldiers, marching between the houses. The rationale for making them soldiers was that soldiers had red coats, and cherries were red. The tyger watched her.

"There are visitors today," he said. The child nodded.

"Uncle Henry and Aunt Elizabeth," she replied. "They came to see John and James. Uncle Henry is going to be their godfather, because he's a curate. They have a little girl, just my size, but she didn't come, or she might have played with me."

"Are you sorry she's not here to play with you?"

The child lifted her head in surprise, struck by the question.

"I don't know," she said. "Would she see me?"

"She might," the tyger said. "Children notice other children, don't they?"

"Sometimes."

"I think someone's coming," the tyger informed her. She looked up, and saw Uncle Henry and Aunt Elizabeth strolling together along the walk.

"...not so well-stocked as it was formerly, alas," said Uncle Henry. He wore black, with a very white wig. Aunt Elizabeth was plump, wore a mulberry-colored gown and a straw hat for the sun.

"Oh, bless us, look there!" she exclaimed, stopping in her tracks as she saw the tyger. "Dear, dear, d'you think it's safe to keep a beast like that about, with so many little children in the house? I'm glad now we kept Jane at home, my love."

"He's never harmed anyone, that I'm aware," Uncle Henry told her, taking her arm and steering her forward. "Poor old Bobo used to scream, and bite, and fling ordure; but I daresay it was because Randall teased him. Randall was frightened of this fellow, however. Kept his distance."

"And very sensible of him too," said Aunt Elizabeth, shuddering. "Oh, look at the size of it! I feel like a mouse must feel before our Tibby."

"The same Providence created them, Bess." Uncle Henry stopped before the pen. "Each creature has its place in the grand design, after all."

"Tibby catches rats, and I'm sure that's very useful indeed, but what's the point of an animal like this one?" protested Aunt Elizabeth. "Great horrid teeth and claws! Unless they have giant rats in India?"

"I don't think they do," said Uncle Henry. "But I trust the Almighty had His reasons."

"Well, I shall never understand how He could make something so cruel," said Aunt Elizabeth firmly. "Look there, what are those? Are those parrots? Dear little things!"

"Budgerigars, I think," said Uncle Henry.

They walked away to inspect the aviary, which was beyond the privet-square.

"Stay where you are," said the tyger.

"Oh, I could never," Mamma was saying distractedly. "I couldn't think of such a thing, with poor Robert's grave scarcely green."

"Tut-tut, Lavinia!" said Uncle Randall, as they approached. "There's none to hear but you and I. Look as pious as you like before the world. The demure widow, meek and holy, if you please! I won't repeat what passes between us; but you and I both knew Robert. He hadn't enough blood in him to keep you contented, a lively girl like you. Had he, now? How long's it been since you had a good gallop, eh? Eh?"

She had been walking quickly ahead of him, and he caught up to her in front of the tyger's pen and seized her arm. Her face was red.

"You don't—oh—"

Uncle Randall stepped close and spoke very quickly. "The blood in your cheeks is honest, Madam Sanctimony. Don't play the hypocrite with me! I know London girls too well. You got your hooks into Robert to climb out of the gutter, didn't you? Well, keep climbing, hussy! I stand ready to help you up the next step, and the old man may be damned. We've got those boys, haven't we? We'll be master and mistress here one day, if you're not an affected squeamish—"

"You hound!" Mamma found her voice at last. "Oh, you base—*thing!*"

Uncle Henry and Aunt Elizabeth came walking swiftly around the privet square, and advanced on the scene like a pair of soldiers marching.

"What's this, Lavinia?" Uncle Henry's eyes moved from Mamma to Uncle Randall and back. "Tears?"

"We were speaking of Robert," said Uncle Randall, standing his ground. "Poor fellow. Were we not, dear Lavinia?"

Shocked back into silence, Mamma nodded. Aunt Elizabeth came and put her arms about her.

"My child, you mustn't vex your heart so with weeping," she said solicitously. "It's natural, in such an affectionate match, but only think! Robert would wish you to be happy, now that all's reconciled. And you must have courage, for the children's sake."

"So I was just saying," said Uncle Randall, helping himself to a pinch of snuff.

"We must endure our sorrows in patience," Uncle Henry advised her, looking at Uncle Randall.

"Come now, Lavinia," said Uncle Randall in quite a kind voice. "Dry your tears and walk with us. Shall we go view the pretty babes? John's the very image of Robert, in my opinion."

They bore her away between them.

"Your Mamma doesn't wish to make trouble, I see," said the tyger.

"She didn't tell on him," said the child, in wonderment.

"Silence is not always wise," said the tyger. "Not when it gives your opponent an opportunity. Perhaps your Uncle Randall hasn't underestimated your Mamma, after all."

"Why didn't she tell on him?" The child stared after the retreating adults.

"Why indeed?" said the tyger. "Something else to remember: even bad strategy can succeed, if your opponent has no strategy at all."

*   *   *

Just beyond the menagerie courtyard, five stone steps led down into a sunken garden. It was a long rectangle of lawn, with rose-beds at its edges and a fountain and small reflecting pool at its center. At its far end five more stone steps led up out of it, and beyond was a dense wood, and further beyond was open heath where deer sometimes grazed.

The roses were briary, and the fountain long clogged and scummed over with green. But there were men working on it today, poking with rakes and sticks, and it had begun to gurgle in a sluggish kind of way; and the gardener had cut back the briars that hung out over the lawn. He was up on a ladder now with his handkerchief, rubbing dust off the sprays of rose haws, so they gleamed scarlet as blood-drops.

The little girl watched them warily, nibbling at a rose haw she'd snatched from one of the cut sprays. It was hard and sour, but interesting. The tyger watched them too, pacing more quickly than usual.

"Your Uncle Randall gave your mother a fine length of sky-blue silk," he said. "Will she have a gown made of it, do you think?"

"No," said the child. "She showed it to Uncle Thomas and Aunt Caroline and asked them if she ought to have a gown made for the christening party."

"Really?" the tyger said. "And what did they say?"

"Aunt Caroline looked cross, and said Mamma mustn't think of such a thing while she's in mourning. Uncle Thomas didn't say anything. But his eyes got very small."

"Rather a clever thing for your Mamma to have done," said the tyger. "What did she say in reply?"

"She said Yes, yes, you're quite right. And Uncle Thomas went and talked to Uncle Randall about it."

The tyger made a low percussive sound in his chest, for all the world like quiet laughter.

"If a rabbit's being chased by a fox, it's wise to run straight to the wolf," he said. "Of course, the question then is, whether it can get away safely after the wolf's taken the fox by the throat. Wolves like a bit of rabbit too."

"It's bad to be a rabbit," said the little girl.

"So it is," said the tyger. "But if one has grown up to be a rabbit, one can do very little about it."

"Only run."

"Just so." The tyger turned his great wide head to regard the sunken garden. "Why, your aunts have come out to take the air."

The little girl retreated to the plum tree. Leaning against its trunk, she watched Aunt Caroline and Aunt Elizabeth coming along the walk.

Aunt Caroline was pale and thin, had a shawl draped about her shoulders, and Aunt Elizabeth half-supported her as she walked.

"Yes, I do think the bloom's returning to your cheeks already," Aunt Elizabeth was saying in a determinedly cheery voice. "Fresh air will do you a world of good, my dear, I'm sure. Whenever I feel faint or bilious at Brookwood, dearest Henry always advises me to take my bonnet and go for a ramble, and after a mile or so I'm always quite restored again, and come home with quite an appetite for my dinner!"

Aunt Caroline said nothing in reply, breathing with effort as they walked. There was a stone seat overlooking the sunken garden, and Aunt Elizabeth led her to it.

"We'll settle ourselves here, shall we, and watch them making it ready?" suggested Aunt Elizabeth, sitting down and making room for Aunt Caroline. "There now. Oh, look, they've got the water going again! Really, this will make the prettiest place for a party. You'll want to put the long table for the collation over there, I suppose, and the trestle tables along the other side. And I would, my dear, have two comfortable chairs brought down and set on a kind of step, 'tis called a dais in London I think, where the nursemaids may sit with the little boys and all may pay their respects conveniently."

Aunt Caroline hissed and doubled over, clutching herself.

"There, my dear, there, courage!" Aunt Elizabeth rubbed her back. "Oh, and you were feeling so much better after breakfast. Perhaps this will help. When I'm troubled with wind, Henry will—"

"It's a judgement from God," gasped Aunt Caroline.

"Dear, you mustn't say such a thing! It may be He sends us our little aches and pains to remind us we ought to be ready at all times to come before Him, but—"

"I prayed the boys would die," Aunt Caroline told her. "I thought of having them suffocated in their cradles. God forgive me, forgive me! And it wasn't a week after that the pains began."

Aunt Elizabeth had drawn away from her. Her face was a study in stupefied horror.

"Never!" she said at last. "Those dear, sweet little lambs? Oh, Caroline, you never! Oh, how could you? Oh, and to think—"

Aunt Caroline had begun to sob hoarsely, rocking herself to and fro in her agony. Aunt Elizabeth watched her a moment, struggling to find words, and at last found them.

"Well," she said, "It's—Henry would say, this is proof of the infinite mercy of the Almighty, you know. For, only think, if you had followed such a wicked thought with a *deed*, what worse torments would await you eternally! As it is, the sin is hideous but not so bad as it might be, and these timely pangs have made you reflect on the peril to your eternal soul, and you have surely repented! Therefore all may yet be well—"

Aunt Caroline toppled forward. Aunt Elizabeth leaped up, screaming, and the men stopped work at once and ran to be of assistance. Upon examination, Aunt Caroline was found not to have died, but merely fainted from her pain, and when revived she begged feebly to be taken to her chamber. Aunt Elizabeth, rising to the occasion, directed the men to improvise a stretcher from the ladder. She paced alongside as they bore Aunt Caroline away, entreating her to call on her Savior for comfort.

The little girl watched all this with round eyes.

"There's one secret out," remarked the tyger. "I wonder whether any others will show themselves?"

*   *   *

The east wind was blowing. It swayed the cloths on the long tables, it swayed the paper lanterns the servants had hung up on lines strung through the trees in the garden. The tyger lashed his tail as he paced.

The little girl was walking from lantern to lantern, peering up at them and wondering how they would light when evening fell.

"Your Uncle Randall asked your Mamma to marry him today," said the tyger.

"He did it in front of Uncle Henry and Aunt Elizabeth," said the child.

"Because he thought she wouldn't like to say no, if they were present," said the tyger. The child nodded.

"But Mamma said no," she concluded. "Then Uncle Randall had a glass of wine."

The tyger put his face close to the bars.

"Something bad is going to happen," he said. "Think very hard, quickly: are you a rabbit, or do you have teeth and claws?"

"What the hell's it doing?" said a hoarse voice from the other end of the courtyard. The child looked up to see Uncle Randall advancing on her swiftly. He had a strange blank look in his eyes, a strange fixed smile.

"Hasn't it ever been told not to go so near a wild brute? Naughty, naughty little thing!" he said, and grabbed her arm tightly. "We'll have to punish it."

He began to drag her away in the direction of the potting shed. She screamed, kicking him as hard as she could, but he laughed and swung her up off her feet. He marched on toward the thicket behind the shed, groping under her skirts.

"We'll have to punish its little soft bum, that's what we'll have to do," he said wildly, "Because a dutiful uncle must do such things, after all, ungrateful little harlot—"

She screamed again, and suddenly he had stopped dead in his tracks and let her fall, because Cousin Louise was standing right before them and staring at Uncle Randall. She was chalk-white. She seemed as though she were choking a long minute, unable to make a sound, as the little girl whimpered and scrambled away on hands and knees.

Uncle Randall, momentarily disconcerted, regained his smile.

"What?" he demanded. "None of your business if we were only playing."

Cousin Louise threw herself at him. Being, as she was, a tall girl, she bore him over so he fell to the pavement with a crash. His wig came off. She beat him in the face with her fists, and found her voice at last, harsh as a crow's:

"*What were you going to tell her?* Were you going to tell her you'd cut her tongue out if she ever told what you did? Were you? *Were you?*"

Uncle Randall snarled and attempted to throw her off.

"Ow! Who'd believe you, stupid bitch? The guests'll be arriving, I'll say you've gone mad—"

The child climbed to her feet and ran, sobbing, and got behind the menagerie wall. There she cried in silence, hiding her face in her skirts.

When she ventured out again at last, neither Uncle Randall nor Cousin Louise were anywhere in sight. The tyger was looking at her steadily.

"That's another secret come to light," he said. "Now, I'll tell you still another."

Rubbing her eyes with her fist, she listened as he told her the secret.

*   *   *

Mamma and Aunt Elizabeth carried the babies into the chapel, so the nurserymaid was able to spare her a moment.

"Lord, lord, how did your face get so dirty? As if I ain't got enough to see to!" she grumbled, dipping a corner of her apron in the horse-trough and washing the little girl's face. "Now, hold my hand and be a good child when we go in. No noise!"

She was a good child through the solemn ceremony. Mamma watched the little boys tenderly, anxiously, and Uncle Henry and Aunt Elizabeth smiled when first John, and then James, screamed and went red-faced at having Satan driven out with cold water. Uncle Thomas was watching Mamma. Aunt Caroline was tranquilly distant: she'd taken laudanum for her pain. Beside her, Cousin Louise watched Uncle Randall with a basilisk glare. Uncle Randall was holding himself upright and defiant, smiling, though his face was puffy with bruises.

Afterward they all processed from the chapel and up the long stairs, to arrange themselves in ranks before Grandpapa, that he might give them his blessing. He stared from his high white bed and had to be reminded who they all were. At last he moved his wasted hand on the counterpane, granting an abbreviated benediction on posterity, and they were able to file from the sickroom into the clean-smelling twilight.

The wind had dropped a little but still moved the lanterns, that had candles inside them now and looked like golden moons glowing in the trees. It brought the sweet smell of wood smoke from an early bonfire. The dusk was lavender, so lambent everything looked slightly transparent, and the milling guests in the garden might have been ghosts. The child wandered among them, unseen as a ghost herself, watching.

There were stout old gentlemen with iron-gray wigs and wide-brimmed hats, who spoke at length with Uncle Henry about harvests and horse fairs. In high white wigs were young men and young ladies, lace-trimmed mincers of both sexes, who wondered why there were no musicians, and were quite put out to be told that there would be no dancing because of mourning for Papa.

Admiring gentlemen in silk stockings, slithery as eels, crowded around Mamma to pay her compliments, and Uncle Thomas held her arm possessively and smiled at them all. Aunt Caroline, on a couch that had been brought out for her, looked on dreamily. Uncle Randall edged through the crowd, telling first one inquirer and then another how his bruises had come at the hands of a low slut of a chambermaid, damn her eyes for a scheming hussy, wanted a guinea for favors as though she were the Queen of Sheba, screamed like a harpy when he'd paid her out in the coin she deserved! Ha-ha.

John and James lay in the arms of the nurserymaid and Aunt Elizabeth, who was glad to get off her feet, and the little boys stared in wide-awake astonishment at the glowing lanterns and ignored all their well-wishers, who moved on speedily to the collation table for cider and ham anyway. Some guests vanished in pairs into shadowy corners. There were perfumes of civet-musk strong in the air, there was wine flowing free. Someone got drunk remarkably quickly and tripped, and his wig went flying. It hit Uncle Henry in the face with a *poof* and a cloud of powder. People tittered with laughter.

The little girl walked through the shadows to the keeper's shed. She found the ring of keys where he had hung it up before hurrying off to the somewhat lesser collation for the servants. Nobody but the tyger saw her as she came and tried the big brass keys, one after another, in the padlock that secured the door of his pen. At last it clicked open.

She slipped it off. The bolt was a simple one, just like the bolt on the nursery door. Sliding it back, she opened the door of the pen.

The tyger paced swiftly forward, his green eyes gleaming. He looked much bigger out of his prison. He turned and gazed at her a moment; put out his warm rough tongue and slicked it along the pulse of her wrist, the palm of her hand. She felt a shock go through her body, an electric thrill of pleasure. She parted her lips but could find no words, only staring back at him in wonderment. He turned his head to regard the party in the sunken garden.

"Now," said the tyger, "We'll see, won't we?"

He stretched his magnificent length, gave a slight wriggle of his shoulders, and bounded across the courtyard. Standing beside the empty cage, she folded her little hands and watched.

He charged the party, vaulting from the top step into the sunken garden. Horrified guests looked up to see him land in the midst of them all, and gilt chairs were knocked over as people scrambled to get away from him, screaming in their panic. Some staggered on their high heels, some kicked off their shoes and ran in their slippery stockinged feet. Aunt Elizabeth went over backward in her chair, clutching young James, and both began to shriek. The servants fled for their lives. Aunt Caroline watched all from her couch, too drugged to care.

But the tyger leapt straight through the garden like a thunderbolt, overtaking Uncle Thomas, whom it felled with a sidelong rake of one paw. Uncle Thomas went down, howling and clutching himself, and blood ran red all down his white silk hose. The tyger didn't even pause, however, it sprang clean over him and continued forward, and the only person left before it now was Uncle Randall, who had broken a heel on the topmost of the opposite steps and was still there, frantically attempting to yank off his tight shoe.

Uncle Randall looked up into the tyger's eyes, but had no time to do more than bleat before it struck him. He broke like a doll, and rolled over with it into the darkness.

There was a second's hush, cries cut off abruptly in those who still crouched or lay sprawled in the sunken garden. Uncle Henry, who had crawled to Aunt Elizabeth's side, rose on his elbow to look and said, "O Lord God!"

The tyger appeared at the top of the steps, dragging Uncle Randall by the back of the neck. Uncle Randall's head hung at a strange angle and his body was limp. The tyger's eyes reflected back the light of the golden lanterns.

It stared at them all a moment before opening its jaws. Uncle Randall dropped like an empty coat. The tyger's beard was red.

It bared its fangs, and turned and bounded away into the night.

*   *   *

When they asked her why, she explained. After she had told them everything, they made her explain it all over, and then explain once more. No matter how often she explained, however, they did not hear what she said.

*   *   *

Finally they sent her away, to a convent school in France. It was by no means as bad as it might have been.

She made no friends, but her eyes being now accustomed to look for detail, she saw keenly the fond possessive looks or angry glances between the other girls, heard the midnight weeping or sighs, saw the notes hastily exchanged; watched the contests for dominance and knew when the cloister gate was locked and when it was left unlocked, and who came and went thereby, and when they came too.

The heavy air buzzed like a hive. She no more thought of participating in the convent's inner life than she would have thrust her hand into a wasp's nest, but she watched in fascination.

Then, one morning at Mass, above the high altar, the crucified Christ opened green blazing eyes and looked at her. He smiled.

Nightmare Mountain

There was once a poor man, and he had a daughter.

He wouldn't for a second have admitted he was poor. He owned a fifty-acre almond ranch in San Jose, after all. He came of fine stock from the South, and all his people on both sides had owned property before the War. It was true their circumstances had been somewhat reduced in the days following the capitulation at Appamattox; it was true he and all his kin had been obliged to flee persecution, and head West. But they were people of account, make no mistake about it.

Great-Aunt Merrion would sit on the front porch and look out over the lion-yellow hills, and recollect: "My daddy once owned three-fifths of Prince County, and the farm proper was seven miles to a side. Nothing like *this*." And she would sniff disdainfully at the dry rows of little almond trees.

And Aunt Pugh, who sat on the other side of the porch and who hated Great-Aunt Merrion only slightly less than she hated the Yankees, would wave her arm at the creaking Aeromotor pump and say: "My daddy once owned a thousand acres of the finest bottom-land on the Mississippi River, as verdant as the gardens of Paradise before the fall. How happy I am he cannot see the extent to which we are reduced, in this desert Purgatory!"

Then they would commence to rock again, in their separate chairs, and little Annimae would sigh and wonder why they didn't like California. She liked it fine. She didn't care much for the ranch house, which was creaking and shabby and sad, and full of interminable talk about the Waw, which she took to be some hideous monster, since it had chased her family clear across the country.

But Annimae could always escape from the house and run through the almond trees, far and far along the rows, in spring when they were all pink and white blossoms. Or she might wander down to the edge by the dry creek, and walk barefoot in the cool soft sand under the cottonwoods. Or she might climb high into the cottonwood branches and cling, swaying with the wind in the green leaves, pretending she was a sailor way high in the rigging of a ship.

But as she grew up, Annimae was told she mustn't do such things anymore. Running and climbing was not proper deportment for a lady. By this time there were two mortgages on the ranch, and Annimae's father went about with a hunted look in his eyes, and drank heavily after dinner, bourbon out of the fine crystal that had been brought from Charleston. As a consequence Annimae very much regretted that she could no longer escape from the house, and sought her escape in the various books that had been her mother's. They were mostly such romances and fairy tales as had been thought proper for genteel young ladies a generation previous.

To make matters worse, the money that had been set aside to send her to a finishing school had gone somehow, so there was no way out there, either; worse yet, Great-Aunt Merrion and Aunt Pugh took it upon themselves to train her up in the manner of a gentlewoman, her dear Mamma (whose sacred duty it would have been) having passed away in the hour of Annimae's birth. They had between them nearly a century's worth of knowledge of what was expected of a fine planter's lady in charge of a great estate, but they so bitterly contradicted each other that Annimae found it next to impossible to please either of them.

When Annimae was fifteen, her father sold off some of the property to the county, though Great-Aunt Merrion and Aunt Pugh warned that this was the beginning of the end. He bought Annimae a pianoforte with some of the money, that she might learn to play. The rest of the money would have paid off the mortgages, if he hadn't speculated in stocks.

By the time Annimae was seventeen she played the pianoforte exquisitely, and across the sold-off fields the new Monterey Road cut straight past the ranch house, within a stone's throw of the window before which she sat as she played. Great-Aunt Merrion and Aunt Pugh were mortified, and thenceforth withdrew from the porch to the parlor, rather than be exposed to the public gaze on the common highway.

One night Annimae came to the end of an air by Donizetti, and fell silent, gazing out into the summer darkness.

"Do play on, child," said Aunt Pugh irritably. "The young have no excuse to sit wool-gathering. A graceful melody will ease your father's cares."

Annimae's father had already eased his cares considerably with bourbon, upstairs at his desk, but ladies did not acknowledge such things.

"I was just wondering, Aunt Pugh," said Annimae, "Who is it that drives by so late?"

"Why, child, what do you mean?" said Great-Aunt Merrion.

"There's a carriage goes by every night, just about half-past nine," said Annimae. "It's very big, quite a fine carriage, and the driver wears a high silk hat. The strangest thing is, the carriage-lamps are all set with *purple* glass, purple as plums! So they throw very little light to see by. I wonder that they are lit at all.

"The horses' hooves make almost no sound, just gliding by. And lately, it goes by so slow! Quite slow past the house, as though they're looking up at us. Who could they be?"

Great-Aunt Merrion and Aunt Pugh exchanged a significant glance.

"Purple glass, you say," said Great-Aunt Merrion. "And a driver in a top hat. Is he an old buck—" and I am afraid Great-Aunt Merrion used a word no true lady ever uses when referring to a member of the Negro race, and Aunt Pugh smiled spitefully at her lapse behind a fan.

"I think so, yes," said Annimae.

"I expect that must be poor crazy Mrs. Nightengale," said Aunt Pugh.

"Poor!" exclaimed Great-Aunt Merrion, with what in anyone less august would have been a snort. "Poor as Croesus, I'd say. *Nouveau Riche,* child; no good breeding at all. Do you know how Talleyrand Nightengale made his money? Selling powder and ball to the Yankees! For which he most deservedly died young, of the consumption (they *said*), and left that bloodstained and ill-gotten fortune to his wife.'

"*I* heard he shot himself in a fit of drunken despondency and shame," asserted Aunt Pugh. "And *she's* nobody. Some storekeeper's daughter from New Orleans. And there was a child, they say; but it was a puny little thing, and I believe she had to put it into a sanatorium—"

"I heard it died," stated Great-Aunt Merrion, and Aunt Pugh glared at her.

"I believe you are misinformed, Miss Merrion. So what should this foolish woman do but take herself off to the Spiritualists' meetings, and venture into the dens of fortune-tellers, like the low-bred and credulous creature she was."

"And what should that foolish woman come to believe," said Great-Aunt Merrion, cutting in with a scowl at Aunt Pugh, "But that all her misfortunes were caused by the unquiet spirits of those who perished due to Northern aggression supplied by Nightengale Munitions! And one evening when she was table-rapping, or some such diabolical nonsense, her departed husband *supposedly* informed her that she had to run clean across the country to California to be safe."

"Nor is that all!" cried Aunt Pugh, leaning forward to outshout Great-

Aunt Merrion. "She believed that if she built herself a house, *and never let the work stop on it,* she would not only escape the predations of the outraged shades of the Confederacy, but would herself be granted life everlasting, apparently in some manner other than that promised by our dear Lord and Savior."

"I do wish," said Great-Aunt Merrion, "Miss Pugh, that you would not raise your voice in that manner. People will think you lack gentility. In any case, child—the Widow Nightengale has built herself a mansion west of town. It is a vile and vulgar thing. *She* calls it Nightengale Manor; but the common children of the street refer to it as Nightmare Mountain. I do hear it has more than a hundred rooms now; and night and day the hammers never cease falling. One wonders that a lady could endure such appalling clamor—"

"But they do say she shuts herself up in there all day, and only ventures forth by night, in that purple carriage of hers," said Aunt Pugh. "Or goes occasionally to make purchases from shopkeepers; yet she never sets a foot to the ground, but they come out to her as though she were the Queen of Sheba, and she picks and chooses from their wares."

"It never ceases to amaze me how common folk will abase themselves before the almighty dollar," said Great-Aunt Merrion with contempt, and Aunt Pugh nodded her head in rare agreement.

But on the very next evening, as Annimae's father was lighting the fire in the parlor himself—for the Chinese servants had all been discharged, and were owed back wages at that—Annimae looked out the window and saw the strange carriage coming up the drive.

"Why, Daddy, we have callers," she exclaimed.

Annimae's father rose up swiftly, white as a sheet, for he was expecting the Marshall. When the gentle knock came, his mouth was too dry to bid Annimae stay, so she got up to open the door; though Great-Aunt Merrion hissed, "Child, mention that our house boy just died, and you do not yourself customarily—"

But Annimae had opened the door, and it was too late.

There on the porch stood an old, old man, leaning on a stick. His hair was snow-white with age, his skin black as Annimae's pianoforte. Though it was a moonless night, he wore smoked spectacles that hid his eyes. He was dressed in a black suit of formal cut, and was just drawing off his tall silk hat. Holding it before him, he bowed. On the drive behind him was the carriage, indeed painted a deep violet, with two great black horses hitched to it. Visible within the carriage was a tiny woman, swathed in a purple lap robe. Perhaps there was something behind her, huddled up in the shadows.

And Annimae felt a wave of summer heat blow in from the night, and it seemed the perfume of strange flowers was on that wind, and the music of insects creaking loud in the darkness.

"Good Evening, Miss. Is Mr. Devereaux Loveland at home?" the old man inquired, in a nasal voice.

"What do you want here, boy?" demanded Great-Aunt Merrion.

"I do beg your pardon, Ma'am, but my mistress is crippled with the rheumatism and hopes you will excuse her if she don't get out of the carriage to speak to you herself," said the old man. "She wishes to know if Mr. Loveland would be so kind as to call on her at Nightengale Manor, at any convenient hour tomorrow."

Annimae's father started forward, and stared past the old man at the carriage.

"You may tell her I would be delighted to do so, boy," he said hoarsely. "What is it your mistress wishes to discuss with me?"

"Matters of mutual advantage, Sir," said the old man, and bowed again.

"Then I shall call on her at one o'clock in the afternoon," said Annimae's father.

When Annimae had closed the door, Aunt Pugh said scornfully:

"A *lady* would have left a calling card."

But the next day Annimae's father dressed in his finest clothes, saddled his white horse and rode away down Monterey Road, well ahead of the hour so as not to be late. It was seven in the evening before he came riding back.

When he had led his horse to the stable himself (for the Mexican groom had been discharged) he returned and came straight into the house, and standing before his hearth he said to Annimae: "Daughter, I have arranged your marriage. You are to become the wife of Daniel Nightengale."

Annimae stood there stunned. Great-Aunt Merrion gasped, and Aunt Pugh sputtered, and then the pair of them raised twenty concerted objections, as her father ignored them and poured himself a glass of brandy from the parlor decanter. But Annimae felt again the strange warm wind, and a reckless joy rising in her heart.

"What d'you mean, that woman has a son?" roared Great-Aunt Merrion. "A *marriageable* son?"

"I am given to understand he is an invalid," said Annimae's father, with a significant look at the old women.

A certain silence fell.

"And he is the only child and heir?" said Aunt Pugh delicately.

"He is, Madam," replied Annimae's father.

"Mm-*hm*," said Great-Aunt Merrion. Adamant was not so hard and bright as the speculative gaze she turned on Annimae. "Well, child, you have indeed been favored by fortune."

Annimae said: "Is he handsome, Daddy?"

"I did not see him," said Annimae's father, studying the ceiling beams. Taking a drink of the brandy, he went on: "The, ah, the young gentleman is unable to receive visitors. Mrs. Nightengale offered his proposal."

"But—how did he fall in love with me, then?" asked Annimae.

The two Aunts pursed their old lips tight. Annimae's father lowered his head, met his child's eyes and said:

"I was informed he goes out riding a'nights in the carriage, and has glimpsed you seated at the window, and was entranced by the vision of beauty and gentility you presented. And he burns for love of you, or so his dear Mamma says."

"Why then, I will surely love him!" said Annimae with firm conviction.

"That is your duty, child," said Great-Aunt Merrion.

But neither Great-Aunt Merrion nor Aunt Pugh were pleased with the conditions set on the match: which were, that there was to be no grand church wedding, blazoned in the Society Pages, no public ceremony or indeed a church ceremony at all, but one conducted in Mrs. Nightengale's private chapel, and that within the next three days. And they were in agonies of mixed emotions about the small trunkful of twenty-dollar gold pieces Mrs. Nightengale had sent to pay for Annimae's trousseau.

"Charity? Who *does* she think we are? How dare she!" said Great-Aunt Merrion.

"Imagine having to buy a wedding dress ready-made! Such a shame!" said Aunt Pugh.

But they spent the gold lavishly, and as a result Annimae looked exquisite, a very magnolia in ivory lace, when she mounted into the hired carriage with her father. They set off in state, with the Aunts following in another carriage behind, and rolled away down dusty commonplace Monterey Road.

As they rode along, Annimae's father cleared his throat and said:

"I expect the old ladies have explained to you your duty to your husband, Daughter?"

"Oh, yes," said Annimae, assuming he meant the selection of suitable house servants and how to entertain guests.

Annimae's father was silent a moment, and at last said:

"I expect any child of mine to be able to withstand adversity with courage. You may find married life a trial. Consider yourself a soldier on the battlefield, Daughter; for the fortunes of our family all depend upon this match. Do not fail us."

"Of course I won't, Daddy," said Annimae, wondering what on earth that had to do with valentine hearts and white doves.

So they came to Nightengale Manor.

Annimae had expected it would be a lofty castle on a crag, and of course this was not so, for it sat on the flat yellow orchard plain of San Jose. But it did rise like a mountain in its way. She glimpsed it out the window a long way off, and caught her breath. High turrets and spires, cupolas, gables, balconies, corbels, cornices, finials and weathercocks, with its walls scaled in every shape of gingerbread shingle and painted all the colors of a fruit bowl! And all rising from a grand park miles long.

They drew up before the gate at last, and Annimae cried out in delight. It was a wildly lush garden, for that dry country. Lawns green as emerald, formal rose beds-edged by boxwood hedges planted in circles, in stars, in crescent moons and diamonds. A double row of palms and oleanders lined the carriage drive. Annimae counted at least three fountains sending up fine sprays through the heavy air. The house itself seemed to spread out in all directions; nowhere could one look, however far out into the park, without catching a glimpse of roofline or a tower somewhere among the trees. Annimae heard the sound of hammering. It seemed far-away and muffled, but it was continuous.

As the carriages drew up before the porch (a fretwork fantasy of spindlewood, scrolls and stained glass), the front door was already being opened by the old black man. He smiled, with fine white teeth, and bowed low.

"Welcome to Nightengale Manor, Sir and Ladies. My mistress is expecting you all in the chapel. If you'll please to follow me?"

They stepped across the threshold, and Annimae heard her aunts breathing heavily, keeping their lips tight together for fear lest they should exclaim aloud. The old man led them through a succession of the most beautiful rooms Annimae had ever seen. Fine carpets, polished paneling of rare inlaid woods, stained glass windows set with crystals that sent rainbows dancing everywhere. Golden rooms, green rooms, red rooms, rooms blue with every color of the sea, and the deeper they went into the house, the more dimly lit it all was. But after they had been walking for fifteen minutes, Aunt Pugh exclaimed:

"Boy, you have been leading us in circles! I declare I have walked five miles!"

"It's a long way to the chapel," said the old man, in tones of sincerest apology. "And the house is designed like a maze, you see. If I was to leave you now, I don't reckon you folks could find your way back. I do beg your pardon. We're nearly there."

And only three rooms and a staircase later they were there, too. They entered a chamber vaulted like a church, set all around with more stained glass, though a curious cold light shone through the panes that was not like daylight at all. Before a little altar of black and porphyry marble stood just three people, two of them looking ill-at-ease.

One was the Reverend Mr. Stevens, clutching his Book of Common Prayer. The other was clearly a workman, middle-aged, dressed in heavy overalls. He was sweating, twisting his cap between his hands. He smelled of sawdust and glue.

The third was the woman Annimae had glimpsed in the carriage. She was merely a plain plump middle-aged little lady, all in purple bombazine, who had been pretty once. Her eyes were still remarkable, though at the moment their stare was rather fixed and hostile.

"Miss Annimae Loveland; Mr. Devereaux Loveland; the Misses Merrion and Pugh," announced the old man, with proper solemnity. The mistress of the house inclined her head in acknowledgement.

"Reverend, you may commence," she said.

"I beg your pardon, but where is the groom?" demanded Great-Aunt Merrion, whose feet were hurting her a great deal.

"Great-Aunt, hush," said Annimae's father. Mrs. Nightengale merely said:

"My son's condition does not permit him to venture from his room at present. The marriage will be conducted with Mr. Hansen standing proxy."

"Why, I never heard of such a thing!" squealed Aunt Pugh.

"Hold your tongue!" said Annimae's father, in a tone of such venom Aunt Pugh went pale.

Annimae scarcely knew what to think, and was further troubled when the Reverend Mr. Stevens leaned forward and said quietly: "My child, do you freely consent to this marriage?"

"Of course I do," she said, "I'd just like to meet my husband, is all."

"Then let us proceed," said Mrs. Nightengale.

The service was brief, and swiftly spoken. Bewildered and disappointed, Annimae spent most of the ceremony staring up at the inscriptions in the two stained glass windows above the altar. One read: *WIDE UNCLASP THE TABLES OF THEIR THOUGHTS*, and the other read, *THESE SAME THOUGHTS PEOPLE THIS LITTLE WORLD*.

Mr. Hansen's hands were shaking as he fitted the wedding band on Annimae's finger, and he mumbled his responses. She in her turn was puzzled at how to put the ring on his hand, for it was much too small for his big thick fingers; but she settled for putting it on the little finger, and as soon as the ceremony was concluded he slipped it off and handed it to the old man, who received it on a velvet cushion and bore it away into the depths of the house.

Then he returned, and with the utmost punctiliousness and grace ushered Annimae's father and aunts away to a cold collation in a room much nearer to the front door than seemed possible, after all the distance they had traveled coming in. Immediately after a glass of champagne and a sandwich apiece, the father and aunts were escorted to their carriages, again with such courtesy that they were halfway back to the ranch before they realized they'd been thrown out.

But Annimae was shown to a splendid dining room, all crystal. Though there were no windows in any of the walls, a domed skylight let in the sun. Mirrors lined every wall and shone inlaid from most other surfaces, so that a hundred thousand Annimaes looked back at her.

Mr. Hansen and the reverend having been dismissed, she found herself seated at the far end of a table empty but for Mrs. Nightengale, who sat at the other end. The old man wheeled in a serving-cart, deftly removed the silver epergne from the middle of the table so the two women could see each other, and served them luncheon.

Annimae racked her memory, desperately trying to recall what she had been taught about Light and Gracious Conversation Appropriate to Dining. Mrs. Nightengale, however, spoke first, shaking out her napkin. The faraway pounding of hammers counterpointed her words, never ceasing once during the ensuing conversation.

"I have something of importance to tell you, girl."

Annimae nearly said "Yes, Ma'am," but recollected herself in time and replied instead: "Certainly, Mother Nightengale."

Mrs. Nightengale stared at her, and then said: "We labor under a curse. I do not use the term in a figurative sense. As you are now one of us, you will be affected. Attend carefully, Daughter-in-Law. Only in this room may we speak of it; for *they* are fascinated by their own reflections, and will pay us no mind."

"Yes, Mother Nightengale," Annimae replied, watching the old man as he ladled soup into her plate, but by neither wink nor smile did he indicate he was hearing anything in the least strange.

"Are you familiar with Spiritualism?" Mrs. Nightengale inquired.

"I—I don't believe so, no," Annimae replied.

"Well, it is simply founded on the discovery that it is possible to converse with the dead," said Mrs. Nightengale in a matter-of-fact way, tasting her soup. "The spirit world is quite real, and sages and ancient mystics have always been aware of it; but in these modern times its existence has at last been accepted by Science."

"I did not know that," said Annimae. "How interesting."

"The thing is," said Mrs. Nightengale, frowning, "That a great many credulous people think that those who have passed over to the other side are just naturally in possession of great truth, and wisdom, and benevolence towards all mankind. And, as anyone who has ever experienced a commonplace haunting knows, that is a lot of fool nonsense."

"Is it really?" said Annimae, cautiously buttering a roll.

"It is, girl. The dead in their ranks are exactly as they were in life. Some are wise and well-intentioned, but others are wicked. Wrathful. Spiteful, and inclined to remorseless persecution of the living," said Mrs. Nightengale sadly. "As I know to my cost, this many a weary year. You see, certain malignant entities are bent upon the destruction of all whom I love."

"Goodness, what a terrible thing," said Annimae.

"They hounded my late husband to an early grave. And both I, and my dear son, have been so fenced and crossed with subtle maledictions that, were we living in an ignorant age, I think we should have perished miserably long ago," said Mrs. Nightengale. "Fortunately, I do have friends in the spirit world, who were able to advise me; and so we are able to take protective measures."

"I am very glad to hear that, Mother Nightengale," said Annimae.

"For example," said Mrs. Nightengale, "I am cursed in such a way that I will die the very moment my feet come into contact with the earth. Dust blown in on the floor of the carriage does me no harm, apparently; but were I ever to step out into the garden, you would see me wither and expire before your eyes. And there are a host of lesser evils, but the wearing of colors with strong vibrational power—purple works the best, you see— helps to ward them off."

"How fascinating," said Annimae, who was running out of pleasant and noncommittal remarks.

"Alas, poor Daniel is not as fortunate," said Mrs. Nightengale. She set her hand on a locket about her neck. "When he was a baby, I despaired of saving his life. It has been only by the most extreme measures that I have preserved him."

So saying, she opened the locket and gazed for a moment on its contents, and for the first time her expression softened.

"I—is that a portrait of Daniel?" Annimae inquired.

Mrs. Nightengale closed the locket with a snap. Then, apparently thinking better of her gesture, she removed the locket and handed it to the old man.

"Sam, please pass this to my daughter-in-law."

The old man obliged, and after fumbling a moment with the clasp Annimae got the locket open. Within was an oval photographic portrait of a baby, perfect as a little angel, staring out at the camera with wide eyes. In the concavity of the lid was a single curl of fine golden hair, enclosed behind crystal.

"How beautiful!" said Annimae.

Mrs. Nightengale held out her hand for the locket. "That was taken before our troubled times," she said, slipping it back about her throat.

"And is Daniel's health very bad?" said Annimae anxiously.

"Why, no, girl; his health is now excellent," said Mrs. Nightengale. "And he owes his survival entirely to the prescription of my spirit friends. His curse is that he must hide from all eyes. To be seen by a living soul, or a dead one for that matter, would be fatal to the poor boy."

"But how does he do anything?" Annimae stammered.

"In utter darkness," said Mrs. Nightengale. "Unrelieved by any ray of light. I have had chambers built for him in the center of this house, without windows or doors, reached only by certain secret means. The wicked dead never find him, for the whole of the house is designed as a maze to confuse them. They are seduced by bright colors and ornamentation, and so they go round and round but never find the dark center."

"But... I was told he saw me, and fell in love with me," said Annimae pitifully.

"And so he did," said Mrs. Nightengale. "Did you think I could keep my boy in eternal darkness? No indeed; the good spirits told me that he might come and go by means of a ruse, though it must be only on moonless nights. He wraps himself in a black shroud, and climbs into a box made to resemble a coffin.

"When he signals, the servants carry it out to where I wait with the carriage. They load his coffin into the back; Sam drives us away; and the foolish dead never follow. Then Daniel climbs out and sits behind me, where he cannot be seen. He is greatly refreshed by the night air, and the chance to see something of the world."

"Oh! You drove past our house every night," exclaimed Annimae.

"So we did," said Mrs. Nightengale, looking grim. "And so he fell under the spell of an image glimpsed through a pane of glass, and would not rest until you became his bride. I must admit to you, Daughter-in-Law, that I was against it. Any disturbance of our domestic arrangements represents a peril to his life. But so taken was he with your beauty, that he threatened to destroy himself unless I spoke with your father. The rest you know."

And Annimae was flattered, and felt beautiful indeed, to have won a man's love at such cost. She warmed with compassion for him, too.

"I promise you, Mother Nightengale, I will be a faithful and loving wife to dear Daniel," she said.

"You will need to be more than that," said Mrs. Nightengale. "You will need to be a comrade-in-arms to *me*, Daughter-in-Law. We must wage a constant battle against the dead, if Daniel is to live." And she pressed her fingertips to her temples, as if in sudden pain.

"What must I do?"

"You will learn," said Mrs. Nightengale, a little distractedly. "Sam and Bridget will explain the arrangements. Oh, my migraine is returning; all these strangers in the house admitted malign influence, as I feared. Sam, I must retire to the thirteenth room. See to the girl."

So saying she rose, dropping her napkin, and walked straight to a wall. Annimae, watching in astonishment with spoon halfway to her mouth, thought her mother-in-law was about to collide with the mirrored surface; but at the last minute a panel opened and Mrs. Nightengale stepped through, to vanish as it slid smoothly into place behind her.

"How did she do that?" Anniemae exclaimed.

"It was a mechanism concealed in the floor, Ma'am," Sam told her, retrieving Mrs. Nightengale's napkin. "Triggered counterweights behind the paneling. There's secret passages all over this house! She designed them herself, you know. My mistress is a most ingenious lady."

"What happens now?" asked Annimae, looking about herself forlornly.

"Why, I'll serve you the rest of your luncheon, Ma'am," said Sam. "And then I'll just clear away the mistress's place, and take myself off to the kitchen. You want anything, you just ring."

"Please—" said Annimae, suddenly afraid to be left alone in this glittering room full of unseen presences. "Won't you stay and talk to me? I need to know things—" And she almost called him *boy,* but it did seem to her ridiculous, as august and white-haired as he was. And, mindful of his bent back, she added: "You can sit down while we speak, if you like. And you can have some dinner, too. I mean—luncheon!"

He smiled at her, and the white flash from his teeth winked in every mirrored surface in the room.

"Thank you, Ma'am, I surely will."

He served out filet of sole to her, then drew up a chair and helped himself to a cup of coffee. Settling back with a sigh, he explained the complex system by which the house ran.

On no account must any room ever be approached in the same way twice. There were a dozen different ways to reach any single destination in the house, and until she memorized them all, either he or another of the servants would guide her. There was no map, lest the dead see it and find their way where they weren't wanted; in any case no map would remain accurate for long, because rooms were continuously being remodeled in order to confuse the dead. Doors and windows were put in and taken out at the direction of the good spirits. Chambers were sealed off and reopened. Some doors opened on blank walls, or into space, even three stories up, so she must be careful; stairs might lead nowhere, or take a dozen turns and landings to go up only one floor.

"I never knew there were such things," said Annimae, feeling as though her head were spinning.

"Oh, folk have always protected themselves from haunts, Ma'am," said Sam, leaning over to serve her a slice of coconut pie. He took a slice of bread for himself. "Horseshoes over the door for good luck, eh? And the red thread, and the witchball, and the clover with the four leaves? They keep away all harm, so people say. Mistress just has the money to do it on a big scale, all modern and scientific too."

"Scientific," Annimae repeated, impressed.

He looked at her a long moment, over his smoked spectacles.

"Don't you be afraid," he said at last. "Just you do like you been told, and it will all fall out pretty as any fairy tale. Romance and a happy ending, yes indeed."

"Can you tell me more about Daniel?" asked Annimae. "Is he handsome?"

Sam shrugged.

"I reckon he is, Ma'am. I haven't laid eyes on the master since he was a baby. But he has a beautiful voice, now. How he sings for love of you!"

"When may I go see—that is, when may I meet him?" Annimae set down her napkin. "Can you take me there now?"

Sam coughed slightly, and rose to his feet. "That would be my old woman's business, Ma'am. You wait; I'll send her."

He left the room, and Annimae shivered. She looked about and met her own timid gaze everywhere. For the first time, she noticed the motif that was repeated on the fine china, in the carpet pattern, in the mosaic arrangement of the mirrored bits and even in the panes of glass that made up the skylight: spiderwebs, perfect geometric cells radiating out from an empty center.

She scarce had time to contemplate the meaning of all this before a door opened and a woman all in black strode in briskly, upright though she too was very old. Her hair must have been red as fire when she'd been a girl, for a few strands of that color trailed still through the rest, which was white as smoke; and her eyes behind their dark spectacles were the hot blue of candle flames.

"I'm to take you to himself, now, Ma'am, am I?" she inquired, politely enough; but her eyes flashed dangerously when Annimae put her hands to her mouth in horror.

"*You're* Sam's wife? But—!"

The old woman looked scornful as she curtsied. "Bridget Lacroix. Bless you, Ma'am, you needn't be surprised. There's no scandal at all in me marrying Sam Lacroix. Don't you know how many of us Irish came to Ameri-kay as slaves? White chimpanzees, that's all we are; or so that fine Mr. Kingsley said. And if the mistress don't mind it, I'm sure you shouldn't."

"I am so sorry!" said Annimae, much distressed. "I never meant offense."

Bridget looked her over shrewdly. "No, I don't suppose you did. Sam told me you was innocent as a little baby. But it's time you grew up, me dear." She grinned. "Especially as it's your wedding day."

She led Annimae out of the dining room and through another, where jets of flame burned brilliantly in wall-mounted glass globes. The globes were all colors, hung with prisms that threw swaying rainbows everywhere. And there were more windows set in the walls, stained glass repeating the spiderweb pattern Annimae had noticed before. They, too, were lit from behind by the strange cold light she had wondered at in the chapel. Annimae, who had only ever seen candles and kerosene lamps after dark, exclaimed:

"What is this place?"

"O, this is just the Room of Eternal Day," said Bridget. "The dead don't like passing through a place so bright, and it shows up that they haven't any shadows besides, and that embarrasses 'em, don't you know. All very up-to-date in here! That's gaslight, of course, but for the windows she's laid on that new electrical light. Clever, isn't it?"

They went on through that room, and came to another that was lined floor to ceiling with clocks, and nothing else. Great inlaid grandfather clocks stood in the corners and ticked solemnly; French bisque clocks sat on shelves and ticked elegantly, as painted Harlequins and Columbines revolved atop them; old wooden regulator clocks thumped along wearily; and little cheap brass clocks beat away the seconds brightly. But no two clocks were set to the same time.

"How strange!" cried Annimae, and Bridget chuckled and said:

"O, this is the Room of All Time and None. It's just to confound the dead. They work very particular shifts, what with midnight being the witching hour and all. If one of 'em strays in to see what o'clock it is, he'll be stuck here guessing with all his might and main."

They left that room and soon came to another, no less curious. There was no spiderweb motif here; rather the recurring image was of a tiny white moth or butterfly, but it was repeated everywhere. It figured in the wallpaper pattern like so many snowflakes, it was woven into the design of the carpet, and into the brocade of the chairs and the inlay of the tables and cabinets, and etched into the very window glass. The curio cabinets held nothing but pressed specimens of white moths, displayed against a blue velvet background.

"What on earth are all these butterflies for?" asked Annimae.

"O, it's only the Soul Trap," said Bridget. "Because, you see, the nasty dead are a bit stupid, and they have a compulsion to count things. Any haunt comes through here, here he must stay until he's numbered every blessed one of the little creatures. Generally by then the ghost will have forgot whatever wickedness he was up to."

"What a good idea," said Annimae, because she could not imagine what else to say.

They proceeded deeper into the house, and as they did it grew dimmer and dimmer, for there were no windows nor light fixtures here, and the corridors turned and turned again ever inward. At last Bridget was only a shadow beside her, that cleared its throat and said:

"Now then, Sam told me you might want a little learning. You know, don't you, what it is a bride does with her husband?"

"Well," said Annimae, "As nearly as I recollect, we're supposed to fall on each other with kisses of passion."

"Hm. Yes, me dear, that's how it starts."

As far as Annimae had been aware, there was nothing more; and in some panic, she racked her brains for what else happened in books and poems.

"I believe that then I'm supposed to swoon away in a transport of love," she said.

"So you must," said Bridget, sounding exasperated. "But there's a great deal goes on between the kissing and swooning, sure. Think of what the stallion does with the mare."

"Oh," said Annimae, who had seen *that* many a time. She walked on in thoughtful silence, drawing certain conclusions, so intent that she scarcely noticed when it became pitch dark at last. Bridget had to take her hand and lead her through the fathomless gloom.

Soon they heard glorious music, close by but muffled. Someone was playing a Spanish guitar with great virtuosity, each note chiming like a bell even through the wall's thickness.

"Why, who's that?" asked Annimae.

"O, the jewel, the darling! He's serenading his bride," Bridget exclaimed with great tenderness. There was a sound suggesting that she had put out her hand and was sliding it along the wall as they walked. Presently she stopped, and rapped twice.

The music halted at once. An eager voice said:

"Annimae?"

"She's here, charming boy," said Bridget. "Hurry now, while it's safe."

There was a click, and then a rush of air that smelled of gentlemen's cologne. Annimae felt herself prodded gently forward, closer to the scent, into a warmer darkness. Something clicked again, behind her now. She fought back a moment of wild terror, realizing she had been locked in; but at once warm hands took her own, and they felt so live and steady that her fear melted away. She touched the wedding ring on his finger.

"I'm here, Daniel Nightengale," she said. "Your own true love—"

"Oh, my own Annimae," said the new voice, breaking on a hoarse sob. And Annimae, feeling brave now, leaned forward in the darkness and sought her husband's lips. She encountered his chin instead, for he was a little taller than she was. He bent to her and they kissed, and the kiss was nicer than anything Annimae had ever known in her whole life. The face of the baby angel in the locket came before her mind's eye; in the table of her thoughts it grew, became the face of a handsome man.

She had compiled a list of rapturous phrases to murmur in his ear, but somehow she couldn't stop kissing, nor could he. Their arms went around each other, they grappled and swayed. Annimae felt once again the dizzy happiness she had known high up in the cottonwood tree, when she seemed about to lift free of the dry earth and soar away, into a green paradise.

The whole time, her young fingers were exploring, touching, tracing out the strange new shape of a man. Such broad shoulders, under his linen shirt! And such smooth skin! Such fine regular features! His hands were exploring too, feverish and fast, and fever woke in her own blood. She thought about mares and stallions. He lifted his mouth from hers and gasped,

"Please, let's lie on the bed—" and she was making sounds of agreement, though she hadn't any idea where his bed or anything else in the room might be. He half-carried her a few yards, and they collapsed together on what must be the counterpane. She understood what he wanted and, remarkably quickly considering how much effort and care had gone into putting on her wedding dress, she writhed out of it.

Then the smooth counterpane was cool under her and he embraced her so close, and, and, and....

Long afterward she recollected the rapturous phrases, and duly murmured them in his ear. Now, however, she knew what they meant.

Now she believed them.

*   *   *

So began Annimae's married life. She was as happy as any new bride in any of her books, even with the strange constraints upon her life. There was no question that she loved Daniel Nightengale with her whole heart, and that he loved her.

"You were the most beautiful thing I'd ever seen in all my life," he sighed, as they lay close together in the dark. "The window shining out across the darkness, and you framed there bright as an angel. I loved you so! You were the very image of everything I'd ever wanted, in the life I'd never be allowed to live. And I thought, I *will* live it! I will marry that girl!"

"Your Mamma said you threatened to die for love of me," said Annimae.

"I would have," he said, with a trace of sullenness. "Just opened that door and walked out through the house, and I'd have kept walking until I found the sunlight."

"Oh, but that would be a terrible thing!" said Annimae. "With so many folks who love you? You mustn't ever do it, my dearest."

"I never will, now that you're here," he conceded, and kissed her.

"And after all," she said, "It's not really so awfully bad, like this. You're no worse off than a blind man would be. Much better, really! You needn't beg for your dinner on a streetcorner, like poor old Mr. Johnson in town. Instead you're my handsome prince, under a spell. And, who knows? Maybe someday we'll find a way to break the spell."

"If only there were a way!" he said. Then, hesitantly, he asked: "Do you think my mother is crazy?"

"Well, I did wonder at first," she admitted. "But I guess she isn't. Spiritualism is a big religion, I hear, and they wouldn't let all those people run around loose if they were crazy, would they? And everything in the house is so modern and scientifical!"

He sighed, and said he guessed she was right.

Their days began around ten o'clock in the morning, when a gentle rap at the panel signified that Sam had brought a wheeled cart with their breakfasts. Annimae would scramble through the heavy velvet curtains that cloaked the bed—only there in case of emergency, for the room was black as ink at all hours—and, finding her dressing gown by touch, slip it on and open the secret panel. Sam would enter along with Gideon, who was Sam's son and Daniel's valet. She became quite skilled at pouring coffee and buttering toast in the dark, as Daniel was shaved and dressed sight unseen, and Sam made the bed and collected their linen, all by touch alone.

The four of them often conversed pleasantly together, for Gideon would bring the news culled from the morning's *Mercury,* and Daniel was eager to hear what was going on in the world. They might have been ordinary people in an ordinary household, Annimae thought; and the reassuring domestic details comforted her, and further convinced her that her life wasn't so strange, after all.

After breakfast she would leave Daniel's suite for a little while, to take the sun. It appeared painfully bright to her now; she saw why all the servants wore smoked spectacles, and begged a pair of her own from Bridget. Then she could wander the gardens, feeding the fish in the reflecting pools, admiring the exotic flowers, picking fruit from the bushes and trees. She brought back bouquets of roses for Daniel, or apron-pockets full of blackberries warm from the sun.

She seldom met the gardeners, the twins Godfrey and Godwin, who were also Sam's sons. Most of the servants had adjusted to a nocturnal schedule over the years, for the mistress of the house kept late hours too. Annimae did wander out now and then to the perimeters of the house, where the workmen were always busy hammering, sawing, extending the vast and gorgeous edifice with raw new redwood that still smelled of the wilderness. They were always too busy to speak, though they doffed their caps to her, blushing.

Sensing that she made them uncomfortable, Annimae stopped coming by to watch their progress. The house would never be finished anyway; and after a week or so her heart beat to the rhythm of the ceaseless hammers. It was a comforting sound. It meant that Daniel was safe, and all was right with the world.

After her morning walks, she was summoned to luncheon with Mrs. Nightengale, which was like having an audience with a gloomy and severe queen. Mrs. Nightengale questioned her in great detail on Daniel's continuing health, though she refrained from asking about the most intimate matters.

"Daniel *seems* to be thriving with your companionship," was the closest she came to a compliment. "Though the good spirits are still concerned for him. You must not grow careless, Daughter-in-Law."

"I do assure you, Mother Nightengale, his life is as precious to me as it must be to you," said Annimae. Mrs. Nightengale regarded her in a chilly kind of way, and then winced and shut her eyes.

"Is it your headache again?" Annimae inquired in sympathy. "Perhaps it's the sun, don't you think? I am sure you would be much more comfortable if you wore dark spectacles too."

"They are not for me," replied Mrs. Nightengale, getting stiffly to her feet. "I gaze into a far brighter light than mortal eyes can imagine, when I commune with the spirits. You'll excuse me, now. I am wanted in the thirteenth room."

So saying, she walked through a wall and vanished.

Annimae went also to the mansion's library each day, once she learned the various routes to get there. It was not really such a big room, relative to the rest of the house. It contained a Bible, and the collected works of Shakespeare, though neither one seemed to have been read much. There were several volumes of fairy-stories, for Mrs. Nightengale had used to sit in the corridor outside Daniel's room and read to him, when he had been small. There were many, many other books, principally by one Andrew Jackson Davis, and both they and the books by Emanuel Swedenborg had pride of place, though there were others by a Countess Blavatsky.

These all treated of the mystical world. Annimae made it a point to sit and read a chapter from one of them each day, in order that she might better understand her husband's plight. She tried very hard to make sense of esoteric wisdom, but it bewildered her.

All the books claimed a great universal truth, simple and pure, revealed by spirit messengers from Almighty God; yet its proponents contradicted one another, sometimes angrily, and not one seemed to be able to state convincingly what the truth *was*. Every time Annimae thought she was coming to a revelation, so that her heart beat faster and she turned the pages eagerly, the promised answers failed to materialize. The great mysteries remained impenetrable.

So with a sigh she would leave the books, and find a way back through the black labyrinth at the house's heart. The deeper the shadows grew, the lighter was her step dancing home to her beloved. And what great truth was there, after all, but that it was sweet delight to pull off all her clothes and leap into bed with Daniel Nightengale?

And when they'd tumbled, when they'd had so much fun they were tired, Daniel would lie beside her and beg her to relate everything she'd seen that day. It was difficult to tell him of the glories of the garden, for he knew very little of colors. Black and purple, midnight blue and the shades of stars or windows were all he could summon to his mind. Red and pink to him were smells, or tastes.

But she could tell him about the swallows that made their nests under the eaves of the carriage-house, queer daubed things like clay jars stuck up there, with the little sharp faces peering out; she could tell him about the squirrel that had tried to climb the monkey-puzzle tree. He wanted to know everything, was hungry for the least detail.

Afterward they would rise in the dark, answerable to no sun or moon, and find their way together into the splendid bathroom, as magnificent in its appointments as any Roman chamber. The spirits had devised ingenious systems to heat the room with jets of warmed air, piped in from below, and to fill the marble tub with torrents of hot water from a spigot. There were silver vessels of scent for the water; there was scented oil too.

When they had luxuriated together they returned to the central room, where Daniel played the guitar for her, as she sprawled in bed with him. And it seemed to Annimae this must be just the way princes and princesses had lived long ago, perhaps even in the days of the Bible: young flesh oiled and perfumed, a silken nest and endless easeful night in which to make sweet music.

It never occurred to her to wonder what the future might hold. Daniel raged against his confinement, and she comforted him, as she felt it was her duty to do. Sometimes they discussed ways in which he might gain more freedom, in the years to come: perhaps a portable room, or even a leather and canvas suit like a deep-sea diver's, with a sealed helmet fronted in smoked glass? Perhaps Daniel might walk in the sunlight. Perhaps he might go to Europe and see all the sights to be seen. Whatever he did, Annimae knew she would always be there beside him; for that was how true lovers behaved, in all the stories in the wide world.

There was no fear in the dark for Annimae, now, ever. Only one thing still made her startle, when it woke her twice each night: the tolling of a vast deep-throated bell somewhere high in the house. Mrs. Nightengale had it struck at midnight, for that was the hour when the good spirits arrived. Mrs. Nightengale, having retired to the thirteenth room and donned one of thirteen ceremonial robes, would commune there with the spirits for two hours, receiving their advice and instruction. At two o'clock the bell would toll again, the spirits depart.

"And then she comes out with a great sheaf of blueprints for the carpenters, you know," said Bridget, sprinkling starch on one of Daniel's shirts and passing it to her daughter, who ironed it briskly. "And whether it's orders to tear out an old room or start a new one, they set to smartly, you may be sure."

"Don't they ever get tired of it?" asked Annimae, gazing about the handsomely appointed washroom—so many modern conveniences!—in wonder. Bridget and Gardenia exchanged amused glances.

"They're paid in gold, Ma'am," Gardenia explained. "And at twice the wage they'd be earning from anybody else. You can bet they just go home at night and fall on their knees to pray old Mrs. Nightengale never finishes her house!"

"Why is it called the thirteenth room?" Annimae asked.

"To confuse the spirits, Ma'am," replied Gardenia. "It's the seventeenth along that corridor, if you count."

"Why does Mother Nightengale spend so much time there?"

"It's by way of being her house of mysteries, isn't it?" said Bridget, sorting through the linen hamper. "Her command post, if you like, where she plans the battle against the wicked dead every night. There's strange things goes on in there! Chanting all hours, and flashes of light, and sometimes screams to freeze the blood in you! She's a brave lady, the mistress. All for our Danny's sake, just to keep his dear heart beating."

"I'm afraid he gets a little restless now and then," said Annimae uncomfortably. "He says that sometimes he doubts that there's any spirits at all."

The mother and daughter were silent a moment, going about their tasks.

"Poor boy," said Bridget at last. "It's to be expected, with him growing up the way he has. Seeing is believing, sure, and he's never seen danger."

"Do *you* believe in the spirits?" Annimae asked.

"Oh, yes, Ma'am," said Gardenia quietly. "Without a doubt."

So the brief bright days blinked past, like images on nickelodeon screens, and the long fevered nights passed in lazy ecstasy. The last of the summer fruit was garnered away in the vast cellars, with Bridget and her daughters carrying down tray after tray of glass jars full of preserves. The orchards were golden. When the leaves began to fall, Godfrey and Godwin raked great red and yellow heaps that were set to smolder in the twilight, like incense.

There came an evening when Annimae was awakened at midnight, as she always was, by the summoning bell. Yet as its last reverberation died away, no customary calm flowed back like black water; instead there came a drumming, ten times louder than the desultory beat of hammers, a thundering music, and faint voices raised in song.

As she lay wondering why anyone would be drumming at this hour of the night, she felt Daniel sit up beside her.

"Listen!" he said eagerly. "Don't you hear? They're dancing!"

"Is that all it is?" said Annimae, a little cross. The sound frightened her for some reason.

"It's their holiday. We must go watch," said Daniel, and she felt him getting out of bed.

"We mustn't!" she cried. "It's not safe for you, honey."

"Oh, there's a safe way," he said, sounding sly. She heard him open a cabinet and take something from a hanger. "I go watch them every year. This year will be the best of all, because you're with me now. Don't be afraid, my darling."

She heard him walk around to her side of the bed. "Now, get up and come with me. I've put my shroud on, and I'll walk behind you all the way; and no one will see us, where we're going."

So she slid from the bed and reached out, encountering a drape of gauze cloth. His hand came up through it and took hers reassuringly, tugged her impatiently to the secret panel. So quickly they left the room that she had no time to pull on even a stitch, and she blushed hot to find herself out in the corridor naked. Yet it was a hot night, and in any case much too dark to be seen.

"Fifty paces straight ahead, Annimae, and then turn left," Daniel told her.

"Left? But I've never gone that way," said Annimae.

"It's all right," Daniel said, so for love's sake she followed his direction. She walked before him the whole way, though she kept tight hold of his hand through the shroud. Left and right and right again he directed her, through so many turns and up and down so many stairs she knew she'd never find her way back alone, even when they reached a place with windows where milky starlight glimmered through. The house was silent, the corridors all deserted. The drumming, however, grew louder, and the clapping and chanting more distinct.

"This is the earliest thing I can remember," Annimae heard Daniel say. "I woke up in the dark and was scared, and I tried to get out. How I stumbled over everything, in my shroud! I must have found the catch in the panel by accident, because the next thing I knew, there was the corridor stretching out ahead of me. It seemed as bright as stars, then. I followed after the music, just as we're doing now. And, look! This is the window I found."

They had come around a corner and entered a narrow passage ending in a wall, wherein was set one little window in the shape of a keyhole. Daniel urged her toward it, pushing gently. She could see something bright flickering, reflecting from below along the beveled edges of the glass.

"My true love, I do believe somebody's lit a fire outside," said Annimae.

"Yes! Don't be afraid. Look out, and I'll look over your shoulder," said Daniel.

So Annimae bent and put her face to the glass, and peered down into a courtyard she had never before seen. There was indeed a fire, a bright bonfire in the center, with a column of smoke rising from it like a ghostly tree. Gathered all around it, swaying and writhing and tossing their heads, were all the servants. Godfrey and Godwin sat to one side, pounding out the beat of the dance on drums, and all their brothers and sisters kept time with their clapping hands, with their stamping feet. They were singing in a language Annimae had never heard, wild, joyful. Now and again someone would catch up an armful of autumn leaves and fling them on the blaze, and the column of smoke churned and seemed to grow solid for a moment.

The beat was infectious, enchanting. It roused desires in Annimae, and for the first time she felt shame and confusion. *This* was neither in fairy tales nor in the Bible. It did not seem right to feel her body moving so, almost against her will. Daniel, pressing hot behind her, was moving too.

"Oh, how I stared and stared," said Daniel. "And how I wanted to be down there with them! They never have to live in fear, as I do. They can dance in the light. How can I dance, in a shroud like this? Oh, Annimae, I want so badly to be free! Watch now, watch what happens."

Annimae saw Gardenia filling her apron with leaves, to pitch a bushel of them on the fire. The flames dimmed momentarily, and when they roared up again she saw that two new dancers had joined the party.

Who was that black man, bigger than all the rest, waving his carved walking stick? How well he danced! The others fell back to the edges and he strutted, twirled, undulated around the fire. Now he was sinuous as a great snake, powerful as a river; now he was comic and suggestive. Annimae blushed to see him thrust his stick between his legs and rock his hips, and the stick rose up, and up, and he waved and waggled in it such a lewd way there were screams of laughter from the crowd. Even Daniel, behind her, chuckled.

Shocked as she was by that, Annimae was astounded to see a white girl down there at the edge of the fire, joining the black man in his dance. Who could she be? What kind of hoydenish creature would pull her skirt up like that and leap over the fire itself? Her hair was as bright as the flame, her face was fierce, her deportment mad as though she had never, ever had elderly aunts to tell her what ladies mustn't do. Oh! Now she had seized a bottle from one of the onlookers, and was drinking from it recklessly; now she spat, she sprayed liquor into the fire, and when the others all applauded she turned and sprayed them too.

Then the black man had slipped his arm around her. He pulled her in and the pace of the dance quickened. Round and round they went, orbiting the fire and each other, and the drumming of their heels drove Annimae almost to guilty frenzy. Rough and tender and insistent, the music pulsed. As she stared, she felt Daniel's hands move over her, and even through the shroud his touch drove her mad. She backed to him like a mare. He rose up like a stallion.

"You're my fire, Annimae," moaned Daniel. "You're my music, you're my dance. You're my eyes in the sunlight and my fever in the dark. We *will* escape this house, some day, my soul!"

It was all Annimae could do to cling to the windowsill, sobbing in pleasure and shame, and the drumbeats never slowed....

Though they did cease, much later. Annimae and Daniel made their unsteady way back through the black labyrinth, and slept very late the next day.

The next afternoon, Gardenia came to Annimae as she walked in the garden and said: "If you please, Ma'am, there's two old ladies come to call on you."

Annimae went at once inside, back through chambers she hadn't entered in months, out to the front of the house. There in a front parlor alarmingly full of the cold light of day sat Great-Aunt Merrion and Aunt Pugh, inspecting the underside of a vase through a pair of lorgnettes.

"Why, child, how pale you are!" cried Aunt Pugh, as Annimae kissed her cheek.

"How you do peer out of those spectacles, child!" said Great-Aunt Merrion, giving her a good long stare through her lorgnette. "Far too much reading in sickrooms, I'll wager. Wifely duty is all very well, but you must think of yourself now and then."

Annimae apologized for being pale, explaining that she had a headache, and wore the glasses against brightness. She bid Gardenia bring coffee for three, and poured as gracefully as she could when it came, though she still spilled a little.

The aunts graciously overlooked this and told her all the news from the almond ranch. Her father's investments had suddenly prospered, it seemed; the mortgages were all paid off, the servants all hired on again. Her father had once more the means to dress as a gentleman, and had bought a fine stable of racehorses. Why, they themselves had come to visit Annimae in a grand new coach-and-four! And all the merchants in town were once again respectful, deferential, as they ought always to have been to ladies of gentle birth.

But Great-Aunt Merrion and Aunt Pugh had heard certain loose talk in town, it seemed; and so they had known it was their duty to call on Annimae, and to inquire after her health and well-being.

They asked all manner of questions about Annimae's daily life, which Annimae fended off as best she might, for she knew it was dangerous to speak much of Daniel. Detecting this, the old ladies looked sidelong at each other and fell to a kind of indirect questioning that had never failed to produce results before.

Annimae was tired, she was still a little shaken and, perhaps, frightened by the violent delight of the previous evening. Her aunts, when all was said and done, had known her all her life. Somehow she let slip certain details, and the aunts pressed her for explanations, and so—

"Do you tell me you've never so much as *seen* your husband, child?" said Aunt Pugh, clutching at her heart.

"Good God Almighty!" Great-Aunt Merrion shook with horror. "Miss Pugh, do you recollect what that Mrs. Delano said outside the milliner's?"

Aunt Pugh recollected, and promptly fainted dead away.

Annimae, terrified, would have rung for a servant at once; but Great-Aunt Merrion shot out a lace-mittened fist and caught her hand.

"Don't you ring for one of *them*," she whispered. She got up and closed the parlor door; then produced a vial of smelling salts from her handbag. Aunt Pugh came around remarkably quickly, and sat bolt upright.

"Child, we must break your heart, but it is for your own sake," said Great-Aunt Merrion, leaning forward. "I fear you have been obscenely deceived."

She proceeded to relate what a Mrs. Delano had told her, which was: that she had a cousin who had known Mrs. Nightengale in Louisiana right after the Waw, when all her cares were first besetting her. This cousin, who had an excellent memory, was pretty sure that Mrs. Nightengale's baby had not merely been sick, it had in fact died. Moreover, there were stories that Mrs. Nightengale was much too familiar with her household staff, especially her coachman.

"If you know what I mean," Great-Aunt Merrion added.

Annimae protested tearfully, and gave her aunts many examples of Daniel's liveliness. Aunt Pugh wept like a spigot, rocking to and fro and moaning about the shame of it all, until Great-Aunt Merrion told her to cease acting like a fool.

"Now, you listen to me, child," she said to Annimae. "There's only one reason that woman would concoct such a cock-and-bull story. I'll tell you why you can't look on the face of that son of hers! *He is a mulatto.*"

"That's not true!" said Annimae. "I saw his baby picture."

"You saw a picture of the baby that died, I expect," said Aunt Pugh, blowing her nose. "Oh, Annimae!"

"There used to be plenty of old families got themselves a little foundling to replace a dead boy, when the estate was entailed," said Great-Aunt Merrion. "So long as there was a male heir, decent folk held their tongues about it. Money kept the nursemaids from telling the truth.

"Well, hasn't she plenty of money? And didn't she move clear out here to the West so there'd be nobody around who knew the truth? And who'll see the color of her sin, if he's kept out of sight?"

"What's his hair like, child? Oh, Annimae, how you have been fooled!" said Aunt Pugh.

"Likely enough he's her *son,*" sneered Great-Aunt Merrion. "But he's not the one who ought to have inherited."

Annimae was so horrified and angry she nearly stood up to her aunts, and as it was she told them they had better leave. The old women rose up to go; but Great-Aunt Merrion got in a parting shot.

"Ghosts and goblins, my foot," she said. "If you're not a fool, child, you'll sneak a penny candle and a match into that bedroom, next time you go in there. Just you get yourself a good look at that Daniel Nightengale, once he's asleep. You'd better be sure than be a lasting disgrace to your father."

Annimae fled to the darkness to weep, that none might see her. Two hours she fought with her heart. All the fond embraces, all the words of love, all the undoubted wisdom of the Spiritualists and her own wedding vows were on her heart's side. But the little quailing child who lived within her breast too thought of the aunts' grim faces as they had spoken, backed up by the dead certainties of all grandmothers and aunts from the beginning of time.

In the end she decided that their dark suspicions were utterly base and unfounded. But she would slip a candle and a match in her apron pocket, all the same, so as to prove them wrong.

And when she came in to Daniel at last, when his glad voice greeted her and his warm hands reached out, she knew her heart was right, and silenced all doubt. Sam came in and served them supper, and she listened and compared the two voices, straining for any similarity of accent. Surely there was none!

And when the supper dishes had been taken away and Daniel took her in his arms and kissed her, she ran her hands through his thick hair. Surely it was golden!

And when they lay together in bed, there was none of the drum-driven madness of the night before, no animal hunger; only Daniel gentle and chivalrous, sane and reasonable, teasing her about what they'd do when he could go to Paris or Rome at last. Surely he was a gentleman!

But she had slipped the candle and the match under her pillow, and they lay there like wise serpents, who wheedled: *Wouldn't you like just a glimpse of his face?*

At last, when he had fallen asleep and lay dreaming beside her, she reached under the pillow and brought out the match. No need to light the candle, she had decided; all she wanted was one look at his dear face. One look only, in a flash no evil ghost would have time to notice. And who would dare harm her darling, if she lay beside him to keep him safe? One look only, to bear in her mind down all the long years they'd have together, one tiny secret for her to keep like a pressed flower....

Annimae touched his face, ran her fingers over his stubbly cheek, and set her hand on his brow to shade his eyes from the light. He sighed and murmured something in his sleep. With her other hand, she reached up and struck the match against the bedpost.

The light bloomed yellow.

Daniel was not there. Nobody was there. Annimae was alone in the bed.

Unbelieving, she felt with her hand that had been touching his cheek, his brow, that very second. There was nothing there.

That was when Annimae dropped the match, and the room was gone in darkness, and she could feel her throat contracting for a scream. But there was a high shriek beginning already, an inhuman whine as though the whole room were lamenting, and that was Daniel's voice rising now in a wail of grief, somewhere far above, as though he were being pulled away from her, receding and receding through the darkness.

"ANNIMAE!"

The bed began to shudder. The room itself, the very house began to shake. She heard a ringing impact from the bathroom, as the silver pitchers were thrown to the tiled floor. The table by the bed fell with a crash. A rending crack, a boom, the sound of plaster falling; a rectangle full of hectic blue-white light, and she realized that the secret panel had been forced open.

Annimae's mind, numb-shocked as it was, registered *Earthquake* with a certain calm. She grabbed her robe and fled over the tilting floor, squeezed through the doorway and ran down the long corridor. Tiny globes of ball lightning crackled, spat, skittered before her, lighting her way at least. But she could see the walls cracking too, she could see the plaster dropping away and the bare laths. The carpet flexed under her feet like an animal's back. The shaking would not stop.

She rounded a corner and saw Mrs. Nightengale flying toward her, hair streaming back and disheveled, hands out as though to claw the slow air. Her face was like a Greek mask of horror and rage, her mouth wide in a cry that Annimae could not hear over the roar of the falling house. She sped past Annimae without so much as a glance, vanishing in the direction of Daniel's rooms.

Annimae ran on, half-falling down a flight of stairs that was beginning to fold up even as she reached the bottom, and then there was a noise louder than any she'd heard yet, loud as an explosion, louder than the cannons must have been at Gettysburg. To her left there was an avalanche of bricks, mortar, splinters and wire, as a tower came down through three floors and carried all before it. It knocked out a wall and Annimae saw flowers glimmering pale through the plaster-dust, and dim stars above them.

She staggered forth into the night and fled, sobbing now, for her heart was beginning to go like the house. On bleeding feet she ran; when she could run no further she fell, and lay still, and wept and knew there was no possible consolation.

Some while later Annimae raised her head, and saw that the sky was just beginning to get light in the east. She looked around. She was lying in a drift of yellow leaves. All around her were the black trunks and arching branches of the orchard, in a silence so profound she might have gone deaf. Turning her head uncertainly, looking for the house, she saw them coming for her.

A throng of shadows, empty-eyed but not expressionless, and at their head walked the dancers from the fire: the black man with his stick, the red-headed hoyden. Beyond them, dust still rising against the dawn, was the nightmare mountain of rubble that had been the home of true love.

Annimae lay whimpering at their approach. With each step they took the figures altered, changed, aged. They became Sam and Bridget Lacroix. The sullen shades in their train began to mutter threateningly, seemed about to surge forward at Annimae; but Sam stopped, and raised his cane in a gesture that halted them. His sad stern face seemed chiseled from black stone.

"Shame on you, girl," he said. "Love and Suspicion can't live together in the same house, no matter how many rooms it has."

Annimae scrambled to her feet and ran again. They did not follow her.

She forgot who she was, or why she was traveling, and she had no destination in mind. By day she huddled in barns or empty sheds, for the sunlight hurt her eyes unbearably. By night she walked on, ducking out of sight when a horseman or a carriage would come along her road. For some days she wandered up a bay shore, following the tideline. The mud felt cool on her cut feet.

At length she came to a great city, that whirred and clattered and towered to the sky. She regarded it in wonder, hiding among the reeds until nightfall, hoping to pass through in the dark. Alas! It was lit bright even after midnight. Annimae edged as close as she dared, creeping through the shadows, and then turned to stare; for she found herself outside a lovely garden, planted all in roses, shaded by high dark cypresses, and the wrought-iron gate was unlocked. It seemed as though it would be a comforting place to rest.

She slipped in, and stretched out on one of the cool white marble beds.

Angels mourned, all around her.

When the pastor at Mission Dolores found her, she was unable to speak. He had his housekeeper feed her, bathe her, and tend to her feet; he sent out inquiries. No one came forward to claim Annimae, however, and the sisters at the Sacred Heart convent agreed to take her in.

In the peace, in the silence punctuated only by matins and evensong, gently bullied by well-meaning maternal women, still she remained mute; but her memory, if not her voice, began to come back to her. There was still too much horror and confusion to absorb, though one fact rose clear and bleak above the rest: she had lost her true love.

He had been dead. He had been imaginary. He had been real, but she had betrayed him. She would never hear his voice again.

She would be alone the rest of her life.

And it seemed a grimly appropriate fate that she should come full circle to end up here, a child in a house full of aunts, confined to the nursery where she clearly belonged, having failed so badly at being a grown woman. Perhaps she would take the veil, though she had always been told to distrust Catholics as minions of the Pope. Perhaps she would take Jesus as her new husband.

But one morning Annimae woke to a welling nausea, and barely made it to the little bathroom at the end of the dormitory hall before vomiting. Afterward she bolted the door, and ran water for a bath.

Stepping into the water, she caught a glimpse of herself in the mirror.

She stared, and stared unbelieving at her swollen body.

Merry Christmas from Navarro Lodge, 1928

That Christmas Eve Dolliver found himself walking south on Highway 1, trying to hitchhike back to San Francisco, in a very unpleasant frame of mind.

He kept trying to find some reason, some pattern of events that had resulted in the present moment. He'd made one stupid decision about living off his unemployment for a while; had that been all it took to bring him here?

That had been all it took. As he trudged along the narrow two-lane above the cliffs Dolliver made another discovery: there wasn't much traffic along that road on Christmas Eve, and what there was wouldn't stop for somebody in a crappy old stained coat. All that long afternoon the sky got grayer and the passing cars got fewer and the dull cold penetrated more deeply into his bones.

It didn't help that the scenery was breathtaking, looming green redwood forests that breathed out a nice seasonal balsam fragrance. In the couple of cliff-perching little bed-and-breakfast towns Dolliver passed, people looked right through him, dressed as he was, though he made no attempt to beg for change. The dogs alone acknowledged his presence, barking and threatening; and the grandeur of the surf beating against the black cliffs began to lure him, as time and the miles went by. Only the thought that suicide during the holidays was a cliché kept him from jumping right over.

Pretty soon it got dark and Dolliver had all he could do to keep from wandering over the edge in the pitch-blackness. The only thing he had to orient himself was the sound of the sea and, miles out on an invisible horizon, the spark of light that was some fishing boat or tanker. He made up his mind to stay at the next little town if he had to break a window and get himself arrested.

He came around a high curve and saw a blaze of light. Following it to the edge of the road, he found himself looking down a hillside into a river gorge. There were buildings down there, where the river met the sea. Right below was the roof of a big gabled place. Painted on its slates in squared black letters, just visible by the reflection of the floodlights, were the words NAVARRO LODGE.

So he followed the road around and down, and found the turnoff from the highway: a gravel drive cutting away through the silver-barked alder trees, following the river bank. Then the gravel was lit up by headlights behind him, and Dolliver looked over his shoulder and had to scramble out of the way of the oncoming car.

He saw that it was an antique, something from the twenties maybe, beautifully restored. Somebody had money. He reflected that he should have let it hit him, and then he might have sued. He felt ashamed immediately, but reflected on the injustice of wealth and felt better.

Dolliver trudged on, beside the river that roared white over boulders, and a few hundred yards farther along he came out into the glow of the lights. There were the parked cars, lined up on the gravel; there were the lit windows of Navarro Lodge, each with its flickering red taper and festoon of evergreen. It was a rambling two-story building with dormer windows looking out on the river and the alder forest.

All the cars were antiques. Gleaming brass and chrome, bug-eyed headlights, green and black and mustard-yellow paint, leather trunks on the back. Oh, thought Dolliver, some classic car club's having a rally. How nice for them. His envy intensified.

He paced along outside, indecisive about going in. Through the windows he could glimpse people moving—the car enthusiasts, probably, he thought, because they all seemed to be wearing costumes for the occasion. There was a smell of wood smoke sweet on the night air, a bite of frost, and how brilliant and chill the stars were! Dolliver could hear slightly drunken laughter and the tinny sound of what he guessed was a television. He could hear the crash of waves in the black winter night, dragging on the shingle beach. Distant on the horizon, the light from the ship was still there.

It occurred to Dolliver that if he took off his coat before he went in, he'd make a better impression, so he hung it on the low fence that ran along the driveway. The cold bit into him at once. Hugging his arms he sprinted up the front steps and shouldered through the doors, rehearsing what he'd made up to say, which was: *Excuse me, I'm afraid I've had something embarrassing happen. My lady friend and I were having an argument and she stopped the car and asked me to get out and look at the right front tire. When I got out, she drove off—she's got my coat, my wallet and all my credit cards, my cell phone—I wonder if I could throw myself on your mercy, since it's Christmas Eve? I'd be happy to sleep in the lobby—*

He went up to the desk, dark wood decorated for the holiday with swags of holly branches. There was a man there writing in a ledger. Dolliver cleared his throat and said, "Excuse me—"

The man didn't look up. Dolliver moved in closer and tried again. "Excuse me—"

Still, the man ignored him. He looked about twenty-five, wore a plain brown sweater over an oxford shirt, wore steel-rimmed glasses: nothing to tip Dolliver off that anything strange had happened, and after all people had been pretending they didn't see him all day.

What did seem weird was the fact that the man was writing in the ledger book using a long wooden pen with a steel nib, and dipping from a little fireplug-shaped bottle of Schaefer's Ink. No computer terminal, there on the desk. No telephone.

Dolliver stepped forward, put both hands flat on the desk and said, as loudly as he could, "EXCUSE ME!"

The man wrote on, with a calm and pleasant expression on his face, giving no acknowledgment Dolliver was there at all.

After a moment of staring Dolliver said huffily, "Well, fine then!" and drew himself up and marched into the main lobby.

There was a big fireplace in there, made of river cobbles, with a bright fire of alder and cottonwood logs. He went straight to it and warmed himself, and as he turned he prepared another speech: *Er—excuse me, but is the person at the counter hearing-impaired? I've been trying to get his attention....*

But as he looked out at the room, he knew.

The people in this room were also oblivious to his presence: a young girl with a powdered face and black pageboy bob sitting on a couch before the fire, right there in front of him, and a young man sitting beside her, leaning close and whispering intently in her ear. A couple of older gentlemen arguing under the deer's head mounted on the wall, as they drank from little glass punch cups. Another old man sitting in a Morris chair, reading a hardcover book and from time to time tipping cigar ash into the smoking stand, with its thick amber bowl.

Dolliver had seen enough movies and *Outer Limits* episodes to guess that he'd fallen into some kind of time slip. He wondered bitterly why couldn't he have been abducted by aliens, which at least would give him a story to sell to the tabloids.

The girl wore '20s flapper garb. The men might have stepped out of an old L. L. Bean catalogue, all hunter flannels. All the details of the room were perfect for the period too, the wainscoting in polished dark wood, the wallpaper with its sporting motif, the duck-hunting print patterns in which the chairs were upholstered. There was a little spruce Christmas tree in one corner with a string of old-style lights, thick mold-blown glass in shapes of fruits, painted in colors, the electrical cord wrapped in woven fabric.

A clock ticked on the mantel, which Dolliver only heard because he was standing right in front of it; otherwise it'd have been drowned out by the Victrola in the corner, on which a scratchy recording of "Adeste Fideles" was playing. He could see the old black phonograph record spinning, just as fast as a CD does now.

The song ended, and the girl jumped away from the young man and got up to change the record. She put on "The Saint Louis Blues" and amused herself by doing a little dance step alone, watching the young man from under her long lashes. She had a piquant little face, but her eyes were rather cold. The young man looked sad and stared into the fire, right through Dolliver's legs.

Interesting as this was, Dolliver was more intrigued by the smell of dinner coming from the dining room beyond. He crossed the room, drawing no attention to himself. One of the two men drinking punch was saying belligerently:

"Sure you could. Say, you could put a radio tower up on that hill that'd pull in China, and he's crazy if he doesn't do it. I told him...."

The dining room had the same sporting decor, except that there were small round tables here and there on the wide plank floor, and a buffet on the far wall. There were a few couples at the tables, girls in bright beaded gowns chatting gaily with more men in plaids and checks. Somebody's little fox terrier was wandering about begging. There was a stockbrokerish guy at the buffet, listening to a thin youth in a waiter's jacket who was affirming:

"Yes, sir, all our own. The salmon's smoked right up the hill in our smokehouse. And that's local venison, sir, and the roast beef too. No, sir, the plum pudding came out of a can, but...."

"Hell with the plum pudding," yelled another stockbrokerish type, bounding up with a cup of punch. "What's in this stuff? It's got plenty of pep, and I mean plenty!" He raised his cup and winked broadly.

"Applejack, what do you think?" said the other stockbroker. "They make their own in the cellar, don't they, kid?"

"Yes, sir. We have the apples brought over special from Sebastopol," agreed the youth.

"Well, say, I think I'll just take a room here permanently," chortled the drinker, and drank. "Hell with the Volstead Act!"

There was somebody else standing at the buffet too. He was helping himself, filling a plate with meat and some of the other fare that was laid out: asparagus, oysters, Stilton cheese and crackers, hot biscuits. He looked up, saw Dolliver and grinned.

"Hey, bro," he said, chewing. He wore blue jeans, a Metallica T-shirt, a down vest; John Deere cap and sneakers. He had a thin beard, long hair. Dolliver was wearing jeans and Nikes, which was presumably how this other person from the present recognized him for a fellow time-traveler.

Dolliver stared, and the other man swallowed and said "Welcome to the Twilight Zone, huh? Doo-de-doo-doo, doo-de-doo-doo!"

"The food's real?" said Dolliver, but he was already crossing the room and reaching for one of the plates.

"Ghost food, I guess, huh? Tasty, though," said the other, stuffing a wad of sliced roast beef into his cheek. Dolliver picked up the plate, weighed it in his hand. It was substantial. There was a green pattern of alder cones and leaves around the rim, and the words NAVARRO LODGE in rustic letters. He took the plate and waved it slowly in front of the face of the nearest stockbroker, who never blinked; in front of the waiter, who never paused in his recitation: "...and the blackberries in the pie were picked right from our own brambles here, our cook makes all our preserves...."

"They ain't gonna see you," said the other. "Really. I've been here since this morning, and nobody's noticed me yet."

"But we can affect their reality," said Dolliver, picking up a sliver of turkey and tasting it experimentally. It was substantial too, and he was famished, so he set to piling food on his plate. "Their buffet's reality, anyway. What's going on?"

"Beats me, friend," said the other. "I figure it's one of those things like on TV. Jesus, don't you wish you had a camera? We could get on one of those programs and make a fortune." He chewed and swallowed and looked Dolliver up and down. "You hitchhiking, huh?"

"Yes," said Dolliver, betting the man lived in a trailer park.

"Where you from?"

"New York."

"Wow," said the other. He lifted a punch cup and drank with relish. "You should try this stuff. Smooth, man!"

"Okay," said Dolliver, spotting the wassail bowl. He filled a punch cup and had a sip. It burned all the way down. He set it carefully aside and began to eat, grimly and seriously, right where he was standing. He hadn't eaten in two days.

"I'm from Navarro, myself," said the other. "Back up the river. So, how'd you come to be here? Long way from home, huh?"

Dolliver introduced himself and told his story in all its humiliating detail: the company layoff, the unemployment error, the closed-out savings account, the eviction; then the ultimate finger from Fate, the old girlfriend who'd invited him out to spend Christmas with her. By the time Dolliver had blown his last cash on bus fare and got to Mendocino she'd made up with her husband and changed her mind about the invitation.

"Wow, man, that happened to me," said the other, looking delighted. "My old lady threw me out of the trailer this afternoon." Bingo, thought Dolliver. "This guy at the Christmas tree lot fucked with me about my bonus, so there was like—no money. I just started walking and wound up here. Verbal Sweet," he said, and Dolliver was mystified until the other extended his hand for a shake and he realized that Verbal Sweet was the man's name.

"Nice meeting you, Verbal," he said.

"You're a college grad, huh?" said Sweet.

Dolliver admitted he was, for all the good it was doing him now, and Sweet closed one eye and nodded shrewdly. "Bingo! I thought so, the way you talk."

Meanwhile the stockbrokers had sat down and begun to eat. The waiter sighed and folded his hands in front of him. Then he looked up sharply: the girl with the black pageboy bob had come in and was approaching the buffet, alone.

"Hello, Billy," she said, picking up a plate.

"I was wondering if you were even going to notice me," said the waiter quietly. He looked anguished.

"I've got a lot to say to you, actually, but this isn't the time," she said, glancing over her shoulder. She tilted her head, staring down with a coy expression at the platters of beef and venison, as though she couldn't make up her mind. She swung a finger to and fro over the dishes. The waiter's eyes widened.

"If you're going to insult me—"

"No." She looked up, and there was nothing playful about her now. "Don't take it like that. So much has happened, Billy. I've been thinking a great deal about this. If we could talk—"

The waiter had looked incredulous, but he glanced up into the room and then hissed: "What good will it do to talk *now*?" Out loud he said: "Yes, Ma'am, that's a thirty-pound turkey. We had it in a pen behind the smokehouse. It's been fed apple mash, so the meat's very rich—"

"Helene." The other man, the one who'd been whispering in her ear, approached and put his hands on her shoulders. "Dear, I'm sorry. But this means an awful lot to Dad."

"Whoa! Lovers' triangle," said Sweet. "What do you want to bet she's cheating on him?"

Dolliver just shrugged and kept eating. The waiter stared straight ahead, expressionless and pale, as the girl sighed and leaned back against the other man. Her voice was querulous as she said: "What does it mean to *you*, Edgar?"

"Well, I—of course I want it too, you know that!" he said.

She just pursed her lips. Beef or venison?

"Dessert time," said Sweet happily, and served himself a piece of blackberry pie. "And you know what's over there at the bar? Honest-to-God French Champagne. I'm getting me a glass. You want any?"

"Sure," said Dolliver. "Thanks."

"Edgar, I don't care to discuss this right now," said the girl, stepping away and selecting the beef at last. Edgar said:

"All right. But think about Christmas, Helene. Think what it could be like in a couple of years. The little tree, a little stocking, toys. Wouldn't that be wonderful?"

"Sweets to the sweet," she said cryptically, and the man smiled. The waiter coughed and excused himself, fleeing through a side door into what was probably the kitchen.

"Here you go," said Sweet, returning from the bar. He handed Dolliver a glass of champagne. Dolliver set down his plate and drank gratefully. Sweet looked furtive and raised two fingers to his lips, miming smoking a joint. He said,

"So, uh, you got any—?" Dolliver stared a moment before he got it.

"Oh! No, sorry."

"Damn. Well, okay. Maybe it's not a good idea to get too messed up, what with us being here and all. We might slip through a time warp or something and I ain't in any hurry to go back yet, are you?"

Dolliver set down his glass and reached into the fruit bowl for an orange. He said, "Not especially. It's not as though I've got anything I'd miss."

"Me either," said Sweet. "But it's kind of a shame we're invisible."

"We were already invisible!" Dolliver snapped. "You think anyone back in our own time sees people like you and I? Even at this time of year? A run of bad luck and a dirty coat makes you a phantom, man."

Sweet listened patiently to his tirade and then went on: "Yeah, but wouldn't it be great if we could wow everybody with computers or something? We could, like, invent TV ahead of its time and get rich."

"Do you know how to make a television set?" Dolliver asked him. Sweet's face fell.

"No."

"Then that wouldn't work, see? But you could buy stock that'll do well," said Dolliver. "Like International Business Machines."

Sweet looked blank. Dolliver tried again:

"Or Coca-Cola, for example."

"Oh, yeah," exclaimed Sweet. He warbled a few bars of the latest Coke jingle, then frowned. "Wait a minute, you mean like the stock market? Oh, no way. You can lose money like that, I always heard. But I got an idea. If this goes on—" At this moment the two men who'd been arguing about radio reception came to the buffet and shouldered Dolliver aside, completely unconscious of his presence.

"No, it was the damnedest thing you ever saw," said one of them, setting down his punch cup and reaching for a plate. "Why, it was nothing like the movies, and all in color, too. But you'd need a lot more than a radio tower for reception, yes, *sir!*"

"The fellow's name was Baird, you say?" inquired the other. "Say, this could be big! I wonder if he's looking for investors over there?"

"Let's go back to the fireplace," suggested Sweet, and he and Dolliver took their desserts and drinks and went into sprawl on the sofa.

"Here's what we do," said Sweet, forking blackberries into his mouth. "We go upstairs to the rooms where everybody's suitcases are, right? And we help ourselves to whatever they got, same as we did with the food."

"Steal?" Dolliver stopped peeling the orange. He thought about it a moment and slowly his hands started moving again. "Why not? They're all a bunch of useless boozers, and dead anyway—I mean, by our time. If they didn't notice the food disappearing, maybe they wouldn't miss jewelry. If they've got any."

"All these rich people?" Sweet looked scornful. "Of course they got jewelry with 'em. Didn't you ever watch any old movies? Ladies used to wear necklaces and stuff a lot more than now. And they'll have cash, too."

"No good," Dolliver told him, having another sip of champagne. "All their cash would be the big old Federal Notes." Sweet frowned at him in incomprehension and just at that moment one of the stockbrokers came to stand in front of them, warming his hands at the fire. "I'll show you," said Dolliver, and feeling absurdly pleased with himself he leaned forward and slipped the man's wallet from his pocket.

"Smooth," laughed Sweet, applauding. Dolliver opened the wallet and fanned the outsized bills. Sweet winced and shook his head.

"That's the weirdest thing I've ever seen, man."

"See? We couldn't spend it in our time without a lot of questions," Dolliver told him, putting the wallet back. "We could sell jewelry, though. If they've got any."

The stockbroker moved away and Edgar came alone to stand in his place, facing out into the room. After a moment he drew from his pocket a red leather case and opened it, staring inside.

"What did I tell you?" Sweet nudged Dolliver. "Jewels! You're so fast with your hands, see can you get it."

"All right." Dolliver drained his glass and stood. Flexing his hands theatrically, he waited until Edgar had slipped the case back into his pocket, sighing; then he slipped the case out again. Edgar remained standing there, staring through him unnervingly as he sat down again and opened the case.

"Diamonds or something," Sweet pronounced, leaning over to see. "Not bad!"

"Maybe it's a Christmas present," said Dolliver, looking up guiltily at Edgar's tense face.

"Well, Merry Christmas to you and me," Sweet replied. "We're both down on our luck a lot worse than these dudes will ever be. So... I guess we're splitting fifty-fifty on this?" He put out his hand and took the necklace from the box, and held it up to the firelight. It winked and threw lights on the wall.

"Sure," Dolliver told him. "Assuming we ever go back to our own time and aren't stuck here like ghosts." He closed the empty case and slipped it back into Edgar's pocket.

"Oh. Well, we could take one of their cars, if we can find some keys," said Sweet.

"We could," Dolliver agreed, "but we couldn't drive away from the past, you see? Just away from this lodge. And even if we managed to take a Packard or a Model T back with us, how would we handle the registration, once we were there?"

"Frigging DMV," Sweet conceded with a sigh, tucking the necklace away inside his vest. "Well, if we never go back, this isn't too bad." He eyed the couples who were leaving the dining room. One of the flappers cranked up the Victrola again and all the younger couples began to dance to a fox trot. One girl tugged an older man to his feet and he cut a few awkward capers. Sweet leaned over and nudged Dolliver. "Hey, wonder if the women are like the buffet? D'you think?"

Dolliver just looked at him a minute and then said, "You'd better be careful. How'd you like to get a dose of something when there's no penicillin yet?"

"There isn't?" Sweet was horrified. "Jesus, what'd people do?"

"Gee, Mr. Wallace, you'd better get a monkey gland," cried the girl gaily, as the wheezing stockbroker retreated from the dance floor.

"Suffered a lot," said Dolliver, standing up. "Come on, let's see what's upstairs."

There was a single red candle burning in the window on the landing, and they took it with them, since the second story did not appear to be wired for electricity. Most of the doors were unlocked. Dolliver and Sweet prowled through the dark rooms and found trunks and suitcases alone that would fetch a nice price in antique stores, plastered as they were with steamer and hotel labels. There wasn't quite the fortune in jewels Sweet had been hoping to find, but they did manage to pilfer a nice little haul in cufflinks and one tie tack with what Dolliver was fairly sure was a diamond on it. There were a couple of art deco brooches and a couple of bracelets of indeterminate value.

"Well, this sucks," complained Sweet as they clumped back downstairs, and the scratchy melody of "Am I Blue" floated up to meet them. One of the younger men was yodeling drunkenly along. Sweet turned on the stairs, eyes brightening. "But you know what? If we take one of the cars we can drive down to San Francisco, rob a bank or a jewelry store! Huh? Nobody'd see us."

"You've got a point there," said Dolliver, deciding not to argue with him.

They settled on the couch again, now and then rising to revisit the buffet. The evening wore on and the young people Charlestoned and shimmied in the glow of the Christmas lights. The older men sat at the edges and talked interminably about the stock market, about Herbert Hoover, about the trouble brewing again among the Serbs and Croats, about surf and stream fishing, about the big breakfast they'd have in the morning.

Everybody drank the Christmas wassail and, when that gave out, drank bootleg booze from flasks they'd brought with them. Dolliver was appalled at the cheerful and reckless way they mixed their liquors, to say nothing of the quantities they seemed to be able to drink without passing out. The dancing just got a little clumsier, the laughter of the girls got louder and shriller; and when "Stille Nacht" was played, with Madame Schumann-Heink crooning tenderly, people wept. At last in ones and twos they began to wander up the narrow staircase to their rooms.

The girl with the black pageboy bob did not drink much, or dance either. She came and sat on the couch by herself, between Dolliver and Sweet, who looked on bemused as Edgar came to crouch beside her.

"Helene, we don't have to live with them," he said quietly.

"Who?" wondered Sweet.

"In-laws, probably," Dolliver told him.

"You haven't got the spine to tell him no," said Helene matter-of-factly, not taking her eyes from the fire. Edgar stiffened and rose again, and left the room.

"Edgar isn't doing very well," remarked Dolliver, yawning. Sweet chuckled, watching Helene, and patted his knee.

"You can come sit on my lap, honey, I'll give you good advice. You don't want to marry that wienie. Marry the other guy, okay? The poor one. Billy."

"Here he comes," Dolliver observed, as Billy came in to build up the fire. He avoided making eye contact with Helene, but she leaned forward.

"You look nice in that jacket," she said.

"It's a waiter's jacket," he snapped. "I'm nobody and I'm going nowhere, remember? Not back east. Not to Europe. Not to Stanford or an office in the City."

Helene put her head in her hands. "All right. But you could do more for yourself, Billy. I know you could. You have the inner strength."

"Strength doesn't matter," Billy replied stonily. "Money matters, Helene. You taught me that well enough."

"Strength matters more than I'd ever imagined," she said, with the suggestion of tears in her voice. He turned in the firelight to stare at her, and his hand opened and he seemed about to reach out; but she looked sidelong at him from under her lashes with those cold eyes, and something about the look made him draw back his hand.

"Crying?" he said. "Or acting, Helene? It would take a lot more than a few tears for me to ever make a fool of myself again. I've got some pride, you know."

"You tell her, bro," said Sweet, slapping his leg.

Edgar had finally re-entered the room. Billy shut his mouth like a trap and turned away from the fire as though Helene weren't there.

"Is everything satisfactory, mister?" he inquired of Edgar, in an excessively servile tone. Edgar just nodded miserably. "Good. Wonderful," said Billy, sounding as though he were about to cry himself. He stalked from the room.

Edgar approached the girl hesitantly.

"Hey!" Sweet stood up. "I know why there's no jewelry in the rooms. It'd be in the hotel safe."

"You think a place like this has one?" said Dolliver, but he got to his feet too. They paced swiftly into the front lobby, as Edgar knelt beside Helene and began to murmur to her in a hesitant voice.

The desk clerk was no longer there, but a quick search behind the desk failed to turn up anything resembling a safe. Sweet got down on his hands and knees to thump the baseboard paneling. Dolliver's attention was drawn by the open ledger, and he paused to examine the list of registered guests.

"Unless maybe it's behind a painting or something, I seen that in movies too—" Sweet was saying, when he heard Dolliver mutter an exclamation. He scrambled up.

"What?" he said. Dolliver didn't answer, so he read over his shoulder. A moment later he caught his breath and pointed a trembling finger at the third entry in the column.

"Shit! Look at that," he croaked.

Mr. Edgar V. Sweet, Palo Alto, California. The next entry was *Miss Helene Thistlewhite, Santa Rosa, California.*

"Same last name," observed Dolliver.

"No! That was my grandfather's name!"

"Uh—" Dolliver blinked at it. "Then—Helene is, what, your grandmother? Which would explain what you're doing here. Maybe. If Helene breaks up with him tonight—"

"I'll never get born," said Sweet. "Oh, my God!"

He turned and bolted into the main lobby, and Dolliver went after him.

There was Edgar, still on his knees, offering the small leather case and saying,

"I swear that's not an empty promise. Merry Christmas, Helene."

"No," cried Sweet, starting forward. Helene, smiling in spite of herself, took the case and opened it. She saw nothing but white silk lining inside. She lifted her eyes to Edgar with a look of flaming contempt.

In that moment, Sweet disappeared. One second he was there, looking on in horror, and the next he was gone. The diamond necklace that had been in his pocket dropped softly to the carpet runner and lay coiled there like a bright snake. Dolliver turned white. For the first time since arriving there he was frightened.

"Not an empty promise?" said Helene with a tight smile. Edgar gaped at the open case a moment before beating frantically at his pockets, and then getting down on hands and knees to peer under the couch.

"Helene, I swear—" he choked. "There was a necklace in there!" He jumped up and started out for the front lobby. Dolliver hesitated a moment before bending quickly to scoop up the necklace and drop it into his own pocket.

"Oh, oh, Lord—" Edgar swept the carpet runner with a desperate stare, and ran to the desk and hammered on the bell. "Oh, jiminy crickets, Helene, it's got to be here—I'll get the staff to help me look—"

"Whatever you like, Edgar," said Helene. "I'm going to go have a cup of coffee. Let me know when you manage to get something right."

There was quite a commotion for a while, as the desk clerk and a couple of waiters—though not Billy—came out and helped Edgar search. Dolliver slunk away to the dining room, where he sat shivering. Helene was not in the dining room. After a while the commotion died down and Edgar went upstairs. Dolliver went back to the main lobby and sank down on the couch, before the fire that was going down to coals. He knew where Helene was, and what she was doing.

A waiter—again, not Billy—made a pass through the room, collecting coffee cups and dessert plates the guests had left. A few minutes later the man in the brown sweater came through, turning out the lamps and blowing out the candles. The surf beat loud on the shingle beach in the night.

Dolliver didn't think he'd ever sleep again after that, but he did doze off sometime before sunrise. When he awoke he was freezing cold and stiff, and sitting up found himself lying on the bare floor of a ruin, as he had half expected. The fireplace was black and yawning, the floor creaking, filthy. There was trash piled in the corners. Blackberry brambles choked the windows. He ran outside and his coat at least was okay, right where he'd left it; but the cars were long gone, the road overgrown, the upstairs gable windows black and staring.

Dolliver shrugged into his coat and went his way.

He pawned one of the brooches in San Francisco and got enough money to buy himself a suit, so he could sell the rest of the jewelry without drawing undue attention to himself. Within a week he'd found a job, which was ironic because his need wasn't desperate now; the necklace alone had brought enough to set him up nicely.

He still felt guilty, though he told himself that neither he nor Sweet could have affected the outcome that night in 1928. It hadn't been his decision. It hadn't been anyone's decision but Helene Thistlewhite's, ever, and she had decided to break her engagement to a young stockbroker and run off with Eustace William Dolliver; or so the family legend went.

Her Father's Eyes

I t was so long ago that fathers were still gaunt from the war, their awful scars still livid; so long ago that mothers wore frocks, made fancy Jell-O desserts in ring molds. And that summer, there was enough money to go for a trip on the train. She was taken along because she had been so sick she had almost died, so it was a reward for surviving.

She was hurried along between her parents, holding their hands, wondering what a *dome coach* was and why it was supposed to be special. Then there was a gap in the sea of adult legs, and the high silver cars of the train shone out at her. She stared up at the row of windows in the coach roof, and thought it looked like the cockpits in the bombers her father was always pointing out.

Inside it was nicer, and much bigger, and there was no possible way any German or Japanese fighter pilots could spray the passengers with bullets; so she settled into the seat she had all for herself. There she watched the people moving down on the platform, until the train pulled out of the station.

Then her parents exclaimed, and told her to look out the wonderful dome windows at the scenery. That was interesting for a while, especially the sight of the highway far down there with its Oldsmobiles and DeSotos floating along in eerie silence, and then, as they moved out into the country, the occasional field with a real horse or cow.

The change in her parents was more interesting. Out of uniform her father looked younger, was neither gloomy nor sarcastic but raucously happy. All dressed up, her mother was today as serene and cheerful as a housewife in a magazine advertisement. They held hands, like newlyweds, cried out in rapture at each change in the landscape, and told her repeatedly what a lucky little girl she was, to get to ride in a dome coach.

She had to admit they seemed to be right, though her gaze kept tracking nervously to the blue sky framed by the dome, expecting any minute steeply banking wings there, fire or smoke. How could people turn on happiness like a tap, and pretend the world was a bright and shiny place when they knew it wasn't at all?

The candy butcher came up the aisle, and her father bought her a bag of mint jellies. She didn't like mint jellies but ate them anyway, amazed at his good mood. Then her mother took her down the car to wash the sugar from her face and hands, and the tiny steel lavatory astonished and fascinated her.

From time to time the train stopped in strange towns to let people off or on. Old neon signs winked from brick hotels, and pointed forests like Christmas trees ran along the crests of hills, stood black against the skyline. The sun set round and red. While it still lit the undersides of the clouds, her parents took her down to the dining car.

What silent terror, at the roaring spaces between the cars where anyone might fall out and die instantly; and people sat in the long room beyond, and sipped coffee and ate breaded veal cutlets as calmly as though there were no yawning gulf rushing along under them. She watched the diners in awe, and pushed the green peas round and round the margin of her plate, while her parents were chatting together so happily they didn't even scold her.

When they climbed the narrow steel stair again, night had fallen. The whole of the coach had the half-lit gloom of an aquarium, and stars burned down through the glass. She was led through little islands of light, back to her seat. Taking her place again she saw that there were now people occupying the seats across the aisle, that had been vacant before.

The man and the lady looked as though they had stepped out of the movies, so elegant they were. The lady wore a white fur coat, had perfect red nails; the man wore a long coat, with a silk scarf around his neck. His eyes were like black water. He was very pale. So was the lady, and so was their little boy who sat stiffly in the seat in front of them. He wore a long coat too, and gloves, like a miniature grownup. She decided they must be rich people.

Presently the Coach Hostess climbed up, and smilingly informed them all that there would be a meteor shower tonight. The elegant couple winked at each other. The little girl scrambled around in her seat, and peering over the back, asked her parents to explain what a meteor was. When she understood, she pressed her face against the cold window glass, watching eagerly as the night miles swam by. Distant lights floated in the darkness; but she saw no falling stars.

Disappointed, cranky and bored, she threw herself back from the window at last, and saw that the little boy across the aisle was staring at her. She ignored him and addressed her parents over the back of the seat:

"There aren't either any meteors," she complained.

"You're not looking hard enough," said her father, while at the same time her mother said,

"Hush," and drew from her big purse a tablet of lined paper and a brand-new box of crayons, the giant box with rows and rows of colors. She handed them over the seat back and added, "Draw some pictures of what you saw from the windows, and you can show them to Auntie when we get there."

Wide-eyed, the little girl took the offerings and slid back into her seat. For a while she admired the pristine green-and-yellow box, the staggered regiments of pure color. All her crayons at home lived in an old coffee can, in a chaos of nub ends and peeled paper.

At last she selected an Olive Green crayon and opened the tablet. She drew a cigar shape and added flat wings. She colored in the airplane, and then took the Sky Blue and drew on a glass cockpit. With the Black, she added stars on the wings and dots flying out the front to signify bullets.

She looked up. The little boy was staring at her again. She scowled at him.

"Those are nice," he said. "That's a lot of colors."

"This is the really big box," she said.

"Can I draw too?" he asked her, very quietly, so quietly something strange pulled at her heart. Was he so quiet because he was scared? And the elegant man said:

"Daniel, don't bother the little girl," in a strange resonant voice that had something just the slightest bit wrong about it. He sounded as though he were in the movies.

"You can share," she told the little boy, deciding suddenly. "But you have to come sit here, because I don't want to tear the paper out."

"Okay," he said, and pushed himself out of his seat as she moved over. The elegant couple watched closely, but as the children opened the tablet out between them and took each a crayon, they seemed to relax and turned their smiling attention to the night once more. The boy kept his gloves on while coloring.

"Don't you have crayons at home?" she asked him, drawing black doughnut-tires under the plane. He shook his head, pressing his lips together in a line as he examined the Green crayon he had taken.

"How can you not have crayons? You're rich," she said, and then was sorry she had said it, because he looked as though he were about to cry. But he shrugged and said in a careless voice,

"I have paints and things."

"Oh," she said. She studied him. He had fair hair and blue eyes, a deep twilight blue. "How come you don't look like your mommy and daddy?" she inquired. "I have my daddy's eyes. But you don't have their eyes."

He glanced over his shoulder at the elegant couple and then leaned close to whisper, "I'm adopted."

"Oh. You were in the War?" she said, gesturing at her airplane. "Like a bomb was dropped on your house, and you were an orphan, and the soldiers took you away?"

"No," he said. He put back the Green crayon, took a Brick Red one instead and drew a house: a square, a triangle on top, a chimney with a spiral of smoke coming out of it. He drew well. "I don't think that's what happened."

She drew black jagged lines under the plane, bombed-out wreckage. She drew little balloon heads protruding from the rubble, drew faces with teardrops flying from the eyes. "This is what happened to the war orphans," she explained. "My daddy told me all about them, and I could see it when he told me. So that didn't happen to you?"

"Nope," he replied, drawing a window in the house. It was a huge window, wide open. It took up the whole wall. He put the Brick Red crayon back in its tier carefully, and selected the Gray crayon. "The War is over now, anyway."

"Everybody thinks so," she replied, glancing uneasily up at the dome. "But my daddy says it isn't really. It could come back any time. There are a lot of bad people. Maybe those people got you from an orphanage."

The boy opened his mouth, closed it, glanced over his shoulder. "No," he whispered. "Something else happened to me. Now I'm their little boy. We came tonight so they could see the meteors from a train. They never did that before. They like trying out new things, you see."

With the Gray crayon, he drew the figure of a stick-man who towered over the house, walking away from the window. He gave it a long coat. He drew its arms up like Frankenstein's monster, and then he drew something in its arms: a white bundle. He put away the Gray crayon, took out the Pink and added a little blob of a face to the bundle.

"See," he said, "That's—"

"What are you drawing, Daniel?" said the elegant lady sharply. The little boy cringed, and the little girl felt like cringing too.

"That's a man carrying wood into his house for the fireplace, Mother," said the little boy, and grabbing the Brown crayon he drew hastily over the bundle in the man's arms, turning it into a log of wood. The little girl looked at it and hoped the lady wouldn't notice that the man in the picture was walking *away* from the house.

"I'm going to be an artist when I grow up," the little boy said. "I go to a studio and they make me take lessons. A famous painter teaches me." He sketched in a row of cylinders in brown, then took the Green crayon and drew green circles above the cylinders. "That's the forest," he added in an undertone. He took the Dark Blue and drew a cold shadow within the forest, and sharp-edged stars above it.

"Is he taking the baby to the forest?" she whispered. He just nodded. When he had drawn the last star he folded the page over, and since she had used up all the room on her page she did not complain, but took the Olive Green crayon again. She laboriously drew in stick-figure soldiers while he watched.

"What are you going to be when you grow up?" he asked.

"A waitress at the dinette," she replied. "If I don't die. And a ballerina."

"I might be a dancer too, if I don't die," he said, reaching for the Gray crayon. He began to draw cylinders like oatmeal boxes, with crenellations: a castle. She took the Black crayon and drew bayonets in the soldiers' hands, remarking:

"Boys aren't ballerinas."

"Some boys have to be," he said morosely, drawing windows in the castle walls. "They have to wear black leotards and the girls wear pink ones. Madame hits her stick on the ground and counts in French. Madame has a hoof on one foot, but nobody ever says anything about it."

"That's strange," she said, frowning as she drew the soldiers bayoneting one another. She glanced over at his picture and asked: "Where's the king and queen?"

He sighed and took the Blue Violet crayon. On the top of one tower he drew an immense crowned figure, leaving the face blank. He drew another crowned figure on the other battlement. "May I have the Black, please?"

"You're *polite*," she said, handing it to him. He drew faces with black eyes on the crowned figures while she took the Red crayon and drew a flag on the ground. She drew a red circle with rays coming off it to the edges of the rectangle, and then drew red dots all over the flag.

"What's that?" he asked.

"That's the blood," she explained. "My daddy has that flag at home. He killed somebody for it. When he told me about it I could see that, too. What did your daddy, I mean, that man, do in the War?"

"He sold guns to the soldiers," said the boy. He drew bars across the windows in the castle and then, down in the bottommost one, drew a tiny round face looking out, with teardrops coming from its eyes.

The little girl looked over at his picture.

"Can't he get away?" she whispered. He shook his head, and gulped for breath before he went on in a light voice:

"Or I might be a poet, you know. Or play the violin. I have lessons in that too. But I have to be very, very good at something, because next year I'm seven and—"

"Have you drawn another picture, Daniel?" said the elegant man with a faint warning intonation, rising in his seat. Outside the night rolled by, the pale lights floated, and the rhythm of the iron wheels sounded faint and far away.

"Yes, Father," said the boy in a bright voice, holding it up, but with his thumb obscuring the window with the face. "It's two people playing chess. See?"

"That's nice," said the man, and sat down again.

"What happens when you're seven?" the little girl murmured. The boy looked at her with terror in his eyes.

"They might get another baby," he whispered back. She stared at him, thinking that over. She took the tablet and opened it out: new fresh pages.

"That's not so bad," she told him. "We've had two babies. They break things. But they had to stay with Grandma; they're too little to come on the train. If you don't leave your books where they can tear the pages, it's okay."

The boy bowed his head and reached for the Red Orange crayon. He began to scribble in a great swirling mass. The girl whispered on:

"And you're rich, not like us, so I bet you can have your own room away from the new baby. It'll be all right. You'll see."

She took the Sky Blue crayon again and drew in what looked at first like ice cream cones all over her page, before she got the Olive Green out and added soldiers hanging from them. "See? These are the parachute men, coming to the rescue."

"They can't help," said the little boy.

She bit her lip at that, because she knew he was right. She thought it was sad that he had figured it out too.

The boy put back the Red Orange, took both Red and Yellow and scribbled forcefully, a crayon in either fist. He filled the page with flame. Then he drew Midnight Blue darkness above it all and more sharp stars. He took the Black and drew a little stick figure with limbs outstretched just above the fire. Flying? Falling in?

"I'm almost seven," he reiterated, under his breath. "And they only like new things."

"What are you drawing now, Daniel?" asked the lady, and both children started and looked up in horror, for they had not heard her rise.

"It's a nice big pile of autumn leaves, Mother," said the little boy, holding up the tablet with shaking hands. "See? And there's a little boy playing, jumping in the leaves."

"What a creative boy you are," she said throatily, tousling his hair. "But you must remember Mr. Picasso's lessons. Don't be mediocre. Perhaps you could do some abstract drawings now. Entertain us."

"Yes, Mother," said the little boy, and the girl thought he looked as though he were going to throw up. When the lady had returned to her seat she reached over and squeezed his hand, surprising herself, for she did not ordinarily like to touch people.

"Don't be scared," she whispered.

In silence, he turned to a fresh pair of pages. He took out a Green crayon and began to draw interlocking patterns of squares, shading them carefully.

She watched him for a while before she took the Silver and Gold crayons and drew a house, with a little stick figure standing inside. Then she took the Olive Green and drew several objects next to the figure.

"That's my bomb shelter, where I'm safe from the War," she explained. "But you can be in it. And that's your knapsack, see it? I made it with big straps for you. And that's your canteen so you can be safe afterwards. They're colored like what soldiers have, so you can hide. And this is the most important thing of all." She pointed. "See that? That's a map. So you can escape."

"I can't take it," he said in a doomed voice.

"That's all right; I'll give it to you," she said, and tore the page out. Folding it up small, she put it into his coat pocket.

Moving with leisurely slowness, he put back the Green crayon. Then, holding his hands close to his chest, he pulled off one of his gloves and took the folded paper out. He thrust it into an inner pocket, glancing over his shoulder as he did so. Nobody had noticed. Hastily he pulled the glove back on.

"Thank you," he said.

"You're welcome," she replied.

At that moment gravity shifted, the steady racketing sound altered and became louder, and there were three distinct bumps. Nobody in the car seemed to notice. Many of the grownups were asleep and snoring, in fact, and did no more than grunt or shift in their seats as the train slowed, as the nearest of the lights swam close and paused outside the window. It was a red blinking light.

"Ah! This is our stop," said the elegant man. "Summerland. Come along, Daniel. I think we've seen enough of the Dome Car, haven't you?"

"Yes, Father," said the boy, buttoning his coat. The elegant lady yawned gracefully.

"Not nearly as much fun as I thought it would be," she drawled. "God, I hate being disappointed. And bored."

"And you bore so easily," said the man, and she gave him a quick venomous glance. The little boy shivered, climbing out of his seat.

"I have to go now," he explained, looking miserable.

"Good luck," said the little girl. The lady glanced at her.

"I'm sure it's past your bedtime, little girl," she said. "And it's rude to stare at people."

She reached down her hand with its long scarlet nails as though to caress, and the little girl dodged. Two fingertips just grazed her eyelid, and with them came a wave of perfume so intense it made her eyes water. She was preoccupied with blinking and sneezing for the next minute, unable to watch as the family walked to the front of the silent car and descended the stair.

But she held her palm tight over her weeping eye and got up on her knees to peek out the window. She looked down onto no platform, no station, but only the verge of the embankment where trees came close to the tracks.

There was a long black car waiting there, under a lamp that swung unsteadily from a low bough. The elegant couple were just getting into the front seat. The little boy was already in the car. She could see his pale face through the windows. He looked up at her and gave a hopeless kind of smile. She was impressed at how brave he was. She thought to herself that he would have made a good soldier. Would he be able to escape?

The train began to move again. People woke up and talked, laughed, commented on the meteor shower. She sat clutching her eye, sniffling, until her mother got up to see if she had fallen asleep.

"Did you get something in your eye?" her mother asked, her voice going sharp with worry.

The little girl thought a moment before answering.

"The rich lady's perfume got in it," she said.

"What rich lady, honey? Don't rub it like that! Bill, hand me a Kleenex. Oh, what have you done to yourself now?"

"The lady with the little boy. They sat there. They just got off the train."

"Don't lie to your mother," said her daddy, scowling. "Those seats have been empty the whole trip."

She considered her parents out of her good eye, and decided to say nothing else about it. By the time she was bundled off the train, wrapped against the dark and cold in her daddy's coat, her eye had swollen shut.

It was red and weeping for days, even after they'd come home again, and her vision in that eye remained blurred. She was taken to an eye doctor, who prescribed an eyepatch for a while. The eyepatch was useful for pretending she was a pirate but did not help, and made her walk into walls besides.

She knew better than to tell anyone about the things she saw out of the other eye, but she understood now why the boy had wanted so badly to escape. She thought about him sometimes, late at night when she couldn't sleep and the long lights of passing cars sent leaf-shadows crawling along her wall.

She always imagined him running through a black night country, finding his way somehow through the maze of wet cobbled alleys, hiding from the Nazis, hiding from worse things, looking for the dome coach so he could escape; and he became clearer in her head as she thought about him, though that always made the headaches come. She would pull the covers over her head and try to hold on to the picture long enough to make the train arrive for him.

But somehow, before he could slip into the safety of the station, bright morning would blind her awake. Sick and crying, she would scream at her mother and knock her head against the wall to make the pain go away.

In the end the doctor prescribed glasses for her. She started kindergarten glaring at the world through thick pink plastic frames, and no one could persuade her she was not hideous in them.

Two Old Men

It was Sunday, January 26, 1961, and Markie Souza was six years old. He sat patiently beside his mother in the long pew, listening to Father Gosse talk about how wonderful it was to have a Catholic in the White House at last. Markie knew this was a good thing, in a general kind of way, because he was a Catholic too; but it was too big and too boring to think about, so he concentrated his attention on wishing his little sister would wake up.

She was limp on his mother's ample shoulder, flushed in the unseasonable heat, and the elastic band that held her straw hat on was edging forward under her chin. Any minute now it was going to ride up and snap her in the nose. Markie saw his opportunity and seized it; he reached up and tugged the band back into place, just incidentally jostling the baby into consciousness. Karen squirmed, turned her head and opened her eyes; she might have closed them again, but just then everybody had to stand up to sing "Tantum Ergo Sacramentum." The little girl looked around in unbelieving outrage and began to protest. Markie put his arms up to her.

"I'll take her out, Mama," he stage-whispered. His mother gratefully dumped the baby into his arms without missing a note. He staggered out of the pew and up the strip of yellow carpet that led to the side door. There was a little garden out there, a couple of juniper bushes planted around a statue of a lady saint. She was leaning on a broken ship's wheel. It had been explained to Markie that she was the patron saint of sailors and fishermen. Markie's daddy was a fisherman, and when he'd lived with them his mother had used to burn candles to this saint. Karen's daddy wasn't a fisherman, though, he only cut up fish at the big market on the other side of the harbor, and Markie assumed this was why Mama had stopped buying the little yellow votive candles anymore.

Karen tottered back and forth in front of the statue, and Markie stood with his hands in his pockets, edging between her and the juniper bushes

when she seemed likely to fall into them, or between her and the parked cars
when she'd make a dash for the asphalt. It was a dumb game, but it was
better than sitting inside. Every so often he'd look away from the baby long
enough to watch the progress of a big ship that was working its way across
the horizon. He wondered if his daddy was on the ship. The baby was quick
to make use of an opportunity too, and the second she saw his attention had
wandered would bolt down the narrow walkway between the church and
the rectory. He would run after her, and the clatter of their hard Sunday
shoes would echo between the buildings.

After a while there was singing again and people started filing out of the
church, blinking in the light. Markie got a firm grip on Karen's fat wrist and
held on until Mama emerged, smiling and chatting with a neighbor. Mama
was a big lady in a flowered tent dress, blonde and blue-eyed like Karen, and
she laughed a lot, jolly and very loud. She cried loud too. She was usually
doing one or the other; Mama wasn't quiet much.

She swept up Karen and walked on, deep in her conversation with Mrs.
Avila, and Markie followed them down the hill from the church. It was hot
and very bright, but the wind was fresh and there were seagulls wheeling and
crying above the town. Their shadows floated around Markie on the sidewalk,
all the way down Hinds Street to the old highway where the sidewalk ended
and the dirt path began. Here the ladies in their Sunday dresses shouted their
goodbyes to each other and parted company, and Markie's Mama swung
round and began a conversation with him, barely pausing to draw breath.

"Got a letter from Grandpa, honey, and he sent nice presents of money
for you and the baby. Looks like you get your birthday after all! What do you
want, you want some little cars? You want a holster and a six-shooter like
Leon's got? Whatever his damn mother buys him, honey, you can have better!"

"Can I have fishing stuff?" Markie didn't like talking about presents
before he got them—it seemed like bad luck, and anyway he liked the idea
of a surprise.

"Or I'll get you more of those green soldiers—what? No, honey, we
talked about this, remember? You're too little and you'd just get the hooks in
your fingers. Wait till you're older and Ronnie can show you." Ronnie was
Karen's daddy. Markie didn't want to go fishing with Ronnie; Ronnie scared
him. Markie just put his head down and walked along beside Mama as she
talked on and on, making plans about all the wonderful things he and Ronnie
would do together when he was older. She was loud enough to be heard
above the cars that zoomed past them on the highway, and when they turned
off the trail and crossed the bridge over the slough her voice echoed off the
water. As they neared their house, she saw Mrs. O'Farrell hanging out a laundry

load, and hurried ahead to tell her something important. Markie got to walk the rest of the way by himself.

Their house was the third one from the end in a half-square of little yellow cottages around a central courtyard. It had been a motor court, once; the rusted neon sign still said it was, but families like Markie's paid by the week to live here year in and year out. It was a nice place to live. Beside each identical clapboard house was a crushed-shell driveway with an old car or truck parked in it, and behind each house was a clothesline. In front was a spreading lawn of Bermuda grass, lush and nearly indestructible, and beyond that low dunes rose, and just beyond them was the sea. Off to the south was a dark forest of eucalyptus trees, and when Markie had been younger he'd been afraid of the monster that howled there; now he knew it was just the freight train, he'd seen where its tracks ran. To the north was the campground, where the people with big silver trailers pulled in; then the bridge that crossed the slough, and the little town with its pier and its general store and hotels.

It was a good world, and Markie was in a hurry to get back to it. He had to change his clothes first, though, and he didn't like going into the house by himself; but Mama looked like she was going to be talking to Mrs. O'Farrell a while, so he was careful not to let the rusty screen bang behind him as he slipped inside.

Ronnie was awake, though, sitting up in bed and smoking. He watched Markie with dead eyes as Markie hurried past the bedroom door. He didn't say anything, for which Markie was grateful. Ronnie was mean when he had that look in his eyes.

Markie's room was a tiny alcove up two stairs, with his bed and a dresser. He shed the blue church suit and the hard shoes, and quickly pulled on a pair of shorts and a cotton shirt. Groping under the bed he found his knapsack. His father had bought it at an Army Surplus store and it had an austere moldy smell, like old wars. He loved it. He put it on, adjusting the straps carefully, and ran from the house.

"Bye, Ma," he shouted as he ran past, and she waved vaguely as she continued telling Mrs. O'Farrell about the fight the people in the next house had had. Markie made for the big state campground; it was the place he always started his search.

There were certain places you could always find pop bottles. Ditches by the side of highways, for example: people pitched them out of speeding cars, in fact a lot of interesting stuff winds up in ditches. Bottles got left in alleyways between houses, and in phone booths, and in flower planters where the flowers had died, and in bushes on the edges of parking lots. The very best place to look was at the campground, just after one of the big silver trailers had pulled away from a space, before the park attendant had emptied the trash can. Beer bottles were worthless, but an ordinary pop bottle was worth two cents on deposit, and the big Par-T-Pak bottles were worth a nickel. Five empty Coca-Cola bottles could be redeemed for ten cents, and ten cents bought a comic book or a soda, or two candy bars—three if you went to Hatta's News, Cigars and Sundries, which carried three-cent Polar Bars. Ten cents bought two rolls of Lifesavers or one box of Crackerjacks, or ten Red Vines, or five Tootsie Roll Pops. Markie knew to the penny what he could do with his money, all right.

The original point of getting the money, though, had been to hand it to Mama in triumph. For a moment he'd completely have her attention, even if she were talking with the other women in the court; she'd yell out that he was her little hero, and engulf him in a hug, and briefly things would be the way they'd been before Karen had been born. Lately this had begun to lose its appeal to him, but the hunt had become more interesting as he got older and better at it, and then one day an idea had hit him like a blow between the eyes—buried treasure! He could save all those dimes in a box and keep it buried somewhere. He was still incredulous at how long it had taken him to think of this, especially since he lived at the beach, which was where people buried treasure.

He thought seriously about this as he scuttled between the campsites, scoring a Bireley's bottle from one trash can and two Frostie Rootbeer bottles from another. The Playtime Arcade had little treasure chests you could buy with blue tickets, real plastic ones with tiny brass locks, but he was too little to play the games that gave out blue tickets and scared to go in the arcades anyway. Well, there were cigar boxes and glass jars and tin cans; any of those might do for a start.

He spotted a good-sized cache of Nehi bottles at one campsite, but the campers were still there; an elderly man and woman seated in folding chairs, talking sadly and interminably about something. He decided to go into the dunes a while, to give them time to leave. Sometimes people wandered into the dunes with pop bottles, too, though usually all there was to find were beer bottles or little whiskey bottles in screwed-up paper bags. Once in a while the sand would drift away from old, old bottles, purple from time and the sun, and those could be sold to the old lady who ran the junk shop on Cypress Street. She'd pay ten cents per bottle, very good money.

So he struggled through the willow thicket, which was swampy and buzzing with little flies, and emerged into the cooler air of the dunes. Trails wound here through the sand, between the lawns of dune grass and big leaning yellow flowers. He knew all the labyrinths between the rows of cypress or eucalyptus trees that had been planted there, a long time ago, when somebody had built a big hotel on the sands. There was a story that one night a storm had come up and blown away the big dune from under the hotel, and the hotel had tipped over like a wrecked ship in the sand. Sometimes the winter storms would blow away enough sand to uncover some of the lost stuff from long ago: old machinery, a grand piano, a box of letters, a Model T Ford.

All the last storm seemed to have uncovered was clamshells. He wandered out from the edge into the full sunlight and the sea wind blew his hair back from his forehead. It was funny: he couldn't hear the waves at all, though they were crashing white with the spray thrown back from their tops. He couldn't hear any sound, though there were little kids playing at the edge of the water, and their mouths were opening as they yelled to one another. He looked around him in confusion.

He was in the place at the edge of the dunes where the trees had died, a long time ago, and they were leafless and silver from fifty years of salt spray, with their silver branches still swept backward from the winds when they were alive. There was a little line of bright water running in a low place beyond the edge, with some green reeds and a big white bird with a crest standing motionless, or moving its neck to strike at a silver fish or a frog. On the other side of the water the high dunes started, the big mountains of sand where there were no trees, only the sand changing color, white or pink or pale gold, and the sky and the pale floating clouds and their shadows on the sand. That was where the old man was sitting. He was looking at Markie.

"Come here, boy," he said, and his voice was so loud in the silence Markie jumped. But he came, at least as far as the edge of the water. The white bird ignored him. The old man was all in white, a long robe like saints wore, and his hair and beard were long and white too. His eyes were as scary as Ronnie's eyes.

"I want you to run an errand for me, boy," he said. His voice was scary, too.

"Okay," said Markie.

"Go into the town, to the arcade with the yellow sign. Ask for Smith."

"Okay," said Markie, though he was scared to go inside the arcades.

"Give him a message for me. Ask him how he likes this new servant of mine. Say to him: My servant has set himself to feed and clothe the poor, and to break the shackles of the oppressed, and to exalt the wise even to the stars. He has invoked the names of the old kings and the days of righteousness. Why should he not succeed? You go to Smith, boy, and you ask him just that. And go along the beach, it'll be faster. Do it, boy."

"Okay," said Markie, and he turned and fled. He made no sound floundering through the hot sand, but as he got to the hard wet sand there was noise again: the roar of the surf, the happy screaming of the little kids playing in the water. He ran up the beach toward the town and never looked back once.

By the time he reached the town and climbed up the ramp from the beach, he had decided to turn in his pop bottles at Hatta's and go home along the state highway. Just as he'd made up his mind on this, however, he passed the yard where the Anderson's big dog slept on its tether, in the shade under a boat up on sawhorses. The dog woke and leapt up barking, as it often did; but to Markie's horror the tether snapped, and the dog came flying over the fence and landed sprawling, right behind him. Markie ran so fast, jolting along the hot sidewalk, that a bottle flew out of his knapsack and broke. The dog stopped, booming out furious threats, but Markie kept going until he got around the corner onto Cypress Street and felt it was safe to slow down.

"Okay," he gasped, "Okay. I'm just going to turn in my bottles and *then* I'm going to the arcade, okay?"

There was a rumble like thunder, but it was only somebody starting up a motorcycle in front of Harry's Bar.

Markie limped into Hatta's News, Cigars and Sundries, grateful for the cool linoleum under his feet. Mr. Hatta wasn't there; only sulky MaryBeth Hatta, who had lately started wearing lipstick. She barely looked up from her copy of *Calling All Girls* as he made his way back to the counter. "Deposit on bottles," he mumbled, sliding his pack off and setting the bottles out one by one.

She gave a martyred sigh. "Eight cents," she told him, and opened the cash register and counted a nickel and three pennies into his sweaty palm. On his way out he slowed longingly by the comic book rack, but her voice came sharply after him:

"If you're not going to buy one of those, don't read them!"

Ordinarily he'd have turned and responded in kind, lifting the tip of his nose or maybe the corners of his eyes up with his fingers; but he remembered the old man in the dunes and it made him feel cold all over, so he hurried out without word or gesture.

At the corner of Pomeroy Avenue he turned and stared worriedly down the street. This was the Bad Part of town. There on the corner was the Peppermint Twist Lounge, and beyond it was the Red Rooster Pool Room, and beyond that the Roseland Ballroom, where fights broke out every Saturday night. Further down toward the pier were the penny arcades; Playland, with its red sign, and the other one with no name. Its yellow sign just said ARCADE.

Markie wasn't ever supposed to go over here, but he had. For a while after his daddy had moved out Markie had been able to see him by walking past the Red Rooster, looking quickly in through the door into the darkness. His daddy would be at the back, leaning listlessly against the wall with a beer bottle or a pool cue in his hand. If he saw Markie he'd look mad, and Markie would run; but one day his daddy hadn't been there anymore, nor had he been there since.

Markie looked in, all the same, as he trotted down the street. No daddy. Markie kept going, all the way down the street, to stand at last outside the doors of the arcade with the yellow sign. He drew a deep breath and went in.

The minute he crossed the threshold into darkness, he wanted to clap his hands over his ears. It was the loudest place he'd ever heard. In a corner there was a jukebox booming, telling him hoarsely that Frankie and Johnny were lovers. Next to that was a glass booth in which a marionette clown jiggled, and as its wooden jaw bobbed up and down a falsetto recording of "The Farmer in the Dell" played nearly as loud as the jukebox. From the back came the monotonous thunder of the skee-ball lanes, and the staccato popping of the shooting gallery: somebody had trapped the grizzly bear in his sights and it stood and turned, stood and turned, bellowing its pain as the ducks and rabbits kept racing by. There were pinball machines ringing and buzzing, with now and then a hollow double knock as a game ended, and a shout of disgust as a player punched a machine or rattled it on its legs. In a booth fixed up with a seat and steering wheel, somebody was flying as grey newsreel skies from the last World War flickered in front of them, and the drone of bomber engines played from a speaker. There were big boys standing around, with slicked-back hair and cigarettes, and some of them were shouting to each other; most of them were silent at their games, though, and dead-eyed as the waxen lady in the booth who swung one arm in a slow arc along her fan of playing cards.

Markie stood shivering. Big boys were scary. If you were lucky they ignored you or just flicked their cigarette butts at you, but sometimes they winked at their friends and grabbed you by the arm and said Hey, Shrimp, C'mere, and then they told you jokes you couldn't understand or asked you questions you couldn't answer, and then everybody would laugh at you. He turned to run outside again, but at that moment a car backfired right outside the door; with a little yelp he ran forward into the gloom.

Then he had to keep going, so he pretended he'd meant to come in there all along, and made for a small machine with a viewscope low enough for him to reach. Silver letters on a red background read IN THE DAYS OF THE INQUISITION. He didn't know what the last word was, but underneath it in smaller letters were the words *One Cent*, so he dug in his pocket for a penny and dropped it in the slot, and looked through the little window.

Clunk, a shutter dropped, and by yellow electric light he saw a tiny mannequin with its head on a block. Whack, another mannequin all in black dropped a tiny axe on its neck, as a third mannequin robed in brown burlap bobbed back and forth in a parody of prayer. The head, no bigger than a pencil eraser, dropped into a tiny basket; just before the light went out Markie could see the head coming back up again on a thread, to snap into place until the next penny was dropped into the slot.

Markie stepped back and looked around. There were other penny machines in this part of the arcade, with titles like SEE YOURSELF AS OTHERS SEE YOU and THE PRESIDENT'S WIFE. He felt in his pocket for more pennies, but a hand on his shoulder stopped him; in all the noise he'd been unable to hear any approach. He turned and stared up at someone very tall, whose face was hideous with lumps and pits and sores.

"Whatcha lookin' for, peanut?" the person shouted.

"Are you Smith?" Markie shouted back. "I got to say something to Smith."

The person jerked a thumb behind them. "Downstairs," he told Markie. Markie followed the direction of the thumb and found himself descending into darkness on a carpeted ramp, booming hollowly under his feet, that led to a long low room. It was a little quieter down here. There were dim islands of light over pool tables, and more dead-eyed boys leaned by them, motionless until an arm would suddenly flash with movement, shoving a cuestick forward. Markie was too short to see the colored balls rolling on the table, but he could hear the quiet clicking and the rumble as they dropped into darkness.

At the back of the room were more pinball machines, brightly lit up, and these did not feature little race horses or playing cards, like the ones upstairs; there were naked ladies and leering magicians. There was an old man seated between two of them, resting his arms on the glass panels. Markie approached cautiously.

This was a wizened old man, heavily tattooed, in old jeans and a T-shirt colorless with dust. The dust seemed to be grained in his skin and thick in his hair and straggly beard. He wore pointed snakeskin boots and a change belt full of nickels, and he was smoking a cigarette. His eyes were heavy-lidded and bored.

"Are you Smith?" Markie asked him. The old man's eyes flickered over him.

"Sure," he replied. It was hard to hear him, so Markie edged closer.

"I talked to this other man, and he said I was supposed to tell you something," he said, loudly, as though the old man were deaf. Smith took a long drag on his cigarette and exhaled. It smelled really bad. Markie edged back a pace or two.

"Oh yeah?" Smith studied his cigarette thoughtfully. "So what's he got to say to me, kid? He bitching about something again?"

"No, he says—" Markie scratched a mosquito bite, trying to remember. "He wants to know how you like his new servant, the one that breaks chains and stuff. He says he talks about old kings and rightness? You know? And he wants to know why he shouldn't, um, s-succeed."

"He does, huh?" Smith stuck his cigarette behind one ear and scratched his beard. "Huh. He's baiting me again, isn't he? Jeeze, whyn't he ever leave well enough alone? Okay. Why shouldn't this servant succeed?" He removed the cigarette and puffed again, then stabbed the air with it decisively. "*Here's* why. His father was unrighteous, and his sins are visited on his kids, right, unto the third and fourth generation? Aren't those the rules? So there, that's one reason. And this man is an adulterer and lusts after the flesh, right? Reason Number Two. Hmmm...." Smith pondered a moment; then his eyes lit up. "And when his son was born dead he despaired in his heart! Sin, Sin and Sin again. That's why his big-shot servant should fail, and you can tell him so from me. Okay, kid? Now beat it."

Markie turned and ran, up the ramp and out through shrieking darkness, and into the clean daylight at the foot of the pier. He pounded to a stop beside the snack stand and caught his breath, looking back fearfully at the arcade. After a moment he wandered out on the pier and looked south toward the dunes. They seemed far away and full of strange shifting lights. He shrugged and ventured further along the pier, stopping to watch with interest as a fisherman reeled in a perch and gutted it there on the spot. There were four telescopes ranged along the pier at intervals, and he stopped and climbed the iron steps to look into the eyepiece of each one, and check the coin slot to see if anyone had jammed a dime in there; no such luck. Further on, he stopped at the bait stand and bought a bag of peanuts for five cents. Just beyond the bait stand was a bench with a clean spot, and he settled down and proceeded to eat the peanuts, dropping the shells through the gaps between the pier planks and watching the green water surge down below.

The last shell felt funny and light, and when he opened it he found inside a little slip of paper printed in red ink. GET GOING, it said.

He jumped up and ran, heart in mouth, and clattered down the stairway to the beach. Near the bottom of the ramp he had to slow down, hobbling along clutching at his side, but he was too scared to stop.

All the way down the beach he watched the place with the silver trees, and he couldn't see the old man's white robes anywhere. The same little kids were still playing on the sand, though, and when he put down his head and plodded across the soft sand the same silence fell over everything; so he was not really much surprised, coming to the foot of the first dune, to lift his head and see the old man leaning against one of the dead trees.

"All right, boy, tell me what his answer was," said the old man without preamble.

Markie gulped for air and nodded. "He says—your servant should be failed because of his father, and the rule about the two and three generations. And he's committed adultery about the flesh, and his son died, and that's why." Markie sank down on the sand, stretching out his tired legs. The old man put his head on one side and stared fixedly into space for a moment.

"Hmm," he said. "Point taken. Very well. Go back and find Smith. Tell him he may therefore afflict my servant with wasting disease, and set scandal to defile his good name; and yet further, that he may confound his judgment among the nations. Go, boy, and tell him that."

Markie didn't want to go anywhere, and he was just tired enough to open his mouth in protest; but before he could make a sound he felt the soft sand begin to run and sink under him, and in terror he scrambled away on all fours. It didn't seem wise not to keep going once he'd started, so once he reached the hard sand he got to his feet and limped away down the beach, muttering to himself.

He left the beach and had started up the ramp at Ocean View Avenue before he remembered that the Andersons' dog was loose. Turning, he picked his way along the top of the seawall, balancing precariously and stepping around the loose bricks. Jumping from the end, he wandered through the courtyard of another small motel, pausing to duck into its row of phone booths and carefully checking to see if any change had been left in the coin return compartment. If none had, sometimes a punch at the coin return lever sent a couple of nickels cascading down; this was another good way to get money. The third booth rewarded his efforts mightily. Not only did he coax a nickel out of the phone, somebody had dropped a dime and it had fallen and stuck between the booth's ventilation slits near the floor. Markie's fingers were little enough to prise it out. He pocketed his small fortune and strolled on along the seafront, feeling pleased with himself.

At the snackbar at the foot of the pier he paused and bought a bottle of Seven-Up. The laconic counterman took off the bottlecap for him and thrust a straw down the neck. Markie carried the bottle carefully to the railings above the sand and sat with his legs dangling through the rails, sipping and not thinking. When the bottle was empty he held it up to his eye like a telescope and surveyed the world, emerald green, full of uncertain shapes. The view absorbed him for a while. He was pulled back to earth by the sound of shouting. One of the shouting voices belonged to Ronnie. Markie scrambled back from the railings and turned around quickly.

Ronnie and another man were over in the parking lot, standing one on either side of a big red and white convertible, yelling across it at one another.

"You were drunk!" the other man was telling Ronnie.

"*Fuck* you!" Ronnie told the man. "I haven't had a drink in two years! Fuck you!"

"Oh, that's some great way to talk when you want your job back," the man laughed harshly, pulling open the car door and getting inside. "It sure is. So you haven't had a drink in two years? So what exactly was that you puked up all over Unit Three, you goddam bum?" He slammed the door and started up his car.

"Come on, man!" Ronnie caught hold of the car door. "You can't do this! I've got an old lady and a kid, for Christ's sake!" But the man was backing up his car, shaking his head, and as he drove away uptown Ronnie ran after him, yelling pleas and threats.

Markie slunk into the arcade, and for a moment the din was almost welcome; at least nobody was fighting in there. He squared his shoulders and marched down the ramp, down into the room where there was no day or night.

Smith was waiting for him, leaning forward with his elbows on his knees. His cigarette was canted up under his nose at a jaunty angle.

"You deliver my answer, kid?" he inquired. Markie nodded. Smith leaned back and exhaled slowly, two long jets of smoke issuing from his nose. He closed his eyes for a moment and when he opened them his attention was riveted on Markie, suddenly interested. "Hey. What's your name, kid?"

"Markie Souza."

"Souza, huh?" Smith narrowed his eyes and pulled at his beard. "So you're a Portugee, huh? Boy, your people have been cheated by some experts. You know it was the Portuguese who discovered the New World really? And a lot of other places, too. They never get credit for it, though. The Spanish and the Italians grabbed all the glory for themselves. Your people used to have a big empire, kid, did you know that? And it was all stolen from them. Mostly by the English, but the Spanish had a hand in that too. Next time you see some Mexican kid, you ought to bounce a rock off his head.

You aren't all Portuguese, though, are you, with that skin?" Smith leaned forward again, studying Markie. "What are you? What's your mother, kid?"

"She's Irish," Markie told him.

"Well, Irish!" Smith grinned hugely. His teeth were yellow and long. "Talk about a people with good reasons to hate! Kid, I could sit here for three days and three nights telling you about the injustices done to the Irish. You got some scores to settle, kid, you can't grow up fast enough. Anytime you want to know about Irish history, you just come down here and ask me."

"Okay," said Markie faintly. The smoke was making him sick. "But the man said to tell you some other stuff."

"What'd he say?"

"That you can do bad things to his servant. Waste and disease, and, uh, scandal. And something about confining his judgment of nations."

"All right," Smith nodded. "All right, that's fair. Will do." He made a circle out of his thumb and index finger and held it up in an affirmative gesture. "But... ask him if he doesn't think we ought to up the ante a little. So what if I punish one sinner with good intentions? He's the leader of a whole people, right? Aren't all his people jumping on his little bandwagon with their Camelot and all that bullshit? But how seriously do they believe in what they're saying? Shouldn't they be tested too?"

Markie didn't know what to say, so he nodded in agreement. Smith stuck his cigarette back between his teeth and laced his gnarled fingers together, popping the knuckles.

"O-kay! We got a whole nation suddenly figuring out that racial injustice is bad, and poverty is bad, and reaching for the stars is good, right? Except they damn well knew that already, they just didn't bother to do anything about it until a pretty boy in the White House announced that righting all wrongs is going to be the latest thing. *Fashion*, that's the only reason they care now. So what'll they do if this servant of his is taken out of the picture? My bet is, they won't have the guts to hang on to those high ideals without a figurehead. What's he want to bet? You go ask him, kid. Does he want to test these people?"

Markie nodded and ran. It was a lot to remember and the words kept turning in his head. He emerged into the brilliant sunlight and stood, dazzled, until he realized that he was still clutching the empty Seven-Up bottle. With a purposeful trot he started up Pomeroy Avenue. The phone booth behind the Peppermint Twist lounge yielded a Nesbitts bottle, and there were two Coca-Cola bottles in the high grass next to the Chinese restaurant, and three pennies lying on the sidewalk in plain view right in front of the Wigwam Motor Inn. He was panting with triumph as he marched into Hatta's, and the cool green linoleum felt good under his bare feet. He lined the bottles up on the counter. Marybeth looked up from her magazine. She was reading *Hit Parade* now.

"Eight cents," she announced. "Are you ever going to buy anything in here, junior?"

"Okay," he said cheerfully, and moved down the counter to the candy display next to the big humidor. The front of the display case was tin rolls of Lifesavers, carefully enameled to look like the real thing. He pretended to grab up a roll of Butter Rum and tugged in feigned surprise when it remained riveted in place. The patience in Marybeth's eyes was withering, so he stopped playing and picked out five wax tubes filled with colored juice. Marybeth gave him his three cents in change and took up her magazine again. He stepped out on the hot pavement and hurried down to the beach.

There was supposed to be a way to bite holes in the wax tubes and play music, once you'd sucked out the sweet juice. All the way down the beach he experimented without success, and his teeth were full of wax by the time he looked up and noticed that he'd reached the silver trees again. He plodded across the sand. The old man was standing by the little stream, watching in silence as the big white bird speared a kicking frog.

"Tell me what he said this time," said the old man, without looking up.

"He said Okay," Markie replied, staring at the dying frog in fascination. "And he wants to bet with you about the people with Camelot and everything. And Fashion. He says, what if the man gets taken out of the picture. You want to test them? I think that was what he said."

"A test!" The old man looked up sharply. "Yes! Very well. Let it be done as he has said; let the people be tested. When he has done unto my servant as I have permitted, let him do more. Let him find a murderer; that man's heart shall I harden, that he may strike down my servant. Let the wife be a widow; let the children weep for their father, and his people mourn. Will they bury righteousness with my servant, and return to their old ways? Or will they be strong in the faith and make his good works live after him? We'll see, won't we? Go back to Smith, boy. Tell him that."

"Okay," Markie turned and plodded away across the sand. His legs were getting tired. He needed more sugar.

He stopped in at Hatta's on his way back down Cypress Street. Marybeth looked up at him in real annoyance, but he dug a nickel and five pennies out of his pocket and smacked them down on the counter.

"I'm *buying* something, ha ha ha," he announced, and after a great deal of forethought selected a Mars Bar. As he wandered back down Pomeroy he ate the bar in layers, scraping away the nougat with his teeth and crunching up the almonds in their pavement of hard chocolate. When the candy was gone you could always chew on the green waxed paper wrapper, which tasted nice and felt interesting between the teeth. He was still chewing on it when he passed the Red Rooster and spotted Ronnie inside, ghastly pale under a cone of artificial light, leaning over a green table and cursing as his shot went wrong. Markie gulped and ran.

Down in the underground room, Smith was watching a fly circle in the motionless air. As Markie approached him, he made a grab for it and missed.

"Shit," he said tonelessly. He noticed Markie and grinned again.

"Well, kid? Did he take me up on it?"

Markie nodded and sat down, rubbing his legs. The red carpet felt sticky.

"He says—yes, test. He says he'll let you find a murderer and he'll make his heart hard. He says let his children cry. He says we'll see about the people and faith."

"So *I'm* supposed to get him a murderer?" Smith leaned back. "That figures. I don't have anything else to do, right? So okay, I'll get him his murderer. This is gonna take some work to get it just right... but, Hell, I like a challenge. Okay." He unrolled his shirtsleeve and took out a pack of cigarettes, and lit one; Markie didn't see just how, because the cloud of smoke was so immediate and thick. Smith waved it away absently and stared into space a moment, thinking. Markie got up on all fours and staggered to his feet, drawing back Smith's attention.

"I bet he's not paying you anything to run all these messages, is he?" Smith inquired. "Hasn't even offered, huh?"

"Nope," Markie sighed.

"That's him all over. Well, kid, here's something for you." Smith leaned down and fished out something from a brown paper bag under his stool. He held up a brown bottle. "Beer! Big kids like beer."

Markie backed away a pace, staring at it. Ronnie had made him taste some beer once; he had cried and spit it out. "No, thank you," he said.

"No? Nobody'll know. Come on, kid, you must be thirsty, the way he's made you run around." Smith held it out. Markie just shook his head. Smith's eyes got narrow and small, but he smiled his yellow smile again.

"You sure? Well, it's yours anyhow, you've earned it. What do you want me to do with it?"

Markie shrugged.

"You want me to give it to somebody else?" Smith persisted. "Okay? What if I give it to the first guy I meet when I go home tonight, huh, kid? Can I do that?"

"Okay," Markie agreed.

"Well, okay then! Now go deliver my message. Tell him I'll get him his murderer. Go on, kid, make tracks!"

Markie turned and limped out. He went slowly down the stairs to the beach, holding on to the sticky metal handrail. It was late afternoon now and a chilly wind had come up; all along the beach families were beginning to pack up to go home, closing their striped umbrellas and collecting buckets and sand spades. Mothers were forcing hooded sweatshirts on protesting toddlers and fathers were carrying towels and beach chairs back to station wagons. The tide was out; as Markie trudged along shivering he saw the keyholes in the sand that meant big clams were under there. Ordinarily he'd stop and dig up a few, groping in the sand with his toes; he was too tired this afternoon.

The sun was red and low over the water when he got to the dead trees, and the dunes were all pink. The old man was pacing beside the water, in slow strides like the white bird. He turned his bright glare on Markie.

"He says okay," Markie told him without prompting. "He'll get a murderer."

The old man just nodded. Markie thought about asking the old man for payment of some kind, but one look into the chilly eyes was enough to silence him.

"Now, boy," said the old man briskly, "Another task. Go home and open the topmost drawer of your mother's dresser. You'll find a gun in there. Take it into the bathroom and drop it into the water of the tank behind the toilet. Go now, and let no one see what you've done."

"But I'm not supposed to go in that drawer, ever," Markie protested.

"Do it, boy!" The old man looked so scary Markie turned and ran, stumbling up the face of the dune and back into the thicket. He straggled home, weary and cold.

Mama was sitting on the front steps with two of the other mothers in the courtyard, and they were drinking beers and smoking. Mama was laughing uproariously at something as he approached.

"Hey! Here's my little explorer. Where you been, boyfriend?" she greeted him, carefully tipping her cigarette ash down the neck of an empty beer bottle.

"Hanging around," he replied, stopping and swatting at a mosquito.

"You seen Ronnie?" Mama inquired casually, and the other two mothers gave her a look, with little hard smiles.

"Uh-uh." He threaded his way through them up the steps.

"Well, that's funny, because he was going to give you a ride home if he saw you," Mama replied loudly, with an edge coming into her voice. Markie didn't know what he was supposed to say, so he just shrugged as he opened the screen door.

"He's probably out driving around looking for you," Mama stated. She raised her voice to follow him as he retreated into the dark house. "I don't want to start dinner until he gets back. Whyn't you start your bath? Don't forget you've got school tomorrow."

"Okay." Markie went into the bathroom and switched on the light. When he saw the toilet, he remembered what he was supposed to do. He crept into Mama's bedroom.

Karen was asleep in the middle of the bed, sprawled with her thumb in her mouth. She did not wake up when he slid the dresser drawer open and stood on tiptoe to feel around for the gun. It was at the back, under a fistful of Ronnie's socks. He took it gingerly into the bathroom and lifted the lid of the toilet tank enough to slip it in. It fell with a splash and a clunk, but to his great relief did not shoot a hole in the tank. He turned on the water in the big old claw-footed tub and shook in some bubble flakes. As the tub was filling, he slipped out of his clothes and climbed into the water. All through his bath he half-expected a sudden explosion from the toilet, but none ever came.

When he got out and dressed himself again, the house was still dark. Mama was still outside on the steps, talking with the other ladies. He was hungry, so he padded into the kitchen and made himself a peanut butter and jelly sandwich and ate it, sitting alone at the kitchen table in the dark. Then he went into his little room and switched on the alcove light. He pulled out the box of comic books from under his bed and lay there a while, looking at the pictures and reading as much as he knew yet of the words.

Later he heard Mama sobbing loudly, and begging the two other mothers to stay with her, and their gentle excuses about having to get home. Heart thudding, he got up and scrambled into his cowboy pajamas, and got under the covers and turned out the light. He lay in a tense knot, listening to her come weeping through the house, bumping into the walls. Was she going to come in and sit on his bed and cry again? No; the noise woke up Karen, who started to scream in the darkness. He heard Mama stumbling into the bedroom, hushing her, heard the creaking springs as she stretched out on the bed beside the baby. Markie relaxed; he was going to be left in peace. Just before he fell asleep, he wondered where Ronnie was.

Ronnie had played badly in the back room of the Red Rooster, all afternoon. He'd come out at last and lingered on the streetcorner, not wanting to have to go home and explain why he wasn't going in to work the next day. As he'd stood there, an old man had come up and pressed a bottle of beer into his hand and walked quickly on, chuckling. Ronnie was too surprised to thank him for the gift, but he was grateful; so he went off and sat on the wall behind the C-Air Motel, sipping his beer and watching the sun go down. From there he went straight into Harry's Bar and had more, and life was good for a while.

But by the time he crawled into his truck and drove out to the old highway, he was in a bad mood again. He was in a worse mood when he climbed from his truck after it ran into the ditch. As he made his way unsteadily through the darkness, a brilliantly simple solution to his problems occurred to him. It would take care of the truck, the lost job, Peggy and the baby, everything. Even the boy. All their problems over forever, with no fights and no explanations. It seemed like the best idea he'd ever had.

He crept into the house, steadying himself by sliding along the wall. Once in the bedroom he groped around in the dresser drawer for a full two minutes before he realized his gun wasn't in there. Peggy was deep unconscious on the bed, and didn't hear him. He stood swaying in the darkness, uncertain what to do next. Then he got mad. All right; he'd show them, and they'd be sorry.

So he left the house, falling noisily down the front steps, but nobody heard him or came to ask if he was all right. Growling to himself he got up and staggered out to the woods, and lay down on the train tracks with a certain sense of ceremony. He passed out there, listening to the wind in the leaves and the distant roar of breakers.

The freight train came through about twenty minutes later.

The Summer People

Don't you call me a townie! I'm too big for this town. I'm too—what's that word? Too *intense.*

You watch me at Harry's Bar on Karaoke Night, now; I burn up that place. I got the audience in the palm of my hand. Born with talent! That's why I didn't go into the family business. What? Firewood delivery and seasonal specialties. Not how you get rich.

A loser like my cousin Verbal likes that kind of work. He's got no ambition at all. He'll just sit there in the flocking shed drinking beer through his face mask until somebody wants a Christmas tree flocked. Now and then he'll have to get up off his ass to go nail on a tree stand or something. Same thing with the pumpkin patches. He'll drive the tractor for the hayrides, he'll load pumpkins off the truck, or firewood. That's about all he's good for.

Not like me. I like a challenge, and also I just am not made to spend my life around clowns like Verbal.

Suellen didn't understand that, though. You'd think, with me bringing home meat for the table and the deck I built for the trailer, plus keeping her satisfied which I did and enough said, you'd think she'd see it was a fair division of labor. But every time she brought home a paycheck she'd start in on me about her brother at the fish packing plant and how he'd hire me.

He'd hire me, sure; but I know how it would go after that. He wants somebody just smart enough to hold on to the right end of the gutting knife, not an idea man who can show him how to run the plant better. Somebody was telling me Einstein didn't do real good in school, and I'm the same way. Too original, you see?

The meat for the table? Well, how do you think I get it? Same way as primeval Man, before there was any Department of Fish and Game. I have been up in front of the judge a few times for poaching but that's chickenshit stuff, and I'd a lot rather do County time for poaching deer than that poor

SOB who was up before me once, who got caught poaching *mushrooms*! Not even the psychedelic kind.

Besides, poaching was how I got my big break. Almost.

I'll tell you about that.

Everybody knows about the big newspaper man who built the castle up there where all the movie stars came, the one that's a museum or something now, right? But back then lots of rich people did that. There's a lot of big fancy houses on this coast, sitting off private roads that ain't paved, cut with kelly ditches, and the gates and padlocks are all rusted because nobody ever comes up from Beverly Hills except in the summer for a couple of weeks.

My other cousin has a caretaking service, he'll go and fill the propane tanks or get the powerhouses started up, WD-40 all the locks, make sure the water's turned on and the pools are filled—me and Verbal worked for him for a month once and you should see the palaces back up in those hills! Every one of them on a hundred acres easy, sometimes more.

So the Forestry Service don't go there, Department of Fish and Game either, because it's all private property! And it's just over the county line too. See where I'm going with this? And why should anybody mind, if you don't try to break into the house or nothing? Go at night, with a night sight on your gun. Moonlight's the best time. That part of the coast's not patrolled after dark and with a good moon you don't run the risk of falling down a mountain. Take a buck, plenty of meat for the freezer.

So I was going up to this one place one bright night in the middle of summer and got a flat tire on Highway 1, in about the worst part where you got the cliff at your back and a thousand-foot drop to the ocean on the other side. I had just room to get the F150 over so I could change the tire. I was crouched down working the jack when I heard them coming, and flattened myself against the truck, because you never know when somebody could swerve over the line and smack you right out of this world.

Around the curve they came with the moonlight sliding off them, big new shiny cars, gleaming like every polished thing you ever saw. I was close enough so I could look into the windows, each one as they went by so quiet, so smooth the motors weren't even purring. Only the whoosh of air and some perfume.

The people inside were just black silhouettes sharp as cut out of black paper, but elegant, you know? And in the last one, a lady had her window down and her white arm resting on the door. It shone in the moonlight like it was made of marble or something. I couldn't see her face but for a second or so, but that was enough to tell me she was from Hollywood.

So I knew then they were summer people up from there, going to some big party probably on one of those estates. I stood up slow and watched after the last one had gone by, and for a few minutes I could see the red lights winding away up the coast road, the moon sparkling on the glossy cars the way it would on bubbles, and the long beams of the headlights winking in and out.

And there I was having to swap bald tires on a rusted-out 1972 F150. But I just told myself, one day that'd be me in one of those fine cars, I'd be one of those summer people, and it'd be my old lady—not Suellen either— with the night air washing in like silver water and floating her perfume out the window. Some people would feel mean and cheap watching all those shiny cars, but not me. If you don't see something like that now and then to tell you what you're missing, you'll be happy selling firewood all your life.

I changed the tire and went on my way, up to this access road the Forestry Service don't maintain anymore, so you can't hardly see it for the brush, and you don't have to park far up the canyon to be hidden from the highway. There's a place where the oaks and the laurels are real thick and there's a leaning old wire fence, which is my favorite place to get in. I took my gun and snaked under and got to cover real fast, walking bent over through the black shadows and moonlight dapples under the bushes, and I fitted up my sight and got to hunting in earnest.

Usually I get what I'm after in no time at all, I'm that good. This one time, though, the deer must have all been over on the Jolon side of the mountains, because I couldn't raise squat. So I went farther up this hill than I usually go, high enough so I could look down on the mist coming in from the sea, white on fire with that moon, and out in the open so I could practically see color like it was day.

Then I heard music coming from somewhere and I turned around, thinking maybe somebody had driven up the Forestry Service road with their radio loud, but I saw the window lights and I thought, oh shit.

All the times I been up there I never even seen the house, back in the trees like it must have been and dark and shut up, but there it was large as life now with every window blazing away and music inside. I picked a bad night to hunt, because obviously this was where the summer people had come to party.

I stepped real quick back under the trees, planning on going away quiet, and I can move like one of those ninjas when I have to but this time it didn't do me jack good, because there was somebody standing right there in the woods with me.

"Nice night, isn't it?" he says, and there's a little flare-up of light from a lighter or something and I look into his eyes as he puffs on this green cigarette.

Then there was just the red dot in the darkness but I could still tell he was there.

I thought it was that pissy-faced little boy actor with the fancy name, you know? That's who he'd looked like in that split second I saw him. So I said how I was sorry, I didn't mean to trespass, I must have got lost in the dark and all, and his voice was real friendly. He said it was okay. He said the garden had gone so wild it was easy to mistake it for the federal land, and I said,

"There's a garden up here?" and he laughed and said,

"See, you can't even tell," and I said,

"Damn! I've lived here all my life and I never knew that," and he said,

"You want to come see?"

Which put me in a dilemma because I figured he was maybe coming on to me. But I was twice as big as him and had a gun and a knife besides. And I was beginning to get some ideas about getting myself discovered, see what I mean? Like he might know a talent scout or somebody.

So I walked on with him, following the little red floating light, further back into the trees, closer to the lights of the house, and son of a bitch if somebody hadn't done some old fancy landscaping up there at one time. Big flowering rhododendron bushes grown up into trees practically, and lots of cement statues and stepping stones and pools all choked with dead oak leaves, and one fountain where you couldn't see what it was supposed to be, there was so much moss, with just a little green slimy water trickling down. All the spots and blobs of moonlight were enough so we could find our way pretty good.

I explained how I was an entertainer too—told him all about my Elvis routine. He just smoked his cigarette, so the red light brightened and dimmed, and I figured he thought he was too good for me, but then he got more friendly and kind of opened up.

It turned out he wasn't that actor at all, even if the house was full of big celebrities. He was just somebody's friend, the good-looking kind they keep around to housesit for them and skim the leaves off their pools and all that! Like that Kato guy. I felt a lot better when I knew that and asked him if there was any way I could maybe meet some of those people in the house who might know if I could get one of those, you know, auditions.

He sounded gloomy and said it wasn't much of a party right now, as the lady in charge and her husband had just had some kind of screaming hissy-fit at each other, which was why he'd ducked out to the garden. But then his cigarette got real bright, I could tell an idea was hitting him, and he said I should come in anyway—maybe I could sing for them and cheer everybody up.

Well, that took my breath away, and I was wishing like hell I'd shaved that morning when he came real close, solid suddenly out of the shadows, and took me by the arm and said,

"But we'd better give you a makeover first, okay?"

I didn't know whether he meant something gay or what, but he was explaining as we went along about Henri-Luc probably having a suit my size, and I could use one of the guest bathrooms to shower and blow-dry my hair, and I caught on. I was kind of sweaty and I'd been changing a tire and all. I wished I'd had my powder blue Karaoke clothes, but he told me it'd be an Armani suit. You know what those are? Real nice.

So anyway we went in the house, through a back entrance, and I could hear the music and smell the perfumes, and I never was nervous before but I was now. It was dark and big in there, kind of dusty but lots of arches and purple drapes and antiques. Bobby, that was my friend, was starting to giggle about what a good idea this would be after all.

He took me to a big old bathroom where, I swear to Jesus, the sink and toilet were purple china and the hardware was all gold. It was even purple tile in the shower stall. When I came out I grabbed for a towel pretty fast but Bobby wasn't around anywhere. He'd left out a suit and everything I needed, though. I got the clothes on and then he came back in and, uh, fussed with my hair and I was starting to get uncomfortable until I saw he was fixing my hair to look like The King's.

He did a real good job too, and did some of those tricks they call slight of hand, pretending to pull combs and hairspray out of nowhere. I guess boys like him have to learn all kinds of ways to make those celebrities laugh, so they can keep on living in their guest houses and don't have to go to work in hair salons.

When he was done he yelled Presto and jumped back. I looked in the mirror at myself in that suit and it was like I saw the real Me, the way I was supposed to look, and God-damn I felt ten feet tall! No wonder I get all those girls coming up to me after I step down from the mike. I could even have understood if Bobby had patted me on the ass, the way I looked right then. Though he didn't; he just grinned and said,

"Let's go introduce you."

So we went out into the big room where the party was going on.

And that was some room, there was a grand piano in one corner and lots of those big potted palms and more antiques and purple velvet drapes. Big mirrors on the walls, but so old they reflected things funny and cloudy. There was so many people in there I could tell right then nobody'd mind a crasher, and I was better-looking than half the men anyhow.

But Bobby was right; it wasn't much of a party, what with the quarrel and all. People seemed sort of scared. A tiny little hunchbacked guy, bald as an egg, sat at the piano and played show tunes, but he was mostly ignored by the lady. Her, you couldn't ignore.

She was the woman I'd seen in the shiny car. She was just as beautiful as she was in the movies, though I couldn't remember what movies she was in but I knew she was somebody. She had on a white dress cut real low, but when I say white I mean that shimmery pearly color like... like pearls, I guess, or the moon. She was sitting under a lamp, sitting on a big white sofa which had draped over it a white tigerskin rug. She'd kicked off her shoes and curled her feet under her, had one arm stretched out along the back of the chair, and her head turned sharp to glare across at the man way across the room.

He was standing way back in the shadows, leaning against a marble column, and he was real dark and wore a dark suit cut almost as nice as mine. He had his arms folded but with one hand up to hold a cigarette between his first two fingers, kind of in a way that looked gay to me, and it was one of those fancy colored cigarettes like Bobby was smoking. No wonder his old lady was mad! He just stared out through the shadows at her with cold black eyes, and every so often he'd flick some ash from that green cigarette.

Between them all the other show people sort of wandered back and forth trying to pretend they were having a good time. There were a lot of little cute boys like Bobby, and some really ugly old women and men, and a whole lot of pretty girls, though some of them seemed awfully young, and none of them were much to look at next to the lady. And everybody had those green cigarettes so the air was all full of swirls of smoke, and it had a sweet smell like perfume. I figured they must be those clove cigarettes, because it wasn't pot. Pot stinks like Rainier Ale, you ever notice?

There were a couple of waiters in green jackets and, it was the damndest thing you ever saw, they were identical twins and must have been seven feet high! And they were bald too. I had to stare when one of them came up to us with a tray and offered me a drink without saying a word, and then I remembered that you don't talk to help, so I just took a glass and nodded. Bobby winked and nudged me.

"See what I mean? Everybody's on edge. This was supposed to be her big birthday blowout, and it's tanked. Baravelli isn't helping any, either. Rodgers and Hammerstein, for God's sake! Could anything be duller? I knew this was a good idea. Why don't I go see if he knows your material?"

"Okay," I said, and took a big slug of my drink and nearly choked, because instead of it being champagne like I figured it was some kind of God-awful salty bubbly water. I shook my head and Bobby stopped to look back at me. He said,

"Oh, no, is there something wrong with the Perrier?"

That was when I realized what it was and I remembered I'd seen it in markets and it comes from France and all, so I just shook my head and waved for him to go on. He winked again and said,

"We're all very health-conscious since she got that guru." Then he went on to go whisper to the piano player and I tried my drink again, and I see why it costs so much if it's got minerals in it, but I couldn't help thinking the party would have livened right up if they'd iced a few twelve-packs of Miller High Life. And if they were so set on health, how come everybody was smoking?

I could see Bobby talking to the little bald man, who was nodding and tipping ash from his cigarette into a big ashtray shaped like a skull. Then one of the ugly old ladies came up to me, and gave me the once over and liked what she saw, if you know what I mean. She was dressed real good, by the way, and I figured she must be one of those New York intellectuals, or maybe a gossip columnist. She said,

"My goodness, I haven't seen you here before," and she had a smart voice, but I could tell she'd had a lot of whiskey in her time, she was kind of hoarse. She took a long suck on her cigarette holder and puffed smoke at me in a teasy way.

"That's because I'm the latest thing, honey," I said, pouring on the charm, and I took her skinny old hand and kissed it and she sure had a lot of big rings. She said,

"Oo! And he's got manners, too. Are you a friend of Bobby's?"

I leaned real close and said, "Not that kind of friend, Ma'am—if you get my drift." And she laughed, husky, and waved her cigarette holder at them all and said,

"What do you think of our little party?" And I said,

"Well, if you ask me, sugar, it could use some excitement. But I hear there's been some quarrel, and that always pees on a parade."

She chuckled and waved away smoke. "It's always something. This particular evening Madam Queen has got it through her beautiful head that she wants to adopt a Romanian orphan. Mister over there hit the ceiling. Children are *not* in the pre-nup, as I understand it. And, you know, the poor little things die on you anyway; they've all got health problems. But he had the *very* bad judgment to tell her she was too old for this kind of thing."

I glared over at Mister where he stood in the gloomy corner. "He did?

That's just sheer stupid mean. Too old! Why, she ain't a day over thirty."

The old lady arched her penciled-in eyebrows at me. She didn't say anything for a minute and then she put her hand on my arm and said, "My dear, I see you have a bright future ahead of you."

Which made me feel so good I almost forgot to hate Mister for a second. We watched as he lifted his hand and beckoned to Bobby, who jumped away from the piano and hurried over to see what he wanted. They talked for a minute real quiet and I could see Mister pointing to the lady, and Bobby turning to look and saying something with a kind of half-assed grin. He nodded in my direction and I stood tall and looked hard at Mister, letting him know that I was just as good as him.

Mister just sort of looked through me. I knew right then I'd settle with him, somehow. Bobby said something else and ducked out of the room, but a split second later he'd come back with whatever he'd fetched. He started across the room to us.

"Bobby, darling!" said the old lady, and she and he sort of kissed cheeks like those folks do, mwah-mwah dry-kissing, and she pulled back and said:

"They're keeping you running tonight, I see," and he rolled his eyes and said,

"Up and down." Then he turned to me and said, "So! I talked to Baravelli. He knows the King's standards. Like to give it a shot?"

"You are damn right I would," I said, and handed my glass to the old lady and marched over to the piano. Bobby ran after me, laughing, and said:

"Hold on, Handsome, I've got to fix your boutonniere." He held up this purple orchid, pulling it out of nowhere like the combs, and stuck it in my buttonhole. I don't wear those things but I could tell this was expensive, so I let him arrange it there, and then he turned up his little grinning face and said, "Let me do your intro, okay?"

He jumped up and got everybody's attention, and made a real nice speech. I felt bad about thinking he was a snippy little you-know, because he told everybody what a fabulous artist I was and how I'd played Vegas, which wasn't true but only because I hadn't had the chance, and it was sure nice of him. I began to wonder if maybe he hadn't caught my act at Harry's, he described it so well.

Then he stepped aside, everybody was applauding and smiling, and I looked around for a mike, because there wasn't one that I could see. Bobby pushed something into my hand and for a second I thought it was just a Perrier bottle, but then I saw it was one of those cordless mikes, only green instead of black for some reason.

And it worked fine when I said, "Thankew, thankew ver'much," just the way the King always did.

The minute I said that the lady turned her beautiful head, like she'd only right then noticed me, and stared. Her eyes were blue like jewels, and hard too but... but like she had *character*, you see what I'm trying to say?

I started into "Heartbreak Hotel" and her eyes got real wide, and not once through that whole song did she ever turn her face away from me.

I might have been nervous before, but I tell you—I had the magic, as usual. I had everybody spellbound! All the gloom went straight out of there, I had those people grinning and hugging themselves. I think a couple of those pretty boys came close to crying, in fact. Even the Mister, over in his corner where Bobby had joined him, looked delighted with me. The little bald guy at the piano was a lot better than the Karaoke tape, seemed to know ahead of time what I was going to do next and never played too loud. He had the biggest damn ears I ever saw in my life, I swear they stuck up above his scalp, and maybe they gave him natural perfect pitch or something.

I could tell they wanted more so I gave them "Hound Dog" after that, and "Suspicious Minds," and "Jailhouse Rock," and the whole time the lady watched me like I was the best thing that had ever come into her life. So then I did "Love Me Tender" just for her, if you get my drift, real soft and leaning to her the whole time. Her face was shining like the moonlight.

And I thought to myself, boy, you have made an impression on these summer people! I thought sure I was going to get an audition now.

I could have been up there all night, but it was starting to get late and folks were sneaking out in ones and twos, though I could tell they hated to leave, and then Bobby came up, really wiping tears out of his eyes, and said:

"You'd better give me the mike now, Elvis, we don't want to wear out that voice. Everybody, a big hand for the King!"

The crowd went wild. They applauded and shouted for more, but I smiled real nice and shook my head as I handed the mike back to Bobby, because I could see some other action getting ready to happen. And if you don't know what I mean, you ain't been listening, friend.

The lady held on to me with that look of hers and patted the couch beside her. In the sweetest voice you ever heard, she asked me to come sit and talk with her. I looked quick over at the Mister but he was talking to Bobby, who was nodding and sipping from a bottle of Perrier. You don't have to ask me twice; I was on that couch in two seconds and, I tell you, she was all over me.

Crazy in love with me! You'd have thought I really was Elvis, the way she went on about how beautiful I was. It was almost embarrassing. Nothing was too good for me; she asked if I wanted anything to drink and I told her a plain beer sure would be nice, and damned if she didn't send one of her little girls running off to the kitchen or somewhere to look for one.

In the meantime she fed me all kinds of chips and crackers from this bowl, health food snacks I guess, and they tasted all right but some of them were pretty strange colors and there was no salt at all. Finally the little girl came back, real apologetic, because all she could find was a real old bottle of something imported, I guess from Japan or somewhere, I couldn't read what the hell was on the label and it tasted funny, like flowers sort of.

I'm too smart to complain about a stupid bottle of beer in a situation like that, though. I just smiled and drank and after the first swallow it wasn't too bad anyhow. I got quite a buzz off of it, in fact.

The lady kept talking about how good-looking I was, which was sweet, but I kind of wanted to get the conversation around to my career, and after a while she saw that and she put her arms around my neck and started talking about all the things she could do for me. Big record producers and club owners and all. She had another of her little girls pull off my shoes and give me a foot massage, if you can believe that, some oriental pressure therapy thing her guru taught her, and I was sure glad I'd had that shower and borrowed that fancy pair of socks.

I looked around to see if the Mister was catching *this* act but I couldn't see him or Bobby anywhere, only some of the ugly old folks standing around here and there talking about Italian museums and some prince or other in the south of France, just as though there wasn't nearly an orgy going on right under their noses. But, you know, that's how morality is in Hollywood.

If I'd been able to keep her talking about my singing, I'd probably be in Vegas right now, but that funny beer was making me, you know, susceptible to her charms and all and she leaned in close and began to whisper things in my ear, and where a lady like her learned to talk like that I do not know. She got me so all I wanted was one thing, and it wasn't a recording contract.

We could have probably done it right there on the couch with the pretty boys looking on, for all those people cared, but I got a little loud and that brought her out of it some, she put her hand over my mouth and whispered that we'd better go to her room. I thought that was a great idea, so we got up and she led me away into that dark old house, not turning on the lights so we wouldn't get caught I guess. Her little girls ran ahead with some kind of colored flashlights, winky bright spots flitting around the old rugs and drapes.

We got to her bedroom and it had this huge antique bed with covers and drapes and hangings all in that Laura Ashby flower pattern, and the moon was pouring in through the arch windows so you could see every detail in the flowers.

"Here," says the lady, and she opened a drawer and took out a baggie of powder and I thought, oh boy, cocaine! Because, you know, those Hollywood people have it all the time. She shook it out in her palms and turned to me and I put my face down and had a real good snort, and she squealed and laughed, and Jesus I thought my nose was on fire but then it felt great, and she threw the rest of the handful up in the air so it floated over us, glittering and sparkling in the moonlight, and I realized maybe it was cut with something unusual, to glow like that.

I was so ready for action it didn't even faze me any when she had all her little giggling boys and girls peel off our clothes. If she'd wanted one of those kinky scenes like some of those Hollywood people you hear about, I'd have done everybody, that's how worked up I was. Well, not the boys, naturally. I'm all man, don't get me wrong.

I was just sorry to see that fine suit come off—but, hell, there was no way she could have told that my underwear came from K-Mart.

Then the rest of them flitted off somewhere and it was just her and me on that flowery bed.

Am I going to tell you what it was like? What do you think it was like? Just sheer poetry, that's all. She was smooth and… and she was cold and hot all at the same time, and she seemed like she was made out of moonlight. And, oh, she wanted me.

I must say I didn't think much of the Mister, because she clearly had never had as good a time as I was giving her. Whatever kind of cocaine that was, it gave a man staying power like that Spurious Spanish Fly in the magazines. We could have gone on all night. I'm not sure we didn't.

I'm not sure what all happened, to tell you the truth, because what with the cocaine and that funny beer I'm a little hazy on the way the evening ended. The last clear thing I remember was making too much noise again, so she was stuffing something sweet and cool in my mouth.

But it must have been like a movie, I know.

*　　*　　*

I guess at some point Bobby must have come and warned us that the Mister was coming, and got me up and helped me get my own clothes on and got me out of the house. I don't exactly remember getting back down to my truck—if you want to know the truth, I don't remember it at all, but it must have happened, because the next thing I knew I was waking up in the back of the pickup bed, and the moon was long gone.

So was everybody else.

I sat up, looking around in the washed-out light, feeling stiff in my dirty clothes, and I spit out what was in my mouth—big fat white rosebuds, can you believe it? She must have grabbed them off of a bouquet or something by her bed when I started to yell.

I figured out right then she had only rushed me out of the way so the Mister wouldn't shoot me, so I didn't mind as much as I might have, though I was kind of queasy to think of Bobby getting my pants on me.

And I was real stiff and cold and had a funny hangover, so I had to pull over three or four times to puke on the way back into San Luis Obispo County. I didn't mind that so much, but when it hit me that I'd lost my big break—because I never got her phone number and, well, I'm not sure about how her name is spelled, and anyway movie people have all kinds of security guards and like that to keep people from contacting them, and most of all she might not recognize me not wearing an Armani suit—that's when I started pounding on the steering wheel and calling myself a sorry bastard.

When I got home, Suellen had already left for work, which I would have been grateful for except she'd left one seriously bitchy note telling me to collect my stuff and get the hell out of there before she got back. The way I felt, I didn't care if I never saw her big old butt (she was five years older than me, by the way) again. I cleaned out everything that was mine and I almost took the deck off too, but I'd have had to take it apart to get all that wood in the truck bed and anyway I'm a bigger man than that. Let her be petty if she wants to.

But I wasn't looking forward to telling my folks I was moving back in, because I knew my daddy had filled up my room with tools. When I got to their doublewide they weren't home anyway, and Verbal was sitting on the deck having himself a Coors Lite. I didn't feel like talking much, but he wanted to tell me all about this idea he had for big money, which was to raise pit bull puppies to sell to the folks that run meth labs out of their trailers back in the canyons.

That's how dumb Verbal is, because everybody knows pit bulls don't really keep the federal agents away, and anyhow if you mess with the meth folks they'll kill you, and Verbal always tries to mess with somebody sooner or later. I told him that, being real short with him because I had a bad headache, and he just grinned and pulled out his eight-inch knife and said nobody'd better try to kill him, and I said,

"Those people got guns, you stupid son of a bitch," and he got huffy and left, and I went inside and lay down on my folks' couch.

I could still smell her. I had been so close to getting out of this town.

Well, I will get out. I have lived my dream and I will live it again. All I have to do is raise some cash, and I've got a plan for that. I'll get enough money for a bus ticket down to Hollywood, and if I can't find her, I'll bet I can track down that Bobby. Of course, I have to save up for one of those Armani suits first. How? The secret word is *recycling*.

Did you know you can make good money at that? You can, if you're smart and you work out a system, which I did.

No, listen: the trick is to go out before sunrise on Thursdays, before the recycling trucks come around. People set those open tubs out on the curb and if you're careful and quiet you can help yourself to their aluminum cans! And another good way is to go out Wednesdays, which is when the freebie advertising papers come out, and their delivery people just drop big bundles of them in front of liquor stores and laundromats. You just follow them at a distance, wait until they're gone and pull up fast, then pitch the bundles of papers into the back of your truck and take off. The recycling plants take them no questions asked, and you don't even get your hands dirty.

No, I'm not lazy—that's a lot of work, getting up when it's still dark. Though I like it, kind of; it reminds me of those summer people and especially her, especially when there's some moonlight. And when I get down to Hollywood, you can bet I'll keep late hours! I like that night life.

Well, of course it'd take forever to save up for an Armani suit that way, if that was all I did. But, now, this is the really good part: you take the money they give you at the recycling plant, and *then* you invest in lottery tickets.

See? I am one smooth operator.

How They Tried to Talk
Indian Tony Down

This happened about ten years ago, out at Tobin Farm.

Back in the sixties, somebody bought Tobin Farm for the purposes of holding a renaissance fair there during the summers. Off-seasons it became a kind of commune for the people involved in putting on the fair. They lived modestly in sheds and trailers scattered on a hundred acres of oak wilderness back of the farm, collecting unemployment between fairs.

They had their own communal security force, in case of problems. Twenty-five years on, though, most of the members of the commune were arthritic and bespectacled and never got up to much in the way of trouble, except for domestic disputes or the occasional DUI.

Abby and Martha Caldecott lived at the foot of a hill, some distance from the center of the little community. Abby was into Wicca and Martha wrote romance novels, and during fairs the sisters ran a beer booth. Remote as their trailer was, it was cozily domestic. There were bright geraniums in coffee cans. There was a small lawn and lawn chairs. There were plastic party lights strung from the awning, bright tropical fish. The lights shone out cheerily in the shadow of the hill. It was a dark cold shadow, because the hill was thought to be haunted.

On the night it happened, Abby was washing dishes after supper and Martha was watching an Alfred Hitchcock movie on the VCR (their television reception was oddly sporadic) when they became aware that somebody was up on the hill, whistling.

It was a plaintive whistle, as though somebody was trying to summon a lost dog, and as the sisters conferred they realized the sound had been going on at intervals since that afternoon. It was now pitch dark and past nine at night. Given that, and given the rumors about the hill, the sisters decided not to investigate. Abby made a pan of cocoa and Martha turned up the volume on *The Birds*.

They were sipping cocoa and watching the film when headlights flashed outside.

The sisters sighed and paused their tape. Abby got up and went out to investigate; a pickup truck had pulled into the gravel space beyond the lawn. Killer Mikey was just getting out.

Killer Mikey had been to Nam, a long time ago, and done very bad things there. He was okay now, though his hands still shook sometimes; but because he was familiar with things like radios and Situations, he had been made security chief for the commune. He stood now doubtfully shining his maglight up into the trees, announcing into his radio that he had arrived at the location. Abby asked him what was going on and he asked her if she knew what the whistling was. She told him she didn't, and he told her it was worrying all the people who lived up on Snob Hill, which was the cluster of trailers on the ridge opposite. He had radioed for backup.

As they stood there talking, the whistling came again, and this time right after it a faint little voice cried out Hey, from way far up in the darkness.

Killer Mikey walked backward, shining his light further up, and asked who was up there. After a long moment the voice replied Tony, and Killer Mikey frowned and then said Indian Tony?

Indian Tony was called that because he claimed to have been an Oglala Sioux shaman in a previous life.

Indian Tony affirmed that it was he. Killer Mikey asked him what he was doing up there.

There followed about five minutes of shouted questions and mostly incoherent answers, but the gist of it was: Indian Tony had gone for a hike and got himself lost, and didn't know how to get off the hill.

Killer Mikey told him all he had to do was walk downhill toward his voice.

Indian Tony said he couldn't do that.

Killer Mikey went to his truck, backed it out a few yards and turned on the headlights. There: all Indian Tony had to do was walk downhill toward the lights, okay?

Indian Tony said he couldn't do that either.

As they were trying to hammer out why, Killer Mikey's backup arrived: Jerry Moss, who had taken the call in his truck as he was returning from town with an order of Chinese food. His truck rattled up to the trailer. He parked beside Killer Mikey and jumped out, complaining that his dinner was going to get cold. When Killer Mikey explained the situation, Jerry grew even more irritable and called Indian Tony a white asshole. Jerry happened to be a full-blooded Miwok and Indian Tony was, in fact, white, so neither Abby nor

Killer Mikey argued the point.

By this time Martha gave up on *The Birds* and came out to see what was going on. As they were explaining to her, Indian Tony began to yell for help again. Now there were answering yells from the ridge, and a procession of headlights came bobbing down as more people were drawn to the scene.

Muttering, Jerry got his portable Hi-Beam out of the bed of his truck and shone it up the hill, walking back and forth to see if he could pinpoint Indian Tony's location. When he did, it was immediately obvious why Indian Tony couldn't come down. In the blue-white beam they spotted his tiny pale face peering out from the branches of a madrone, very far up the hill and about fifty feet above the ground.

Jerry cursed and called Indian Tony a jackass. Killer Mikey shouted up to tell Indian Tony they'd keep the light on him so he could climb down.

Indian Tony replied that he couldn't do that. He sounded as though he were crying now.

The people from Snob Hill were arriving by this time, getting out of their trucks and staring up the hill at Indian Tony trapped against the stars. Old Ricker the fiddler, who lived in the trailer next to Indian Tony's, came up to tell the security team that he had seen Indian Tony go out that afternoon wearing his ceremonial regalia (a plains war bonnet replica he'd found at a swap meet), which usually meant that Indian Tony was going on a vision quest. It also generally meant that Indian Tony had dropped acid.

Killer Mikey sighed. Jerry cursed again and clipped the Hi-Beam to the hood ornament of his truck. He got out his carton of chow mein and a pair of chopsticks and climbed up on the hood of the truck to eat. Killer Mikey made a megaphone of his hands and asked Indian Tony if the reason he couldn't climb down was because he was still all messed up.

Indian Tony replied that he couldn't come down because *they* were down there. Martha shook her head and expressed her opinion that Indian Tony was still all messed up, and wondered what they ought to do now?

Nobody wanted to call the sheriff's department, because little incidents like this tended to contribute to the slightly unsavory reputation Tobin Farm had developed over the years. Killer Mikey called up to ask Indian Tony what *they* were and was informed *they* were some kind of animals, man. What kind? He didn't know. What did they look like? They had big pointed ears.

Martha went running back to her trailer and came out with the Roger Tory Peterson *Field Guide to Western Mammals*. Through Killer Mikey's patiently shouted interrogation they built up a gradual description of what Indian Tony thought he was seeing, as Martha paged through the book by the headlights, and at last narrowed the possibilities down to either a lynx, *Lynx canadensis,* or a bobcat, *Lynx rufus.* Then they narrowed it further to bobcat, because Tobin Farm was much too far south for lynxes. The only problem was, Indian Tony insisted that *they* were all white, which bobcats were not; and that he could see three pairs of eyes, though the field guide stated that bobcats were solitary hunters.

Jerry looked up from his chow mein long enough to observe that Indian Tony might be seeing spirit animals, and it would serve the dumb bastard right if a spirit guide chased his white ass up a tree. He added a few crotchety words about people who had the nerve to co-opt other people's sacred stuff, after taking their land away too. Then he flipped his long gray braid back over his shoulder and went on eating.

Killer Mikey nodded sadly and lifted his hands to his mouth again. He told Indian Tony that *they* were probably not really there, and if *they* were *they* were probably just little wild kitties, and if he threw something at *them, they'd* probably go away, so why didn't he just break off a branch and throw it at *them* and then climb down in the light of the Hi-Beam?

Indian Tony said he didn't want to do that.

They argued back and forth for several minutes on the subject, as Martha continued to search through the field guide. Abby asked if anybody would like cocoa and went off to the trailer to make more. Ricker asked Jerry whether or not somebody ought to go up the hill and bring Indian Tony down. Jerry replied that he wasn't about to, because all that undergrowth up there was poison oak. Ricker replied that he thought Native Americans were immune to poison oak. Jerry said like hell they were and told Ricker about the time he'd gone fishing at Rincon and walked through a thicket of it, not seeing the leaves because it was winter, but how even that much exposure had been enough to make his dick swell up like a beer can. Ricker tsked sympathetically.

He was telling Jerry about the time he got itch mites from sitting on an infested hay bale when Killer Mikey at last persuaded Indian Tony to break off a branch and throw it down at whatever it was that had him treed. Everyone there heard the slight crack and then the crash as the branch went down through the underbrush.

RRRrrrAOOM, protested something, sounding seriously Big Cat in nature and quite angry. The sound echoed off the surrounding hills. Everybody froze. Jerry had lifted a big hunk of noodles and bean sprouts halfway to his open mouth, but now they slipped from his chopsticks, plop, on the hood of his truck.

Indian Tony began to gibber and scream. Killer Mikey observed that that had sounded like a goddamn tiger, man. His hands were shaking; not a good sign. Martha wondered if they maybe shouldn't call Animal Control?

Ricker volunteered. He jumped into his VW van and went puttering off in the direction of the phone booth out on Highway 37.

Killer Mikey staggered to his truck and leaned into the cab. He pulled the seat forward and rummaged among the various guns he had back there. Jerry finished his chow mein in a hurry and jumped down. Abby opened the trailer door and stood silhouetted against the light, calling out to know what was going on. Everyone told her to get back inside.

There was a crash up the hill and Indian Tony cried out that *they* were coming up the tree after him.

Jerry grabbed the Hi-Beam and directed it at the tree, and those present could see the distant branches thrashing in a manner that suggested that something really was climbing up from below.

Killer Mikey found his AK-47 and pulled it out, and aimed it up the hill, but his hands were trembling really badly now. Indian Tony, shrieking, was trying to get higher up in the madrone and breaking branches in his efforts. Jerry shouted up to him to stop, to hold on to the trunk with his arms and legs or he'd fall and break his neck. He handed off the Hi-Beam to Martha and pulled a handgun from the glove box of his truck.

Then the Hi-Beam went out. So did the truck lights and the lights at the trailer.

Flash, a second later the madrone was lit again, blue-white as before but not by the Hi-Beam. A column of radiance was stabbing down from the bottom of some kind of black aircraft, hovering just above the hill.

Below, they saw Indian Tony turn his face up, staring in astonishment. He rose, pulled by the light, gliding with a few broken branches upward into the craft. Something fell fluttering down: the war bonnet he'd been wearing.

There was another feline roar, a distinctly disappointed sound. Something very large made a last lunge at Indian Tony and they caught a glimpse of it for a second in the light; and it wasn't any *Lynx rufus*, or *Lynx canadensis*, either, though it was obvious why Indian Tony had been seeing three pairs of eyes.

There followed a moment of shock, in which all persons present quietly decided that they couldn't possibly have seen what they'd just seen.

Killer Mikey blinked rapidly and then took aim again, gamely trying to draw a bead on the aircraft, it being less of an insult to his rational mind. Jerry grabbed his arm and told him not to be an idiot; if the aircraft crashed the Government would be all over the farm, like what happened at Roswell.

Nobody wanted that, of course, because geraniums weren't the only plants grown on the farm. Killer Mikey lowered the gun and they all watched as the aircraft moved slowly off to the north, a darkness silently occluding stars where it passed. Something big was crashing through the woods below, following vainly after it. Gradually the sound died away.

The lights came back on, startling everybody, and Killer Mikey accidentally blasted hell out of Abby's and Martha's lawn chairs. Nobody said anything, though, until Ricker came puttering back and leaned out of his van to announce that the Animal Control Department was sending a unit over as soon as possible. Then he realized they were all staring like zombies and wanted to know what had happened.

Jerry explained that Indian Tony had seriously offended something but that the Star Brothers appeared to have bailed out his sorry ass. Ricker thought that over and announced he was going back to his trailer. It seemed like a good idea. When the Amador County Animal Control Department van crossed the tracks and bumped along the farm's dark rutted access road half an hour later, they couldn't find a soul to direct them. Finally they gave it up and left.

Nobody ever saw Indian Tony again. His disappearance went unreported and, because he had no family or job, unnoticed.

That was the end of the matter, except that the inhabitants of the commune stayed well away from the hill after that. Abby and Martha, in fact, paid Jerry fifty dollars to hook up their trailer to his truck and move them over to the other side of the ridge. Everybody knew what had rescued Indian Tony, but nobody knew what it had rescued him from, and that was a little worrisome.

Abby and Martha liked the new place. There was room to put in a vegetable garden.

Pueblo, Colorado Has the Answers

Marybeth Hatta had survived a lot. Not as much as her parents, certainly; her one failed marriage had ended without drama. The fact that she had been a Customer Serviceperson for a financial institution, and had worked her patient way over years to within inches of the glass ceiling before being laid off when the company was purchased and dismantled for corporate looting—well, that wasn't noteworthy either, given the state of California's economy.

It *had* happened to Marybeth three times in a row, however, over a period of twenty years, and even the girl at the unemployment office had agreed the odds against that were probably high. It looked funny on a resume, too. At the age of forty she found herself with no job, no Wilshire Boulevard apartment, and no prospects at all. Under the circumstances she was grateful to be able to go home to the tiny coastal town where she'd grown up, to do what she'd adamantly refused to do twenty years earlier when her life hadn't been irrelevant: take a job in her parents' store.

Nothing had changed there. Not the stained green linoleum, not the candy display rack with its rolls of tin Lifesavers, not the ceiling fan describing the same wobbling circle it had described since June 1948, not the bright plastic beach toys and bottles of sun lotion. The little town hadn't changed either, with its rusted hotel signs and weatherbeaten cottages. It was lively with tourists on weekends, but by five P.M. on Sunday afternoon you could still fire a shotgun down Pomeroy Street without hitting a living soul. Once it had made her want to scream with frustration; now the permanence of the past was comforting. She had learned that the future, far from being inevitable, sometimes drains away like water vanishing into sand.

So she was the Branch Postmistress in the little store now, selling stamps and weighing envelopes for the year-round population, who were mostly pensioned retirees living in the trailer park on the edges of the dunes. All day she sat behind the humidor cabinet and watched the bright glare of the sea outside, or watched the fog advance or recede between the old pool hall and the secondhand store.

On this particular afternoon her view was occluded for a moment by an old man limping in. The limp identified him for her, because otherwise he looked like most of her customers: past seventy, in a stained nylon windbreaker, wearing a baseball cap pinned with military insignia. He had neither the pink plastic hearing aid nor the reading glasses in black plastic frames that went with the geriatric uniform, however.

"How are you today, Mr. Lynch?" she inquired.

"So-so. Something gave me the runs last night like you wouldn't believe." He smacked an envelope down on the counter and stared at her earnestly.

"Really."

"I think I inhaled some of that bug spray, that's what I think did it," he affirmed.

"Working in your garden?" This one was proud of his garden, she remembered. He had an acre behind his trailer, enclosed by snow fence to keep the dunes from encroaching. He leaned forward now and his voice dropped to a loud whisper.

"Have you ever heard," he wanted to know, "of a bug or a virus or anything that makes the bottom of corn stalks go *soft?*" Wow, his breath was like a crypt. She tried not to draw back involuntarily as she frowned and shook her head.

"Gosh, no. You mean like, rotten or something?"

"Not rotten, no, they're still green and all right—but they're all bent over! Like the stalk went soft and they melted, then got hard again. Damnedest thing I ever saw. You ever heard of that?"

She had, in fact. Her gaze darted momentarily to the rack of magazines with titles like *Paranormal Horizon, Journal of the Unproven* and *Alien Truth!!!* But she blinked and replied "No, I can't imagine what would do that."

"I just thought, you being Japanese and all, you might know. Your father might garden or something." Mr. Hatta didn't garden; he sat on the couch in his black bathrobe doing crossword puzzles. So did Mrs. Hatta, in her pink bathrobe. As far as Marybeth could tell, they had done nothing else since she'd been home. Marybeth smiled apologetically and shook her head.

"Nope. No idea."

"Well, I'll tell you who will know." He reached for his wallet. "U.S. Government will, that's who. You know those commercials they put on about writing to Pueblo, Colorado for free Government information on everything? No? They're on at five a.m. I get up at four-thirty most mornings, earlier when I got the runs like I did, and you can learn a lot from those. I mail this, they'll send me a free booklet on garden pests special for our area—this part of the coast right here. Now, isn't that a deal?"

"Sounds great." She weighed the envelope in her hand. "One stamp ought to do it, Mr. Lynch."

"Okey-doke." He counted out change. "You should write to them, you know. Pueblo, Colorado. People don't know about all the free stuff they're missing out on."

"I'll have to remember to do that." She smiled, peeling off a stamp and fixing it to the envelope.

"There's the Post Office Box number right there." He reached out to tap the address insistently. "You want to copy it down before I mail it?"

"Okay, sure." She took a pen and copied out the address on the back of a scrap of paper. When she had finished, he took the envelope and dropped it through the OVERSEAS—OUT OF STATE slot in the wall.

"She's on her way now, all right," he stated cheerily. "Now, you can sell me a bottle of Milk of Magnesia. The cherry kind."

*   *   *

A week later the fan was still going around and Marybeth was arranging the various needlecraft monthly magazines in their places when Mr. Lynch came through the door. He looked troubled.

"Good morning, Mr. Lynch." She looked up from a cover featuring a particularly hideous hooked rug. "What can I do for you today?"

"Well, I sort of thought—" He waved a booklet at her helplessly. It was printed on newsrag, like a tax form guide. "You remember I sent off to Pueblo, Colorado, for free information on garden pests? Well, they sent it, all right, but I think they must be Army guys wrote it—the language is awful technical. And I remembered your father said you went to College, so I wondered if you couldn't tell me—"

"You want me to look at it for you?" Marybeth returned to her seat behind the humidor and held out her hand for the booklet. She skimmed through it, reading about Artichoke Plume Moths, Meadow Spittlebugs, Corn Earworms and a host of others.

Mr. Lynch shifted uneasily from foot to foot.

"And the problem's getting worse," he told her.

"The diarrhea?" She looked up in mild alarm.

"No, the... the whatever it is. I can't find anything like what's happening to my corn in that book. It's just laying right over."

"Maybe it's jack rabbits." She went on reading.

"No it ain't, because there's no holes under the fence and no tracks. At first I thought it was those God-damned kids, because I caught somebody looking in my window, but then the glowing started."

"Glowing?" She looked up again.

"I don't know, maybe it's phosphorus or something. Maybe it's something to do with the wilt or whatever's bending the stalks. I look out my window last night and a whole row's shining like it was broad daylight. That ain't normal, is it?"

"It doesn't sound normal." She wondered how to phrase her next question. "Um—you haven't heard any funny noises, have you? High-pitched whistling or anything?"

"Well, I'll tell you, I couldn't hear it if there was because there's so God-damned much interference on my radio lately. I think they must be running some big machinery over at that Air Force base. It's driving me nuts."

"Okay." She bit her lower lip. "Maybe that's what's doing it, you know, something electromagnetic? I don't think it's a garden pest in this booklet, Mr. Lynch."

"No? Didn't seem like it to me, but the way it was written I couldn't tell anything. Well, you know what? I'm going to write back to Pueblo, Colorado and tell 'em about this. Maybe it's something to do with rocket testing." He dug in his pocket for his wallet. "So I need you to sell me some stamps and a writing tablet. Another box of envelopes, too."

When he had limped out the door with the paper sack that held his purchases, she went straight to the nearest copy of *Paranormal Horizons* and retired behind the humidor case with it for an hour of uninterrupted reading.

That night she waited until the TV trays had been cleared away and a commercial had interrupted *Jeopardy* to ask: "Daddy, when Grandpa had the truck farm out behind the dunes before the war... did he ever mention anything funny happening to the corn?"

"Didn't grow corn." Her father did not look away from the screen. "We grew peas, artichokes, lettuce and cauliflower. No corn."

"Well... did he ever talk about anything he couldn't explain? Any kind of really strange pests in his fields?"

"No." Mr. Hatta turned his head and the lamplight hit his glasses in such a way that his eyes looked like glowing ovals. He gave a bitter laugh. "Except God-damned G.I.s!"

Jeopardy returned and Alex Trebek saved her from another visit to Manzanar. She sighed and went in to wash the dinner dishes.

*   *   *

The next Saturday dawned bright and hot, but then the wind shifted and a wall of cold fog rolled in, blanketing the town. Tourists retreated, complaining, to their hotel rooms, and discovered they would be charged extra for cable TV. The salt mist beaded on everything. Mr. Lynch's nylon jacket was slick and damp with it when he came in.

"Good morning, Mr. Lynch. How's your garden doing?" she asked. By way of a reply, he laid a thick manila envelope on the top of the humidor.

"Well, they wrote back from Pueblo, Colorado," he told her. "But, you know, I was right—it *is* some Army guy who writes this stuff. They sent me a letter and a thing I'm supposed to fill out. Now I just wondered, since I know you went to College and all, if you couldn't explain this in plain English?"

"Okay." She tipped out the contents of the envelope and unfolded the cover letter. Below the superscription and date it began:

> Dear Mr. Lynch,
> Thank you for your interest in our programs. We received your recent letter describing the unusual problem affecting your Early Golden Wonder Hybrid.
>
> It is our opinion that your plants may be suffering from a condition known as Australian Anthracnose Sclerotinia, which is uncommon but not unknown in the United States, especially in cool coastal areas adjacent to military bases. However, this diagnosis cannot be confirmed without further information.
>
> You may be aware that as an honorably discharged member of our Armed Forces, you are entitled to a number of benefits auxiliary to your pension and medical coverage. Pest control is included among these. If you will take the time to complete the enclosed detailed questionnaire and return it in the enclosed postage-paid envelope, we will endeavor to respond within ten (10) working days from the arrival of your reply.
> Sincerely,
> Lt. John C. Collins
> Dept. of Agricultural Safety

"Agricultural Safety?" Marybeth looked over her glasses at Mr. Lynch.

"That's right. People don't know there's government departments where the Army will do things free for them, but it's true, you know." He nodded his head for emphasis. "Now, I got a pen here—if you wouldn't mind taking a look at the test for me?"

"It's not a test, it's a questionnaire." She unfolded five sheets of closely typed, crudely photocopied paper. She read aloud: *"Please circle either YES or NO after each of the following questions. One. Have any unusual marks appeared on the ground adjacent to the affected plants? These may be fungal blights resembling scorch or burn marks and may be circular in shape, or may appear in a pattern. YES or NO?"*

"Yep, yep, I've had those." Mr. Lynch nodded again.

"Okay." Marybeth took the pen and circled *YES.* *"Two. Have you noticed a continuous high-pitched noise that may or may not be described as trilling, warbling or whistling?"*

There were many more questions of this kind, some of them seemingly repetitive. Mr. Lynch gave his Yes or No answer to each of them and Marybeth circled appropriately, though with a growing sense of unease. Some of the questions really couldn't have any imaginable connection with gardening, and many were of a quite personal nature. They didn't seem to bother Mr. Lynch, however. When the questions had all been answered, Marybeth folded the pages, slipped them into the envelope that had been provided, and sealed it. She stole a quick look at the stamps, half-expecting a franking mark from Langley, Virginia. No; two ordinary stamps celebrating the Lighthouses of America.

"Well, there you go, Mr. Lynch." She gave it to him. "I hope this helps."

"Hey, those guys know what they're doing." He stuck the envelope in *OVERSEAS—OUT OF TOWN*. He seemed relieved, energized. "You know what? I could go for a Hoffman's Cup o' Gold. You restock those yet?"

When he had gone she roamed unhappily up and down the aisles, straightening the magazines on doll collecting, on guns and ammo, on Victorian furniture. Finally she drifted over to the paperback kiosks, and spent a long while perusing them. She found the latest title by Whitley Streiber. She took it back to the humidor cabinet and barely looked up from it the rest of the afternoon.

*   *   *

"Some old guy's got a package," grunted the mail carrier, sliding it across the counter at her. Surf was up and he was anxious to be done with his route for the day.

Marybeth examined it and saw Mr. Lynch's name. "He wasn't home?"

"Nah. I knocked. Left the sticker on his door so he can pick it up here."

The carrier crossed the green linoleum with rapid steps and was out again in the sunlight, in the fresh salt air. Marybeth leaned down and turned the box slowly. It was just big enough to contain a head of lettuce, perhaps, or a jar of candy. It didn't weigh much, nor did it rattle. She looked for a return address. There it was: a Post Office Box in Pueblo, Colorado. She gnawed her lower lip, wondering why Mr. Lynch hadn't answered the mail carrier's knock.

But he limped in an hour later, face alight with anticipation. "My trap here yet?" he wanted to know.

"Is that what it is?" Marybeth reached under the counter and brought it out for him.

"Uh-huh. Got a letter the other day from Pueblo, Colorado saying they were sending it separate." He thrust the yellow delivery slip at her. "Here. Where do I sign for it?"

"Right there. Did they say if they'd figured out what the problem is?"

"Well, as near as I can make out they *think* it's that thing they said in the other letter, and they think it's carried by some kind of—I don't remember what they said it was, bugs or spores or something. One of them Latin names. Anyhow, here's this trap or repellent or whatever it is for me to try on 'em, absolutely free. You have to have an FCC license for it, but they said they'd waive that since I'm a Veteran of Foreign Wars." He completed his wandering signature with effort. "Don't tell *me* this government don't take care of its servicemen!"

"You mean it's electronic?" Marybeth frowned.

"I guess so. They sent instructions with it." He hefted the box and limped toward the door. "I'll let you know how it works!"

"Okay. Good luck, Mr. Lynch," she called after him, craning her head to watch his shadow limp away after him down the sidewalk.

*   *   *

There were gulls circling in the air outside, wheeling and crying, and their shadows danced over the street. An old car pulled up and parked under the swirling cloud of wings, a 1953 BelAir, black and pink, beautifully restored. She nodded in appreciation. A child came in through the doorway, silhouetted against the light, and moved down the aisle toward her. She pulled her attention away from the car and looked down into her own eyes. *Mommie, can I have a U-No Bar?*

Blue school uniform, white Peter Pan collar, saddle oxfords, yes, and there was the pink Barbie purse that had been stolen from her desk in third grade. She heard her mother's voice answering: *You know what your father said about candy. Here, have some raisins.*

Just as the child began to pout, it vanished. She jumped to her feet, staring. The car was gone, too. She felt an urge to make the sign of the cross. But here came Mr. Lynch, limping in haste, and he looked out of breath and upset. She drew on years of Customer Service sangfroid and inquired: "Is anything the matter, Mr. Lynch?"

"Well, that trap don't work, for one," he gasped. "*All* my corn knocked clean over this morning, and these damn things all over the place!" He held up a white sphere. It had a cloudy, frosted-glass quality, like a fist-sized mothball. "All there is in here's a moth! There's bugs and moths and mosquitoes in every damn one of 'em, but they're not the problem. There's tracks now. Looks like some kind of big chicken feet. Say, you got a phone in here?"

Wordlessly she pointed him to the dark oak booth in the corner. He hurried into it and she heard him fumbling around in there, dropping nickels and cursing. After several attempts at dialing he yelled in frustration: "This God-damned phone don't work."

"Yes it does, Mr. Lynch." She went to the door of the booth. "Who are you trying to call?"

"This Eight-Oh-Oh number that came with the instructions." He held out a letter, creased and dogeared from having been in his pocket. She glimpsed the words: —*Temporal Displacement Unit not perform to specifications, please do not hesitate to call us day or night at the following number*—

"Did you dial One first?"

"Are you supposed to?" He stared at her in distraction. On the little hammered steel shelf under the telephone, the white sphere was glowing softly. "Listen, could I ask you to dial?—these God-damned long numbers they got now—"

"Sure, Mr. Lynch." She leaned in and took the receiver from him. "What's the number again?" He read it out to her and she dialed it. Abruptly there was a jarring clang on the other end of the line and the number began ringing. She handed the receiver back to him and walked quickly away.

Trying not to listen to his conversation, she stared at the postal wall. Under the LOCAL slot was a decal of the little cartoon figure the Postal Service had used to convince its customers that zip codes were wonderful, convenient and necessary. The years had not worn away his crazy little smile. Mr. Lynch raised his voice, pulling her attention back. He was waving the sphere as though the person on the other end of the line could see it.

"NOPE. NOPE. YESSIR. I THOUGHT IT WAS ON FIRE. SEE, I—UH HUH. UH-HUH. NO, I DIDN'T. ABOUT THREE INCHES.

NOPE. SEE, I THOUGHT—UH HUH. TWO MONTHS AGO. NO, JUST FLAT DOWN. SEE, WHAT I THOUGHT AT FIRST—UH HUH. YESSIR. YOU WHAT?"

A pair of tourists came in. They bought a *San Francisco Chronicle* and a package of Hostess Honeybuns. They were unpleasantly surprised at the price of the newspaper, but went ahead with the purchase anyway. When they walked out, Marybeth glanced over at the phone booth. Mr. Lynch looked happy now, he was smiling and nodding as he scrawled something on the back of the letter.

"OKAY. RIGHT. OKAY. *RELATIVITY CONDENSER?* WHERE DO I FIND THAT? IT'S WHERE? *WHERE* DID YOU SAY? OH. OKAY." He listened a moment longer and then said, "ALL RIGHT, AND IT'S BEEN A PLEASURE TALKING TO YOU, SIR."

He emerged from the booth, tucking the letter inside his nylon jacket. "I got to go to the market," he told her. "Thanks for your help."

"What did they say about the trap?"

"They think maybe I adjusted it wrong. It's set too small and that's why it's just catching bugs instead of that thing with the chicken feet. Said that's what's carrying the spores, like deer carry that Lyme Tick stuff? They gave me some suggestions, though." He winked at her. "We'll see what's cookin' now!"

He left with an air of importance. Ten minutes later she realized that he'd left the sphere in the phone booth. With some reluctance she retrieved it and walked over to the front window, examining the thing in the light.

Something inside, a vague outline of tiny wings. Yes, that was a moth in there, trapped in a cue ball of etched glass. What happened when you *condensed Relativity?* Was this a sphere of frozen Time? Could you turn Time into a solid so things got trapped in it? It had no unusual coldness now, no glow. She walked slowly back to the humidor cabinet and sat down, thoughtfully turning the sphere in her hands. A customer came in and paced up and down in front of the magazines, looking for something in particular. Marybeth lifted a little square of plywood set into the floor, revealing the squared cavity in cement that had once held her father's safe. She dropped the sphere inside and covered it again.

"Can I help you find something?" she inquired, standing up.

*   *   *

She did not see Mr. Lynch for a week after that. One morning she had just arrived and was unlocking the door when a local customer approached, being tugged along by a Pomeranian in a hurry.

"'Morning, Marybeth!"

"Good morning, Mrs. Foster."

"Say, if those movie people aren't done shooting in your store, do you think they might want to hire any extras? I used to work at RKO back before the war, you know."

She just stared, her hand motionless on the key. "Excuse me?"

"I tell you, it looked just like old times in there! All those beautiful old cars parked along the street outside, too. I saw a De Soto and a Packard just like Jerry used to have. Good-looking kid they had behind the counter—was that Jason Scott Lee?"

"Yes," she said, for no reason she understood.

"I thought so, but I didn't want to get too close. Will they be shooting again tonight?"

She shook her head. Mrs. Foster looked rueful. "Darn. I knew I should have gone home and gotten my autograph book. Well, she who hesitates is lost. Can I get in there and buy an air mail stamp, honey?"

"Certainly, Mrs. Foster." She woke from her trance and pushed the door open, and reversed the hanging sign to let the town know everything was business as usual. It clearly wasn't, but she didn't know what else to do.

After Mrs. Foster had gone, Marybeth did a quick check of the store. Nothing out of the ordinary; no copies of *Look* or *The Saturday Evening Post* on the racks. A succession of octogenarians came in for crossword books, laxatives and cigars. A man in a dark suit and sunglasses came in and bought a souvenir: a plastic snow-globe with sparkles instead of snow, swirling around a tiny plastic treasure chest full of clams.

Shortly before noon Mr. Lynch looked hesitantly around the door. His expression was most odd: scared and elated together. He was carrying a small suitcase.

"Why, Mr. Lynch, what's happened?" She stood up.

"Oh, just having my place exterminated," he said casually. "Got to take a hotel room for a couple of days, that's all." He set the suitcase inside the doorway and looked up and down the street before coming the rest of the way in. "You know that trap I sent off for? I got it to work, finally. Got the little bastard, too. It didn't look like any animal to me—hell, at first I thought it was a circus dwarf or something, but that nice boy from the Government said it was a Giant Rat of Sumatra. It's all froze solid inside one of them glow-balls, only this is a real big one. Took a lot of my corn with it, but I about decided I wasn't going to eat that stuff anyway, not with whatever's wrong with it."

"You mean the—the whatever it is—the trap generated a *big* white sphere."
Marybeth glanced involuntarily at the piece of plywood set in the floor.

"That's what I've been telling you!"

"And it caught something that looked to you like a little man."

"Yep. The boy explained about the trap generating a Temporary Field."
Marybeth wondered if he meant *Temporal.* "Says it's just like that new equipment
that freezes termites. See, those people from Pueblo, Colorado sent some
men out here to see if the trap was working okay. They were right there at
my trailer this morning, right after I got up. They're going to clean it all up for
me, too, even all those bugs I got by mistake. I ask you now, is that thoughtful?
And look at this." He lowered his voice and dug in his pants for his wallet.
"Look here!" He pulled out and fanned three twenty-dollar bills. "That's to
pay for my hotel room. Now, then. Do they know how to treat an old
soldier or do they know how to treat an old soldier?"

The only thing she managed to say was, "I don't think you can get two
nights for sixty dollars at this time of year, Mr. Lynch. Except maybe over at
the Beachcomber."

"The Beachcomber will do me fine," he asserted. "Hell, I don't need the
frills. I need to buy a toothbrush and some toiletries from you, though. They
said I couldn't use mine any more. Too many rodent genes from the
extermination."

"You don't mean *roentgens,* do you?" She thought about the UFO articles
she'd read.

"Yeah! That was it." He looked cheerful. "And I got to go get some
underwear at the Thrift Shop, too."

"O-okay." She helped him find a new toothbrush, as well as a can of
tooth powder and a tube of Burma-Shave, and rang up his purchases on the
cash register. When he had limped out in triumph, she leaned down and lifted
the piece of plywood. The sphere was exactly where she had put it, and it
was not glowing. Another customer came in. She let the plywood drop back
into place.

*   *   *

After she had locked up that night, she walked up Hinds Avenue as far as
the corner of the old state highway, where she could get a good view
south to the edges of the dunes. She saw nothing out of the ordinary, and
didn't know what she'd expected to see: a glowing white sphere the size of
the Hollywood Cinerama Dome, maybe, with scores of hapless trailer park
residents trapped in an eternal *Now* inside? As she walked back down in the

direction of her parent's house, a baby blue 1958 Lincoln Continental zoomed up past her, radio playing loud. It sounded like it was playing "That'll Be The Day." Not the Linda Ronstadt version, though.

*   *   *

After dinner she opened the kitchen drawers and poked through them. "Mom? Don't we have a pair of kitchen tongs?"

"They're in there somewhere." Her mother's voice drifted over the back of the sofa.

She found them at last, and took them to the front hall with a plastic grocery bag. Slipping on a sweater, she reached for her keys.

"Are you going out?" inquired her mother sleepily.

"Just down to the store. I think I left my book."

It was cold on the front porch, and the little figure in flowered pajamas was shivering as she looked up at the stars. She was waiting for one to fall out of the sky, Marybeth remembered; and she almost stepped forward and advised herself to go inside, because the stars would never come within reach. She was not a cruel woman by nature, however, so she just stared fixedly at the child until she vanished, and then moved carefully past the place where she had been, down the steps into the street.

Kon-Tiki Liquors was still open as she crossed the street, but the red and yellow neon beer signs were being shut off one by one. The rest of the town was dark and silent. She experienced a peculiar disappointment as she came around the corner and found her parent's store as dark and silent as the rest. Well, better safe than sorry. She unlocked it, stepped inside and turned to lock the door behind her.

When she turned back, the counter was bathed in daylight, and her young father (God, he *had* looked like Jason Scott Lee) was having a conversation with a stranger in a red Hawaiian shirt.

Man, oh, man, they must have been going a hundred miles an hour, the stranger was moaning. Her father was nodding in agreement. *And they say he probably couldn't even see them in the dusk. Believe you me, that is one dangerous intersection even in broad daylight.* He stubbed out a cigarette under the counter. She drew a deep breath and edged past them. Her father barely glanced at her. *Honey, the new issues of* Holiday Magazine *came in.*

"Okay. Thanks," she said, guessing that the ball of concentrated Time was doing more than warping the temporal flow around itself; Past and Present were becoming interactive. She leaned down to prize up the square of plywood. The sphere was glowing in there like a light bulb. She reached in with the kitchen tongs and pulled it out, and dropped it into the grocery bag. It flickered and went out, and when it did the daylight vanished and she was alone in the darkness of the store.

Out on Pomeroy Street again, she paused and wondered what to do next. After considering a number of possibilities, she walked over two blocks to the empty lot where the C-Air Motor Hotel had been before it burned down in 1966. A rusted standpipe protruded from a patch of cracked pink tiles there, nearly hidden by weeds. Using the tongs, she dropped the sphere into the pipe. She heard it rattling down into darkness. She dropped the tongs in after it and then wadded up the plastic bag and jammed that in too. Maybe the lead in the pipe would somehow shield against the temporal distortion. Or not; maybe it was an iron pipe. In any case, there was nothing she could do about it now. She walked home quickly and washed her hands as soon as she got in.

In the morning, she noticed that her watch was running backward. She replaced the battery when she got to the store, but it made no difference. Finally she turned it upside down and wore it that way.

The next time she saw Mr. Lynch, he looked crestfallen. He shuffled toward her down the aisle, clutching an envelope.

"You got any alarm clocks here?"

"Hi, Mr. Lynch. No, but Bob's Hardware has them. Did those people finish fumigating your trailer?" she inquired.

"What? Oh. Oh, yeah. It was too bad, though—I lost the whole garden." He blinked. Was he on the point of tears?

"Well, you probably wouldn't have wanted to eat anything from that crop anyway, you said so yourself," she reminded him.

"Yeah, but all my topsoil's gone too. There's a big round hole now, must be eight feet deep. The boy from the Government said it was Geologic Subsidence. Said it didn't have anything to do with the other problem. Gave me some good advice, though." He nodded somberly and waved the envelope. "I can get free clean fill dirt. All I got to do is write to this Post Office Box in Pueblo, Colorado."

*　　*　　*

As the summer wore on, there were occasional reports of odd occurrences—somebody thought they saw a ghost in the Elks Lodge, and the instances of red tides causing phosphorescence in the surf increased. There were more surfers with old-style longboards in the water, and more little boys with crewcuts playing on the beach—but Retro was In these days, wasn't it? And the occasional sightings of classic cars, gleaming as if lovingly restored, caused nothing but sentimental pleasure for the witnesses.

She was still a little uneasy about what she'd done with the sphere, but its effect seemed weak and dissipated. No phantom C-Air Motor Hotel rose from the weeds and at least Hatta's News, Cigars and Sundries was no longer the center of the phenomena.

And, really, how could it hurt business? Don't people come to little seaside towns to stop Time, to pretend they'll never grow old or haven't grown old, to relive a summer afternoon forgotten thirty years?

Marybeth went on working in the store, going home to fix dinner for her parents each night. She put a radio behind the counter, tuned to an oldies station, and hummed along as she waited on customers or arranged new stock on the shelves. The older customers complained bitterly about the God-damned Rock and Roll, and she'd apologize at once and turn the volume down until they left the store. Sometimes the news broadcasts mentioned the wrong President, but not often enough to draw attention. Secure, with a watch resolutely running backward, Marybeth Hatta was really rather happy. The past was pleasant at least. You have to live somewhere, after all.

Mother Aegypt

"Speak sweetly to the Devil, until
you're both over the bridge."
Transylvanian proverb

I n a country of mad forests and night, there was an open plain, and pitiless sunlight.

A man dressed as a clown was running for his life across the plain.

A baked-clay track, the only road for miles, reflected the sun's heat and made the man sweat as he ran along it. He was staggering a little as he ran, for he had been running a long while and he was fat, and the silken drawers of his clown costume had begun to work their way down his thighs. It was a particularly humiliating costume, too. It made him look like a gigantic dairymaid.

His tears, of terror and despair, ran down with his sweat and streaked the clown-white, graying his big mustache; the lurid crimson circles on his cheeks had already run, trickling pink down his neck. His straw-stuffed bosom had begun to slip, too, working its way down his dirndl, and now it dropped from beneath his petticoat like a stillbirth. Gasping, he halted to snatch it up, and peered fearfully over his shoulder.

No sign of his pursuers yet; but they were mounted and must catch up with him soon, on this long straight empty plain. There was no cover anywhere, not so much as a single tree. He ran on, stuffing his bosom back in place, whimpering. Gnats whined in his ears.

Then, coming over a gentle swell of earth, he beheld a crossroads. There was his salvation!

A team of slow horses drew two wagons, like the vardas of the Romanies but higher, and narrower, nor were they gaily painted in any way. They were black as the robe of scythe-bearing Death. Only: low, small and ominous, in white paint in curious antiquated letters, they bore the words: *MOTHER AEGYPT*.

The man wouldn't have cared if Death himself held the reins. He aimed himself at the hindmost wagon, drawing on all his remaining strength, and pelted on until he caught up with it.

For a moment he ran desperate alongside, until he was able to gain the front and haul himself up, over the hitch that joined the two wagons. A moment he poised there, ponderous, watching drops of his sweat fall on hot iron. Then he crawled up to the door of the rear wagon, unbolted it, and fell inside.

The driver of the wagons, hooded under that glaring sky, was absorbed in a waking dream of a place lost for millennia. Therefore she did not notice that she had taken on a passenger.

*   *   *

The man lay flat on his back, puffing and blowing, too exhausted to take much note of his surroundings. At last he levered himself up on his elbows, looking about. After a moment he scooted into a sitting position and pulled off the ridiculous lace milkmaid's cap, with its braids of yellow yarn. Wiping his face with it, he muttered a curse.

In a perfect world, he reflected, there would have been a chest of clothing in this wagon, through which he might rummage to steal some less conspicuous apparel. There would, at least, have been a pantry with food and drink. But the fates had denied him yet again; this was nobody's cozy living quarters on wheels. This wagon was clearly used for storage, holding nothing but boxes and bulky objects wrapped in sacking.

Disgusted, the man dug in the front of his dress and pulled out his bosom. He shook it by his ear and smiled as he heard the *clink-clink*. The gold rings were still there, some of the loot with which he'd been able to escape.

The heat within the closed black box was stifling, so he took off all his costume but for the silken drawers. Methodically he began to search through the wagon, opening the boxes and unwrapping the parcels. He chuckled.

He knew stolen goods when he saw them.

Some of it had clearly been lifted from Turkish merchants and bureaucrats: rolled and tied carpets, tea services edged in gold. But there were painted ikons here too, and family portraits of Russians on wooden panels. Austrian crystal bowls. Chased silver ewers and platters. Painted urns. A whole umbrella-stand of cavalry sabers, some with ornate decoration, some plain and ancient, evident heirlooms. Nothing was small enough to slip into a pocket, even if he had had one, and nothing convenient to convert into ready cash.

Muttering, he lifted out a saber and drew it from its scabbard.

As he did so, he heard the sound of galloping hooves. The saber dropped from his suddenly nerveless fingers. He flattened himself against the door, pointlessly, as the hoofbeats drew near and passed. He heard the shouted questions. He almost—not quite—heard the reply, in a woman's voice pitched very low. His eyes rolled, searching the room for any possible hiding place. None at all; unless he were to wrap his bulk in a carpet, like Cleopatra.

Yet the riders passed on, galloped ahead and away. When he realized that he was, for the moment, safe, he collapsed into a sitting position on the floor.

After a moment of listening to his heart thunder, he picked up the saber again.

*   *   *

It was night before the wagon halted at last, rumbling over rough ground as it left the road. He was still crouched within, cold and cramped now. Evidently the horses were unhitched, and led down to drink at a stream; he could hear splashing. Dry sticks were broken, a fire was lit. He thought of warmth and food. A light footfall approached, followed by the sound of someone climbing up on the hitch. The man tensed.

The door opened.

There, silhouetted against the light of the moon, was a small pale spindly-looking person with a large head. A wizened child? It peered into the wagon, uncertainty in its big rabbitlike eyes. There was a roll of something—another carpet?—under its arm.

"Hah!" The man lunged, caught the other by the wrist, hauling him in across the wagon's threshold. Promptly the other began to scream, and he screamed like a rabbit too, shrill and unhuman. He did not struggle, though; in fact, the man had the unsettling feeling he'd grabbed a ventriloquist's dummy, limp and insubstantial within its mildewed clothes.

"Shut your mouth!" the man said, in the most terrifying voice he could muster. "I want two things!"

But his captive appeared to have fainted. As the man registered this, he also became aware that a woman was standing outside the wagon, seeming to have materialized from nowhere, and she was staring at him.

"Don't kill him," she said, in a flat quiet voice.

"Uh—I want two things!" the man repeated, holding the saber to his captive's throat. "Or I'll kill him, you understand?"

"Yes," said the woman. "What do you want?"

The man blinked, licked his lips. Something about the woman's matter-of-fact voice disturbed him.

"I want food, and a suit of clothes!"

The woman's gaze did not shift. She was tall, and dark as a shadow, even standing in the full light of the moon, and simply dressed in black.

"I'll give you food," she replied. "But I haven't any clothing that would fit you."

"Then you'd better get me some, hadn't you?" said the man. He made jabbing motions with the saber. "Or I'll kill your little… your little…." He tried to imagine what possible relationship the creature under his arm might have with the woman. Husband? Child?

"Slave," said the woman. "I can buy you a suit in the next village, but you'll have to wait until morning. Don't kill my slave, or I'll make you sorry you were ever born."

"Oh, you will, will you?" said the man, waving the saber again. "Do you think I believe in Gypsy spells? You're not dealing with a village simpleton, here!"

"No," said the woman, in the same quiet voice. "But I know the police are hunting you. Cut Emil's throat, and you'll see how quickly I can make them appear."

The man realized it might be a good idea to change strategies. He put his head on one side, grinning at her in what he hoped was a charmingly roguish way.

"Now, now, no need for things to get nasty," he said. "After all, we're in the same trade, aren't we? I had a good look around in here." He indicated the interior of the wagon with a jerk of his head. "Nice racket you've got, fencing the big stuff. You don't want me to tell the police about it, while I'm being led away, do you?"

"No," said the woman.

"No, of course not. Let's be friends!" The man edged forward, dragging his captive—Emil, had she called him?—along. "Barbu Golescu, at your service. And you'd be Madam…?"

"Amaunet," she said.

"Charmed," said Golescu. "Sure your husband hasn't a spare pair of trousers he can loan me, Madam Amaunet?"

"I have no husband," she replied.

"Astonishing!" Golescu said, smirking. "Well then, dear madam, what about loaning a blanket until we can find me a suit? I'd hate to offend your modesty."

"I'll get one," she said, and walked away.

He stared after her, momentarily disconcerted, and then put down the saber and flexed his hand. Emil remained motionless under his other arm.

"Don't you get any ideas, little turnip-head," muttered Golescu. "Hey!

Don't get any ideas, I said. Are you deaf, eh?"

He hauled Emil up by his collar and looked at him critically. Emil whimpered and turned his face away. It was a weak face. His head had been shaved at one time, and the hair grown back in scanty and irregular clumps.

"Maybe you *are* deaf," conceded Golescu. "But your black mummy loves you, eh? What a useful thing for me." He groped about and found a piece of cord that had bound one of the carpets. "Hold still or I'll wring your wry neck, understand?"

"You smell bad," said Emil, in a tiny voice.

"Bah! You stink like carpet-mold, yourself," said Golescu, looping the cord about Emil's wrist. He looped the other end about his own wrist and pulled it snug. "There, so you can't go running away. We're going to be friends, you see? You'll get used to me soon enough."

He ventured out on the hitch and dropped to the ground. His legs were unsteady and he attempted to lean on Emil's shoulder, but the little man collapsed under him like so much cardboard.

"She doesn't use you for cutting wood or drawing water much, does she?" muttered Golescu, hitching at his drawers. Amaunet came around the side of the wagon and handed him the blanket, without comment.

"He's a flimsy one, your slave," Golescu told her. "What you need is a man to help with the business, if you'll pardon my saying so." He wrapped his vast nakedness in the blanket and grinned at her.

Amaunet turned and walked away from him.

"There's bread and tomatoes by the fire," she said, over her shoulder.

*   *   *

Clutching the blanket around him with one hand and dragging Emil with the other, Golescu made his way to the fire. Amaunet was sitting perfectly still, watching the flames dance, and only glanced up at them as they approached.

"That's better," said Golescu, settling himself down and reaching for the loaf of bread. He tore off a hunk, sopped it in the saucepan of stewed tomatoes and ate ravenously. Emil, still bound to his wrist and pulled back and forth when he moved, had gone as limp and unresponsive as a straw figure.

"So," said Golescu, through a full mouth, "No husband. Are you sure you don't need help? I'm not talking of bedroom matters, madame, you understand; perish the thought. I'm talking about security. So many thieves and murderers in this wicked old world! Now, by an astounding coincidence,

I need a way to get as far as I can from the Danube, and *you* are headed north. Let's be partners for the time being, what do you say?"

Amaunet's lip curled. Contempt? But it might have been a smile.

"Since you mention it," she said, "Emil's no good at speaking to people. I don't care to deal with them, much, myself. The police said you were with a circus; do you know how to get exhibition permits from petty clerks?"

"Of course I do," said Golescu, with a dismissive gesture. "The term you're looking for is *advance man*. Rely on me."

"Good." Amaunet turned her gaze back to the fire. "I can't pay you, but I'll lie for you. You'll have room and board."

"And a suit of clothes," he reminded her.

She shrugged, in an affirmative kind of way.

"It's settled, then," said Golescu, leaning back. "What business are we in? Officially, I mean?"

"I tell people their futures," said Amaunet.

"Ah! But you don't look like a Gypsy."

"I'm not a Gypsy," she said, perhaps a little wearily. "I'm from Egypt."

"Just so," he said, laying his finger beside his nose. "The mystic wisdom of the mysterious east, eh? Handed down to you from the ancient pharaohs. Very good, madame, that's the way to impress the peasants."

"You know a lot of big words, for a clown," said Amaunet. Golescu winced, and discreetly lifted a corner of the blanket to scrub at his greasepaint..

"I am obviously not a real clown, madame," he protested. "I am a victim of circumstances, calumny and political intrigue. If I could tell you my full story, you'd weep for me."

She grinned, a brief white grin so startling in her dark still face that he nearly screamed.

"I doubt it," was all she said.

*   *   *

He kept Emil bound to him that night, reasoning that he couldn't completely trust Amaunet until he had a pair of trousers. Golescu made himself comfortable on the hard floor of the wagon by using the little man as a sort of bolster, and though Emil made plaintive noises now and then and did in fact smell quite a lot like moldy carpet, it was nothing that couldn't be ignored by a determined sleeper.

Only once Golescu woke in the darkness. Someone was singing, out there in the night; a woman was singing, full-throated under the white moon. There was such throbbing melancholy in her voice Golescu felt tears stinging his eyes; yet there was an indefinable menace too, in the harsh and unknown syllables of her lament. It might have been a lioness out there, on the prowl. He thought briefly of opening the door to see if she wanted comforting, but the idea sent inexplicable chills down his spine. He snorted, rolled on his back and slept again.

Golescu woke when the wagons lurched back into motion, and stared around through the dissipating fog of vaguely lewd dreams. Sunlight was streaming in through cracks in the plank walls. Though his dreams receded, certain sensations remained. He sat upright with a grunt of outrage and looked over his own shoulder at Emil, who had plastered himself against Golescu's backside.

"Hey!" Golescu hauled Emil out. "What are you, a filthy sodomite? You think because I wear silk, I'm some kind of Turkish fancy boy?"

Emil whimpered and hid his face in his hands. "The sun," he whispered.

"Yes, it's daylight! You're scared of the sun?" demanded Golescu.

"Sun hurts," said Emil.

"Don't be stupid, it can't hurt you," said Golescu. "See?" He thrust Emil's hand into the nearest wavering stripe of sunlight. Emil made rabbity noises again, turning his face away and squeezing his eyes shut, as though he expected his hand to blister and smoke.

"See?" Golescu repeated. But Emil refused to open his eyes, and Golescu released his hand in disgust. Taking up the saber, he sliced through the cord that bound them. Emil promptly curled into himself like an angleworm and lay still, covering his eyes once more. Golescu considered him, setting aside the saber and rubbing his own wrist.

"If you're a *vampyr,* you're the most pathetic one I've ever heard of," he said. "What's she keep you around for, eh?"

Emil did not reply.

*   *   *

Some time after midday, the wagons stopped; about an hour later, the door opened and Amaunet stood there with a bundle of clothing.

"Here," she said, thrusting it at Golescu. Her dead stare fell on Emil, who cringed and shrank even further into himself from the flood of daylight. She removed one of her shawls and threw it over him, covering him completely. Golescu, pulling on the trousers, watched her in amusement.

"I was just wondering, madame, whether I should maybe get myself a crucifix to wear around our little friend, here," he said. "Or some bulbs of garlic?"

"He likes the dark," she replied. "You owe me three piastres for that suit."

"It's not what I'm accustomed to, you know," he said, shrugging into the shirt. "Coarse-woven stuff. Where are we?"

"Twenty kilometers farther north than we were yesterday," she replied.

Not nearly far enough, Golescu considered uneasily. Amaunet had turned her back on him while he dressed. He found himself studying her body as he buttoned himself up. With her grim face turned away, it was possible to concede that the rest of her was lovely. Only in the very young could bodily mass defy gravity in such a pert and springy-looking manner. How old *was* she?

When he had finished pulling on his boots, he stood straight, twirled the ends of his mustaches and sucked in his gut. He drew one of the gold rings from his former bosom.

"Here. Accept this, my flower of the Nile," said Golescu, taking Amaunet's hand and slipping the ring on her finger. She pulled her hand away at once and turned so swiftly the air seemed to blur. For a moment there was fire in her eyes, and if it was more loathing than passion, still, he had gotten a reaction out of her.

"Don't touch me," she said.

"I'm merely paying my debt!" Golescu protested, pleased with himself. "Charming lady, that ring's worth far more than what you paid for the suit."

"It stinks," she said in disgust, snatching the ring off.

"Gold can afford to smell bad," he replied. His spirits were rising like a balloon.

*   *   *

Uninvited, he climbed up on the driver's seat beside her and the wagons rolled on, following a narrow river road through its winding gorge.

"You won't regret your kindness to me, dear madam," said Golescu. "A pillar of strength and a fountain of good advice, that's me. I won't ask about your other business in the wagon back there, as Discretion is my middle name, but tell me: what's your fortunetelling racket like? Do you earn as much as you could wish?"

"I cover my operating expenses," Amaunet replied.

"Pft!" Golescu waved his hand. "Then you're clearly not making what you deserve to make. What do you do? Cards? Crystal ball? Love potions?"

"I read palms," said Amaunet.

"Not much overhead in palm reading," said Golescu, "But on the other hand, not much to impress the customers either. Unless you paint them scintillating word-pictures of scarlet and crimson tomorrows, or warn them of terrifying calamity only *you* can help them avoid, yes? And, you'll excuse me, but you seem to be a woman of few words. Where's your glitter? Where's your flash?"

"I tell them the truth," said Amaunet.

"Ha! The old, 'I-am-under-an-ancient-curse-and-can-only-speak-the-truth' line? No, no, dear madam, that's been done to death. I propose a whole new approach!" said Golescu.

Amaunet just gave him a sidelong look, unreadable as a snake.

"Such as?"

"Such as I would need to observe your customary clientele before I could elaborate on," said Golescu.

"I see," she said.

"Though *Mother Aegypt* is a good name for your act," Golescu conceded. "Has a certain majesty. But it implies warmth. You might work on that. Where's your warmth, eh?"

"I haven't got any," said Amaunet. "And you're annoying me, now."

"Then, *taceo*, dear madame. That's Latin for 'I shall be quiet,' you know."

She curled her lip again.

Silent, he attempted to study her face, as they jolted along. She must be a young woman; her skin was smooth, there wasn't a trace of gray in her hair or a whisker on her lip. One could say of any ugly woman, *Her nose is hooked,* or *Her lips are thin,* or *Her eyes are too close together.* None of this could be said of Amaunet. It was indeed impossible to say anything much; for when Golescu looked closely at her he saw only shadow, and a certain sense of discord.

*   *   *

They came, by night, to a dismal little town whose slumped and rounded houses huddled with backs to the river, facing the dark forest. After threading a maze of crooked streets, they found the temporary camp for market fair vendors: two bare acres of open ground that had been a cattle pen most recently. It was still redolent of manure. Here other wagons were drawn up, and fires burned in iron baskets. The people who made their livings offering rides on painted ponies or challenging all comers to games of skill stood about the fires, drinking from bottles, exchanging news in weary voices.

Yet when Amaunet's wagons rolled by they looked up only briefly, and swiftly looked away. Some few made gestures to ward off evil.

"You've got quite a reputation, eh?" observed Golescu. Amaunet did not reply. She seemed to have barely noticed.

Golescu spent another chilly night on the floor in the rear wagon—alone this time, for Emil slept in a cupboard under Amaunet's narrow bunk when he was not being held hostage, and Amaunet steadfastly ignored all Golescu's hints and pleasantries about the value of shared body warmth. As a consequence, he was stiff and out of sorts by the time he emerged next morning.

Overnight, the fair had assumed half-existence. A blind man, muscled like a giant, cranked steadily at the carousel, and thin pale children rode round and round. A man with a barrel-organ cranked steadily too, and his little monkey sat on his shoulder and watched the children with a diffident eye. But many of the tents were still flat, in a welter of ropes and poles. A long line of bored vendors stood attendance before a town clerk, who had set up his permit office under a black parasol.

Golescu was staring at all this when Amaunet, who had come up behind him silent as a shadow, said:

"Here's your chance to be useful. Get in line for me."

"Holy Saints!" Golescu whirled around. "Do you want to frighten me into heart failure? Give a man some warning."

She gave him a leather envelope and a small purse instead. "Here are my papers. Pay the bureaucrat and get my permit. You won't eat tonight, otherwise."

"You wouldn't order me around like this if you knew my true identity," Golescu grumbled, but he got into line obediently.

The town clerk was reasonably honest, so the line took no more than an hour to wind its way through. At last the man ahead of Golescu got his permit to sell little red-blue-and-yellow paper flags, and Golescu stepped up to the table.

"Papers," said the clerk, yawning.

"Behold." Golescu opened them with a flourish. The clerk squinted at them.

"Amaunet Kematef," he recited. "Doing business as 'Mother Aegypt.' A Russian? And this says you're a woman."

"They're not my papers, they're—they're my wife's papers," said Golescu, summoning an outraged expression. "And she isn't Russian, my friend, she *is* a hot-blooded Egyptian, a former harem dancer if you must know, before an unfortunate accident that marred her exotic beauty. I found her starving in the gutters of Cairo, and succored her out of Christian charity. Shortly, however, I discovered her remarkable talent for predicting the future based on an ancient system of—"

"A fortune-teller? Two marks," said the clerk. Golescu paid, and as the clerk wrote out the permit he went on:

"The truth of the matter is that she was the only daughter of a Coptic nobleman, kidnapped at an early age by ferocious—"

"Three marks extra if this story goes on any longer," said the clerk, stamping the permit forcefully.

"You have my humble gratitude," said Golescu, bowing deeply. Pleased with himself, he took the permit and strutted away.

"Behold," he said, producing the permit for Amaunet with a flourish. She took it without comment and examined it. Seen in the strong morning light, the indefinable grimness of her features was much more pronounced. Golescu suppressed a shudder and inquired, "How else may a virile male be of use, my sweet?"

Amaunet turned her back on him, for which he was grateful. "Stay out of trouble until tonight. Then you can mind Emil. He wakes up after sundown."

She returned to the foremost black wagon. Golescu watched as she climbed up, and was struck once more by the drastically different effect her backside produced on the interested spectator.

"Don't you want me to beat a drum for you? Or rattle a tambourine or something? I can draw crowds for you like a sugarloaf draws flies!"

She looked at him, with her white grimace that might have been amusement. "I'm sure you can draw flies," she said. "But I don't need an advertiser for what I do."

Muttering, Golescu wandered away through the fair. He cheered up no end, however, when he discovered that he still had Amaunet's purse.

Tents were popping up now, bright banners were being unfurled, though they hung down spiritless in the heat and glare of the day. Golescu bought himself a cheap hat and stood around a while, squinting as he sized up the food vendors. Finally he bought a glass of tea and a fried pastry, stuffed with plums, cased in glazed sugar that tasted vaguely poisonous. He ate it contentedly and, licking the sugar off his fingers, wandered off the fairground to a clump of trees near the river's edge. There he stretched out in the shade and, tilting his hat over his face, went to sleep. If one had to babysit a *vampyr* one needed to get plenty of rest by day.

*   *   *

By night the fair was a different place. The children were gone, home in their beds, and the carousel raced round nearly empty but for spectral riders; the young men had come out instead. They roared with laughter and shoved one another, or stood gaping before the little plank stages where the exhibitions were cried by mountebanks. Within this tent were remarkable freaks of nature; within this one, an exotic dancer plied her trade; within another was a man who could handle hot iron without gloves. The lights were bright and fought with shadows. The air was full of music and raucous cries.

Golescu was unimpressed.

"What do you mean, it's too tough?" he demanded. "That cost fifteen groschen!"

"I can't eat it," whispered Emil, cringing away from the glare of the lanterns.

"Look." Golescu grabbed up the ear of roasted corn and bit into it. "Mm! Tender! Eat it, you little whiner."

"It has paprika on it. Too hot." Emil wrung his hands.

"Ridiculous," said Golescu through a full mouth, munching away. "It's the food of the gods. What the hell *will* you eat, eh? I know! You're a *vampyr*, so you want blood, right? Well, we're in a slightly public place at the moment, so you'll just have to make do with something else. Taffy apple, eh? Deep fried sarmale? Pierogi? Pommes Frites?"

Emil wept silently, tears coursing from his big rabbit-eyes, and Golescu sighed and tossed the corn cob away. "Come on," he said, and dragged the little man off by one hand.

They made a circuit of all the booths serving food before Emil finally consented to try a Vienna sausage impaled on a stick, dipped in corn batter and deep-fried. To Golescu's relief he seemed to like it, for he nibbled at it uncomplainingly as Golescu towed him along. Golescu glanced over at Amaunet's wagon, and noted a customer emerging, pale and shaken.

"Look over there," Golescu said in disgust. "One light. No banners, nobody calling attention to her, nobody enticing the crowds. And one miserable customer waiting, look! That's what she gets. Where's the sense of mystery? She's *Mother Aegypt*! Her other line of work must pay pretty well, eh?"

Emil made no reply, deeply preoccupied by his sausage-on-a-spike.

"Or maybe it doesn't, if she can't do any better for a servant than you. Where's all the money go?" Golescu wondered, pulling at his mustache. "Why's she so sour, your mistress? A broken heart or something?"

Emil gave a tiny shrug and kept eating.

"I could make her forget whoever it was in ten minutes, if I could just get her to take me seriously," said Golescu, gazing across at the wagon. "And the best way to do that, of course, is to impress her with money. We need a scheme, turnip-head."

"Four thousand and seventeen," said Emil.

"Huh?" Golescu turned to stare down at him. Emil said nothing else, but in his silence the cry of the nearest hawker came through loud and clear:

"Come on and take a chance, clever ones! Games of chance, guess the cards, throw the dice, spin the wheel! Or guess the number of millet-grains in the jar and win a cash prize! Only ten groschen a guess! *You* might be the winner! You, sir, with the little boy!"

Golescu realized the hawker was addressing him. He looked around indignantly.

"He is not my little boy!"

"So he's your uncle, what does it matter? Take a guess, why don't you?" bawled the hawker. "What have you got to lose?"

"Ten groschen," retorted Golescu, and then reflected that it was Amaunet's money. "What the hell."

He approached the gaming booth, pulling Emil after him. "What's the cash prize?"

"Twenty thousand lei," said the hawker. Golescu rolled his eyes.

"Oh, yes, I'd be able to retire on *that*, all right," he said, but dug in his pocket for ten groschen. He cast a grudging eye on the glass jar at the back of the counter, on its shelf festooned with the new national flag and swags of bunting. "You've undoubtedly got rocks hidden in there, to throw the volume off. Hm, hm, all right... how many grains of millet in there? I'd say..."

"Four thousand and seventeen," Emil repeated. The hawker's jaw dropped. Golescu looked from one to the other of them. His face lit up.

"That's the right answer, isn't it?" he said. "Holy saints and patriarchs!"

"No, it isn't," said the hawker, recovering himself with difficulty.

"It is so," said Golescu. "I can see it in your eyes!"

"No, it isn't," the hawker insisted.

"It is so! Shall we tip out the jar and count what's in there?"

"No, and anyway you hadn't paid me yet—and anyway it was your little boy, not you, so it wouldn't count anyway—and—"

"Cheat! Shall I scream it aloud? I've got very good lungs. Shall I tell the world how you've refused to give this poor child his prize, even when he guessed correctly? Do you really want—"

"Shut up! Shut up, I'll pay the damned twenty thousand lei!" The hawker leaned forward and clapped his hand over Golescu's mouth. Golescu smiled at him, the points of his mustaches rising like a cockroach's antennae.

Wandering back to Amaunet's wagon, Golescu jingled the purse at Emil. "Not a bad night's work, eh? I defy her to look at this and fail to be impressed."

Emil did not respond, sucking meditatively on the stick, which was all that was left of his sausage.

"Of course, we're going to downplay your role in the comedy, for strategic reasons," Golescu continued, peering around a tent and scowling at the wagon. There was a line of customers waiting now, and while some were clearly lonely women who wanted their fortunes told, a few were rather nasty-looking men, in fact rather criminal-looking men, and Golescu had the uneasy feeling he might have met one or two of them in a professional context at some point in his past. As he was leaning back, he glanced down at Emil.

"I think we won't interrupt her while she's working just yet. Gives us more time to concoct a suitably heroic and clever origin for this fine fat purse, eh? Anyway, she'd never believe that *you*—" Golescu halted, staring at Emil. He slapped his forehead in a gesture of epiphany.

"Wait a minute, wait a minute! She *knows* about this talent of yours! That's why she keeps you around, is it? Ha!"

He was silent for a moment, but the intensity of his regard was such that it penetrated even Emil's self-absorption. Emil looked up timidly and beheld Golescu's countenance twisted into a smile of such ferocious benignity that the little man screamed, dropped his stick and covered his head with both hands.

"My dear shrinking genius!" bellowed Golescu, seizing Emil up and clasping him in his arms. "Puny friend, petite brother, sweetest of *vampyrs!* Come, my darling, will you have another sausage? No? Polenta? Milk punch? Hot chocolate? Golescu will see you have anything you want, pretty one. Let us go through the fair together."

The purse of twenty thousand lei was considerably lighter by the time Golescu retreated to the shadows under the rear wagon, pulling Emil after him. Emil was too stuffed with sausage and candy floss to be very alert, and he had a cheap doll and a pinwheel to occupy what could be mustered of his attention. Nonetheless, Golescu drew a new pack of cards from his pocket, broke the seal and shuffled them, looking at Emil with lovingly predatory eyes.

"I have heard of this, my limp miracle," crooned Golescu, making the cards snap and riffle through his fat fingers. "Fellows quite giftless as regards social graces, oh yes, in some cases so unworldly they must be fed and diapered like babies. And yet, they have a brilliance! An unbelievable grasp of systems and details! Let us see if you are one such prodigy, eh?"

An hour's worth of experimentation was enough to prove to Golescu's satisfaction that Emil was more than able to count cards accurately; if a deck was even fanned before his face for a second, he could correctly identify all the cards he had glimpsed.

"And now, dear boy, only one question remains," said Golescu, tossing the deck over his shoulder into the night. The cards scattered like dead leaves. "Why hasn't Madame Amaunet taken advantage of your fantastic abilities to grow rich beyond the dreams of avarice?"

Emil did not reply.

"Such a perfect setup. I can't understand it," persisted Golescu, leaning down to peer at the line stretching to the door of the forward wagon. A woman had just emerged, wringing her hands and sobbing. Though the fairground had begun to empty out now, there were still a few distinct thugs waiting their turn to… have their fortunes told? It seemed unlikely. Three of them seemed to be concealing bulky parcels about their persons.

"With a lucky mannekin like you, she could queen it at gambling houses from Monte Carlo to St. Petersburg," mused Golescu. "In fact, with a body like hers, she could be the richest whore in Rome, Vienna or Budapest. If she wore a mask, that is. Why, then, does she keep late hours fencing stolen spoons and watches for petty cutthroats? Where's the money in that? What does she want, Emil, my friend?"

"The Black Cup," said Emil.

*   *   *

When the last of the thugs had gone his way, Amaunet emerged from the wagon and looked straight at Golescu, where he lounged in the shadows. He had been intending to make an impressive entrance, but with the element of surprise gone he merely waved at her sheepishly.

"Where's Emil?" demanded Amaunet.

"Safe and sound, my queen," Golescu replied, producing Emil and holding him up by the scruff of his neck. Emil, startled by the light, yelled feebly and covered his eyes. "We had a lovely evening, thank you."

"Get to bed," Amaunet told Emil. He writhed from Golescu's grip and darted into the wagon. "Did you feed him?" she asked Golescu.

"Royally," said Golescu. "And how did I find the wherewithal to do that, you ask? Why, with *this*." He held up the purse of somewhat less than twenty thousand lei and clinked it at her with his most seductive expression. To his intense annoyance, her eyes did not brighten in the least.

"Fetch the horses and hitch them in place. We're moving on tonight," she said.

Golescu was taken aback. "Don't you want to know where I got all this lovely money?"

"You stole it?" said Amaunet, taking down the lantern from its hook by the door and extinguishing it.

"I never!" cried Golescu, genuinely indignant. "I won it for you, if you must know. Guessing how many grains of millet were in a jar."

He had imagined her reaction to his gift several times that evening, with several variations on her range of emotion. He was nonetheless unprepared for her actual response of turning, swift as a snake, and grabbing him by the throat.

"How did you guess the right number?" she asked him, in a very low voice.

"I'm extraordinarily talented?" he croaked, his eyes standing out of his head.

Amaunet tightened her grip. "It was Emil's guess, wasn't it?"

Golescu merely nodded, unable to draw enough breath to speak.

"Were you enough of a fool to take him to the games of chance?"

Golescu shook his head. She pulled his face close to her own.

"If I ever catch you taking Emil to card-parlors or casinos, I'll kill you. Do you understand?"

She released him, hurling him back against the side of the wagon. Golescu straightened, gasped in air, pushed his hat up from his face and said:

"All right, so I discovered his secret. Does Madam have any objections to my asking why the hell she isn't using our little friend to grow stinking rich?"

"Because Emil doesn't have a secret," Amaunet hissed. "He *is* a secret."

"Oh, that explains everything," said Golescu, rubbing his throat.

"It had better," said Amaunet. "Now, bring the horses."

Golescu did as he was told, boiling with indignation and curiosity, and also with something he was barely able to admit to himself. It could not be said, by any stretch of the imagination, that Amaunet was beautiful in her wrath, and yet....

Something about the pressure of her fingers on his skin, and the amazing strength of her hands... and the scent of her breath up close like that, like some unnamable spice....

"What strange infatuation enslaves my foolish heart?" he inquired of the lead horse, as he hitched it to the wagon-tongue.

*   *   *

They traveled all the rest of the moonless night, along the dark river, and many times heard the howling of wolves, far off in the dark forest.

Golescu wove their cries into a fantasy of heroism, wherein he was possessed of an immense gun and discharged copious amounts of shot into a pack of ferocious wolves threatening Amaunet, who was so grateful for the timely rescue she... she threw off her disguise, and most of her clothing too, and it turned out that she'd been wearing a fearsome mask all along. She was actually beautiful, though he couldn't quite see how beautiful, because every time he tried to fling himself into her arms he kept tangling his feet in something, which seemed to be pink candy-floss someone had dropped on the fairground....

And then the pink strands became a spiderweb and Emil was a fly caught there, screaming and screaming in his high voice, which seemed odd considering Emil was a *vampyr*. "Aren't they usually the ones who do the biting?" he asked Amaunet, but she was sprinting away toward the dark river, which was the Nile, and he sprinted after her, pulling his clothing off as he went too, but the sun was rising behind the pyramids....

Golescu sat up with a snort, and shielded his eyes against the morning glare.

"We've stopped," he announced.

"Yes," said Amaunet, who was unhitching the horses. They seemed to have left the road in the night; they were now in a forest clearing, thickly screened on all sides by brush.

"You're camping here," Amaunet said. "I have an appointment to keep. You'll stay with the lead wagon and watch Emil. I should be gone no more than three days."

"But of course," said Golescu, stupid with sleep. He sat there rubbing his unshaven chin, watching her lead the horses out of sight through the bushes. He could hear water trickling somewhere near at hand. Perhaps Amaunet was going to bathe in a picturesque forest pool, as well as water the horses?

He clambered down from the seat and hurried after her, moving as silently as he could, but all that rewarded his stealthy approach was the sight of Amaunet standing by the horses with her arms crossed, watching them drink from a stream. Golescu shuddered. Strong morning light was really not her friend.

Sauntering close, he said:

"So what does the little darling eat, other than sausages and candy?"

"Root vegetables," said Amaunet, not bothering to look at him. "Potatoes and turnips, parsnips, carrots. He won't eat them unless they're boiled and mashed, no butter, no salt, no pepper. He'll eat any kind of bread if the crusts are cut off. Polenta, but again, no butter, no salt. He'll drink water."

"How obliging of him," said Golescu, making a face. "Where'd you find our tiny friend, anyway?"

Amaunet hesitated a moment before replying. "An asylum," she said.

"Ah! And they had no idea what he was, did they?" said Golescu. She turned on him, with a look that nearly made him wet himself.

"And *you* know what he is?" she demanded.

"Just—just a little idiot savant, isn't it so?" said Golescu. "Clever at doing sums. Why you're not using his big white brain to get rich, I can't imagine; but there it is. Is there anything else Nursie ought to know about his care and feeding?"

"Only that I'll hunt you down and kill you if you kidnap him while I'm gone," said Amaunet, without raising her voice in the slightest yet managing to convince Golescu that she was perfectly sincere. It gave him another vaguely disturbing thrill.

"I seek only to be worthy of your trust, my precious one," he said. "Where are you going, anyway?"

"That's none of your business."

"To be sure," he agreed, bowing and scraping. "And you're taking the rear wagon, are you? One can't help wondering, my black dove of the mysteries, whether this has anything to do with all the loot hidden back there. Perhaps you have a rendezvous with someone who'll take it off your hands, eh?"

Her look of contempt went through him like a knife, but he knew he'd guessed correctly.

*   *   *

The first thing Golescu did, when he was alone, was to go into Amaunet's wagon and explore.

Though his primary object was money, it has to be admitted he went first to what he supposed to be her underwear drawer. This disappointed him, for it contained instead what seemed to be alchemist's equipment: jars of powdered minerals and metals, bowls, alembics and retorts. All was so spotlessly clean it might never have been used. When he found her underwear at last, in a trunk, he was further disappointed. It was plain utilitarian stuff; evidently Amaunet didn't go in for frills. Nevertheless, he slipped a pair of her drawers into his breast pocket, like a handkerchief, and continued his search.

No money at all, nor any personal things that might give him any clue to her history. There were a few decorative items, obviously meant to give an Egyptian impression to her customers: a half-size mummy case of papier-mâché. A hanging scroll, hieroglyphs printed on cloth, of French manufacture.

No perfumes or cosmetics by the washbasin; merely a bar of yellow soap. Golescu sniffed it and recoiled; no fragrance but lye. Whence, then, that intoxicating whiff of not-quite-cinnamon on her skin?

No writing desk, no papers. There was something that might have been intended for writing, a polished box whose front opened out flat to reveal a dull mirror of green glass at its rear. It was empty. Golescu gave it no more than a cursory glance. After he'd closed it, he rubbed the fingertips of his hand together, for they tingled slightly.

Not much in the larder: dry bread, an onion, a few potatoes. Several cooking pots and a washing copper. Golescu looked at it thoughtfully, rubbing his chin.

"But no money," he said aloud.

He sat heavily on her bed, snorting in frustration. Hearing a faint squeak of protest, he rose to his feet again and looked down. "Yes, of course!" he said, and opened the drawer under the bed. Emil whimpered and rolled away from the light, covering his face with his hands.

"Hello, don't mind me," said Golescu, scooping him out. He got down on his hands and knees, ignoring Emil's cries, and peered into the space. "Where does your mistress keep her gold, my darling? Not in here, eh? Hell and Damnation."

He sat back. Emil attempted to scramble past him, back into the shadows, but he caught the little man by one leg.

"Emil, my jewel, you'll never amount to much in this world if you can't walk around in the daytime," he said. "And you won't be much use to me, either. What's your quarrel with the sun, anyway?"

"It burns my eyes," Emil wept.

"Does it?" Golescu dragged him close, prized down his hands and looked into his wet eyes. "Perhaps there's something we can do about that, eh? And once we've solved that problem...." His voice trailed off, as he began to smile. Emil wriggled free and vanished back into the drawer. Golescu slid it shut with his foot.

"Sleep, potato-boy," he said, hauling himself to his feet. "Don't go anyplace, and dear Uncle Barbu will be back with presents this afternoon."

Humming to himself, he mopped his face with Amaunet's drawers, replaced them in his pocket, and left the wagon. Pausing only to lock its door, he set off for the nearest road.

*　　*　　*

It took him a while to find a town, however, and what with one thing and another it was nearly sundown before Golescu came back to the wagon.

He set down his burdens—one large box and a full sack—and unlocked the door.

"Come out, little Emil," he said, and on receiving no reply he clambered in and pulled the drawer open. "Come out of there!"

"I'm hungry," said Emil, sounding accusatory, but he did not move.

"Come out and I'll boil you a nice potato, eh? It's safe; the sun's gone down. Don't you want to see what I got you, ungrateful thing?"

Emil came unwillingly, as Golescu backed out before him. He stepped down from the door, looking around, his tiny weak mouth pursed in suspicion. Catching sight of the low red sun, he let out a shrill cry and clapped his hands over his eyes.

"Yes, I lied," Golescu told him. "but just try *these*—" He drew from his pocket a pair of blue spectacles and, wrenching Emil's hands away, settled them on the bridge of his nose. They promptly fell off, as Emil's nose was far too small and thin to keep them up, and they only had one earpiece anyway.

Golescu dug hastily in the sack he had brought and drew out a long woolen scarf. He cut a pair of slits in it, as Emil wailed and jigged in front of him. Clapping the spectacles back on Emil's face and holding them in place a moment with his thumb, he tied the scarf about his head like a blindfold and widened the slits so the glass optics poked through.

"Look! Goggles!" he said. "So you're protected, see? Open your damned eyes, you baby!"

Emil must have obeyed, for he stood still suddenly, dropping his hands to his sides. His mouth hung open in an expression of feeble astonishment.

"But, wait!" said Golescu. "There's more!" He reached into the sack again and brought out a canvas coachman's duster, draping it around Emil's shoulders. It had been made for someone twice Emil's size, so it reached past his knees, indeed it trailed on the ground; and Golescu had a difficult three minutes' labor working Emil's limp arms through the sleeves and rolling the cuffs up. But, once it had been painstakingly buttoned, Emil stood as though in a tent.

"And the crowning touch—" Golescu brought from the sack a wide-brimmed felt hat and set it on Emil's head. Golescu sat back to admire the result.

"Now, don't you look nice?" he said. Emil in fact looked rather like a mushroom, but his mouth had closed. "You see? You're protected from the sun. The *vampyr* may walk abroad by day. Thanks are in order to good old Uncle Barbu, eh?"

"I want my potato," said Emil.

"Pah! All right, let's feast. We've got a lot of work to do tonight," said Golescu, taking up the sack and shaking it meaningfully.

Fairly quickly he built a fire and set water to boil for Emil's potato. He fried himself a feast indeed from what he had brought: rabbit, bacon and onions, and a jug of wine red as bull's blood to wash it down. The wine outlasted the food by a comfortable margin. He set it aside and lit a fine big cigar as Emil dutifully carried the pans down to the stream to wash them.

"*Good* slave," said Golescu happily, and blew a smoke ring. "A man could get used to this kind of life. When you're done with those, bring out the laundry-copper. I'll help you fill it. And get some more wood for the fire!"

When Emil brought the copper forth they took it to the stream and filled it; then carried it back to the fire, staggering and slopping, and set it to heat. Golescu drew from the sack another of his purchases, a three-kilo paper bag with a chemist's seal on it. Emil had been gazing at the bright fire, his vacant face rendered more vacant by the goggles; but he turned his head to stare at the paper bag.

"Are we making the Black Cup?" he asked.

"No, my darling, we're making a golden cup," said Golescu. He opened the bag and dumped its contents into the copper, which had just begun to steam. "Good strong yellow dye, see? We'll let it boil good, and when it's mixed—" he reached behind him, dragging close the box he had brought. He opened it, and the firelight winked in the glass necks of one hundred and forty-four little bottles. "And when it's cooled, we'll funnel it into these. Then we'll sell them to the poultry farmers in the valley down there."

"Why?" said Emil.

"As medicine," Golescu explained. "We'll tell them it'll grow giant chickens, eh? That'll fill the purse of twenty thousand lei back up again in no time. This never fails, believe me. The dye makes the yolks more yellow, and the farmers think that means the eggs are richer. Ha! As long as you move on once you've sold all your bottles, you can pull this one anywhere."

"Medicine," said Emil.

"That's right," said Golescu. He took a final drag on his cigar, tossed it into the fire, and reached for the wine jug.

"What a lovely evening," he said, taking a drink. "What stars, eh? They make a man reflect, indeed they do. At times like this, I look back on my career and ponder the ironies of fate. I was not always a vagabond, you see.

"No, in fact, I had a splendid start in life. Born to a fine aristocratic family, you know. We had a castle. Armorial devices on our stained glass windows. Servants just to walk the dog. None of that came to me, of course; I was a younger son. But I went to University, graduated with full honors, was brilliant in finance.

"I quickly became Manager of a big important bank in Bucharest. I had a fine gold watch on a chain, and a desk three meters long, and it was kept well polished, too. Every morning when I arrived at the bank, all the clerks would line up and prostrate themselves as I walked by, swinging my cane. My cane had a diamond set in its end, a diamond that shone in glory like the rising sun.

"But they say that abundance, like poverty, wrecks you; and so it was with me. My nature was too trusting, too innocent. Alas, how swiftly my downfall came! Would you like to hear the circumstances that reduced me to the present pitiable state in which you see me?"

"...What?" said Emil. Golescu had another long drink of wine.

"Well," he said, "My bank had a depositor named Ali Pasha. He had amassed a tremendous fortune. Millions. Millions in whatever kind of currency you could imagine. Pearls, rubies, emeralds too. You should have seen it just sitting there in the vault, winking like a dancing girl's... winky parts. Just the biggest fortune a corrupt bureaucrat could put together.

"And then, quite suddenly, he had to go abroad to avoid a scandal. And, bam! He was killed in a tragic accident when his coal-black stallion, startled by a pie wagon, threw him from its back and trampled him under its hooves..

"Being an honest man, I of course began searching for his next of kin, as soon as I heard the news of his demise. And you would think, wouldn't you, that he'd have a next of kin? The way those lustful fellows carry on with all their wives and concubines? But it was revealed that the late Ali Pasha had had an equally tragic accident in his youth, when he'd attracted the attention of the Grand Turk because of his sweet singing voice, and, well... he was enabled to keep that lovely soprano until the time of his completely unexpected death.

"So no wives, no children, a yawning void of interested posterity.

"And this meant, you see, that the millions that lay in our vault would, after the expiration of a certain date, become the property of the Ottoman Empire.

"What could I do? The more I reflected on the tyranny under which our great nation suffered for so long, the more my patriotic blood began to boil.

I determined on a daring course of action.

"I consulted with my colleagues in the international banking community, and obtained the name of an investor who was known far and wide for his integrity. He was a Prussian, as it happened, with a handsome personal fortune. I contacted him, apologized for my presumption, explained the facts of the case, and laid before him a proposition. If he were willing to pose as the brother of the late Ali Pasha, I could facilitate his claim to the millions sitting there on deposit. He would receive forty per cent for his part in the ruse; the remaining sixty per cent I would, of course, donate to the Church.

"To make a long story short, he agreed to the plan. Indeed, he went so far as to express his enthusiastic and principled support for Romanian self-rule.

"Of course, it was a complicated matter. We had to bribe the law clerks and several petty officials, in order that they might vouch for Smedlitz (the Prussian) being a long-lost brother of Ali Pasha, his mother having been kidnapped by Barbary Coast pirates with her infant child and sold into a harem, though fortunately there had been a birthmark by which the unfortunate Ali Pasha could be posthumously identified by his sorrowing relation.

"And Smedlitz was obliged to provide a substantial deposit in order to open an account in a bank in Switzerland, into which the funds could be transferred once we had obtained their release. But he agreed to the expenditure readily—too readily, as I ought to have seen!" Golescu shook his head, drank again, wiped his mustache with the back of his hand and continued:

"How I trusted that Prussian! Alas, you stars, look down and see how an honest and credulous soul is victimized."

He drank again and went on:

"The fortune was transferred, and when I went to claim the agreed-upon sixty per cent for charity—imagine my horror on discovering that Smedlitz had withdrawn the entire amount, closed the account, and absconded! As I sought him, it soon became apparent that Smedlitz was more than a thief—he was an impostor, a lackey of the international banking community, who now closed ranks against me.

"To make matters worse, who should step forward but a new claimant! It developed that Ali Pasha had, in fact, a real brother who had only just learned of his death, having been rescued from a remote island where he had been stranded for seven years, a victim of shipwreck.

"My ruin was complete. I was obliged to flee by night, shaming my illustrious family, doomed to the life of an unjustly persecuted fugitive." Golescu wiped tears from his face and had another long drink. "Never again to sit behind a polished desk, like a gentleman! Never again to flourish my walking-stick over the heads of my clerks! And what has become of its diamond, that shone like the moon?" He sobbed for breath. "Adversity makes a man wise, not rich, as the saying goes; and wisdom is all I own now. Sometimes I think of self-destruction; but I have not yet sunk so low."

He drank again, belched, and said, in a completely altered voice:

"Ah, now it's beginning to boil! Fetch a long stick and give it a stir, Emil darling."

*   *   *

Golescu woke in broad daylight, grimacing as he lifted his face from the depths of his hat. Emil was still sitting where he had been when Golescu had drifted off to sleep, after some hours of hazily remembered conversation. The empty jug sat where Golescu had left it; but the hundred and forty-four little glass bottles were now full.

"What'd you…." Golescu sat up, staring at them. He couldn't recall filling the bottles with concentrated yellow dye, but there they were, all tidily sealed.

"The medicine is ready," said Emil.

Golescu rose unsteadily. The empty copper gleamed, clean as though it were new.

"No wonder she keeps you around," he remarked. "You must be part kitchen fairy, eh? Poke up the fire, then, and we'll boil you another potato. Maybe a parsnip too, since you've been such a good boy. And then, we'll have an adventure."

He picked up the sack and trudged off to attend to his toilet.

*   *   *

Two hours later they were making their way slowly along a country lane, heading for a barred gate Golescu had spotted. He was sweating in the heat, dressed in the finest ensemble the rag shop had had to offer: a rusty black swallowtail coat, striped trousers, a black silk hat with a strong odor of corpse. On his left breast he had assembled an impressive-looking array of medals, mostly religious ones dressed up with bits of colored ribbon, and a couple of foil stickers off a packet of Genoa biscuits. In one hand he carried a heavy-looking satchel.

Emil wore his duster, goggles and hat, and was having to be led by the hand because he couldn't see very well.

When they came within a hundred yards of the gate, two immense dogs charged and collided with it, barking at them through the bars.

"Take the bag," said Golescu, handing it off to Emil.

"It's heavy," Emil complained.

"Shut up. Good morning to you, my dear sir!" He raised his voice to address the farmer who came out to investigate the commotion.

"I'm too hot."

"Shut up, I said. May I have a moment of your time, sir?"

"Who the hell are you?" asked the farmer, seizing the dogs by their collars.

Golescu tipped his hat and bowed. "Dr. Milon Cretulescu, Assistant Minister of Agriculture to Prince Alexandru, may all the holy saints and angels grant him long life. And you are?"

"Buzdugan, Iuliu," muttered the farmer.

"Charmed. You no doubt have heard of the new edict?"

"Of course I have," said Farmer Buzdugan, looking slightly uneasy. "Which one?"

Golescu smiled at him. "Why, the one about increasing poultry production on the farms in this region. His highness is very concerned that our nation become one of the foremost chicken-raising centers of the world! Perhaps you ought to chain up your dogs, dear sir."

When the dogs had been confined and the gate unbarred, Golescu strode through, summoning Emil after him with a surreptitious shove as he passed. Emil paced forward blindly, with tiny careful steps, dragging the satchel. Golescu ignored him, putting a friendly hand on Buzdugan's shoulder.

"First, I'll need to inspect your poultry yard. I'm certain you passed the last inspection without any difficulties, but, you know, standards are being raised nowadays."

"To be sure," agreed Buzdugan, sweating slightly. In fact, there had never been any inspection of which he was aware. But he led Golescu back to the bare open poultry yard, an acre fenced around by high palings, visible through a wire-screen grate.

It was not a place that invited lingering. Poultry yards seldom are. The sun beat down on it mercilessly, so that Golescu felt the hard-packed earth burning through the thin soles of his shoes. A hundred chickens stood about listlessly, quite unbothered by the reek of their defecation or the smell of the predators impaled on the higher spikes of the fence: two foxes and something so shrunken and sun-dried its species was impossible to identify.

"*Hmmm*," said Golescu, and drew from his pocket a small book and a pencil stub. He pretended to make notes, shaking his head.

"What's the matter?" asked Buzdugan.

"Well, I don't want to discourage you too much," said Golescu, looking up with a comradely smile. "Good pest control, I'll say that much for you. Make an example of them, eh? That's the only way foxes will ever learn. But, my friend! How spiritless your birds are! Not exactly fighting cocks, are they? Why aren't they strutting about and crowing? Clearly they are enervated and weak, the victims of diet."

"They get nothing but the best feed!" protested Buzdugan. Smiling, Golescu waved a finger under his nose.

"I'm certain they do, but is that enough? Undernourished fowl produce inferior eggs, which produce feeble offspring. Not only that, vapid and tasteless eggs can ruin your reputation as a first-class market supplier. No, no; inattention to proper poultry nutrition has been your downfall."

"But—"

"Fortunately, I can help you," said Golescu, tucking away the book and pencil stub.

"How much will I have to pay?" asked Buzdugan, sagging.

"Sir! Are you implying that a representative of his highness the prince can be bribed? That may have been how things were done in the past, but we're in a new age, after all! I was referring to Science," Golescu admonished.

"Science?"

"Boy!" Golescu waved peremptorily at Emil, who had just caught up with them. "This loyal subject requires a bottle of Golden Formula Q."

Emil did nothing, so Golescu grabbed the satchel from him. Opening it, he drew forth a bottle of the yellow dye. He held it up, cradling it between his two hands.

"This, dear sir, is a diet supplement produced by the Ministry of Agriculture. Our prince appointed none but university-trained men, ordering them to set their minds to the problem of improving poultry health. Utilizing the latest scientific discoveries, they have created a tonic of amazing efficacy! *Golden Formula Q.* Used regularly, it produces astonishing results."

Buzdugan peered at the bottle. "What does it do?"

"Do? Why, it provides the missing nourishment your birds so desperately crave," said Golescu. "Come, let me give you a demonstration. Have you a platter or dish?"

When a tin pan had been produced, Golescu adroitly let himself into the chicken yard, closely followed by Buzdugan. Within the yard it was, if possible, even hotter. "Now, observe the behavior of your birds, sir," said Golescu, uncorking the bottle and pouring its contents into the pan. "The poor things perceive instantly the restorative nature of Golden Formula Q. They hunger for it! Behold."

He set the pan down on the blistering earth. The nearest chicken to notice turned its head. Within its tiny brain flashed the concept: THIRST. It ran at once to the pan and drank greedily. One by one, other chickens had the same revelation, and came scrambling to partake of lukewarm yellow dye as though it were chilled champagne.

"You see?" said Golescu, shifting from one foot to the other. "Poor starved creatures. Within hours, you will begin to see the difference. No longer will your egg yolks be pallid and unwholesome, but rich and golden! All thanks to Golden Formula Q. Only two marks a bottle."

"They *are* drinking it up," said Buzdugan, watching in some surprise. "I suppose I could try a couple of bottles."

"Ah! Well, my friend, I regret to say that Golden Formula Q is in such limited supply, and in such extreme demand, that I must limit you to one bottle only," said Golescu.

"What? But you've got a whole satchel full," said Buzdugan. "I saw, when you opened it."

"That's true, but we must give your competitors a chance, after all," said Golescu. "It wouldn't be fair if you were the only man in the region with prize-winning birds, would it?"

The farmer looked at him with narrowed eyes. "Two marks a bottle? I'll give you twenty-five marks for the whole satchel full, what do you say to that?"

"Twenty-five marks?" Golescu stepped back, looking shocked. "But what will the other poultry producers do?"

Buzdugan told him what the other poultry producers could do, as he dug a greasy bag of coin from his waistband.

*   *   *

They trudged homeward that evening, having distributed several satchels' worth of Golden Formula Q across the valley. Golescu had a pleasant sense of self-satisfaction and pockets heavy with wildly assorted currency.

"You see, dear little friend?" he said to Emil. "This is the way to make something of yourself. Human nature flows along like a river, never changes; a wise man builds his mill on the banks of that river, lets foibles and vanities drive his wheel. Fear, greed and envy have never failed me."

Emil, panting with exhaustion, made what might have been a noise of agreement.

"Yes, and hasn't it been a red-letter day for you? You've braved the sunlight at last, and it's not so bad, is it? Mind the path," Golescu added, as Emil walked into a tree. He collared Emil and set his feet back on the trail.

"Not far now. Yes, Emil, how lucky it was for you that I came into your life. We will continue our journey of discovery tomorrow, will we not?"

*   *   *

And so they did, ranging over to the other side of the valley, where a strong ammoniac breeze suggested the presence of more chicken farms. They had just turned from the road down a short drive, and the furious assault of a mastiff on the carved gate had just drawn the attention of a scowling farmer, when Emil murmured: "Horse."

"No, it's just a big dog," said Golescu, raising his hat to the farmer. "Good morning, dear sir! Allow me to introduce—"

That was when he heard the hoofbeats. He began to sweat, but merely smiled more widely and went on: "—myself. Dr. Milon Cretulescu, of the Ministry of Agriculture, and I—"

The hoofbeats came galloping up the road and past the drive, but just as Golescu's heart had resumed its normal rhythm, they clattered to a halt and started back.

"—have been sent at the express wish of Prince Alexandru himself to—"

"Hey!"

"Excuse me a moment, won't you?" said Golescu, turning to face the road. He beheld Farmer Buzdugan urging his horse forward, under the drooping branches that cast the drive into gloom.

"Dr. Cretulescu!" he said. "Do you have any more of that stuff?"

"I beg your pardon?"

"You know, the—" Buzdugan glanced over at the other farmer, lowered his voice. "That stuff that makes the golden eggs!"

"Ah!" Golescu half-turned, so the other farmer could see him, and raised his voice. "You mean, *Golden Formula Q*? The miracle elixir developed by his highness's own Ministry of Agriculture, to promote better poultry production?"

"Shush! Yes, that! Look, I'll pay—"

"*Golden eggs*, you say?" Golescu cried.

"What's that?" The other farmer leaned over his gate.

"None of your damn business!" said Buzdugan.

"But, dear sir, *Golden Formula Q* was intended to benefit everyone," said Golescu, uncertain just what had happened but determined to play his card. "If this good gentleman wishes to take advantage of its astonishing qualities, I cannot deny him—"

"A hundred marks for what you've got in that bag!" shouted Buzdugan.

"What's he got in the bag?" demanded the other farmer, opening his gate and stepping through.

"Golden Formula Q!" said Golescu, grabbing the satchel from Emil's nerveless hand and opening it. He drew out a bottle and thrust it up into the morning light. "Behold!"

"What was that about golden eggs?" said the other farmer, advancing on them.

"Nothing!" Buzdugan said. "Two hundred, Doctor. I'm not joking. Please."

"The worthy sir was merely indulging in hyperbole," said Golescu to the other farmer. "Golden eggs? Why, I would never make that claim for Golden Formula Q. You would take me for a mountebank! But it is, quite simply, the most amazing dietary supplement for poultry you will ever use."

"Then, I want a bottle," said the other farmer.

Buzdugan gnashed his teeth. "I'll buy the rest," he said, dismounting.

"Not so fast!" said the other farmer. "This must be pretty good medicine, eh? If you want it all to yourself? Maybe I'll just buy two bottles."

"Now, gentlemen, there's no need to quarrel," said Golescu. "I have plenty of Golden Formula Q here. Pray, good Farmer Buzdugan, as a satisfied customer, would you say that you observed instant and spectacular results with Golden Formula Q?"

"Yes," said Buzdugan, with reluctance. "Huge eggs, yellow as gold. And all the roosters who drank it went mad with lust, and this morning all the hens are sitting on clutches like little mountains of gold. Two hundred and fifty for the bag, Doctor, what do you say, now?"

*   *   *

Golescu carried the satchel on the way back to the clearing, for it weighed more than it had when they had set out that morning. Heavy as it was, he walked with an unaccustomed speed, fairly dragging Emil after him. When they got to the wagon, he thrust Emil inside, climbed in himself and closed the door after them. Immediately he began to undress, pausing only to look once into the satchel, as though to reassure himself. The fact that it was filled to the top with bright coin somehow failed to bring a smile to his face.

"What's going on, eh?" he demanded, shrugging out of his swallowtail coat. "I sold that man bottles of yellow dye and water. Not a *real* miracle elixir!"

Emil just stood there, blank behind his goggles, until Golescu leaned over and yanked them off.

"I said, we sold him fake medicine!" he said. "Didn't we?"

Emil blinked at him. "No," he said. "Medicine to make giant chickens."

"No, you silly ass, that's only what we *told* them it was!" said Golescu, pulling off his striped trousers. He wadded them up with the coat and set them aside. "We were lying, don't you understand?"

"No," said Emil.

Something in the toneless tone of his voice made Golescu, in the act of pulling up his plain trousers, freeze. He looked keenly at Emil.

"You don't understand lying?" he said. "Maybe you don't. And you're a horrible genius, aren't you? And I went to sleep while the stuff in the copper was cooking. Hmmm, hm hm." He fastened his trousers and put on his other coat, saying nothing for a long moment, though his gaze never left Emil's slack face.

"Tell me, my pretty child," he said at last. "Did you put other things in the brew, after I was asleep?"

"Yes," said Emil.

"What?"

In reply, Emil began to rattle off a string of names of ingredients, chemicals for the most part, or so Golescu assumed. He held up his hand at last.

"Enough, enough! The nearest chemist's is three hour's walk away. How'd you get all those things?"

"There," said Emil, pointing at the papier-mâché mummy case. "And some I got from the dirt. And some came out of leaves."

Golescu went at once to the mummy case and opened it. It appeared to be empty; but he detected the false bottom. Prizing back the lining he saw rows of compartments, packed with small jars and bags of various substances. A faint scent of spice rose from them.

"Aha," he said, closing it up. He set it aside and looked at Emil with narrowed eyes. He paced back and forth a couple of times, finally sitting down on the bed.

"How did you know," he said, in a voice some decibels below his customary bellow, "what goes into a medicine to make giant chickens?"

Emil looked back at him. Golescu beheld a strange expression in the rabbity eyes. Was that... scorn?

"I just know," said Emil, and there might have been scorn in his flat voice too.

"Like you just know how many beans are in a jar?"

"Yes."

Golescu rubbed his hands together, slowly. "Oh, my golden baby," he said. "Oh, my pearl, my plum, my good-luck token." A thought struck him. "Tell me something, precious," he said. "On several occasions, now, you have mentioned a Black Cup. What would that be, can you tell your Uncle Barbu?"

"I make the Black Cup for her every month," said Emil.

"You do, eh?" said Golescu. "Something to keep the babies away? But no, she's not interested in love. Yet. What happens when she drinks from the Black Cup, darling?"

"She doesn't die," said Emil, with just a trace of sadness.

Golescu leaned back, as though physically pushed. "Holy saints and angels in Heaven," he said. For a long moment ideas buzzed in his head like a hive of excited bees. At last he calmed himself to ask;

"How old is Madame Amaunet?"

"She is old," said Emil.

"Very old?"

"Yes."

"How old are you?"

"I don't know."

"I see." Golescu did not move, staring at Emil. "So that's why she doesn't want any attention drawn to you. You're her philosophers' stone, her source of the water of life. Yes? But if that's the case...." He shivered all over, drew himself up. "No, that's crazy. You've been in show business too long, Golescu. She must be sick with something, that's it, and she takes the medicine to preserve her health. Ugh! Let us hope she doesn't have anything catching. Is she sick, little Emil?"

"No," said Emil.

"No? Well. Golescu, my friend, don't forget that you're having a conversation with an idiot, here."

His imagination raced, though, all the while he was tidying away the evidence of the chicken game, and all that afternoon as the slow hours passed. Several times he heard the sound of hoofbeats on the road, someone riding fast—searching, perhaps, for Dr. Cretulescu?

As the first shades of night fell, Golescu crept out and lit a campfire. He was sitting beside it when he heard the approach of a wagon on the road, and a moment later the crashing of branches that meant the wagon had turned off toward the clearing. Golescu composed an expression that he hoped would convey innocence, doglike fidelity and patience, and gave a quick turn to the skillet of bread and sausages he was frying.

"Welcome back, my queen," he called, as he caught sight of Amaunet. "You see? Not only have I not run off with Emil to a gambling den, I've fixed you a nice supper. Come and eat. I'll see to the horses."

Amaunet regarded him warily, but she climbed down from the wagon and approached the fire. "Where is Emil?"

"Why, safe in his little cupboard, just as he ought to be," said Golescu, rising to offer his seat. Seeing her again up close, he felt a shiver of disappointment; Amaunet looked tired and bad-tempered, not at all like an immortal being who had supped of some arcane nectar. He left her by the fire as he led the horses off to drink. Not until he had come back and settled down across from her did he feel the stirring of mundane lust.

"I trust all that unsightly clutter in the wagon has been unloaded on some discreet fence?" he inquired pleasantly.

"That's one way of putting it," said Amaunet, with a humorless laugh. "You'll have all the room you need back there, for a while."

"And did we get a good price?"

Amaunet just shrugged.

Golescu smiled to himself, noting that she carried no purse. He kept up a disarming flow of small talk until Amaunet told him that she was retiring. Bidding her a cheery good night without so much as one suggestive remark, he watched as she climbed into the wagon—her back view was as enthralling as ever—and waited a few more minutes before lighting a candle-lantern and hurrying off to the other wagon.

On climbing inside, Golescu held the lamp high and looked around.

"Beautifully empty," he remarked in satisfaction. Not a carpet, not a painting, not so much as a silver spoon anywhere to be seen. As it should be. But—

"Where is the money?" he wondered aloud. "Come out, little iron-bound strongbox. Come out, little exceptionally heavy purse. She must have made a fortune from the fence. So...."

Golescu proceeded to rummage in the cupboards and cabinets, hastily at first and then with greater care, rapping for hollow panels, testing for hidden drawers. At the end of half an hour he was baffled, panting with exasperation.

"It must be here somewhere!" he declared. "Unless she made so little off the bargain she was able to hide her miserable share of the loot in her cleavage!"

Muttering to himself, he went out and banked the fire. Then he retrieved his satchel of money and the new clothes he had bought, including Emil's daylight ensemble, from the bush where he had stashed them. Having re-secured them in a cupboard in the wagon, he stretched out on the floor and thought very hard.

"I've seen that dull and sullen look before," he announced to the darkness. "Hopeless. Apathetic. Ill-used. She might be sick, but also that's the way a whore looks, when she has a nasty brute of a pimp who works her hard and takes all her earnings away. I wonder...."

"Perhaps she's the hapless victim of some big operator? Say, a criminal mastermind, with a network of thieves and fences and middlemen all funneling profits toward him? So that he sits alone on a pyramid of gold, receiving tribute from petty crooks everywhere?

"What a lovely idea!" Golescu sat up and clasped his hands.

*   *   *

He was wakened again that night by her singing. Amaunet's voice was like slow coals glowing in a dying fire, or like the undulation of smoke rising when the last glow has died. It was heartbreaking, but there was something horrible about it.

*   *   *

They rolled on. The mountains were always ahead of them, and to Golescu's relief the valley of his labors was far behind them. No one was ever hanged for selling a weak solution of yellow dye, but people have been hanged for being too successful; and in any case he preferred to keep a good distance between himself and any outcomes he couldn't predict.

The mountains came close at last and were easily crossed, by an obscure road Amaunet seemed to know well. Noon of the second day they came to a fair-sized city in the foothills, with grand houses and a domed church.

Here a fair was setting up, in a wide public square through which the wind gusted, driving yellow leaves before it over the cobbles. Golescu made his usual helpful suggestions for improving Amaunet's business and was ignored. Resigned, he stood in the permit line with other fair vendors, whom he was beginning to know by sight. They also ignored his attempts at small talk. The permit clerk was rude and obtuse.

By the time evening fell, when the fair came to life in a blaze of gaslight and calliope music, Golescu was not in the best of moods.

"Come on, pallid one," he said, dragging Emil forth from the wagon. "What are you shrinking from?"

"It's too bright," whimpered Emil, squeezing his eyes shut and trying to hide under Golescu's coat.

"We're in a big modern city, my boy," said Golescu, striding through the crowd and towing him along relentless. "Gaslight, the wonder of the civilized world. Soon we won't have Night at all, if we don't want it. Imagine that, eh? You'd have to live in a cellar. You'd probably like that, I expect."

"I want a sausage on a stick," said Emil.

"Patience," said Golescu, looking around for the food stalls. "Eating and scratching only want a beginning, eh? So scratch, and soon you'll be eating too. Where the hell is the sausage booth?"

He spotted a vendor he recognized and pushed through the crowd to the counter.

"Hey! Vienna sausage, please." He put down a coin.

"We're out of Vienna sausage," said the cashier. "We have sarmale on polenta, or tochitura on polenta. Take your pick."

Golescu's mouth watered. "The sarmale, and plenty of polenta."

He carried the paper cone to a relatively quiet corner and seated himself on a hay bale. "Come and eat. Emil dear. Polenta for you and nice spicy sarmale for me, eh?"

Emil opened his eyes long enough to look at it.

"I can't eat that. It has sauce on it."

"Just a little!" Golescu dug his thumb in amongst the meatballs and pulled up a glob of polenta. "See? Nice!"

Emil began to sob. "I don't want that. I want a sausage."

"Well, this is like sausage, only it's in grape leaves instead of pig guts, eh?" Golescu held up a nugget of sarmale. "Mmmm, tasty!"

But Emil wouldn't touch it. Golescu sighed, wolfed down the sarmale and polenta, and wiped his fingers on Emil's coat. He dragged Emil after him and searched the fairground from end to end, but nobody was selling Vienna sausage. The only thing he found that Emil would consent to eat was candy floss, so he bought him five big wads of it. Emil crouched furtively under a wagon and ate it all, as Golescu looked on and tried to slap some warmth into himself. The cold wind pierced straight through his coat, taking away all the nice residual warmth of the peppery sarmale.

"This is no life for a red-blooded man," he grumbled. "Wine, women and dance are what I need, and am I getting any? It is to laugh. Wet-nursing a miserable picky dwarf while the temptress of my dreams barely knows I exist. If I had any self-respect, I'd burst into that wagon and show her what I'm made of."

The last pink streamer of candy floss vanished into Emil's mouth. He belched.

"Then, of course, she'd hurt me," Golescu concluded. "Pretty badly, I think. Her fingers are like steel. And that excites me, Emil, isn't that a terrible thing? Yet another step downward in my long debasement."

Emil belched again.

The chilly hours passed. Emil rolled over on his side and began to wail to himself. As the fair grew quieter, as the lights went out one by one and the carousel slowed through its last revolution, Emil's whining grew louder. Amaunet's last customer departed; a moment later her door flew open and she emerged, turning her head this way and that, searching for the sound. Her gaze fell on Emil, prostrate under the wagon, and she bared her teeth at Golescu.

"What did you do to him?"

"Nothing!" said Golescu, backing up a pace or two. "His highness the turnip wouldn't eat anything but candy, and now he seems to be regretting it."

"Fool," said Amaunet. She pulled Emil out from the litter of paper cones and straw. He vomited pink syrup and said, "I want a potato."

Amaunet gave Golescu a look that made his heart skip a beat, but in a reasonable voice he said: "I could take us all to dinner. What about it? My treat."

"It's nearly midnight, you ass," said Amaunet.

"That café is still open," said Golescu, pointing to a garishly lit place at the edge of the square. Amaunet stared at it. Finally she shrugged. "Bring him," she said.

Golescu picked up Emil by the scruff of his neck and stood him on his feet. "Your potato is calling, fastidious one. Let us answer it." Emil took his hand and they trudged off together across the square, with Amaunet slinking after.

They got a table by the door. For all that the hour was late, the café was densely crowded with people in evening dress, quite glittering and cosmopolitan in appearance. The air was full of their chatter, oddly echoing, with a shrill metallic quality. Amaunet gave the crowd one surly look, and paid them no attention thereafter. But she took off her black shawl and dropped it over Emil's head. He sat like an unprotesting ghost, shrouded in black, apparently quite content.

"And you're veiling him because...?" said Golescu.

"Better if he isn't seen," said Amaunet.

"What may we get for the little family?" inquired a waiter, appearing at Golescu's elbow with a speed and silence that suggested he had popped up through a trap door. Golescu started in his chair, unnerved. The waiter had wide glass-bright eyes, and a fixed smile under a straight bar of mustache like a strip of black fur.

"Are you still serving food?" Golescu asked. The waiter's smile never faltered; he produced a menu from thin air and presented it with a flourish.

"Your *carte de nuit*. We particularly recommend the black puddings. Something to drink?"

"Bring us the best you have," said Golescu grandly. The waiter bowed and vanished again.

"It says the *Czernina Soup* is divine," announced Golescu, reading from the menu. "Hey, he thought we were a family. Charming, eh? You're Mother Aegypt and I'm...."

"The Father of Lies," said Amaunet, yawning.

"I shall take that as a compliment," said Golescu. "Fancy French cuisine here, too: *Boudin Noir*. And, for the hearty diner, *Blutwurst*. So, who do you think will recognize our tiny prodigy, Madam? He wouldn't happen to be a royal heir you stole in infancy, would he?"

Amaunet gave him a sharp look. Golescu sat up, startled.

"You can't be serious!" he said. "Heaven knows, he's inbred enough to have the very bluest blood—"

The waiter materialized beside them, deftly uncorking a dusty bottle. "This is very old wine," he said, displaying the label.

" 'Egri Bikaver,' " read Golescu. "Yes, all right. Have you got any Vienna sausage? We have a little prince here who'll hardly eat anything else."

"I want a potato." Emil's voice floated from beneath the black drape.

"We will see what can be done," said the waiter, unblinking, but his smile widened under his dreadful mustache. "And for Madam?"

Amaunet said something in a language with which Golescu was unfamiliar. The waiter chuckled, a disturbing sound, and jotted briefly on a notepad that appeared from nowhere in particular. "Very wise. And for Sir?"

"Blutwurst. I'm a hearty diner," said Golescu.

"To be sure," said the waiter, and vanished. Golescu leaned forward and hissed, "Hey, you can't mean you actually stole him from some—"

"Look, it's a gypsy!" cried a young woman, one of a pair of young lovers out for a late stroll. Her young man leaned in from the sidewalk and demanded, "What's our fortune, eh, gypsy? Will we love each other the rest of our lives?"

"You'll be dead in three days," said Amaunet. The girl squeaked, the boy went pale and muttered a curse. They fled into the night.

"What did you go and tell them that for?" demanded Golescu. Amaunet shrugged and poured herself a glass of wine.

"Why should I lie? Three days, three hours, three decades. Death always comes, for them. It's what I tell them all. Why not?"

"No wonder you don't do better business!" said Golescu. "You're supposed to tell them *good* fortunes!"

"Why should I lie?" repeated Amaunet.

Baffled, Golescu pulled at his mustaches. "What makes you say such things?" he said at last. "Why do you pretend to feel nothing? But you love little Emil, eh?"

She looked at him in flat astonishment. Then she smiled. It was a poisonous smile.

"Love *Emil?*" she said. "Who could love that thing? I could as soon love you."

As though to underscore her contempt, a woman at the bar shrieked with laughter.

Golescu turned his face away. Immediately he set about soothing his lacerated ego, revising what she'd said, changing her expression and intonation, and he had nearly rewritten the scene into an almost-declaration of tender feeling for himself when the waiter reappeared, bearing a tray.

"See what we have for the little man?" he said, whisking the cover off a dish. "Viennese on a stake!"

The dish held an artful arrangement of Vienna sausages on wooden skewers, stuck upright in a mound of mashed potato.

"Well, isn't that cute?" said Golescu. "Thank the nice man, Emil."

Emil said nothing, but reached for the plate. "He says Thank You," said Golescu, as smacking noises came from under the veil. The waiter before Amaunet a dish containing skewered animal parts, flame-blackened to anonymity.

"Madame. And for Sir," said the waiter, setting a platter before Golescu. Golescu blinked and shuddered; for a moment he had the strongest conviction that the blutwurst was pulsing and shivering, on its bed of grilled onions and eggplant that seethed like maggots. Resolutely, he told himself it was a trick of the greenish light and the late hour.

"Be sure to save room for cake," said the waiter.

"You'll be dead in three days, too," Amaunet told the waiter. The waiter laughed heartily.

*   *   *

They journeyed on to the next crossroads fair. Two days out they came to the outskirts of another town, where Amaunet pulled off the road onto waste ground. Drawing a small purse from her bosom, she handed it to Golescu.

"Go and buy groceries," she said. "We'll wait here."

Golescu scowled at the pouch, clinked it beside his ear. "Not a lot of money," he said. "But never mind, dearest. You have a man to provide for you now, you know."

"Get potatoes," Amaunet told him.

"Of course, my jewel," he replied, smiling as he climbed down. He went dutifully off to the main street.

"She is not heartless," he told himself. "She just needs to be wooed, that's all. Who can ever have been kind to her? It's time to drop the bucket into your well of charm, Golescu."

The first thing he did was look for a bathhouse. Having located one and paid the morose Turk at the door, he went in, disrobed, and submitted to being plunged, steamed, scraped, pummeled, and finally shaved. He declined the offer of orange flower water, however, preferring to retain a certain manly musk, and merely asked to be directed to the market square.

When he left it, an hour later, he was indeed carrying a sack of potatoes. He had also onions, flour, oil, sausages, a bottle of champagne, a box of Austrian chocolates, and a bouquet of asters.

He had the satisfaction of seeing Amaunet's eyes widen as he approached her.

"What's this?" she asked.

"For you," he said, thrusting the flowers into her arms. Golescu had never seen her taken aback before. She held them out in a gingerly sort of way, with a queer look of embarrassment.

"What am I supposed to do with these?" she said.

"Put them in water?" he said, grinning at her as he hefted his other purchases.

*   *   *

That night, when they had made their camp in a clearing less cobwebbed and haunted than usual, when the white trail of stars made its way down the sky, Golescu went into the wagon to retrieve his treats. The asters had drooped to death, despite having been crammed in a jar of water; but the champagne and chocolates had survived being at the bottom of his sack. Humming to himself, he carried them, together with a pair of chipped enamel mugs, out to the fireside.

Amaunet was gazing into the flames, apparently lost in gloomy reverie. She ignored the popping of the champagne cork, though Emil, beside her, twitched and started. When Golescu opened the chocolates, however, she looked sharply round.

"Where did you get that?" she demanded.

"A little fairy brought it, flying on golden wings," said Golescu. "Out of his purse of twenty thousand lei, I might add, so don't scowl at me like that. Will you have a sweetmeat, my queen? A cherry cream? A bit of enrobed ginger peel?"

Amaunet stared fixedly at the box a long moment, and then reached for it. "What harm can it do?" she said, in a quiet voice. "Why not?"

"That's the spirit," said Golescu, pouring the champagne. "A little pleasure now and again is good for you, wouldn't you agree? Especially when one has the money."

Amaunet didn't answer, busy with prizing open the box. When he handed her a mug full of champagne, she took it without looking up; drained it as though it were so much water, and handed it back.

"Well quaffed!" said Golescu, as a tiny flutter of hope woke in his flesh. He poured Amaunet another. She meanwhile had got the box open at last, and bowed her head over the chocolates, breathing in their scent as though they were the perfumes of Arabia.

"Oh," she groaned, and groped in the box. Bringing out three chocolate creams, she held them up a moment in dim-eyed contemplation; then closed her fist on them, crushing them as though they were grapes. Closing her eyes, she licked the sweet mess from her hand, slowly, making ecstatic sounds.

Golescu stared, and in his inattention poured champagne in his lap. Amaunet did not notice.

"I had no idea you liked chocolates so much," said Golescu.

"Why should you?" said Amaunet through a full mouth. She lifted the box and inhaled again, then dipped in with her tongue and scooped a nut cluster straight out of its little paper cup.

"Good point," said Golescu. He edged a little closer on the fallen log that was their mutual seat, and offered her the champagne once more. She didn't seem to notice, absorbed as she was in crunching nuts. "Come, drink up; this stuff won't keep. Like youth and dreams, eh?"

To his astonishment, Amaunet threw back her head and laughed. It was not the dry and humorless syllable that had previously expressed her scorn. It was full-throated, rolling, deep, and so frightful a noise that Emil shrieked and put his hands over his head, and even the fire seemed to shrink down and cower. It echoed in the night forest, which suddenly was darker, more full of menace.

Golescu's heart beat faster. When Amaunet seized the mug from him and gulped down its contents once more, he moistened his lips and ventured to say:

"Just let all those cares wash away in the sparkling tide, eh? Let's be good to each other, dear lady. You need a man to lessen the burden on those poor frail shoulders. Golescu is here!"

That provoked another burst of laughter from Amaunet, ending in a growl as she threw down the mug, grabbed another handful of chocolates from the box and crammed them into her mouth, paper cups and all.

Scarcely able to believe his luck (*one drink and she's a shameless bacchante!*) Golescu edged his bottom a little closer to Amaunet's. "Come," he said, breathing heavily, "Tell me about yourself, my Nile lily."

Amaunet just chuckled, looking at him sidelong as she munched chocolates. Her eyes had taken on a queer glow, more reflective of the flames perhaps than they had been. It terrified Golescu, and yet….

At last she swallowed, took the champagne bottle from his hand and had a drink.

"Hah!" She spat into the fire, which blazed up. "You want to hear my story? Listen, then, fat man."

"A thousand thousand years ago, there was a narrow green land by a river. At our backs was the desert, full of jackals and demons. But the man and the woman always told me that if I stayed inside at night, like a good little girl, nothing could hurt me. And if I was a very good little girl always, I would never die. I'd go down to the river, and a man would come in a reed boat and take me away to the Sun, and I'd live forever.

"One day, the Lean People came out of the desert. They had starved in the desert so long, they thought that was what the gods *meant* for people to do. So, when they saw our green fields, they said we were Abomination. They rode in and killed as many as they could. We were stronger people and we killed them all, threw their bodies in the river—no boats came for *them*! And that was when I looked on Him, and was afraid."

"Who was He, precious?" said Golescu.

"Death," said Amaunet, as the firelight played on her face. "The great Lord with long rows of ivory teeth. His scales shone under the moon. He walked without a shadow. I had never seen any boat taking good children to Heaven; but I saw His power. So I took clay from the riverbank and I made a little Death, and I worshipped it, and fed it with mice, with birds, anything I could catch and kill. *Take all these,* I said, *and not me; for You are very great.*

"Next season, more riders came out of the desert. More war, more food for Him, and I knew He truly ruled the world.

"Our people said: *We can't stay here. Not safe to farm these fields.* And many gave up and walked north. But the man and woman waited too long. They tried to take everything we owned, every bowl and dish in our house, and the woman found my little image of Him. She beat me and said I was wicked. She broke the image.

"And He punished her for it. As we ran along the path by the river, no Sun Lord came to our aid; only the desert people, and they rode down the man and the woman.

"I didn't help them. I ran, and ran beside the river, and I prayed for Him to save me." Amaunet's voice had dropped to a whisper. She sounded young, nearly human.

Golescu was disconcerted. It wasn't at all the mysterious past he had imagined for her; only sad. Some miserable tribal struggle, in some backwater village somewhere? No dusky princess, exiled daughter of pharaohs. Only a refugee, like any one of the hatchet-faced women he had seen along the roads, pushing barrows full of what they could salvage from the ashes of war.

"But at least, this was in Egypt, yes? How did you escape?" Golescu inquired, venturing to put his arm around her. His voice seemed to break some kind of spell; Amaunet turned to look at him, and smiled with all her teeth in black amusement. The smile made Golescu feel small and vulnerable.

"Why, a bright boat came up the river," she said. "There was the Sun Lord, putting out his hand to take me to safety. He didn't come for the man and woman, who had been good; He came for *me,* that had never believed in him. So I knew the world was all lies, even as I went with him and listened to his stories about how wonderful Heaven would be.

"And it turned out that I was right to suspect the Sun, fat man. The price I paid for eternal life was to become a slave in Heaven. For my cowardice in running from Death, they punished me by letting the sacred asps bite me. I was bitten every day, and by the end of fifteen years, I was so full of poison that nothing could ever hurt me. And by the end of a thousand years, I was so weary of my slavery that I prayed to Him again.

"I went out beside the river, under the light of the moon, and I tore my clothes and bared my breasts for Him, knelt down and begged Him to come for me. I wailed and pressed my lips to the mud. How I longed for His ivory teeth!

"But He will not come for me.

"And the Sun Lord has set me to traveling the world, doing business with thieves and murderers, telling foolish mortals their fortunes." Amaunet had another drink of champagne. "Because the Sun, as it turns out, is actually the Devil. He hasn't got horns or a tail, oh, no; he looks like a handsome priest. But he's the master of all lies.

"And I am so tired, fat man, so tired of working for him. Nothing matters; nothing changes. The sun rises each day, and I open my eyes and hate the sun for rising, and hate the wheels that turn and the beasts that pull me on my way. And Him I hate most of all, who takes the whole world but withholds His embrace from me."

She fell silent, looking beyond the fire into the night.

Golescu took a moment to register that her story was at an end, being still preoccupied with the mental image of Amaunet running bare-breasted beside the Nile. But he shook himself, now, and gathered his wits; filed the whole story under *Elaborate Metaphor* and sought to get back to business in the real world.

"About this Devil, my sweet," he said, as she crammed another fistful of chocolates into her mouth. "and these thieves and murderers. The ones who bring you all the stolen goods. You take their loot to the Devil?"

Amaunet didn't answer, chewing mechanically, watching the flames.

"What would happen if you didn't take the loot to him?" Golescu persisted. "Suppose you just took it somewhere and sold it yourself?"

"Why should I do that?" said Amaunet.

"So as to be rich!" said Golescu, beginning to regret that he'd gotten her so intoxicated. "So as not to live in wretchedness and misery!"

Amaunet laughed again, with a noise like ice splintering.

"Money won't change that," she said. "For me or you!"

"Where's he live, this metaphorical Devil of yours?" said Golescu. "Bucharest? Kronstadt? I could talk to him on your behalf, eh? Threaten him slightly? Renegotiate your contract? I'm good at that, my darling. Why don't I talk to him, man to man?"

That sent her into such gales of ugly laughter she dropped the chocolate box.

"Or, what about getting some real use out of dear Emil?" said Golescu. "What about a mentalist act? And perhaps we could do a sideline in love philtres, cures for baldness. A little bird tells me we could make our fortunes," he added craftily.

Amaunet's laugh stopped. Her lip curled back from her teeth.

"I told you," she said, "No. Emil's a secret."

"And from whom are we hiding him, madame?" Golescu inquired.

Amaunet just shook her head. She groped in the dust, found the chocolate box and picked out the last few cordials.

"*He'd* find out," she murmured, as though to herself. "And then he'd take him away from me. Not fair. *I* found him. Pompous fool; looking under hills. Waiting by fairy rings. As though the folk tales were real! When all along, he should have been looking in the lunatic asylums. The ward keeper said:

here, madame, we have a little genius who thinks he's a *vampyr*. And I saw him and I knew, the big eyes, the big head, I knew what blood ran in his veins. Aegeus's holy grail, but *I* found one. Why should I give him up? If anybody could find a way, he could…."

More damned metaphors, thought Golescu. "Who's Aegeus?" he asked. "Is that the Devil's real name?"

"Ha! He wishes he were. The lesser of two devils…." Amaunet's voice trailed away into nonsense sounds. Or were they? Golescu, listening, made out syllables that slid and hissed, the pattern of words.

If I wait any longer, she'll pass out, he realized.

"Come, my sweet, the hour is late," he said, in the most seductive voice he could summon. "Why don't we go to bed?" He reached out to pull her close, fumbling for a way through her clothes.

Abruptly he was lying flat on his back, staring up at an apparition. Eyes and teeth of flame, a black shadow like cloak or wings, claws raised to strike. He heard a high-pitched shriek before the blow came, and sparks flew up out of velvet blackness.

*   *   *

Golescu opened his eyes to the gloom before dawn, a neutral blue from which the stars had already fled. He sat up, squinting in pain. He was soaked with dew, his head pounded, and he couldn't seem to focus his eyes.

Beside him, a thin plume of smoke streamed upward from the ashes of the fire. Across the firepit, Emil still sat where he had been the night before. He was watching the east with an expression of dread, whimpering faintly.

"God and all His little angels," groaned Golescu, touching the lump on his forehead. "What happened last night, eh?"

Emil did not respond. Golescu sorted muzzily through his memory, which (given his concussion) was not at its best. He thought that the attempt at seduction had been going rather well. The goose egg above his eyes was clear indication *something* hadn't gone as planned, and yet….

Emil began to weep, wringing his hands.

"What the hell's the matter with you, anyway?" said Golescu, rolling over to get to his hands and knees.

"The sun," said Emil, not taking his eyes from the glow on the horizon.

"And you haven't got your shade-suit on, have you?" Golescu retorted, rising ponderously to his feet. He grimaced and clutched at his head. "Tell me, petite undead creature, was I so fortunate as to get laid last night? Any idea where black madame has gotten to?"

Emil just sobbed and covered his eyes.

"Oh, all right, let's get you back in your cozy warm coffin," said Golescu, brushing dust from his clothing. "Come on!"

Emil scuttled to his side. He opened the wagon door and Emil vaulted in, vanishing into the cupboard under Amaunet's bed. Emil pulled the cupboard door shut after himself with a bang. A bundle of rags on the bed stirred. Amaunet sat bolt upright, staring at Golescu.

Their eyes met. *She doesn't know what happened either!* thought Golescu, with such a rush of glee, his brain throbbed like a heart.

"If you please, madame," he said, just a shade reproachfully, "I was only putting poor Emil to bed. You left him out all night."

He reached up to doff his hat, but it wasn't on his head.

"Get out," said Amaunet.

"At once, madame," said Golescu, and backed away with all the dignity he could muster. He closed the door, spotting his hat in a thorn bush all of ten feet away from where he had been lying.

"What a time we must have had," he said to himself, beginning to grin. "Barbu, you seductive devil!"

And though his head felt as though it were splitting, he smiled to himself all the while he gathered wood and rebuilt the fire.

*   *   *

On the feast days of certain saints and at crossroad harvest fairs, they lined up their black wagons beside the brightly-painted ones. Amaunet told fortunes. The rear wagon began to fill once more with stolen things, so that Golescu slept on rolls of carpet and tapestry, and holy saints gazed down from their painted panels to watch him sleep. They looked horrified.

Amaunet did not speak of that night by the fire. Still, Golescu fancied there was a change in her demeanor toward him, which fueled his self-esteem: an oddly unsettled look in her eyes, a hesitance, what in anybody less dour would have been *embarrassment*.

"She's dreaming of me," he told Emil one night, as he poked the fire. "What do you want to bet? She desires me, and yet her pride won't let her yield."

Emil said nothing, vacantly watching the water boil for his evening potato.

Amaunet emerged from the wagon. She approached Golescu and thrust a scrap of paper at him.

"We'll get to Kronstadt tomorrow," she said. "You'll go in. Buy what's on this list."

"Where am I to find this stuff?" Golescu complained, reading the list. "An alchemist's? I don't know what half of it is. Except for...." He looked up at her, trying not to smile. "Chocolate, eh? What'll you have, cream bonbons? Caramels? Nuts?"

"No," said Amaunet, turning her back. "I want a brick of the pure stuff. See if you can get a confectioner to sell you some of his stock."

"Heh heh heh," said Golescu meaningfully, but she ignored him.

*   *   *

Though Kronstadt was a big town, bursting its medieval walls, it took Golescu three trips, to three separate chemists' shops, to obtain all the items on the list but the chocolate. It took him the best part of an hour to get the chocolate, too, using all his guile and patience to convince the confectioner's assistant to sell him a block of raw material.

"You'd have thought I was trying to buy state secrets," Golescu said to himself, trudging away with a scant half-pound block wrapped in waxed paper. "Pfui! Such drudge work, Golescu, is a waste of your talents. What are you, a mere donkey to send on errands?"

And when he returned to the camp outside town, he got nothing like the welcome he felt he deserved. Amaunet seized the carry-sack from him and went through it hurriedly, as he stood before her with aching feet. She pulled out the block of chocolate and stared at it. She trembled slightly, her nostrils flared. Golescu thought it made her look uncommonly like a horse.

"I don't suppose you've cooked any supper for me?" he inquired.

Amaunet started, and turned to him as though he had just asked for a roasted baby in caper sauce.

"No! Go back into Kronstadt. Buy yourself something at a tavern. In fact, take a room. I don't want to see you back here for two days, understand? Come back at dawn on the third day."

"I see," said Golescu, affronted. "In that case I'll just go collect my purse and an overnight bag, shall I? Not that I don't trust you, of course."

Amaunet's reply was to turn her back and vanish into the wagon, bearing the sack clutched to her bosom.

Carrying his satchel, Golescu cheered up a little as he walked away. Cash, a change of clothes, and no authorities in pursuit!

He was not especially concerned that Amaunet would use his absence to move on. The people of the road had a limited number of places they could ply their diverse trades, and he had been one of their number long enough to know the network of market fairs and circuses that made up their itinerary.

He had only to follow the route of the vardas, and sooner or later he must find Amaunet again. Unless, of course, she left the road and settled down; then she would be harder to locate than an egg in a snowstorm. Or an ink bottle in a coal cellar. Or… he amused himself for at least a mile composing unlikely similes.

Having returned to Kronstadt just as dusk fell, Golescu paused outside a low dark door. There was no sign to tell him a tavern lay within, but the fume of wine and brandy breathing out spoke eloquently to him. He went in, ducking his head, and as soon as his eyes had adjusted to the dark he made out the bar, the barrels, the tables in dark corners he had expected to see.

"A glass of schnapps, please," he said to the sad-faced publican. There were silent drinkers at the tables, some watching him with a certain amount of suspicion, some ignoring him. One or two appeared to be dead, collapsed over their drinks. Only a pair of cattle herders standing near the bar were engaged in conversation. Golescu smiled cheerily at one and all, slapped down his coin, and withdrew with his glass to an empty table.

"…Hunting for him everywhere," one of the drovers was saying. "He was selling this stuff that was supposed to make chickens lay better eggs."

"Has anybody been killed?" said the other drover.

"I didn't hear enough to know, but they managed to shoot most of them—"

Golescu, quietly as he could, half-rose and turned his chair so he was facing away from the bar. Raising his glass to his lips, he looked over its rim and met the eyes of someone propped in a dark corner.

"To your very good health," he said, and drank.

"What's that you've got in the satchel?" said the person in the corner.

"Please, sir, my mummy sent me to the market to buy bread," said Golescu, smirking. The stranger arose and came near. Golescu drew back involuntarily. The stranger ignored his reaction and sat down at Golescu's table.

He was an old man in rusty black, thin to gauntness, his shabby coat buttoned high and tight. He was bald, with drawn and waxen features, and he smelled a bit; but the stare of his eyes was intimidating. They shone like pearls, milky as though he were blind.

"You travel with Mother Aegypt, eh?" said the old man.

"And who would that be?" inquired Golescu, setting his drink down. The old man looked scornful.

"I know her," he said. "Madame Amaunet. I travel, too. I saw you at the market fair in Arges, loafing outside her wagon. You do the talking for her, don't you, and run her errands? I've been following you."

"You must have me confused with some other handsome fellow," said Golescu.

"Pfft." The old man waved his hand dismissively. "I used to work for her, too. She's never without a slave to do her bidding."

"Friend, I don't do anyone's bidding," said Golescu, but he felt a curious pang of jealousy. "And she's only a poor weak woman, isn't she?"

The old man laughed. He creaked when he laughed.

"Tell me, is she still collecting trash for the Devil?"

"What Devil is that?" said Golescu, leaning back and trying to look amused.

"Her master. I saw him, once." The old man reached up absently and swatted a fly that had landed on his cheek. "Soldiers had looted a mosque, they stole a big golden lamp. She paid them cash for it. It wasn't so heavy, but it was, you know, awkward. And when we drove up to the Teufelberg to unload all the goods, she made me help her bring out the lamp, so as not to break off the fancy work. I saw him there, the Devil. Waiting beside his long wagons. He looked like a prosperous Saxon."

"Sorry, my friend, I don't know what you're talking about," said Golescu. He drew a deep breath and plunged on: "Though I *have* heard of a lord of thieves who is, perhaps, known in certain circles as the Devil. Am I correct? Just the sort of powerful fellow who has but to pull a string and corrupt officials rush to do his bidding? And he accumulates riches without lifting a finger?"

The old man creaked again.

"You think you've figured it out," he said. "And you think he has a place for a fast-talking fellow in his gang, don't you?"

Taken aback, Golescu just stared at him. He raised his drink again.

"Mind reader, are you?"

"I was a fool, too," said the old man, smacking the table for emphasis, though his hand made no more sound than an empty glove. "Thought I'd make a fortune. Use her to work my way up the ladder. I hadn't the slightest idea what she really was."

"What is she, grandfather?" said Golescu, winking broadly at the publican. The publican shuddered and looked away. The old man, ignoring or not noticing, leaned forward and said in a lowered voice:

"There are *stregoi* who walk this world. You don't believe it, you laugh, but it's true. They aren't interested in your soul. They crave beautiful things. Whenever there is a war, they hover around its edges like flies, stealing what they can when the armies loot. If a house is going to catch fire and burn to the ground, they know; you can see them lurking in the street beforehand,

and how their eyes gleam! They're only waiting for night, when they can slip in and take away paintings, carvings, books, whatever is choice and rare, before the flames come. Sometimes they take children, too.

"*She's* one of them. But she's tired, she's lazy. She buys from thieves, instead of doing the work herself. The Devil doesn't care. He just takes what she brings him. Back she goes on her rounds, then, from fair to fair, and even the murderers cross themselves when her shadow falls on them, but still they bring her pretty things. Isn't it so?"

"What do you want, grandfather?" said Golescu.

"I want her secret," said the old man. "I'll tell you about it, and then you can steal it and bring it back here, and we'll share. How would you like eternal youth, eh?"

"I'd love it," said Golescu patiently. "But there's no such thing."

"Then you don't know Mother Aegypt very well!" said the old man, grinning like a skull. "I used to watch through the door when she'd mix her Black Cup. Does she still have the little mummy case, with the powders inside?"

"Yes," said Golescu, startled into truthfulness.

"That's how she does it!" said the old man. "She'd put in a little of this— little of that—she'd grind the powders together, and though I watched for years I could never see all that went in the cup, or what the right amounts were. Spirits of wine, yes, and some strange things—arsenic, and paint! And she'd drink it down, and weep, and scream as though she was dying. But instead, she'd live. My time slipped away, peering through that door, watching her live. I could have run away from her many times, but I stayed, I wasted my life, because I thought I could learn her secrets.

"And one night she caught me watching her, and she cursed me. I ran away. I hid for years. She's forgotten me, now. But when I saw her at Arges, and you with her, I thought—he can help me.

"So! You find out what's in that Black Cup of hers, and bring it back to me. I'll share it with you. We'll live forever and become rich as kings."

"Will I betray the woman I love?" said Golescu. "And I should believe such a story, because—?"

The old man, who had worked himself into a dry trembling passion, took a moment to register what Golescu had said. He looked at him with contempt.

"Love? *Mother Aegypt?* I see I have been wasting my breath on an idiot."

The old man rose to his feet. Golescu put out a conciliatory hand. "Now, now, grandfather, I didn't say I didn't believe you, but you'll have to admit that's quite a story. Where's your proof?"

"Up your ass," said the old man, sidling away from the table.

"How long were you with her?" said Golescu, half rising to follow him.

"She bought me from the orphan asylum in Timisoara," said the old man, turning with a baleful smile. "I was ten years old."

Golescu sat down abruptly, staring as the old man scuttled out into the night.

After a moment's rapid thought, he gulped the rest of his schnapps and rose to follow. When he got out into the street, he stared in both directions. A round moon had just lifted above the housetops, and by its light the streets were as visible as by day, though the shadows were black and fathomless. Somewhere, far off, a dog howled. At least, it sounded like a dog. There was no sign of the old man, as far as Golescu could see.

Golescu shivered, and went in search of a cheap hotel.

*   *   *

Cheapness notwithstanding, it gave Golescu a pleasant sense of status to sleep once again in a bed. Lingering over coffee and sweet rolls the next morning, he pretended he was a millionaire on holiday. It had long been his habit not to dwell on life's mysteries, even fairly big and ugly ones, and in broad daylight he found it easy to dismiss the old man as a raving lunatic. Amaunet clearly had a bad reputation amongst the people of the road, but why should he care?

He went forth from the hotel jingling coins in his pocket, and walked the streets of Kronstadt as though he owned it.

In the Council Square his attention was drawn by a platform that had been set up, crowded with racks, boxes and bins of the most unlikely-looking objects. Some twenty citizens were pawing through them in a leisurely way. Several armed policemen stood guard over the lot, and over two miserable wretches in manacles.

Catching the not-unpleasant scent of somebody else's disaster, Golescu hurried to investigate.

"Am I correct in assuming this is a debtors' sale, sir?" he asked a police sergeant.

"That's right," said the sergeant. "A traveling opera company. These two bankrupts are the former managers. Isn't that so?" He prodded one of them with his stick.

"Unfortunately so," agreed the other gloomily. "Please go in, sir, and see if anything catches your fancy. Reduce our debt and be warned by our example. Remember, the Devil has a stake in hell especially reserved for defaulting treasurers of touring companies."

"I weep for you," said Golescu, and stepped up on the platform with an eager expression.

The first thing he saw was a rack of costumes, bright with tinsel and marabou. He spent several minutes searching for anything elegant that might fit him, but the only ensemble in his size was a doublet and pair of trunk hose made of red velvet. Scowling, he pulled them out, and noticed the pointy-toed shoes of red leather, tied to the hanger by their laces. Here was a tag, on which was scrawled FAUST 1-2.

"The Devil, eh?" said Golescu. His eyes brightened as an idea began to come to him. He draped the red suit over his arm and looked further. This production of *Faust* had apparently employed a cast of lesser demons; there were three or four child-sized ensembles in black, leotards, tights and eared hoods. Golescu helped himself to the one least motheaten.

In a bin he located the red tights and skullcap that went with the Mephistopheles costume. Groping through less savory articles and papier-mâché masks, he found a lyre strung with yarn. He added it to his pile. Finally, he spotted a stage coffin, propped on its side between two flats of scenery. Giggling to himself, he pulled it out, loaded his purchases into it, and shoved the whole thing across the platform to the cashier.

"I'll take these, dear sir," he said.

*   *   *

By the time Golescu had carried the coffin back to his hotel room, whistling a cheery tune as he went, the Act had begun to glow in his mind. He laid out his several purchases and studied them. He tried on the Mephistopheles costume (it fit admirably, except for the pointy shoes, which were a little tight) and preened before the room's one shaving mirror, though he had to back all the way to the far wall to be able to see his full length in it.

"She can't object to this," he said aloud. "Such splendor! Such classical erudition! Why, it would play in Vienna! And even if she does object... you can persuade her, Golescu, you handsome fellow."

Pleased with himself, he ordered extravagantly when he went down to dinner. Over cucumber salad, flekken and wine he composed speeches of such elegance that he was misty-eyed by the bottom of the second bottle. He rose at last, somewhat unsteady, and floated up the stairs from the dining room just as a party of men came in through the street door.

"In here! Sit down, poor fellow, you need a glass of brandy. Has the bleeding stopped?"

"Almost. Careful of my leg!"

"Did you kill them both?"

"We got one for certain. Three silver bullets, it took! The head's in the back of the wagon. You should have seen..."

Golescu heard no more, rounding the first turn of the stair at that point, and too intent on visions of the Act to pay attention in any case.

*   *   *

So confident was Golescu in his dream that he visited a printer's next day, and commissioned a stack of handbills. The results, cranked out while he loafed in a tavern across the street in the company of a bottle of slivovitz, were not as impressive as he'd hoped; but they were decorated with a great many exclamation points, and that cheered him.

The Act was all complete in his head by the time he left Kronstadt, just before dawn on the third day. Yawning mightily, he set down the coffin and his bag and pulled out his purse to settle with the tavern keeper.

"And a gratuity for your staff, kind sir," said Golescu, tossing down a handful of mixed brass and copper in small denominations. "The service was superb."

"May all the holy saints pray for you," said the tavern keeper, without enthusiasm. "Any forwarding address in case of messages?"

"Why, yes; if my friend the Archduke stops in, let him know that I've gone on to Paris," said Golescu. "I'm in show business, you know."

"In that case, may I hire a carriage for you?" inquired the tavern keeper. "One with golden wheels, perhaps?"

"I think not," Golescu replied. "I'm just walking on to Predeal. Meeting a friend with a private carriage, you know."

"Walking, are you?" The tavern keeper's sneer was replaced with a look of genuine interest. "You want to be careful, you know. They say there's a new monster roaming the countryside!"

"A monster? Really, my friend," Golescu waggled a reproving finger at him. "Would I ever have got where I am in life if I'd believed such stories?"

He shouldered the coffin once more, picked up his bag and walked out.

Though the morning was cool, he was sweating by the time he reached the outskirts of Kronstadt, and by the time he stepped off to the campsite track Golescu's airy mood had descended a little. Nonetheless, he grinned to see the wagons still there, the horses cropping placidly where they were tethered. He bellowed heartily as he pounded on Amaunet's door:

"Uncle Barbu's home, darlings!"

Not a sound.

"Hello?"

Perhaps a high thin whining noise?

"It's meeee," he said, trying the door. It wasn't locked. Setting down the coffin, he opened the door cautiously.

A strong, strong smell: spice and sweetness, and blood perhaps. Golescu pulled out a handkerchief and clapped it over his nose. He leaned forward, peering into the gloom within the wagon.

Amaunet lay stretched out on her bed, fully dressed. Her arms were crossed on her bosom, like a corpse's. Her skin was the color of ashes and her eyes were closed. She looked so radiantly happy that Golescu was unsure, at first, who lay there. He edged in sideways, bent to peer down at her.

"Madame?" He reached down to take her hand. It was ice-cold. "Oh!"

She just lay there, transfigured by her condition, beautiful at last.

Golescu staggered backward, and something fell from the bed. A cup rolled at his feet, a chalice cut of black stone. It appeared at first to be empty; but as it rolled, a slow black drop oozed forth to the lip.

"The Black Cup," stated Golescu, feeling the impact of a metaphorical cream pie. He blinked rapidly, overwhelmed by conflicting emotions. It was a moment before he was able to realize that the whining noise was coming from the cabinet under Amaunet's bed. Sighing, he bent and hauled Emil forth.

"Come out, poor little maggot," he said.

"I'm hungry," said Emil.

"Is that all you have to say?" Golescu demanded. "The Queen of Sorrow is dead, and you're concerned for a lousy potato?"

Emil said nothing in reply.

"Did she kill herself?"

"The cup killed her," Emil said.

"Poison in the cup, yes, I can see that, you ninny! I meant—*why?*"

"She wanted to die," said Emil. "She was too old, but she couldn't die. She said, 'Make me a poison to take my life away.' I mixed the cup every month, but it never worked. Then she said, 'What if you tried Theobromine?'. I tried it. It worked. She laughed."

Golescu stood there staring down at him a long moment, and finally collapsed backward onto a stool.

"Holy God, Holy mother of God," he murmured, with tears in his eyes. "It was true. She was an immortal thing."

"I'm hungry," Emil repeated.

"But how could anyone get tired of being alive? So many good things!

Fresh bread with butter. Sleep. Making people believe you. Interesting possibilities," said Golescu. "She had good luck handed to her, how could she want to throw it away?"

"They don't have luck," said Emil.

"And what are *you*, exactly?" said Golescu, staring at him. "You, with all your magic potions? Hey, can you make the one that gives eternal life, too?"

"No," said Emil.

"You can't? You're sure?"

"Yes."

"But then, what do you know?" Golescu rubbed his chin. "You're an idiot. But then again...." He looked at Amaunet, whose fixed smile seemed more unsettling every time he saw it. "Maybe she did cut a deal with the Devil after all. Maybe eternal life isn't all it's cracked up to be, if she wanted so badly to be rid of it. What's that in her hand?"

Leaning forward, he opened her closed fist. Something black protruded there: the snout of a tiny figure, crudely sculpted in clay. A crocodile.

"I want a potato," said Emil.

Golescu shuddered.

"We have to dig a grave first," he said.

*   *   *

In the end he dug it himself, because Emil, when goggled and swathed against daylight, was incapable of using a shovel.

"Rest in peace, my fair unknown," grunted Golescu, crouching to lower Amaunet's shrouded body into the grave. "I'd have given you the coffin, but I have other uses for it, and the winding sheet's very flattering, really. Not that I suppose you care."

He stood up and removed his hat. Raising his eyes to heaven, he added: "Holy angels, if this poor creature really sold her soul to the Devil, then please pay no attention to my humble interruption. But if there were by chance any loopholes she might take advantage of to avoid damnation, I hope you guide her soul through them to eternal rest. And, by the way, I'm going to live a much more virtuous life from now on. Amen."

He replaced his hat, picked up the shovel once more and filled in the grave.

*   *   *

That night Golescu wept a little for Amaunet, or at least for lost opportunity, and he dreamed of her when he slept. By the time the sun rose pale through the smoke of Kronstadt's chimneys, though, he had begun to smile.

"I possess four fine horses and two wagons now," he told Emil, as he poked up the fire under the potato-kettle. "Nothing to turn up one's nose at, eh? And I have you, you poor child of misfortune. Too long has your light been hidden from the world."

Emil just sat there, staring through his goggles at the kettle. Golescu smeared plum jam on a slab of bread and took an enormous bite.

"Bucharest," he said explosively, through a full mouth. "Constantinople, Vienna, Prague, Berlin. We will walk down streets of gold in all the great cities of the world! All the potatoes your tiny heart could wish for, served up on nice restaurant china. And for me...." Golescu swallowed. "The life I was meant to live. Fame and universal respect. Beautiful women. Financial embarrassment only a memory!

"We'll give the teeming masses what they desire, my friend. What scourges people through life, after all? Fear of old age. Fear of inadequacy. Loneliness and sterility, what terrible things! How well will people pay to be cured of them, eh? Ah, Emil, what a lot of work you have to do."

Emil turned his blank face.

"Work," he said.

"Yes," said Golescu, grinning at him. "With your pots and pans and chemicals, you genius. Chickens be damned! We will accomplish great things, you and I. Future generations will regard us as heroes. Like, er, the fellow who stole fire from heaven. Procrustes, that was his name.

"But I have every consideration for *your* modest and retiring nature. I will mercifully shield you from the limelight, and take the full force of public acclaim myself. For I shall now become..." Golescu dropped his voice an octave, "Professor Hades!"

*   *   *

It was on Market Day, a full week later, that the vardas rolled through Kronstadt. At the hour when the streets were most crowded, Golescu drove like a majestic snail. Those edged to the side of the road had plenty of time to regard the new paint job. The vardas were now decorated with suns, moons and stars, what perhaps might have been alchemical symbols, gold and scarlet on black, and the words:

PROFESSOR HADES
MASTER OF THE MISERIES

Some idle folk followed, and watched as Golescu drew the wagons up in a vacant field just outside the Merchants' Gate. They stared, but did not offer to help, as Golescu unhitched the horses and bustled about with planks and barrels, setting up a stage. They watched with interest as a policeman advanced on Golescu, but were disappointed when Golescu presented him with all necessary permits and a handsome bribe. He left, tipping his helmet; Golescu climbed into the lead wagon and shut the door. Nothing else of interest happened, so the idlers wandered away after a while.

But when school let out, children came to stare. By that time, scarlet curtains had been set up, masking the stage itself on three sides, and handbills had been tacked along the edge of the stage planking. A shopkeeper's son ventured close and bent to read.

" 'FREE ENTERTAINMENT,' " he recited aloud, for the benefit of his friends. 'Health and Potency can be Yours!! Professor Hades Knows All!!! See the Myrmidion Genius!!!!' "

" '*Myrmidion*?' " said the schoolmaster's son.

" 'Amazing Feats of Instant Calculation,' " continued the shopkeeper's son. " 'Whether Rice, Peas, Beans, Millet or Barley, The Myrmidion Genius will Instantly Name the CORRECT Number in YOUR JAR. A Grand Prize will be Presented to Any Person who can Baffle the Myrmidion Genius!' "

"What's a Myrmidion?" wondered the blacksmith's son.

"What's a Feat of Instant Calculation?" wondered the barber's son. "Guessing the number of beans in a jar?"

"That's a cheat," said the policeman's son.

"No, it isn't!" a disembodied voice boomed from behind the curtain. "You will see, little boys. Run home and tell your friends about the free show, here, tonight. You'll see wonders, I promise you. Bring beans!"

The boys ran off, so eager to do the bidding of an unseen stranger that down in Hell the Devil smiled, and jotted down their names for future reference. Dutifully they spread the word. By the time they came trooping back at twilight, lugging jars and pots of beans, a great number of adults followed them. A crowd gathered before the wagons, expectant.

Torches were flaring at either side of the stage now, in a cold sweeping wind that made the stars flare too. The scarlet curtain flapped and swayed like the flames. As it moved, those closest to the stage glimpsed feet moving beneath, accompanied by a lot of grunting and thumping.

The barber cleared his throat and called, "Hey! We're freezing to death out here!"

"Then you shall be warmed!" cried a great voice, and the front curtain was flung aside. The wind promptly blew it back, but not before the crowd had glimpsed Golescu resplendent in his Mephistopheles costume. He caught the curtain again and stepped out in front of it. "Good people of Kronstadt, how lucky you are!"

There was some murmuring from the crowd. Golescu had applied makeup to give himself a sinister and mysterious appearance, or at least that had been his intention, but the result was that he looked rather like a fat raccoon in a red suit. Nevertheless, it could not be denied that he was frightening to behold.

"Professor Hades, at your service," he said, leering and twirling the ends of his mustache. "World traveler and delver-into of forbidden mysteries!"

"We brought the beans," shouted the barber's son.

"Good. Hear, now, the story of my remarkable—"

"What are you supposed to be, the Devil?" demanded someone in the audience.

"No indeed! Though you are surely wise enough to know that the Devil is not so black as he is painted, eh?" Golescu cried. "No, in fact I bring you happiness, my friends, and blessings for all mankind! Let me tell you how it was."

From under his cloak he drew the lyre, and pretended to twang its strings.

"It is true that in the days of my youth I studied the Dark Arts, at a curious school run by the famed Master Paracelsus. Imagine my horror, however, when I discovered that every seven years he offered up one of his seven students as a sacrifice to Hell! And I, I myself was seventh in my class! I therefore fled, as you would surely do. I used my great wealth to buy a ship, wherewith I meant to escape to Egypt, home of all the mysteries.

"Long I sailed, by devious routes, for I lived in terror that Master Paracelsus would discover my presence by arcane means. And so it happened that I grew desperately short of water, and was obliged to thread dangerous reefs and rocks to land on an island with a fair spring..

"Now, this was no ordinary island, friends! For on it was the holy shrine of the great Egyptian god Osiris, once guarded by the fierce race of ant-men, the Myrmidions!"

"Don't you mean the *Myrmidons*?" called the schoolmaster. "They were—"

"No, that was somebody else!" said Golescu. "These people I am talking about were terrors, understand? Giant, six-limbed men with fearsome jaws and superhuman strength, whom Osiris placed there to guard the secrets of his temple! Fangs dripping venom! Certain death for any who dared to set foot near the sacred precinct! All right?

"Fortunately for me, their race had almost completely died out over the thousands of years that had passed. In fact, as I approached the mysterious temple, who should feebly stagger forth to challenge me but the very last of the ant-men? And he himself such a degraded and degenerate specimen, that he was easily overcome by my least effort. In fact, as I stood there in the grandeur of the ancient moonlight, with my triumphant foot upon his neck, I found it in my heart to pity the poor defeated creature."

"Where do the beans come in?" called the policeman's son.

"I'm coming to that! Have patience, young sir. So I didn't kill him, which I might easily have done. Instead, I stepped over his pathetic form and entered the forbidden shrine of Osiris.

"Holding my lantern high, what should I see but a towering image of the fearsome god himself, but this was not the greatest wonder! No, on the walls of the shrine, floor to ceiling, wall to wall, were inscribed words! Yes, words in Ancient Egyptian, queer little pictures of birds and snakes and things. Fortunately I, with my great knowledge, was able to read them. Were they prayers? No. Were they ancient spells? No, good people. They were nothing more nor less than recipes for medicine! For, as you may know, Osiris was the Egyptians' principal god of healing. Here were the secret formulas to remedy every ill that might befall unhappy mankind!

"So, what did I do? I quickly pulled out my notebook and began to copy them down, intending to bring this blessing back for the good of all.

"Faster I wrote, and faster, but just as I had cast my eye on the last of the recipes—which, had I been able to copy it, would have banished the awful specter of Death himself—I heard an ominous rumbling. My lamp began to flicker. When I looked up, I beheld the idol of Osiris trembling on its very foundation. Unbeknownst to me, my unhallowed feet crossing the portal of the shrine had set off a dreadful curse. The shrine was about to destroy itself in a convulsive cataclysm!

"I fled, thoughtfully tucking my notebook into my pocket, and paused only to seize up the last of the Myrmidions where he lay groveling. With my great strength, I easily carried him to my ship, and cast off just before the shrine of Osiris collapsed upon itself, with a rumble like a hundred thousand milk wagons!

"And, not only that, the island itself broke into a hundred thousand pieces and sank forever beneath the engulfing waves!"

Golescu stepped back to gauge his effect on the audience. Satisfied that he had them enthralled, and delighted to see that more townfolk were hurrying to swell the crowd every minute, he twirled his mustache.

"And now, little children, you will find out about the beans. As we journeyed to a place of refuge, I turned my efforts to taming the last of the Myrmidions. With my superior education, it proved no difficulty. I discovered that, although he was weak and puny compared with his terrible ancestors, he nevertheless had kept some of the singular traits of the ant!

"Yes, especially their amazing ability to count beans and peas!"

"Wait a minute," shouted the schoolmaster. "Ants can't count."

"Dear sir, you're mistaken," said Golescu. "Who doesn't remember the story of Cupid and Psyche, eh? Any educated man would remember that the princess was punished for her nosiness by being locked in a room with a huge pile of beans and millet, and was supposed to count them all, right? And who came to her assistance? Why, the ants! Because she'd been thoughtful and avoided stepping on an anthill or something. So the little creatures sorted and tided the whole stack for her, and counted them too. And that's in classical literature, my friend. Aristotle wrote about it, and who are we to dispute him?"

"But—" said the schoolmaster.

"And NOW," said Golescu, hurrying to the back of the platform and pushing forward the coffin, which had been nailed into a frame that stood it nearly upright, "Here he is! Feast your astonished eyes on—*the last of the Myrmidions!*"

With a flourish, he threw back the lid.

Emil, dressed in the black imp costume that had been modified with an extra pair of straw-stuffed arms, and in a black hood to which two long antenna of wire had been attached, looked into the glare of the lights. He screamed in terror.

"Er—yes!" Golescu slammed the lid, in the process trapping one of the antennae outside. "Though you can only see him in his natural state in, er, the briefest of glimpses, because—because, even though weak, he still has the power of setting things on fire with the power of his gaze! Fortunately, I have devised a way to protect you all. One moment, please."

As the crowd murmured, Golescu drew the curtain back across the stage. Those in the front row could see his feet moving to and fro for a moment. They heard a brief mysterious thumping and a faint cry. The curtain was opened again.

"*Now,*" said Golescu. "Behold the last of the Myrmidions!"

He opened the lid once more. Emil, safely goggled, did not scream. After a moment of silence, various members of the audience began to snicker.

"Ah, you think he's weak? You think he looks harmless?" said Golescu, affecting an amused sneer. "Yet, consider his astonishing powers of calculation! You, boy, there." He lunged forward and caught the nearest youngster who was clutching a jar, and lifted him bodily to the stage. "Yes, you! Do you know—don't tell me, now!—do you know exactly how many beans are in your jar?"

"Yes," said the boy, blinking in the torchlight.

"Ah! Now tell me, good people, is this child one of your own?"

"That's my son!" cried the barber.

"Very good! Now, is there a policeman here?"

"I am," said the Captain of Police, stepping forward and grinning at Golescu in a fairly unpleasant way.

"Wonderful! Now, dear child, will you be so kind as to whisper to the good constable—whisper, I say—the correct number of beans in this jar?"

Obediently, the barber's son stepped to the edge of the planking and whispered into the Police Captain's ear.

"Excellent! And now, brave oliceman, will you be so good as to write down the number you have just been given?" said Golescu, sweating slightly.

"Delighted to," said the Police Captain, and pulling out a notebook he jotted it down. He winked at the audience, in a particularly cold and reptilian kind of way.

"Exquisite!" said Golescu. "And now, if you will permit—?" He took the jar of beans from the barber's son and held it up in the torchlight. Then he held it before Emil's face. "Oh, last of the Myrmidions! Behold this jar! *How many beans?*"

"Five hundred and six," said Emil, faint but clear in the breathless silence.

"How many?"

"Five hundred and six."

"And, sir, what is the figure you have written down?" demanded Golescu, whirling about to face the Police Captain.

"Five hundred and six," the Police Captain responded, narrowing his eyes.

"And so it is!" said Golescu, thrusting the jar back into the hands of the barber's son and more or less booting him off the stage. "Let's have more proof! Who's got another jar?"

Now a half-dozen jars were held up, and children cried shrilly to be the next on stage. Grunting with effort, Golescu hoisted another boy to the platform.

"And you are?" he said.

"That's *my* son!" said the Police Captain.

"Good! How many beans? Tell your papa!" cried Golescu, and as the boy was whispering in his father's ear, "Please write it down!"

He seized the jar from the boy and once more held it before Emil. "Oh last of the Myrmidions, *how many beans?*"

"Three hundred seventeen," said Emil.

"Are you certain? It's a much bigger jar!"

"Three hundred seventeen," said Emil.

"And the number you just wrote down, dear sir?"

"Three hundred seventeen," admitted the Police Captain.

"I hid an onion in the middle," said his son proudly, and was promptly cuffed by the police captain when Golescu had dropped him back into the crowd.

Now grown men began to push through the crowd, waving jars of varied legumes as well as barley and millet. Emil guessed correctly on each try, even the jar of rice that contained a pair of wadded socks! At last Golescu, beaming, held up his hands.

"So, you have seen one proof of my adventure with your own eyes," he cried. "But this has been a mere parlor entertainment, gentle audience. Now, you will be truly amazed! For we come to the true purpose of my visit here. *Behold the Gifts of Osiris!*"

He whisked a piece of sacking from the stacked boxes it had concealed. The necks of many medicine bottles winked in the torchlight.

"Yes! Compounded by me, according to the ancient secret formulas! Here, my friends, are remedies to cure human misery! A crown a bottle doesn't even cover the cost of its rare ingredients—I'm offering them to you practically as a charity!"

A flat silence fell at that, and then the Police Captain could be heard distinctly saying, "I thought it would come to this."

"A crown a bottle?" said somebody else, sounding outraged.

"You require persuasion," said Golescu. "*Free* persuasion. Very good! You, sir, step up here into the light. Yes, you, the one who doesn't want to part with his money."

The man in question climbed up on the planks and stood there looking defiant, as Golescu addressed the audience.

"Human misery!" he shouted. "What causes it, good people? Age. Inadequacy. Inability. Loneliness. All that does not kill you, but makes life not worth living! Isn't it so? Now you, good sir!" He turned to the man beside him. "Remove your hat, if you please. I see you suffer from baldness!"

The man turned red and looked as though he'd like to punch Golescu, but the audience laughed.

"Don't be ashamed!" Golescu told him. "How'd you like a full growth of luxurious hair, eh?"

"Well—"

"Behold," said Golescu, drawing a bottle from the stack. "The Potion of Ptolemy! See its amazing results."

He uncorked the bottle and tilted it carefully, so as to spill only a few drops on the man's scalp. Having done this, he grabbed the tail of his cloak and spread the potion around on the man's scalp.

"What are you doing to me?" cried the man. "It burns like Hell!"

"Courage! Nothing is got without a little pain. Count to sixty, now!"

The audience obliged, but long before they had got to forty they broke off in exclamations: for thick black hair had begun to grow on the man's scalp, everywhere the potion had been spread.

"Oh!" The man clutched his scalp, unbelieving.

"Yes!" said Golescu, turning to the audience. "You see? Immediately, this lucky fellow is restored to his previous appearance of youth and virility. And speaking of virility!" He smacked the man's back hard enough to send him flying off the platform. "What greater source of misery can there be than disappointing the fair ones? Who among you lacks that certain something he had as a young buck, eh?

"Nobody here, I'm sure, but just think: someday, you *may* find yourself attempting to pick a lock with a dead fish. When that day comes, do you truly want to be caught without a bracing bottle of the Pharaoh's Physic? One crown a bottle, gentlemen! I'm sure you can understand why no free demonstrations are available for this one."

There was a silence of perhaps five seconds before a veritable tidal wave of men rushed forward, waving fistfuls of coin.

"Here! One to a customer, sirs, one only. That's right! I only do this as a public service, you know, I love to make others happy. Drink it in good health, sir, but I'd suggest you eat your oysters first. Pray don't trample the children, there, even if you can always make more. And speaking of making more!" Golescu stuffed the last clutch of coins down his tights and retreated from the front of the stage, for he had sold all his bottles of Pharaoh's Physic and Potion of Ptolemy.

"What's the use of magnificent potency when your maiden is cold as ice, I ask you? Disinterest! Disdain! Diffidence! Is there any more terrible source of misery than the unloving spouse? Now, you may have heard of love philtres; you may have bought charms and spells from mere gypsies. But what your little doves require, my friends, is none other than the *Elixir of Isis*! Guaranteed to turn those chilly frowns to smiles of welcome!"

A second surge made its way to the front of the platform, slightly less desperate than the first but moneyed withal. Golescu doled out bottles of Elixir of Isis, dropped coins down his tights, and calculated. He had one case of bottles left. Lifting it to the top of the stack, he faced his audience and smiled.

"And now, good people, ask yourselves a question: what is it that makes long life a curse? Why, the answer is transparent: it is *pain*. Rending, searing, horrible agony! Dull aches that never go away! The throb of a rotten tooth! Misery, misery, misery, God have mercy on us! But! With a liberal application of Balm Bast, you will gain instant relief from unspeakable torment."

There was a general movement toward the stage, though not such a flood as Golescu had expected; some distraction was in the crowd, though he couldn't tell what it was. Ah! Surely, this was it: an injured man, with bandaged head and eye, was being helped forward on his crutches.

"Give way! Let this poor devil through!"

"Here, Professor Hades, here's one who could use your medicine!"

"What about a free sample for *him*?"

"What's this, a veteran of the wars?" said Golescu, in his most jovial voice. "Certainly he'll get a free sample! Here, for yo—" He ended on a high-pitched little squeak, for on leaning down he found himself gazing straight into Farmer Buzdugan's single remaining eye. Mutual recognition flashed.

"Yo—" began Farmer Buzdugan, but Golescu had uncorked the bottle and shoved it into his mouth quick as thought. He held the bottle there, as Buzdugan choked on indignation and Balm Bast.

"AH, YES, I RECOGNIZE THIS POOR FELLOW!" said Golescu, struggling to keep the bottle in place. "He's delusional as well! His family brought him to me to be cured of his madness, but unfortunately—"

Unfortunately the distraction in the crowd was on a larger scale than Golescu had supposed. It had started with a general restlessness, owing to the fact that all those who had purchased bottles of Pharaoh's Physic had opened the bottles and gulped their contents straight down. This had produced general and widespread priapism, at about the time Golescu had begun his spiel on the Elixir of Isis.

This was as nothing, however, to what was experienced by those who had purchased the Potion of Ptolemy and, most unwisely, decided to try it out before waiting to get it home. Several horrified individuals were now finding luxuriant hair growing, not only on their scalps but everywhere the potion had splashed or trickled in the course of its application, such as ears, eyelids, noses and wives. More appalled still were those who had elected to rub the potion well in with their bare hands.

Their case was as nothing, however, compared to the unfortunate who had decided that all medicines worked better if taken internally. He was now prostrate and shrieking, if somewhat muffledly, as a crowd of horrified onlookers stood well back from him.

Buzdugan threw himself back and managed to spit out the bottle.

"Son of a whore!" he said. "This is him! This is the one who sold us the—"

"MAD, WHAT DID I TELL YOU?" said Golescu.

"He sold us the stuff that created those—" Buzdugan said, before the Balm Bast worked and he abruptly lost all feeling in his body. Nerveless he fell from his crutches into the dark forest of feet and legs.

But he was scarcely noticed in the excitement caused by the man who had purchased both Pharaoh's Physic and Elixir of Isis, with the intention of maximizing domestic felicity, and in the darkness had opened and drunk off the contents of the wrong bottle. Overcome by a wave of heat, and then inexplicable and untoward passion, and then by a complete loss of higher cerebral function, he had dropped his trousers and was now offering himself to all comers, screaming like a chimpanzee. Several of those afflicted by the Pharaoh's Potion, unable to resist, were on the very point of availing themselves of his charms when—

"Holy saints defend us!" cried someone on the edge of the crowd. "Run for your lives! *It's another demon cock!*"

This confused all who heard it, understandably, but only until the demon in question strode into sight.

Golescu, who had been edging to the back of the platform with tiny little steps, smiling and sweating, saw it most clearly: a rooster, but no ordinary bird. Eight feet tall at the shoulder, tail like a fountain of fire, golden spurs, feathers like beaten gold, comb like blood-red coral, and a beak like a meat cleaver made of brass! Its eyes shone in the light of the torches with ferocious brilliance, but they were blank and mindless as any chicken's. It beat its wings with a sound like thunder. People fled in all directions, save for those folk who were so crazed with lust they could not be distracted from what they were doing.

"Oh why, oh why do these things happen?" Golescu implored no one in particular. "I have *such* good intentions."

The great bird noticed the children crowded together at the front of the platform. Up until this point, they had been giggling at the behavior of their elders. Having caught sight of the monster, however, they dove under the platform and huddled there like so many mice. The bird saw them nonetheless, and advanced, turning its head to regard them with one eye and then the other. Terrified, they hurled jars of beans at it, which exploded like canisters of shot. Yet it came on, raking the ground as it came.

And Golescu became aware that there was another dreadful noise below the cries of the children, below Buzdugan's frenzied cursing where he lay, below the ever-more-distant yells of the retreating audience. Below, for it was low-pitched, the sort of noise that makes the teeth vibrate, deep as an earthquake, no less frightening.

Something, somewhere, was growling. And it was getting louder.

Golescu raised his head, and in a moment that would return to him in nightmares the rest of his life saw a pair of glowing eyes advancing through the night, eyes like coals above white, white teeth. The nearer they came, floating through the darkness toward the wagon, the louder grew the sound of growling. Nearer now, into the light of the torches, and Golescu saw clearly the outstretched arms, the clawing fingers caked with earth, the murderous expression, the trailing shroud.

"Good heavens, it's Amaunet," he observed, before reality hit him and he wet himself. The Black Cup had failed her again after all, and so—

"rrrrrrrkillYOU!" she roared, lunging for the platform. Golescu, sobbing, ran to and fro only a moment; then fear lent him wings and he made one heroic leap, launching himself from the platform to the back of the chicken of gold. Digging his knees in its fiery plumage, he smote it as though it were a horse.

With a squawk that shattered the night, his steed leaped in the air and came down running. Golescu clung for dear life, looking over his shoulder. He beheld Emil, antennae wobbling, scrambling frantically from the coffin.

"Uncle Barbu!" wailed Emil. But Amaunet had Emil by the ankle now. She pulled him close. He vanished into the folds of her shroud, still struggling. Golescu's last glimpse was of Amaunet lifting Emil into her bosom, clutching him possessively, horrific Madonna and limp Child.

Golescu hugged the neck of his golden steed and urged it on, on through the night and the forest. He wept for lost love, wept for sour misfortune, wept for beauty, and so he rode in terrible glory through water and fire and pitiless starlight. When bright day came he was riding still. Who knows where he ended up?

Though there is a remote village beyond the forests, so mazed about with bogs and streams no roads lead there, and every man has been obliged to marry his cousin. They have a legend that the Devil once appeared to them, riding on a golden cock, a fearful apparition before which they threw themselves flat. They offered to make him their prince, if only he would spare their lives.

And they say that the Devil stayed with them awhile, and made a tolerably good prince, as princes go in that part of the world. But he looked always over his shoulder, for fear that his wife might be pursuing him. He said she was the Mother of Darkness. His terror was so great that at last it got the better of him and he rode on, rather than let her catch him.

The men of the village found this comforting, in an obscure kind of way. *Even the Devil fears his wife,* they said to one another. They said it so often that a man came from the Ministry of Culture at last, and wrote it down in a book of proverbs.

But if you travel to that country and look in that great book, you will look in vain; for unfortunately some vandal has torn out the relevant page.